# IRON PROOF

A CACHE IRON MYSTERY

ALEX BLAKELY

# COPYRIGHT

# 1

Relationships are complicated, so why is murder easy? Cache thought as she stared down at the bandage on her leg. Some people break up with you simply by telling you they don't want to see you anymore. Cache's latest partner had decided to send the message home with a bullet to the leg. Her trip to California to visit a friend had proven anything but relaxing. But now she had to deal with the aftermath, when everyone knows your name and wants to have a piece of you.

She glanced around her shipping-container home. Her brothers had welded three shipping containers together while she was overseas in the army, giving her her own place on the ranch that was home to four generations of Irons. After all, what self-respecting woman in her thirties would still live at home with her parents? She lay back in her bed, blankets pulled up around her, leaving her wounded right leg exposed to the elements. Cache looked over at the alarm clock. It was now nine o'clock in the morning. Oh well, I overslept, she thought. She pulled herself from her blanketed tomb and made her way down the ladder that connected the top shipping container to the bottom, where there was a small seating area and kitchen. A third container jutting off at the end of the hall provided needed washroom facilities and storage. Cache reached for a pod of coffee, medium roast; plopped it into the coffee machine; sat down at the small table; and stared up at the ranch house where her parents lived. Her brother Tommy's truck was in the gravel driveway in front of the large log-and-brick structure built by her great-grandfather. She could see their dog Duke running in the field as she spotted her brother and dad pointing at something in the distance and then her brother moving his hand like he was swatting a fly. Her brother turned to look in her direction and went off into the house. She could hear the hissing sound of the coffee machine and smell that wonderful scent of freshly brewed coffee in the air. Cache grabbed a mug from the top shelf above the sink, retrieved the cream from her small fifties-style fridge and poured a shot of cream and dropped two sugar cubes into the mug, and returned to her seat to look out onto the ranch. She reached for her phone, which she had plugged in to charge before going to bed, and saw that she had received texts and emails from her best friend, Vanny, and her friend and ex-whatever Jake, checking in with her to see how she was faring. She scrolled through a series of messages from other friends, from college and those who lived around Hart, congratulating her and telling her how proud of her they were.

Cache sipped on the coffee and reflected on the events that had led her to solving the murders committed by the Pinup Killer. The sequence of incidents had left her feeling bewildered, as if nothing in her life would ever feel normal again. She could taste the hazelnut in the coffee creamer and the concoction drifted over her tastebuds. Cache leaned back and stretched out her hands. She could feel a creak in her back. Oh, that can't be good. A heavy sigh and a release of tension coming out in one breath, she wondered what was for breakfast and finished off her coffee, pulled on her jeans and boots and threw a fleece pullover on over the tank top she had worn to bed. Cache walked out of her home, which was situated close to the barn, and Duke came running up to her for his morning ear rub. As she bent down to rub his face, she could hear noise off to her left in the distance in the same direction where her brother had been pointing earlier. She stood up and covered the top of her eyes with her hand to keep out the glare of the morning sun and could see what looked like satellite dishes in the distance, just outside the fencing that surrounded the ranch. The hilly terrain blocked sight of whatever they were fixed to, but her brother probably knew what they were, and she would simply ask him. Cache walked up to the main house. Opening the door, she could hear bacon sizzling from the kitchen. Her father and brother sat in the family room by the fireplace, a cup of coffee in her brother's hand; a mug sat on the table next to her father.

"Well, good morning, sleepyhead," her father, Thomas, said.

Her brother glanced over at her. "You know, we strung fifty feet of fence while you slept this morning."

"Bullshit, if you had to string fifty feet of fence there is no way you would have let me sleep." Cache tilted her head in the direction of the satellite dishes. "What's with the satellite dishes?"

"Your fan club," her brother said.

"What fan club?" she asked.

Her mother, Julie, came into the family room. "Don't pay any attention to him, dear. Come, I have some eggs, bacon and toast for you."

As Cache walked into the kitchen, she could hear a beeping sound and noticed the phone on the wall was off the hook. "Mom, do you want me to hang the phone back up?"

"No, it's been ringing nonstop, so I took it off the receiver."

"Who's been calling?"

"Everyone," her father said from behind her as he made his way to the kitchen.

"Who is everyone?"

"I mean everyone. Friends wanting to congratulate you, telling us how proud they are of you, and media outlets wanting an interview with you, wanting to know if they can talk to you."

Her brother Tommy joined them in the kitchen. "That's what the satellite dishes are. There is a whole bunch of news vans camped out along Interstate 90 hoping to get a picture of you."

"I'm sorry, I was hoping this wouldn't follow me home."

"Oh, don't worry about it, something will come up eventually and it will be their new shiny object to chase. In the meantime, I would suggest you stay close to the ranch or go on another vacation."

"No thanks, it will be a while before I take another vacation."

Cache ate her breakfast and finished her coffee as her parents and brother filled her in on what had been going on since she'd made the national news. The small community of Hart, Montana, population twenty-three hundred, had caught the attention of media from all over the country. Her brother shared stories about how friends they'd grown up with were cashing in on their fifteen minutes of fame as they were stopped on the street to be asked what it was like to grow up with her. Everyone wanted to know about Cache Iron. Cache finished her breakfast, went into the family room with her parents and brother and sat down. Her mother put the phone back on the hook, and not more than ten minutes later, it began to ring repeatedly.

"Just leave it," her father said, "the answering machine will get it and we can check on it later."

"You okay, honey?" her mother asked as she rubbed Cache's shoulder.

"Still just processing some things. Need to work them out on my own." She smirked in her mother's direction.

Cache left the main house and walked out toward the gravel driveway. A cloud of dust could be spotted coming toward her, obscuring the sight of the satellite dishes. A gunmetal pickup truck pulled in alongside Tommy's, and her brother Cooper and his wife, Beth, climbed out of the rig.

"Did you see all those trucks out there?"

"Nah, Tommy told me about them."

"You should go down there and charge them a grand each to talk with them, you could make a killing." Her sister-in-law Beth made her way into the house as Cache continued to walk down to her place. She put her mug in her small sink, sat down at her table and stared in silence out to the highway. The one person she wanted to talk to probably would not take her calls. As she sat there and reflected, she found her mood changing, becoming more depressed with each passing second. She'd thought when she got home everything would go back to normal, and a lot of things had, but that was the problem. Something had changed for her. Cache had left the army four years ago, and while she had settled back into ranching in Montana, the exhilaration she had once felt being a military police officer had started to become a ship in the distance, moving farther away from the shore. This recent series of events had brought the ship back to the dock, and she craved the excitement again. What she was feeling now was like the reaction you have after going to see your favorite band in concert. Afterward there is a sense of being let down as the event fades into the background of your memories.

Cache gazed at her smartwatch and saw that the time was now a quarter after eleven. She looked at her coffeemaker and knew another cup of coffee wasn't going to cut it. Cache rose, walked over to the small cupboard below the sink, opened it up and revealed a few different bottles of rye whiskey. She grabbed the one that was half full by the neck, pulled down a shot glass from above the sink, poured two fingers of whiskey and fired it back. Maybe I can numb the feeling, she thought. She grabbed the bottle by the neck and walked out of her place and down toward the barn. Hopefully, the horses wouldn't mind some company this morning. She reached the foot of the ladder that extended up into the hayloft. Cache tucked her tank top into her jeans and put the bottle down her top so the neck of it wedged between her breasts. The touch of the glass against her bare skin was cold as she looked down to see the long neck of the bottle peering up at her, and a thought came to her mind that made her smile. Cache climbed up the ladder, sat down on the old wooden floor, rested against a bale of hay and reached down for the bottle. She pulled the top from the bottle, took a big swig and pushed the upper doors to the barn open so she could see all the trucks parked along Interstate 90.

Cache counted maybe nine vehicles in total; some were vans, some were trucks like delivery companies use, all with large letters and numbers painted on the side, as the news media talked to one another hoping someone would emerge from the ranch to give them something worthy to put on the air. She looked down at the bottle and started to peel the label from it. Meticulously, she pulled every inch of the label from the body and neck of the bottle until there was nothing but clear glass and the amber appearance of the liquid inside. Cache continued to look at the trucks and pondered. What if I went down there and told them every juicy detail? Would that change anything? Would it horrify the people around here or would no one care? She was struggling to figure out what the direction forward was for her when she heard the creaking of the ladder and spotted the black matted hair of her brother Tommy climbing up into the loft.

"So this is where you've gotten off to?" he asked.

"Mom sent you to look for me?"

"I don't need Mom to know something is not right with you. Do you want to talk about it?"

"You want me to share my sex life with you?"

"No, I would prefer to believe you haven't had sex, kind of like Dad does. Is it about Jake?"

She shook her head. "If it was Jake, I think it would be easier to process."

He reached for the bottle, took a swig of it and sat down opposite her, resting his foot up against the bale of hay she was leaning back on.

"There's no label on the bottle," he said.

In a very philosophical tone, Cache looked at him and said, "Why do we need to put labels on everything?"

"So we know what's inside, so we don't drink paint varnish by mistake."

Cache reached for the bottle and took another gulp of whiskey, and it put a fire to the back of her throat as it made its way down deep inside of her.

"Do you remember what Grandpa used to say about the family? He said, 'Nothing penetrates Iron.' Whatever you're going through, all of us are here for you, whether or not you want to talk."

"Circling the wagons?" she asked.

"We always have, when one of us is in trouble; no matter what it is, we will always protect our own."

He extended his hand, reached for the bottle and took it from Cache; he wiped the top of the bottle with his hand and took another gulp. They looked out of the upper door of the barn and saw their brother Cooper making his way down to them.

"Is this a private party, or can anyone join?" he asked, looking up at them in the loft.

"Come on up," Cache said, motioning with her hand for him to come join them. Cooper walked into the barn, climbed up into the loft, took a seat beside his older brother and reached for the bottle.

"Everything okay?" he asked.

"Just talking," she said.

He looked to his right at his brother. "Did you give her the penetrating-iron speech?"

Tommy extended his arm around Cooper's neck, pulled him in close and vigorously rubbed his head, trying to make it hurt with each passing stroke.

"Now all we need is Pauly and the family will be all together. Where is he?"

"Dad sent him into town for supplies this morning. With his desire to be on camera, we'll probably see him on the evening news." Tommy put his hands up, creating a frame with his hands with Cache in the middle. "'What was it like to have a sister like Cache?'" he said in an ominous tone.

The three of them laughed as they passed the bottle around for a few minutes. Cache was the third of four children, two older brothers and one younger, and was the only daughter in four generations of Irons.

"I almost forgot why I came down here. Mom said you got a message on the machine that you should listen to," Cooper said.

"Another news reporter wanting a story?" she asked.

"No, this was some guy wanting to hire you."

"To do what?"

"Investigate something I guess. Anyway he was calling from Boston, left a number for you to call him back at."

Tommy looked at her. "Might be what you need to get away from all of this crazy for a little while."

"I'm not an investigator. Why would he want me?"

"Maybe because you solved a mystery that everyone can't shut up about. Sorry, that came out wrong," Cooper said.

"Cache, it's not like you've never done this before, you did it for six years, it's in your blood now."

"That was different, that was the army."

"Is it really different or is that just an excuse you're telling yourself?"

Cache looked at him, annoyed at his calling her out on it. "Jake said you can be an asshole."

"But I tell the truth. Call him back. What do you have to lose?"

Cache thought about it for a few minutes. The bottle was almost empty. If nothing else, it would give her a chance to get another bottle from the house. She climbed down from the loft and walked toward the main house, as her brothers yelled from the loft that she should ask them about their baked beans.

Cache walked into the house. Her mother and Beth sat talking at the kitchen table.

"I heard there was a phone message from Boston for me?"

Beth handed her a piece of paper with a phone number scribbled on it and the name Graydon Quill above it.

"He sounded like a nice man on the phone, had a real strong voice," her mother said.

Cache walked into the family room, sat down in the seat normally occupied by her father when he was in the room and picked up the phone. Her mother and sister-in-law came into the room to join her. Evidently they were just as curious about the call as Cache was.

Cache punched the ten-digit number, beginning with a one followed by the 617 area code. The phone rang once, twice, and was picked up on the third ring.

"Hello, this is Cache Iron, I heard you called looking for me?"

"I did, Ms. Iron. I was wondering how long it was going to

take before you got back to me. I might have had to get the local sheriff to come out and see if you were still in the area."

"Why would you do that?"

"I'm in need of an investigator and my gut tells me you're what I am looking for."

"I am not an investigator. I mean I was, but not anymore. Surely you can find someone better suited for whatever you need than me."

"You're what I want, and you're what I expect to get. I didn't pick your name out of a phone book; I looked into you, talked to a three-star general about you."

Cache pulled the receiver back from her head and stared at it. The audience in the room watched her, appearing equally puzzled. "You talked to a general about me?"

"I did, and he talked to your commanding officer, who endorsed you. Said good things about you. I saw your story on the news and that was my starting point; from there, my people did a background check on you until I was positive you are who I want to hire."

"To do what?"

"I can't talk about it over the phone. What I want you to do is to come out here to Boston. I will fill you in on the details, then you will get to work. What do you charge?"

Cache covered the receiver with her hand and looked at her mother. "He wants to know what I would charge."

Her mom thought about it for a second and blurted out, "Tell him two hundred and fifty dollars a day."

Cache pulled her hand from the receiver. "Two hundred and fifty—"

At which point she was interrupted midsentence: "Two hundred and fifty an hour, that sounds more than reasonable." She was going to correct him, but he just continued talking. "So I will expect you here in about seven hours and we can go over the details."

"I don't know if I can get there in seven hours. I have to drive to an airport that flies to Boston. I'm not sure if I'll have to get a connection somewhere along the way."

"No, no, no," he said. "Flight time to Boston is a little over four hours straight through. My private jet left Boston heading to Ford Airfield just outside Hart, Montana, about two hours ago. Should be there in about two hours. Given time to refuel, I expect I will see you here in seven hours. Don't worry about getting to the airport, my assistant has arranged for a limo to come get you."

"Seems like you made a lot of assumptions. How did you know I would say yes?"

"I'm not the CEO of Quillchem Industries because I take no for an answer. On board the jet is one of our senior legal counselors, Ms. Chase Flynn. She will go over a few things with you. We need you to sign a nondisclosure agreement before we can talk. Things will become clearer after our meeting. Does that work for you?"

Cache felt like she had been run over by a speeding eighteen-wheeler. "Okay."

"Splendid, I will see you in Boston shortly, and we can get you going on this project. And don't worry about a hotel. We have several rooms here in our complex you can stay in while you lead your investigation."

She heard the click as he hung up the phone.

"What did he say? Was he okay with the rate?"

"He is paying me two hundred and fifty dollars an hour."

"An hour? You got to be kidding me!"

"No, he seemed quite fine with the rate, and he has dispatched a private jet to come get me and will be sending a limousine out to the ranch to pick me up."

"Pick you up from where?" her father asked as he made his way into the house.

"Cache is going to Boston for a possible job as an investigator and they are paying two hundred and fifty an hour," her mother said.

Cache talked to her father, filling him in on the details of the conversation. He said that while under normal circumstances, he might be more skeptical, getting away from the circus that was surrounding the ranch might do her some good. He told her that opportunities might open up for her. Given her involvement in solving the pinup killings, she should take advantage of all that came her way. Cache got up and walked down to her place, passing her brothers, who were now heading to the house, and shared the details of the phone call with them. She grabbed her duffel bag and packed a couple of tops, a spare pair of jeans, socks, panties and toiletries; Cache had ditched her bras for good when she left the service. She went through a mental checklist in her head to ensure she had everything. The only thing that she wanted to bring with her but decided to leave home was her 9 millimeter pistol. It had saved her on more than one occasion, but she didn't know how they would react to her bringing a weapon onto the plane and felt it might be better to leave it at home on this trip. Cache grabbed her laptop and charger and slid it down inside a protective sleeve in her duffel bag. She went to her dresser and pulled out a black nylon pouch containing a small gray metal flashlight and lock pick set. Cache pulled two black dresses from a closet—one a little black dress, a staple in every woman's wardrobe, and one with a skirt that fell around the knees—and a set of shoes. She grabbed a black sequined clutch and then grabbed her phone and sent a brief text to Jake and Vanny that she had gotten their messages and that she had to go out of town, heading back east. Cache had met Vanny when they roomed together at Dartmouth, and she figured Vanny would think she was just going back to visit her old college. Since her time out west, Jake had been making suggestions that they get back together. But Cache's head was not there. She didn't quite know how to explain it to him, so it surprised her when he texted back asking her why and whether she had thought about what they'd talked about before she headed back to Montana.

Cache grabbed her duffel bag, made sure everything was off in her little home and walked back up to the main house to wait out the next few hours. After two hours passed, Duke was the first to pick up that someone was coming into the driveway as a big long black SUV arrived with blacked-out windows everywhere but the driver's side. A cloud of dust followed the vehicle until it came to a stop at the foot of the pickup trucks parked outside the house. Cache was uncertain what awaited her, but she hugged everyone goodbye and walked outside as a tall, slender gentleman, dressed in a black suit, white shirt with black tie and spit-polished black leather shoes, emerged from the vehicle. He introduced himself as Lee Jackson. Cache's parents and brothers walked out onto the porch to see her off. Cache looked in the direction of her brother Cooper. "Coop, can you do me a favor while I'm gone?"

"Depends. What is it?"

"Can you take a look at my truck? I picked up a strange rattle on the way home from California and can't figure out where it'd be coming from."

"If I have time, I'll see what Grandpa's old Whiticker has going on." Lee opened up the passenger-side door, allowing Cache to escape into the vehicle, putting her duffel bag alongside of her. For the first time in the past week, she felt that her life had begun again and was eager to see what was coming next for her.

# 2

As the limousine pulled out of the Iron & Sons ranch, Cache pushed a switch to bring down the privacy screen that separated her from Lee.

"Are all these people here for you?" he asked. As they drove past the news vans, men with cameras and large lenses took aim at the limousine to try to capture who was hiding in its internal compartments.

"I'm afraid so."

"Are you a musician or an actress? I'm sorry, the name didn't ring a bell when I was told to come fetch you."

"No, just a private citizen who was hoping to stay private. Have you been with Mr. Quill long?"

"Only for the past four hours. We got a call to come pick someone up; truth be told we were fully booked, but when they offered to pay triple our going rate, there was no turning that down. Plus, they're a big outfit; who knows if it could mean more business down the road."

"Funny, I never heard of them."

"From what I read online, they're a big company out east,

been around for years. You know we don't have many big companies around here like that."

"You mean in Hart?"

"Well, definitely bigger than anything in Hart. I knew where you were. Everyone around these parts knows where your ranch is. Are you married to one of the Iron brothers?"

"No, I'm the only daughter, and before you ask about the ranch name, it's been that way for years and isn't about to change any time soon."

Cache glanced around the back of the vehicle. The armrest had two bottles of water in it. There was a series of magazines in a magazine holder attached to the front of her compartment. She flipped through the magazines and pulled out a travel guide with the headline "Best Places to Travel in the Orient" on the cover.

"So, Lee, what are the best places to travel in the orient?"

"What are you talking about?"

Cache held up the magazine so he could see it in his review mirror.

"Oh, they seem to like Criza as number one. It discusses things to see if you visit Criza, China and Japan."

"Well, I lived in Japan for two years, so I think I would either go to Criza or China. What about you, which one would you go to?"

"I would choose Japan, I'm not a fan of Communist governments, which leaves the other two out."

Cache returned the magazine to the rack and sat back in her seat, opening a bottle of water and looking out the window.

They continued to drive east toward Hart and then veered off down Presidential Boulevard, heading for Ford Airfield. The airfield had been built back in the forties and later renamed in honor of the thirty-eighth president. The airfield was small, with two long runways that intersected each other in the middle of the airport. To the south of the runways, there were three large hangars that could accommodate any number of smaller jets, and there were stalls where local pilots parked their planes when not in use. The control tower sat at the southernmost part of the airport with two attached buildings, one serving as a weather center where pilots could gather information before a flight and the other a small restaurant and lounge for anyone waiting for a charter flight that could take you to one of the larger airports in the area.

The limo pulled up to the gate, and an attendant stepped out from his booth as Lee rolled down his window.

"Where are you heading, sir?"

"I've got a passenger for Quillchem Industries. They're supposed to have a jet here. I don't know if it has landed yet."

The man stepped back into the booth as Cache rolled down her window. "Don't make me late, Jerry."

The man stepped out of the booth and walked over to her window. "Well, Cache, how are you? Look at you all fancy, limousine, private jet—looks like you absorbed a little of the LA lifestyle when you were out there. Hey, we are all proud of you for what you did out there."

"I appreciate it. So are you going to make me late?"

Jerry scratched his forehead, walked back to the booth, picked up a yellow phone and returned to talk to Lee.

"They just landed about ten minutes ago and are getting refueled. Drive out to the stop sign, hang a left and they will be in bay three. It's a corporate jet, midnight blue with a silver Q on the tail. Can't miss it, we don't get many like that in here." He walked back to Cache's window. "Where are you heading?"

"Boston."

"Went to the West Coast, now going to the East; you are a seasoned traveler. What's out there, if you don't mind me asking?"

"A job, I think. I'll know more in a little bit." Cache reached out and took his hand in hers. "You take care of yourself."

"Will do." And with that Lee pulled away and followed the directions to take Cache to hangar bay three. There on the tarmac was a long jet with two engines attached to the tail behind the wings of the aircraft. Seven small, round porthole-style windows sat along the side of the plane. They had painted it a midnight blue with a large silver Q on the tail and a red lightning bolt coming down from the middle of the Q. The limousine pulled up about thirty feet from the plane, and as Lee got out of the vehicle to open up her door, she told him she had it, grabbed her duffel bag and exited the limousine, thanking him for bringing her to the airport. Cache walked over toward the plane as the side door popped open and a young man in his early thirties climbed down the stairs.

"Are you Ms. Iron? I'm Chip Martin, the steward. Can I take your bag?"

Cache handed her olive-green duffel bag to him. He was dressed in dark blue pants and a white pressed shirt. He had dark hair and green eyes, was clean shaven and stood at around five foot eleven, just three inches taller than her.

"Ms. Flynn is on board waiting for you. Once you're on board and settled in, I'll let Captain Nowak know."

Cache boarded the private jet. This was the first time she had been on a private plane. She'd spent most of her flight time either on the cheapest flight she could find, stuck in the back, wedged between two passengers, or on a military transport plane. The jet was long and narrow; it wasn't like boarding a big commercial airliner. A cream leather couch that could seat four people ran along one wall, while two cream leather full-size chairs sat opposite one another, separated by a rich mahogany-looking table. There was a deep colored wood trim running along the roof of the plane with beautiful lighting highlighting the elegant-looking interior, and there was a wall toward the back of the plane made out of cherrywood with black inlaid lines running vertically and a small door that led to either

washroom facilities or perhaps a private bedroom in the back
of the plane.

Seated in one of the chairs facing the entrance on the plane
was a woman, strikingly beautiful. She had on a white shirt
rolled up to her elbows; the pressed linen sat against her dark
skin. Her black wavy hair fell down past her shoulders, and she
had a cute little nose and lips painted a deep red. She got up
from her seat, walked over to the door and extended her hand.
"You must be Cache. My name is Chase Flynn, I'm one of the
senior legal counselors for Quillchem Industries. Did you have
any problem getting here?"

"No, I'm familiar with the airport, and your driver Lee was
great."

"Excellent, that's what I wanted to hear." She motioned to
the chair opposite where she had been seated. "Why don't
you sit down and buckle up? Chip, can you tell Amanda we
are all set back here and she can take off whenever she's
ready?"

"Will do, and, Ms. Iron, I've stored your bag in the small
closet behind you if you need anything from it."

"Thanks, I should be good."

Chip walked to the front of the plane, entered the cockpit
and closed the door behind him. As Chase returned to her seat,
she bent over, leaving a gap between her shirt and her breasts,
which were held in by a soft pink lace bra. Cache thought,
Would I have noticed this before I had my first romantic
encounter with someone of the same sex? Cache now looked at
beautiful women the same way guys used to eye her when she
would emerge from dirty jeans and cowboy boots into a long
gown and high heels.

Cache reached down for her seat belt and pulled it in tight
against her waist as Chase did the same and then leaned back
and relaxed.

"Once we get in the air, Chip will be able to get you something to drink and eat if you like. It should be a smooth flight, we hardly felt any turbulence on the way here."

"What time do you think we'll arrive?"

"Let's see." Flynn looked down at her watch. "It's four o'clock now; we should land in Boston by eight thirty this evening and then I have strict orders to take you right to Quillchem Industries."

"Will anyone still be there?"

"Graydon will be. He wants to talk to you right away. Some scientists could still be in the labs. Security is tight, so there are armed guards on the premises around the clock. We have a small corporate hotel on the campus. They've set aside a room for you while you're in Boston. I also have a room there. I used to rent but was spending so much time at the office, it just made sense for me to keep a room there. They're more business suites than rooms; they have a small kitchen, two bedrooms, a small living room and two washrooms."

The plane started moving. Cache looked out through one of the porthole windows as the jet taxied to the far end of one runway. A voice came from a speaker above Cache's head.

"Everyone should be buckled up back there. If you're not, please do so. We are about to go."

With that Cache could feel the jet moving fast down the runway and after a few moments she could see out of her window that it was climbing as the nearby town of Hart, Montana, became smaller and smaller. Cache sat there and closed her eyes as the jet pushed its way up to its cruising altitude. After a few minutes, Chip came back into the cabin. "Can I get you ladies something to drink?"

"Rye whiskey if you have it," Cache said, "with ice."

"Ms. Flynn, would you care for your usual?"

"Please, Chip, thank you."

Chip put a napkin down in front of both women, followed by two crystal rocks glasses, Cache's filled with whiskey and ice.

"What are you drinking?" Cache asked.

"Eighteen-year-old scotch. If you like scotch you should try it, Graydon keeps only the best on the plane."

Cache sipped her whiskey. "It tastes smooth."

"Well, Ms. Iron—"

"Call me Cache."

"Okay, Cache, you can call me Chase. As I mentioned, I'm one of the senior legal counselors at Quillchem Industries. They have asked me to go over a standard nondisclosure agreement that we have with you, which I need you to sign before you meet with Graydon."

"And why am I signing this?"

"Do you know much about Quillchem Industries?"

"Can't say that I do."

"Quillchem Industries was founded by Graydon Quill the First back in the early nineteen hundreds. They started with textiles and then expanded into various chemical compounds, and then transitioned to technology in the late sixties. Several projects that we're involved in are joint projects with the Pentagon and are highly classified."

"I get it now. And whatever Graydon wants to talk to me about is one of those projects."

"Exactly, and you, being former military, can appreciate why sensitive subjects need to be protected."

"Gotcha."

Chase spent the next hour and a half going over the agreement with Cache in-depth so that she understood what she was signing. There were also clauses that covered not only the current project, whatever it was, but any future work that might occur between her and Quillchem Industries. In the end, Cache saw nothing to be concerned about and signed the agreement, and then Chip witnessed it.

Chase reached down for the agreement, picked it up,

swiveled around to reach her briefcase behind her and tucked the papers down into it, then turned to face Cache.

"Now that we've got that out of the way, what can you tell me about why I'm flying to Boston?"

"I can't say much, simply because Graydon wants to talk to you about it. I will tell you that part of it has to do with his son, Mack, who was killed in the Iraq War sixteen years ago. It's been a driving force behind what Graydon wants to talk to you about."

"So you're not going to tell me anything?"

"For now, that is all I can say. Once you and Graydon have spoken, if you decide to stay on to help us out, come see me and we can talk game plan. If you decide it's not for you, then Amanda will fly you back home tomorrow. Oh, and he plans to pay you for your time."

"Come on, you have to tell me something more than that."

She looked at Cache, smiled and sipped her scotch. "So is everything they say about you on the news true?"

"Lot of it's just speculation on the media's part. They've asked me not to say anything until after the trial takes place and then I think I'll just want to forget about it."

"Well, for what it's worth, if you hadn't been on the news, you might not be here. This could be an opportunity for you; it was for me."

"What do you mean?"

"I mean Quillchem could have hired any lawyer. I was involved in some high-profile cases and caught their attention. Next thing I know, I'm moving to Boston, and that was eight years ago. Everyone acts like family there. You know, a lot of companies talk about that like it's a marketing pitch. Quillchem doesn't talk about it, it just does it."

"Where did you go to school?"

"I started out at Columbia and then went to Stanford for law. After that I spent time with one of the big New York law firms, until Quillchem came looking for me. Now I get involved in all sorts of projects and various parts of the business."

"Does Graydon have any other children?"

"No, Mack was it, that's why his death has been a driving engine behind some of the Quillchem Industries military contracts. Mack thought of himself as a career soldier. He was a lieutenant when he was killed. Graydon said he had hoped that Mack would eventually leave the military and take over the company." Chase took a large gulp of her drink and held it in silence for a moment before swallowing. "Now we don't know who will be the head of the company when Graydon is no longer there."

"They could always hire someone."

"Yeah, and that is what they will have to do, but it's family owned, no external shareholders, so who they'll hire is anyone's guess."

"Maybe it will be a hotshot lawyer."

"Or maybe it will be a private investigator." With that she reached over and clanked her glass against Cache's.

"Yeah, that ain't going to happen."

"Say that now. Tell me you feel the same way after spending twenty minutes with Graydon. He has this ability to make you want to see things, to believe anything is possible. Besides that, whoever he leaves his stock to, that is the new owner of a multi-billion-dollar company."

Cache looked around the plane. "Is there a washroom on board?"

Chase swiveled her chair and pointed at the door at the back of the plane. "Just through those doors."

Cache got up and made her way to the back of the plane and through the wooden door. There was a full-size washroom with a toilet, sink, vanity and small shower. She just wanted to throw some cold water on her face and freshen up for a few minutes. She opened the door an inch to walk out and then pulled back inside and closed the door slightly to watch something going on in the cabin. Chase had Cache's duffel bag open on the table as she and Chip went through the contents. "What are they doing?" she muttered, and softly opened the door and crept back to the front of the plane so they did not hear her approach.

"You know, if you want to get into my panties, there's a shower back there we could try."

Chase, flustered, and Chip, embarrassed at being caught, stood back from the table. "I'm sorry, Cache, we just needed to check to see if you had a weapon with you."

"Nope, left it at home. Now I wish I brought it." She grabbed the bag from Chip's hands and pulled out the contents one by one until the bag was empty. "Happy?"

Chase sat down in her chair, and Chip walked off to the cockpit and closed the door behind him.

"Can I put my stuff away, or do you want to sniff them now?" she said, looking directly at Chase.

"I don't apologize for it. You'll appreciate it why we needed to do it after you talk to Graydon. Do you want me to help you put them away?"

"I can take care of it," Cache said, and proceeded to put everything back into her bag and then threw it on the leather couch beside her.

She walked over to Chase and bent down so that she was about two inches from her face. "Maybe you should pat me down now." She could feel the steam coming from Chase's breath, the smell of roses and lilies coming from her neck. She thought about reaching down and unbuttoning her blouse to see what reaction that would get.

"I think we have invaded your privacy enough for one day," she whispered to Cache.

Cache leaned in even closer to her. "Are you sure you don't want to invade it some more?"

Chase ran her tongue over her lips and looked Cache straight in the eye. "No, I'm good."

Cache returned to her seat and sat down, looking at Chase, who seemed noticeably agitated from their encounter, and grabbed her glass of whiskey and downed the remaining amount in one large gulp.

"You could have just asked."

"Would you have said yes?"

"Sure, I have nothing to hide. I'll strip down naked in front of you right here and now, if that's going to make you feel more comfortable."

"Most people wouldn't. Most people lie, they try to conceal things."

"I am not most people."

"I can see that."

"Not a good way to start off getting to know someone."

Cache and Chase sat in silence for the next sixty minutes. Cache took the time to go up to the bar and make herself another glass of whiskey. Chip did not seem too eager to leave the cockpit, and she sat back down and sipped on her glass and stared out the window, eventually closing her eyes and stretching out her legs, plunking her boots across from her up on the leather couch.

"I'm sorry."

Cache opened her eyes and looked at Chase.

"I should have asked. If you decide to stay on and help us with our issue, we could be working a lot together and it's not the best way to start a relationship."

Cache sat there staring at Chase as she watched her sip on her scotch.

"This is usually the part where you say something back," Chase said.

Cache looked at her and thought about walking over, wrapping her hand around her head and pulling her mouth in tight against hers. That would send an obvious message that every-thing was forgiven. But she resisted the urge. She was still trying to figure out whether her encounter with Kathryn was just a one-time event in her life or something more.

"I forgive you, for wanting to know what my panties looked like."

Chase laughed and the tension that had filled the plane for more than an hour disappeared. The door to the cockpit opened and a timid-looking Chip Martin stepped back into the cabin. "Captain Nowak wanted me to tell you we are coming into Boston and you should buckle up, and, Ms. Iron, I'm sorry for that incident earlier." Chip returned to the cockpit and closed the door behind him.

About twenty minutes later, Cache could feel the wheels of the jet coming into contact with the ground of the runway. The skies were dark and she could spot rain drops bursting against the plane's windows. The jet rolled along until it reached the Quillchem Industries hangar, and Cache disembarked with Chase, who had now pulled on a beige trench coat and held her briefcase in her hand.

"Is there a limo or do I need to get a taxi?" Cache asked.

"I'll drive you, we're going to the same place."

Cache followed Chase out of the hangar to a yellow Mini Cooper S parked in one of the reserved parking spots. Cache threw her bag into the trunk and the two women climbed into the vehicle. Chase put her wipers on a medium setting to whisk away the water falling on the windshield.

"The corporate campus is about forty minutes away from here. I'll take you upstairs to meet Graydon and can drop your bag off at your suite if you trust me with it."

They left the airport and made their way down the road to a four-way intersection with a traffic light. No other vehicles could be spotted in any direction as the red light reflected off of the wet pavement. As they continued to travel away from the airport, Cache could see the glow coming from Boston in the direction in which they were heading.

The headlights of a car behind them caught Cache's attention in the mirror. Two vehicles traveling in the same direction as the rain pounded them. Chase slowed down, providing the car behind her with the opportunity to pass them, but it never did. It just kept pace with them as they made their way down Oakcreek Drive and a series of large glass buildings with modern architecture appeared on the horizon with the glow of Boston some miles behind them. The main building that they were heading to had angles jutting out in different directions. Cache could see large circular windows at the top of the building that looked like they were encased in some sort of shiny metal. A big sign appeared to Cache's right, lit up by white floodlights that announced that she had found her way to the corporate campus for Quillchem Industries. As they pulled into the main gate, which was closed, to talk with the security personnel in the booth, Cache observed the car that had been following them passed by them down the road. The vehicle looked like an American-made four-door black sedan, but further details were hidden because of the rain.

"Good evening, Ms. Flynn, can you advise me on who your passenger is?"

"Hey, Roger, yeah, this is Ms. Iron. She has an appointment with Mr. Quill."

Roger returned to the security building, and a few minutes later, returned to the car. The gates opened up. "Yep, he's expecting her."

The car drove through the gates. Cache watched as the gates closed behind her. She noted that a black metal fence about twelve feet high ran along the perimeter of the campus and she could observe security cameras throughout the complex. Chase drove into the parking garage and down to a parking spot reserved for her by name. Cache grabbed her bag from the trunk and followed Chase into the building. As they walked through the parking garage, which was well lit and patrolled by security teams, Cache noted for the first time her long legs and black stiletto heels.

Chase walked up to a scanner, scanned her security card and held the door open for Cache. They approached the main security checkpoint for the building, where three armed guards were stationed, two men and one woman. They asked Cache to put her bag down and scanned it for any dangerous items, and then Cache proceeded through a metal detector, followed by Chase.

It struck Cache as odd that Chase had felt the need to go through her bag on the flight, given that security was going to check it for weapons anyway. Chase walked past the four main elevator doors to an elevator door on the far side of the building. The doors to this elevator were different, made of brass with artistic etchings. Chase put her badge against a reader and rested her chin on a plastic arm jutting out from the wall in front of a camera lens. A blue light covered her face as a computer said, "Chase Deborah Flynn, senior legal counsel, access approved."

The doors to the elevator opened. "Do you want to hold on to your bag, or do you want me to drop it in your room?"

Cache thought about it for a second, then handed her the bag and walked into the elevator. The door closed behind her. It was a small compartment made of wood and polished steel. The elevator panel only housed one button, which read, "To the Top." Cache pressed the button, uncertain what awaited her.

# 3

---

Cache continued to ride to the top. A display on the top right-hand side of the elevator illuminated with a blue arrow pointing upwards with the phrase "You're almost there." The elevator came to an abrupt halt and opened up to a large foyer. White marble floors and an odd green wall about thirty feet from the elevator doors blocked sight of what lay behind. Cache poked out her head. A woman in her midfifties, a little plump with gray curly hair, pale white skin and a funky pair of glasses in a teal color, spoke up.

"You must be Ms. Iron, or do you prefer Cache?"

Cache walked over to the desk she was seated behind. It was a large desk in cherrywood with brass fixtures. There were flowers in a variety of vases surrounding her, a computer, pens, and an assortment of office paraphernalia.

"Cache is fine."

"I'm Nancy Grant, Mr. Quill's personal assistant. He is expecting you."

She turned to her computer, typed something into the keyboard, stood up from her desk and walked over to a small door built into the wall. She opened the door up and pulled out a machine that looked like something you would put your head against at an optometrist's office while having your eyes checked.

"Come, come here." She motioned to Cache. "I need you to rest your chin here and then put your palm down on this pad." Cache looked down and could see an outline of a handprint on the pad.

"Why am I doing this?" she asked.

"Security is everywhere in the building—biometric locks, iris scans—so I just need to take a picture so that I can add it to your security profile. Don't want to be locked out of the washrooms, do we?"

"I haven't said yes to the job."

"Oh, but you will. I have been here twenty years and I can count on one hand the number of times someone could say no to Mr. Quill."

"You may need to use the other hand, in my case."

"I knew I was going to like you," said a loud male voice from over her shoulder. "Nancy, if she doesn't want to do it, we can do it another time, if she decides to stay on."

He extended his hand. He was tall, about six foot two, with silver-white hair, a slight tan and an average build, though he was not overweight, at least as far as Cache could assess. He wore a dark gray suit with a vest, a pressed white shirt, gold cufflinks and a silvery-blue tie. Cache put his age around his mid-sixties, and he presented himself with a sense of polish that very few gentlemen still exhibited in this day and age.

"I'm Graydon Quill, Ms. Iron. Thank you for coming all this way. Can you come with me?"

As Cache left with Graydon, she turned back to look at Nancy, who motioned at the equipment.

"I'll leave this out just in case." And she returned to her desk.

Cache followed Graydon around the green wall to a wall of

glass that extended the entire length of the floor, a frosted glass door in the middle. Graydon reached for the door handle and held the door open as Cache entered the room. The room had round windows, some facing the exterior of the building while others showed the interior works of Quillchem Industries. There was a big chair behind a large mahogany desk to the right, with a computer and stacks of papers on it. A large oil painting of a gentleman bearing some resemblance to Mr. Quill hung on the wall behind the chair. To the left was a seating area that comprised two leather couches and two large leather chairs, with a round table with a glass insert in the middle. A cup of coffee sat in front of one chair. He motioned for Cache to sit down in the chair opposite him.

"Would you care for coffee?"

"Please."

"How do you take it?"

"Two creams, two sugars."

She expected him to walk to his desk and call for Nancy to get her a coffee, but much to her surprise he walked over to a set of cabinet doors, prepared the coffee himself and brought it over to her, and sat back down opposite her.

"Did you have a pleasant flight?"

"It was relatively uneventful."

"Which means something happened and you're not prepared to tell me."

"Nothing worth sharing. So why I am I here?"

"Straight to the point, I like that. We're going to get along great."

He got up from his seat, walked over to his desk, picked up a picture, brought it over to her and handed it to her.

The photograph had to have been taken about twenty years ago. It had two people in the picture: a much younger Graydon Quill, silver-gray hair replaced with dark chestnut hair, showing few wrinkles, with his arm around a young man in his early twenties wearing an army dress uniform. Their facial features were similar, only different due to age.

"That's my son, Mackory, before he left for Iraq. He is no longer with us, killed in battle along with several other soldiers, shot three times before they killed him."

Cache looked at the picture, set it down gently on the table in front of her and picked up her coffee.

"My great-grandfather started Quillchem Industries." He motioned with his hand, pointing at the oil painting behind his desk. "That's a painting of him there. It started off in textiles and then chemicals. In the sixties my father took it into technology, which is where we are today. We develop a lot of our own products, we license our technology out to other companies and we work on several joint projects, including ones for the military."

"It's quite impressive. I still don't know what I have to do with any of this."

He took a sip of his coffee and stayed silent for a few minutes before continuing. "My son and others died because bullets entered their body, but what if... what if there was a way that we could prevent that from ever happening again? For more than a decade since Mack died I have been assembling a team of brilliant scientists to engineer a fabric that will repel bullets. Not large ordnance from something like a tank or a bomber, but everyday bullets fired from guns and rifles manufactured all over the world. Something that's lightweight that could be woven into the field uniforms and headwear that would keep our troops alive. What do you think about that?"

"Truthfully, it sounds like fantasy stuff. If it was possible it would be off the charts, but it's just fantasy, right?"

"Others would have agreed with you until a few months ago when our lead scientist, Dr. Lucas Fischer, made a breakthrough and created what we call Electrified Ballistic Stopping Material, or EBSM for short. And this is where you come in.

Last week he went missing. No one has seen him. His wife is concerned, he hasn't been in the lab and we can't find him."

"Have you called the police?"

"I did one better. I called the army. The police have been here, taken statements, his wife filed a missing persons report, but they don't always get the attention they need. I reached out to our contact at the Pentagon, General Douglas, who, when doing some research, suggested I bring in a bright young former soldier who was making the news recently for her investigative work."

"Meaning me?"

"Meaning you. You know full well the army has a certain protocol that they have to adhere to. You as a private citizen may not be as constrained by those protocols but you have the experience, and I need that—I need you."

"I'm not an investigator, any more, I don't think I would be helpful to you, and this sounds too important to trust to an amateur who got lucky."

He stood up, picked up the framed photograph and placed it back on his desk. He returned to her, put his finger to his mouth and thought for a few seconds, then pointed at her. "I don't think you know what you are."

Cache thought that he had hit the nail on the head in more ways than one.

"I know talent, even before they can see it for themselves. I see it in you. I would rather trust your amateurish ways than trust anyone else with this. Can you do this for me? Can you do this for your country?"

"The country part was a little much."

"I thought so too as it was coming out of my mouth, but you were in the army. You can see the importance of this. Will you help me? There is no indication anywhere of what the formula is, and without Dr. Fischer we might be going back to the drawing board and starting over." He sat down, leaned over and put his hand on her knee. "Will you help me?"

Cache could picture Nancy's smug expression if she agreed, but she thought this might be what she needed at this moment in her life.

"If I agree to this, I will need a few things from you."

"What do you need? I have all the resources in the world."

"I will need to talk with everyone connected to Dr. Fischer to see if I can figure out what happened."

"Done. What else do you need?"

"I need a gun. Call it a safety blanket, but we don't know who we're dealing with on this." Graydon got up and walked to the cabinet doors to the right of the coffee station and opened them up. He looked around inside, pulled out a wooden box, walked back and sat it down in front of her. She pulled back the lid to reveal an automatic handgun.

"It's a subcompact, nine millimeter, small enough for you to keep it concealed, owned by Quillchem Industries and registered to you by tomorrow morning, the new head of investigations for Quillchem Industries."

"It's nice, but I'm not sure the local police are going to be too happy with me carrying it around."

He scratched his nose and thought for a moment. He rose and opened up the cabinet to the left of the coffeemaker station, revealing a sixty-five-inch flat-panel television set. "Let's see if he's in."

"Who?"

Graydon went back to his desk and punched something into his computer. The television screen opened up to reveal a man in military dress uniform with two lower-ranking officers flanking him.

"General, did I get you at a bad time?"

"Have you found our missing scientist?"

"No, but I have our new lead investigator here." Cache stood at attention, saluting the general.

"At ease, soldier. I'm glad Mr. Quill took my advice and brought you on. Heard good things about you, don't make me regret recommending you."

"No, sir."

"General, Ms. Iron needs a gun as part of her duties here at Quillchem. Given we don't know what she might be up against, can you arrange a state carry permit for her?"

The general leaned over to one of the junior officers beside him, and he nodded. "Yes, we can take care of that. It might take a few days but given that she is effectively also working for the military in this capacity, it shouldn't be a problem. We'll need to talk with the right people to fast track the process, she might need to meet with someone from local law enforcement. Is there anything else you require?"

Graydon looked back at Cache, who shook her head. "No, General, not at this time, sorry to disturb you."

"Just find our missing scientist." And with that she could see the general press something on his desk and the screen went dark.

Graydon went over and sat back down beside Cache. "Welcome to Quillchem Industries. I hope you are successful in your pursuit here."

"Chase mentioned that you have hotel rooms here?"

"We have set you up in one. We have suites at the far end of the facilities. Mainly there for people who are forced to work late, or for employees from one of our other facilities. There are four in total; one has Ms. Flynn in it, we have assigned the one next to hers to you and the other two are vacant."

"Did Dr. Fischer ever use them?"

"He might have. Nancy can check to see who we have assigned them to and when."

"Who should I report to?"

"You report to me and only me. The team around here will provide support as necessary but if they give you any guff, it's me they will have to deal with. This is too important to get bogged down in petty squabbling."

They continued talking for about thirty minutes, sharing personal insights as she got to know her new boss better. As she finished her coffee, she got up, and Graydon gathered his personal effects and walked back out into the lobby with her.

"Nancy, would you call Jack and have him bring the car around? I better get home before my wife worries. Cache, thank you for doing this for me. If you need anything, you contact me, Nancy knows to put you straight through. Or talk to her or Flynn; they'll be tremendous resources for you here."

Graydon patted her on the back, made his way to the elevator and disappeared.

Nancy held up five fingers. "Which one of these were you again?"

"He got me with the 'do it for your country' part."

"He always does," Nancy said as she walked to her desk and fiddled with her computer. She had Cache rest her chin on the contraption jutting out from the wall.

The pad that registered her palm print glowed red for a few seconds, and then a green outline around her palm lit up. The machine said, "Julie Cache Iron, lead investigator, Quillchem Industries, confirmed." Next Cache could see a soft blue light scan down over her face to her chin and then back up to her forehead. The machine said, "Julie Cache Iron, lead investigator, Quillchem Industries, confirmed."

Nancy motioned for her to step back and then pushed the contraption back into the wall.

"Don't you have a head of security to do all of this?"

"We do, but there are some things, especially when it comes to the military, that Graydon insists are done outside of our security office."

Nancy sat back at her desk and began typing on her computer.

"Your height is...?"

"Five foot eight and a half."

Nancy looked at her for a second. "Do I need to get a measuring tape?"

"Fine, five foot eight."

"Let's see, hair color, obviously brunette; eye color?"

"Blue."

Nancy pushed down her glasses and looked at Cache. "Yes, blue. Any tattoos?"

"Two."

"Visible?"

"Sometimes; right shoulder and left forearm."

"Scars?"

"Three: one lower back—a steer wasn't happy with me; one on my right leg—an ex wasn't happy with me; and one on the back of my left leg—a rock formation wasn't happy with me."

"Weight?"

"Do you really need to know?"

"Weight?"

"One hundred and twenty pounds, give or take something, I haven't weighed myself recently."

Nancy continued typing for a few minutes. "That should be everything we need. Human Resources may have a few questions about home address and other things but we can get that from you later."

She opened up a drawer on her left-hand side and pulled out a brown billfold. She then pressed a couple of buttons on her computer and a device behind her printed out a card with Cache's name on it that she took and inserted into the wallet. Cache noticed a silver metal badge on the right-hand side of the billfold as Nancy handed it to her and she examined the contents. The badge was a silver metal Q with a lightning bolt coming from the center, with the word *investigator* emblazoned on the bottom.

"You're now our top cop."

She proceeded to turn off everything on her desk and power down her computer.

"I'll take you over to the accommodation wing and then I need to get home."

"Do you always work this late?"

"Not usually, but Graydon was convinced that you would take the job, and he wanted to get you up and running as soon as possible."

Cache had the small wooden box tucked into the gap of her left arm.

"What's in the box?" Nancy asked.

Cache opened it to show her the firearm with thirty rounds of ammunition.

"Nice. I think all I got when I started here was a black leather portfolio case that read 'Quillchem' on it."

Nancy turned off all the lights and walked Cache to the elevator. They took the elevator down to the lobby, passed the security officers and walked down the hallway. The left side of the hallway was all glass. The windows looked out onto a green space that was well lit, with floodlights and light poles scattered throughout the grounds. To the right was a series of rooms with solid walls covered in paintings and illustrations from various artists. Cache observed that there appeared to be cameras everywhere. Every corner had a camera covering a portion of the hallway. Some doors to the offices had keyed locks on them, while others had facial scanning devices attached to the wall. They wandered down the hall, which was marked "Tesla Avenue" in white paint on a black marquee on the wall housing the offices, and turned right when the hallway came into conjunction with Edison Avenue. Nancy pointed out various areas to Cache to give her the lay of the land. The corporate campus covered 135 acres, with the building they were in as the primary facility. There were five other buildings on the campus; the perimeter was covered by a twelve-foot black metal fence with security cameras at different points and armed security patrols with dogs walking around the property at all hours.

As they passed the food court on the hallway designated Bell Street, which intersected with Edison Avenue, Nancy shared that some stations were open twenty-four hours while others only operated from seven a.m. to six p.m. Being a resident in the facility would give her twenty-four-hour access to the kitchen. As they continued down Edison Avenue, they came to a small hallway called Curie Causeway and hung a left until they reached a set of elevators.

"What's with all the hallway names?" Cache asked.

"They're all famous inventors from around the world. It makes finding something in this place a lot easier. In the morning, the tech group will have you set up on the intranet, where you will be able to find any place you want to go by the door number and the street that was assigned to that hallway."

"Dr. Fischer's lab. Is it here in the building?"

Nancy pushed the button to call the elevator. "No, his team is located in the Franklin Facility, where all military work is conducted. The security there is tighter than in here. When you want to go over, let me know and I'll let Greg Drewison, the head of security, know. You should meet Greg sooner than later. He's one of those who could easily get his nose out of joint with you being here, whether or not Graydon hired you."

They boarded the elevator and Nancy instructed Cache to swipe her key card against the key card reader. There were two buttons on the panel, for the second and third floors. "We have you assigned to Suite B on the third floor. Ms. Flynn is in Suite A if you need anything." They arrived at the third floor and got off, and walked down the hall. Suite A appeared on the left-hand side and Suite B on the right. Nancy instructed Cache to swipe her card again to open the door.

"Here is where I leave you. If you have any questions, I'll be in by eight o'clock tomorrow morning. I've left a list of extensions by your phone. I've also left the extension for the kitchen if you're hungry and would like anything. I bid you good night."

Cache waved at her as Nancy headed for the elevator and disappeared from sight. She walked into the room and flipped on the light. There was a large circular sitting area in the middle of the room made up of a long fabric couch and two leather chairs perched in front of a large, black flat-panel television set. To the right of Cache was a door that opened onto a small closet, and then another door that revealed a powder room with all the necessary items. Cache walked past the second door into a small kitchen that was circular. Stove, microwave, fridge, dishwasher, sink, cupboards filled with plates, glasses, mugs and silverware. She exited the kitchen and continued around the room to a set of double doors that opened onto a large bedroom with a king-sized bed. The far wall was all glass, which continued beyond the bedroom into a second bedroom next door and then into the sitting room. The wall opposite one chair in the sitting room had a sliding glass door that led to a balcony with two chairs and a small table. In the master bedroom, at the foot of the bed was a small rectangular ottoman that had her olive-green duffel bag resting on it. The bedroom contained a walk-in closet and a large master bathroom with walk-in shower and bathtub for two.

Cache stepped back and looked around the room. It was possibly one of the nicest suites she had ever been in. She went to the couch, sat down and looked at the portable phone and the list of numbers that Nancy had written beside it. She picked up the phone and called home, and talked to her mother. Cache explained that she couldn't share the details of the work that she would be doing, but that she had accepted the job and could be in Boston for the next little while. She promised her mother that she would stay safe and to phone regularly so they could know what she was up to and that she was okay. As she sat on the couch, kicking her boots off and resting her bare feet up on the table, she heard a knock at the door.

"Hey, Mom, someone is at the door, I have to let you go... yes, I love you too, say hello to everyone."

She got up off the couch and walked over to the door. In a facility with this much security, there was only one person this could be, and she opened the door.

The trench coat and high heels had been exchanged for a pair of Daisy Duke jean shorts and a blue T-shirt with a faded white print of some location in Boston on it. Her long black hair swept down behind her, and her red-painted lips matched the red toenail polish she was sporting. She held two wine-glasses in her hand and a bottle of white.

"Hope you like wine, neighbor. Thought I would come say hello."

"Come on in." Cache waved as if she were making a grand gesture.

"So, did you take the job that Graydon offered, or are you heading back in the morning?"

"He is one very convincing gentleman. It looks like I'm going to be staying on for a while, at least until I can figure out what happened to Dr. Fischer. I assume it's okay for me to mention him to you, I assume you know."

Chase put the wineglasses down on the table with the bottle of white wine, went into the kitchen and returned with a corkscrew. She opened the wine and poured them each a glass. "I know of Dr. Fischer and can fill you in on some of his back-ground, but as to what happened to him, that is what Graydon is hoping you will bring to the puzzle."

Cache reached for her glass of wine and took a sip as she ran her eyes up and down Chase. She still wasn't sure why

Chase had gone through her belongings on the plane and decided to file that in a drawer she visualized in her mind where she kept things she didn't immediately want to deal with but would need to come back to.

"So do you have a plan?"

"I plan to start at the beginning. Tonight I'll try to get some rest, and tomorrow I'll meet with the people who worked with Dr. Fischer to see what they can tell me. Then I would like to talk to his wife if she'll meet with me. It would be helpful if you can tell me what you know about the Fischer's before I speak with her, and I should touch base with the Boston Police Department to introduce myself and ensure I don't step on any toes unless it becomes necessary."

"Sounds like you have a busy few days ahead of you."

Cache reached into her back pocket, pulled out the brown leather billfold that Nancy had given her, opened it up and put her badge down in front of Chase.

"What's that?"

"I think it means my life has just taken an unexpected detour."

## 4

Cache opened her eyes and flipped on her smartwatch. Eight o'clock, that can't be right. As a child, someone had always hustled her out of bed between five and six a.m. to do chores with her brothers before heading off to school. She looked around the room. Cache pulled herself to the edge of the bed and opened the double doors that led to the main living space. Time zone change, she thought, and she sat down on the couch and looked at the extensions that Nancy had left for her. She punched in extension 308 on the phone.

"Hello, Maurice here. What can I get for you this morning, Ms. Iron?"

"Can I get eggs sunny side up, bacon, brown toast and coffee?"

"Absolutely, we'll have that up to you in about twenty-five minutes."

"Perfect." Cache hung up the phone, walked to the bathroom, dropped her top and shorts, pulled herself into the shower and turned on the hot water. The water burned as it fell onto her skin and she breathed in the steam coming from the showerhead. She stood in there for about ten minutes, feeling the hot water flow over her skin and then washed her hair, and then walked out. The mirrors were all steamed up as she walked back out into the bedroom to change for the day. She had just finished combing her hair when she heard a knock at the door. Cache went over to open it up, and a server with deep red hair brought in her breakfast and left. Cache munched through breakfast and then called Nancy to see how she could get over to the Franklin Facility. She punched extension 206 into the phone.

"Good morning, Nancy Grant here."

"Nancy, it's Cache."

"Good morning, Cache, I trust you slept all right?"

"Yeah, it was great. I'm kind of eager to get started today. How do I get to the Franklin Facility?"

"I have arranged for Greg Drewison, our head of security, to take you over. Cars aren't allowed inside the campus, so people either walk or use a golf cart. How about I have him meet you at nine thirty this morning?"

Cache looked at her watch. It was coming up on nine and the extra thirty minutes would give her a chance to finish her breakfast. "That works. Where do I meet him and what does he look like?"

"Go to the elevator at the end of your hall and go down to the main floor. We came from the right last night, so I want you to go left and proceed down the hall to a set of doors. There will be a few parking spots with golf carts there. I can have one assigned to you if you like?"

"That might come in handy."

"Greg is about late forties, dark skin, black thinning hair cut close to the scalp and a black goatee with gray running through it. He'll probably be wearing something that says 'security' on it and will be the one carrying a gun."

"The one carrying a gun. Great, I'll see him then. Thanks, Nancy, for your help."

Cache finished her breakfast and pulled on her boots underneath her jeans. The day looked a little cooler, so she pulled her fleece over her tank top. She grabbed the handgun that Graydon had provided, loaded the clip and tucked it down inside of her jeans, and pulled her fleece over it so as not to show the grip from behind. She grabbed a pad of paper and pen from the desk and jotted down a couple of to-dos for the day.

1. Talk with the head of security.

2. Meet people who worked with Dr. Fischer and see what they know.

3. Reach out to contact at Boston PD. See if they have heard anything.

Cache exited her suite, tucking her badge in her back pocket, and took the elevator to the ground floor and followed Nancy's directions, taking her to the back parking lot. A tall man with dark skin in mirrored pilot shades and a blue sweater with the word *security* printed on the upper left-hand side sat there in a midnight-blue two-seater golf cart with a white top and the words *Quillchem Security* in silver painted across the front.

"Ms. Iron, I presume? I'm Greg Drewison, head of security here at Quillchem. They have asked me to take you over to the Franklin Facility to meet everyone."

Cache walked over to the golf cart and climbed in the passenger side. She extended her hand. "You can call me Cache, and what would you like me to call you?"

"Mr. Drewison is fine." Cache felt a shiver that she wasn't sure was directly attributable to the brisk weather outside.

They drove away from the main building down a two-sided paved path toward a glass building about ten minutes away from the primary facility. The building was surrounded with lush green lawns with sprinklers on in places and trees, benches and walking paths scattered throughout. Cache noticed that there were no other buildings close to the Franklin Facility, as other buildings existed to the east but would be a ten-to-fifteen-minute walk away.

"You know, I wasn't consulted about your hiring."

"Does Mr. Quill seek your permission often?"

He chuckled. "No he doesn't, but given that there is some overlap in what we do, it would have been nice to have a say. So I hear you're ex-army?"

"Six years."

"Why did you leave?"

"Just seemed like the right thing to do at the time."

They continued down the path until they pulled into the Franklin Facility. The building was three stories tall, all mirrored glass, so no one could see in. A bronze sign welcomed them to the facility and a bronze figure of Benjamin Franklin stood atop a marble column out front. The building had twelve golf carts parked out front. Men and women in white lab coats entered and exited the building.

"Did you talk with the Boston PD?" Cache asked.

"Yeah, they came out and did some interviews the other day."

"Do you remember who the lead detective was that came out?"

"Yeah, I brought his card with me." He fished inside his pocket and handed it to her. "You can keep it, I took a copy for my records."

Cache looked at the card. Detective Michael Boone, with a phone number and email. "Thanks, someone else I'll have to reach out to today. Who am I meeting with here?"

"There are about twenty scientists that were working on the project that Dr. Fischer headed up. Most of the people report to one of four lead scientists who worked under Dr. Fischer's supervision. There is Dr. Zhou, Dr. Tanaka, Dr. Wright and Dr. Allen. We advised them that the new lead investigator for the company wanted to meet with them, so they know you're coming."

Cache exited the golf cart and followed Mr. Drewison into the building. She noted that the front of the building had two security cameras facing the doors and several on top of the building, scanning the exterior. The facility sat in the middle of the grounds at that end of the campus, and the security fence running along the perimeter could be spotted in the distance. Mr. Drewison placed his security card against the card reader to open the front doors as they passed through into the main lobby. The lobby had black slate floors and a manned security checkpoint requiring people to enter a vertical tube to pass through to the other side as security officers sat behind the desk scanning the individuals for unauthorized items entering the premises. Mr. Drewison waved at the officers behind the desk, took his firearm out and placed it in a tray, walked inside the scanner and then exited out the other side. Cache followed suit, placing her badge and firearm in a tray and entering the scanner. The two of them collected their belongings and made their way to the elevators.

"Dr. Fischer's labs are on the top floor."

"Does everyone go through that process?"

"Everyone, and for every camera you see, we have two or three hidden ones in various locations, except for the third floor."

"Why none on the third floor?"

Mr. Drewison pressed the elevator call button. "Pentagon didn't want cameras filming the work that was being done out of fear that hackers might be able to tap into the feed. There is no access to the roof from the third floor and the only way up or down is via the elevator or the stairs, which only open in case of an emergency. There are cameras in the elevators and throughout the second floor, but once you enter the third, you are in a dark area of the building." Cache boarded the elevator with Mr. Drewison and made her way to the third floor. As the doors opened, she saw a wall of glass that separated the people working from those getting on or off the elevator. The facilities were in a sterile white color throughout, with microscopes spaced out along the various desks and apparatuses hanging from the ceiling in several locations. Cache could spot areas where Bunsen burners were boiling different colored solutions in glass beakers as scientists huddled around holding test tubes, swirling the contents, while others observed and made notes.

In the middle of the glass wall was a large glass tube that looked like a turnstile setup that you might encounter in the subway. The top and bottom of the tube were covered in a polished steel with thick steel beams fixing the tube to white cinder-block columns that held the glass walls in place. Mr. Drewison walked over to a scanner attached to one column, placed his palm on top of a palm reader and placed his face into a contraption similar to the one Cache had experienced the previous night. A blue light came down over his face and the computer read "approved."

"It's one in, one out," he commented to her, and proceeded into the frosted glass tube. Cache was next; she placed her palm on the hand scanner and her chin on the chin grip, allowing the computer to scan her retinas. "Approved."

Cache entered the tube and came out the other side. A long hallway continued down past the tube, with doors entering the various lab facilities with card readers attached to the walls. Cache followed Mr. Drewison down to the end of the hallway and walked into a boardroom that had a long white table with twelve white leather chairs with chrome frames and swivel wheels surrounding it. The exterior of the room was all mirrored glass, allowing the occupants to view the outside grounds, and a button on the wall brought down window shades.

"This is where I leave you. If you open up the far cabinet over there, you'll find a selection of coffees, teas and mugs."

"You're not staying?"

"I was told to bring you here and then leave. We will have a golf cart with your name on it downstairs shortly, so you can take that back to the primary facility when you're done. My office is located in room twenty-eight on Newton Lane if you're looking for me. Good luck." Mr. Drewison exited the conference room, and Cache went over to the cabinet on the far wall and made herself a coffee, then returned to take a seat at the end of the table with her pen and pad of paper.

She sat there in silence for about twenty minutes. Security had confiscated her smartphone and smartwatch, so she had nothing to play with to pass the time.

She could hear chatter from outside of the room getting louder and louder until a knock came from the door.

"Come on in."

Four individuals walked into the room, two men and two women. The women had brought notepads and pens with them to take notes; the men had chosen not to. All were wearing white lab coats and different styles of dress under the coats that could easily have separated their personalities right then and there. The first person Cache met was Dr. Emily Zhou. She was beautiful, of East Asian descent, with long auburn hair, a small oval face and dark red lipstick with just a touch of makeup. Underneath her lab coat, Cache could spot a brown knitted top, a gray skirt that came just above her knees and a pair of black leather heels. Behind Dr. Zhou in the introduction line was Dr. Ian Wright. He stood at five foot eleven and was in his late fifties with a large, rugged oval face; he was bald, though whether by fate or choice, Cache could not determine. He spoke with an English accent and wore khakis and a polo shirt with a pair of brown casual shoes.

The next person Cache had the pleasure of meeting was Dr.

Jeffrey Allen. He was younger than Dr. Wright, and had gray hair that was messy and a gray beard and mustache of probably a week's growth. He had a slight accent, though Cache thought he might have originally hailed from the Southern part of the US. He wore a black turtleneck, blue jeans and white running shoes. The last member of the group of four was Dr. Akiko Tanaka. She was shorter than Dr. Zhou, with black hair that fell just above her shoulders. She had a small round face and was likely of Japanese descent. Cache reflected on her time stationed in Tokyo as she shook Dr. Tanaka's hand, noting the wedding ring on her left hand. She wore a pink blouse, blue jeans and shiny black leather shoes.

Cache greeted them, trying to note different things about each person that she would record later when they were no longer in the room. She invited them to take a seat around the table and to make themselves a coffee or tea if they liked.

Cache let out a heavy sigh, noticeable to everyone. "My name is Cache Iron, and they have brought me to Quillchem Industries to investigate the disappearance of Dr. Fischer."

"Have they found Lucas yet?" Dr. Tanaka asked.

Dr. Zhou, who positioned herself closest to Cache, turned to face her colleague. "You nitwit, if they had found him, she wouldn't be here to investigate."

"Hey, don't call her a nitwit, you twat," Dr. Allen said.

Cache could see Dr. Allen giving Dr. Zhou an odd look. Clearly this was not a harmonious bunch, she thought.

"Ms. Iron, you don't know Lucas. He's not missing, he is just being dramatic—always needs to be in the limelight, always needs to steal the thunder," Dr. Wright said.

"Ian, that's not fair. What if something happened to him?" Dr. Tanaka said.

Cache could see Dr. Zhou twirling her hair as the others bantered back and forth about whether Dr. Fischer was missing or gone of his own choice.

"You know who suffers the most when Lucas does this bull-shit?" Dr. Wright said as he pointed his finger in Cache's direction.

"Oh, are you going to go on again about poor Petra?" Dr. Allen said.

"She deserves a hell of a lot better than that fool," Dr. Wright said.

"Petra, is she someone else that works here in the lab?" Cache asked.

Dr. Zhou spoke up. "Petra is Dr. Fischer's wife, and don't listen to them, they can't appreciate Lucas's brilliance and neither can she."

"Of course you would say that. You fawn all over him, and he just laps up all your praise. Oh, Dr. Fischer, you're just so brilliant," Dr. Wright said.

"Emily, you have to admit it, you are a little too close to be objective," Dr. Allen said.

"What do you mean by that?" Dr. Zhou said, gritting her teeth and raising her eyebrows.

"You know exactly what it means, you're not dumb, and we can all see right through you," Dr. Tanaka said as she leaned forward and pointed a finger at Dr. Zhou.

"Okay, I can see we are all a cheerful group of campers here," Cache said. "Let's start by asking when was the last time each of you saw Dr. Fischer here."

"Thursday of last week," Dr. Zhou said.

"Last Thursday," Dr. Tanaka said.

"Same," Dr. Allen said.

"Last Friday," Dr. Wright said.

His colleagues looked at Dr. Wright and Cache asked, "Why did you see him on Friday and the others saw him on Thursday?"

"Friday was a holiday, a reward for our success in making a breakthrough with EBSM. We don't get many of them."

"Then why were you here?" Dr. Tanaka asked, looking at Dr. Wright.

"I had a personal matter to talk to Lucas about and I knew, holiday or not, he would be here in the lab."

"And it was just the two of you here?" Cache asked.

"Yes. You can check the security footage, but when I left Lucas was still here working on his code."

"What code?" Cache asked.

"Oh, you haven't seen it?" Dr. Allen asked. "Lucas has this special code he writes all of his notes down in. I mean, if you didn't know there was a method to it, you would think it all gibberish. Pictures and numbers—it made no sense to any of us, and when we asked him to explain it so that we could refer to his notes, he would tell us it was beyond our limited intellects."

"None of you know how to read this code?" Cache asked.

The group of four all shook their heads, while Cache observed Dr. Tanaka looking crossly at Dr. Zhou.

"No, I don't know the code. I asked him to teach me a few times, and he just dismissed my requests. Are you happy?" Dr. Zhou asked.

"So, where did Dr. Fischer use this code?" Cache asked.

"He kept a series of manila journals and would write all his notes in his made-up gibberish," Dr. Wright said.

"The journals, are they here, can I see one of them?" Cache asked.

"We don't know where they are and I suspect—though I can't say with complete certainty—that the reason you are here is to find the journals and the code keeper himself and to get the formula. That's what Quillchem is really interested in," Dr. Allen said.

"Okay, so if I have this straight, you guys had a breakthrough recently on EBSM. Dr. Fischer documented the formula in the journals, in some unrecognizable language, and the journals are now missing as well as Dr. Fischer," Cache said.

Dr. Wright leaned back in his chair and held his hands over his head. "Eureka, I think she's got it. And now you know why he is such a fucking asshole. Years of work, and we may be back to starting over again."

"Can't you just reverse-engineer the product?" Cache asked.

"If we had kept an abundance of the finished product, it might have been possible. We only had a small sample produced, and Mr. Quill and the army wanted it tested against all kinds of ordnance to see how it would hold up. Since Lucas had the formula, they didn't think it to be a concern. Under normal ballistic fire the material did what it was supposed to. Under major firepower, it didn't hold up. Now we don't have enough. I mean, we might be able to figure out a starting point that is farther ahead than starting over again, but it's still going to take years to get back to this point. That is why you need to find Dr. Fischer," Dr. Tanaka said.

Dr. Zhou leaned forward, gripped Cache's hand in hers and squeezed it tight. "Please find Dr. Fischer for us, we are all worried about him."

Cache pulled her hand away. "That's why I'm here." Cache jotted down some notes on her pad of paper as she observed everyone getting a little agitated. She leaned back in her chair, sipped on her coffee and contemplated what to ask next.

"You guys don't know why Dr. Fischer would just disappear on his own without telling a colleague or his wife, who filed a missing persons report?"

Dr. Wright said "No", Dr. Tanaka said, "Not a clue" and Dr. Allen said, "No, idea."

Dr. Zhou said, "He might just need some time on his own to get away from that shrew."

Hearing the word *shrew* caused Dr. Wright to jump to his feet and head over to where Dr. Zhou was sitting. Cache, seeing the anger in his eyes, leaped up from her seat and put herself in the middle of the two parties.

"How dare you call her that? You will never be half the scientist she is, you little bitch," he shouted, and waved his hands in the air.

"Maybe you need some air," Cache said. "I don't think you want me to restrain you."

"Are we done here?" he asked.

"For now. I may need to talk to each one of you again, though I think we'll do the interviews one-on-one. This group dynamic that you have kind of sucks."

Dr. Wright retreated from his position and threw open the conference room door, almost tearing it from its hinges. Dr. Allen left, giving Cache a quick smirk. Dr. Tanaka gathered her belongings and said, "If you need to reach me, call me anytime."

As Dr. Zhou began to leave, Cache asked her to remain for a few minutes, and she returned to the chair closest to Cache.

"What was that all about?"

"Ian has a thing for Petra. They've known each other for years. In fact, Lucas and Ian go way back."

"Really?"

"Yes. Ian thinks he should have been allowed to head the project instead of Lucas. They were both rising scientists in Quillchem's overseas operations, Lucas got picked and Ian didn't."

"Was there bad blood between them?"

She struggled with the question for a few moments, and Cache could see she was trying to formulate the proper response. "The two of them drive each other. Lucas wouldn't be half as good as he is without competing with Ian, and the same goes for Ian, though neither one of them would admit it. I suspect Petra had some influence over Lucas's bringing Ian in on the team. I can't say for certain, just a gut feeling."

"Do you guys have private offices or do you always work in the labs?"

"There are five offices. Four of them are in the respective corners of the building. Ian's is farthest away from Lucas's, and then in one corner there is Lucas's and mine."

"You didn't get a corner office?"

"There are only four corner offices. Besides, Lucas and I work well together and he relies on me as a sounding board, so our offices are closer than the others."

"Can you show me Dr. Fischer's office? I want to have a look around before I head out, but I think we should talk again, if you don't mind."

"No, anything I can do to help. I'm in and out over the next few days to deal with some personal matters that have come up." She reached over to Cache's pad of paper, flipped it to a clean page and wrote down an address and phone number. "If I'm not here and you need to reach me, you can call me or come by. I want to help in any way that I can."

The two of them got up and Dr. Zhou led Cache to the back of the facility through part of the lab. There was a small office next to an even larger corner office. The door was unlocked, and the office was sterile. There was a desk, two black vinyl chairs, textbooks on a bookshelf in different fields of science. A family photo sat on the desk, showing Dr. Fischer, his wife and a young boy.

"I'm just next door, if you need anything," Dr. Zhou said as she departed and walked to her office.

Cache sat down at the desk and looked through the drawers. There were pens, paper, paper clips, a stapler, but no personal items could be found other than the photo on the desk. The office walls were white, the floor a white linoleum; it looked like an office that belonged in a laboratory or hospital. Cache leaned back in the chair and stared out the window. "Where are you, Dr. Fischer?" she muttered. As she turned her head, the sun coming in the window reflected off something small hidden behind the leg of the desk closest to the wall. Cache pushed the chair out of the area, got down on her hands and knees and fished for the object. As she grabbed hold of it, she picked it up. It was a gold button with blue thread hanging from the back clasp. An image of a dragon was etched on the front. She rolled it around in her fingers. "What are you doing here?" she asked.

## 5
---

Cache sat down on the couch inside of her suite and fished the small button from her pocket. She rolled it around between her thumb and index finger and stared at it. "What do you have to tell me?" she asked. She grabbed her smartphone, took a picture of the front and back of the button, put it into a small bag and went to tuck it down deep inside of her duffel bag. A safe is what this room needs, she thought. She returned to the couch, pulled up the photos on her phone and zoomed in on the image. The front depicted a dragon etched into the top of the button. The back showed the setting of a normal button and the words *Made in Criza*. "Well, that isn't much of a clue." A single blue thread clung to the loop that was used to attach the button to the garment it rested on.

Cache reached into her pocket and fished out the business card for the detective in the Boston Police Department who had been assigned to the case. She grabbed the portable phone and punched in his number and extension. The phone rang once, twice, and on the third ring his voice mail kicked in.

"Hello, you have reached Detective Michael Boone of the

Boston Police Department. If this is an emergency, please hang up and dial 911. If not, leave a message after the beep and I will get back to you." *Beep.*

"Hello, Detective Boone, my name is Cache Iron. I'm the new lead investigator for Quillchem Industries. I'm just reaching out to find out if you have learned any new information about the disappearance of our Dr. Fischer. I can be reached at Quillchem Industries." She glanced down at the piece of paper that Nancy had put together for her. "You can reach me at my extension, number 5008. I look forward to speaking with you."

Cache sat the phone down and went over to the coffee machine to brew herself a cup of coffee. She figured she would take the afternoon to compose some notes on her meeting with the group of four. Her next stop would be to go out to the Fischer residence and meet with Mrs. Fischer to see what she might learn there. As the coffeemaker made its hissing sound, telling her that her brew was near completion, her phone rang. She looked at it oddly and wondered who would be calling her. Cache picked it up.

"Hello, Cache Iron here."

"Ms. Iron, Detective Boone, Boston Police Department. You called me?"

"That was only a few minutes ago. I didn't expect to hear from you for a few days and figured I would need to hound you for a response."

"What is your role in this case?"

"Graydon Quill has hired me to oversee the investigation and try to find Dr. Fischer from our company's perspective. We recognize that the Boston police have many other cases, whereas I can put my full attention on this one."

"Well, we found Dr. Fischer, so you don't have to worry about that. As the company's representative, can I ask you to come down to his residence in town? We have a couple of questions that you might be able to help us with."

"Is he all right?"

"I hate to tell you this over the phone, but he was found dead this morning by the cleaning service the Fischer's use."

"Okay, let me gather a few things and I'll be there shortly."

Cache stepped back and thought this might be the shortest job she'd ever had. They knew where Dr. Fischer was. Now hopefully the journals would be with him and she could be on her way back to Montana. She grabbed her coffee, added cream and sugar, and went back to the couch and grabbed the phone. She dialed Nancy and told her she needed to speak with Graydon immediately.

"Hello, Cache, you have news for me?"

"I just got off the phone with the Boston Police Department. They found the body. Dr. Fischer is dead." There was a pause for a few moments. "Graydon, did you hear me?"

"Yes, I heard you. Do we know how? And where are his journals, did they find them?"

"To answer your questions, we don't know the how; I'm going down there after we speak, he was found at his residence in town. I will need to know where that is, and I don't know about the journals; we'll know more once I get there."

"All right, keep me posted. Lucas kept a residence at the Dawes here in town. Preferred it to staying in one of the suites. The condo number is 2905. Cache, I don't want to sound insensitive but we need to find those journals. I will let General Douglas know of the developments." And then he hung up.

Cache gathered her belongings and debated whether it was smart to bring her gun with her but did not want to be caught without it. She called Nancy back to find out how she could get a taxi to go downtown. Nancy told her they had a car service on standby to take her wherever she needed to go and that it would meet her out at the front of the building. Cache made her way to the lobby and, after getting lost once in the maze of hallways and asking for directions, found her way to the entrance of the primary facility. A black German luxury Baumann sedan was parked there, and a tall, thin man with a mop of gray hair, in a black suit, stood beside the back door.

"Ms. Iron, my name is Aaron Wells. I will be your driver when you're in town. Just call Nancy or me directly and I can bring the car around for you."

Aaron handed her a card that she took and pushed down into her jeans pocket. She extended her hand. "Aaron, it's nice to meet you. Do you know where the Dawes is? We need to get there as soon as possible."

"Absolutely." He opened the back door for her and she sat down inside.

The interior differed from those of other Baumann's she had been in. The back compartment had walnut trim throughout, with a folding desk to work on, USB and power ports, and a phone in the middle attached to a console of buttons. It was like sitting in a miniature office. Aaron jumped into the driver's seat and they sped off, heading toward downtown Boston.

"Aaron, what can you tell me about the Dawes?"

"It's one of a few luxury condominiums down near the water. I believe it was built nine or ten years ago, approximately thirty-nine or forty stories."

Cache could hear a buzzing sound in the back of the vehicle and looked around for the source. Aaron glanced in his rearview mirror. "Ms. Iron, it's the phone that's buzzing."

"Thanks, and please call me Cache."

She picked up the phone to talk with Nancy, who had been asked to relay a message to her. The Pentagon was dispatching military police officers to the Dawes and would be on site to provide any help to her as was required. Cache hung up the phone. Traffic picked up as Aaron made his way into downtown Boston and then pulled up to a large condominium complex in the heart of the city. Several police cruisers and unmarked sedans lined the street. Cache even spotted a dark green sedan with military markings on it and a red bubble lamp on the dash. As she pulled up, a uniformed police officer approached the car. "Sir, you can't park here."

"It's okay, Aaron, I'll jump out and call you when I need to go back."

Cache exited the car and leaned over it to speak with the officer, "I'm here to see Detective Boone, is he upstairs in 2905?"

The officer grabbed the microphone attached to the top of his jacket and called it in. "Are you Ms. Iron?"

"I am."

"He is upstairs waiting for you."

Cache entered the building and showed her credentials to the officer manning the lobby. She jumped into the elevator and took it upstairs. As the doors opened she could see a round mirror with a gold frame on the wall opposite the elevators. There was a mirrored table and two leather high-backs on either side of the table. She looked down to her right to see a hallway that was pretty much empty, with the odd person popping out of their home to see what the fuss was about. To her left, at the end of the hall, stood two members of the army outside of a residence. That must be the place, she thought, and proceeded down the hallway. She spoke with the military personnel and then walked inside the condo.

———

There was a flurry of activity in the home. Forensics personnel were photographing the scene and various markers laid out in the room. On the floor facing upward was Dr. Lucas Fischer, dead. A little older than he was in the pictures she had viewed of him, he had thinning gray hair on the top of his head and a stern oval face with silver-framed glasses.

He was wearing a gray cardigan sweater, blue pants and white socks. There was no sign of blood around him, no evidence of bullet holes or knife wounds that Cache could see. In a circled area close to the body, a crime marker sat beside a red striped tie with a pattern of repeating red and blue stripes. A man in dark pants and a sport coat in his late thirties, with dark brown hair to his shoulders and about two days of facial growth, was talking to the forensic personnel as Cache entered the room.

"Are you the one responsible for those gentlemen outside?"

Cache showed her credentials to the man making the inquiry. "Yeah, my name is Cache Iron. They don't work for me but they're here to provide support if I need it. Do I need it?"

He walked closer to her. She could smell the tangy scent of citrus and leather. His sapphire-blue eyes held her attention for a moment.

"Detective Boone, we spoke on the phone," he said as he extended his hand. "This is a homicide that we will look after."

"Obviously we will be cooperative as best we can, Detective, but as you can appreciate from my friends out there, there are national security interests at stake here and we can't ignore those. Can you tell me how he died?"

"We'll know more when we get him down to the lab, but the preliminary investigation suggests strangulation."

Cache pointed at the tie on the ground. "You suspect that as the murder weapon?"

"There are similar fibers from the tie around Dr. Fischer's neck and bruising that leads us to believe that the necktie was the murder weapon."

"Do you have any suspects?" she asked.

"Funny, I was going to ask you the same question."

"Given what he was working on, there are foreign players that may have had some interest in the doctor's work. Would you mind if I have a look around?"

"Sure, but don't touch anything. If you find something let our guys know so that it can be processed properly."

Cache wandered around the condo. The windows faced onto Boston Harbor. It was a two-bedroom condominium with a small living room, a kitchen, three washrooms and a study. As Cache entered the study, she saw a large Victorian-style desk of dark mahogany with polished brass fixtures stood in the center of the room. Behind the desk three large bookcases stood with a collection of hardback and paperback books on a variety of subjects, including chemistry, chemical engineering, biology, physics, philosophy, art and pulp fiction. Stacks of papers and reports covered the desk, making it hard to see the wood underneath. Two chairs sat at the entrance to the room, with file folders of paper stacked five inches high on one and almost a foot higher on the other. Cache walked around the room and surveyed the contents. There were notes written in the gibberish his colleagues had spoken about and others that were printed and easily readable. A laptop sat on the far left of the desk in a docking station, with a large computer screen behind it.

"Find anything interesting?" Detective Boone said as he entered the room.

"Have you searched the desk?"

"Yes, we looked through the room, doesn't look like anything was disturbed in here."

"Any chance it was a robbery?" Cache asked as she sat behind the desk.

"He is wearing an expensive watch, wedding ring and insignia ring, and they were all left behind."

Cache looked around the room. "And nothing in here was missing?"

"Not that we can tell, but look at the mess. And besides that, that laptop would be worth a few thousand."

"It's more than likely our property," she said.

As she swirled around to face the cabinet behind her, she looked at the hardcover books staring out at her behind the glass-paneled doors. She opened the doors up and noticed what looked like a seam running over the covers of several of the books, and applied pressure to them. She heard a click.

"What have you got there?" Detective Boone asked.

Cache pulled back several books that were indeed fake on a hinge to reveal a safe. There was a palm print reader on the outside of it, and a handle.

"Can you bring him in here so I can open this up?"

"You can't do that, we don't have a warrant."

Cache got up and left the room and went out into the hall to speak with the military personnel on guard. She returned to the study, sat back down and pulled out her phone.

"Hi, it's Cache. Hey, I can fill you in on the details later but we discovered a safe in Dr. Fischer's study that can only be opened by a handprint. The police say we need a warrant. Okay, I will advise them." Cache hung up the phone.

"A federal judge should issue a warrant shortly; until then we sit and wait."

"Sorry, miss, this is a police matter and we have a body to take downtown."

"Afraid not. The armed soldiers at the front are not letting anyone in or out until the warrant arrives, and there are more federal troops on standby, in case they are needed."

"You can't keep us prisoners here, we're police officers."

"You're not prisoners. You are free to go any time you want. You just can't take the body, not just yet. Unless you want to take the hand off and leave me just that."

"This isn't over," he said as he pointed at her, grabbed his mobile phone and walked out into the other room.

Cache swiveled in her chair. She hated waiting for things, but she needed to know if what she was hunting for was hidden behind the safe's steel wall. After fifteen minutes had passed,

Detective Boone reentered the study, walked to the chair with the smaller collection of files on it, picked them up and put them on the floor against the wall, and pulled the chair up closer to Cache.

"What did your superiors say?" she asked.

"We wait for the warrant. You know, smugness doesn't suit you," he said as he sat in the chair and stared at her. "What's so important in the safe, anyway?"

"Can't tell you that, national security and all that fine stuff."

"You know when we get that open, I have to take the contents of the safe."

"Nope, can't let you do it."

"And you're going to stop me? You and what army?" He thought about his comment for a second. "You're a lot cuter than when you think you're right."

"Look, there is only one thing we are interested in; anything else, you can deal with, and you can make your arguments to a judge if you think you should keep custody of what I am hoping is in there. That's not up for me to decide. My goal is to recover Quillchem Industries' property. So you think I'm cute?"

"What? No! Yes—it's just a figure of speech, don't read too much into it. You're not my type."

After an hour had passed, there was some commotion in the principal part of the condominium as a woman in a two-piece dark business suit with short blond hair and narrow facial features was escorted by one of the military police officers to the study.

"Hello, I'm Olivia Sutton," she said as she pulled out her credentials for Detective Boone. "I'm with the Justice Department. Here is the warrant you requested to open the safe. All contents of a personal nature are to be turned over to the detective; any property of Quillchem Industries is to go to Ms. Iron. Can we get on with this?"

Detective Boone got up from his chair and spoke with the

forensics people, who had placed Dr. Fischer in a black body bag. They carried his remains into the study, pulled his right hand from the bag and positioned it against the safe. The palm print scanner turned green and clicked open.

"He is all yours," Cache said as the forensics team carried the body out to a waiting stretcher and headed back to their facilities.

Cache was about to open the safe. "Wait, put these on first," Detective Boone said, and handed her a pair of latex gloves.

Cache obliged him and opened the safe. There were seventeen manila journals marked *Quillchem* on the spine, and nothing else. She pulled out the books and put them down on a small area of the desk not already covered with papers and folders. Detective Boone walked over, looked inside the safe and noted that it was now empty.

"Was that what you were looking for?"

"I think so." Cache flipped through the journals. Each one had a number in blue or red pen in the top right-hand corner. She counted out seventeen journals, starting with number one and finishing with number eighteen. She re-counted.

"One of them is missing. Looks like number fifteen is not here."

"Is that significant?" Detective Boone said.

"I don't know." As she opened up journal number one, everyone in the room could see the pages comprised a series of odd shapes and numbers that looked like a child had doodled them. She flipped through all the pages in the journals as everyone watched, and there were no words in the English language present other than the name *Quillchem* on the outside of the journal.

"Detective, are we done here? I trust you have no interest in what Ms. Iron has in her possession."

"No, not at this time. How are you supposed to read those?"

"Dr. Fischer's colleagues said he had his own code for

keeping his notes. We will need to try to figure out what they say and then we need to know where journal fifteen is at."

"Well, I have a murder to solve, so I will leave you, Ms. Iron. I wish I could say it was a pleasure, but I would be lying." He left the room, escorted out by one of the military officers.

"For what it's worth, he doesn't hurt the eyes too much," Olivia said.

"I hadn't noticed, plus he seems rather full of himself."

"If you don't need me any further, I have a mountain of work to get back to." She handed a business card to Cache. "If you need me for anything else, please call me."

Cache walked with her out of the condo and thanked her for her help. There were still uniformed police officers stationed inside of the condominium. But Cache had what she had come for. She asked the military police officers to wait for her and escort her down to her vehicle given the significance of the journals she'd recovered. She grabbed her phone, called Aaron to bring the car around and told him that they would head back to Quillchem Industries shortly.

Cache returned to the study and gathered up the journals in her arms. She then walked back to the living room in the condo, where Dr. Fischer's body had been discovered, she saw that the tie that had sat a few feet away from his body had been removed, as had other evidence that had been flagged in the home. Cache was escorted down to her black Baumann sedan, where Aaron stood waiting for her to get back in. She thanked the military police officers for their help as they made their way to their parked vehicle. She climbed inside the back of the vehicle and rested the journals beside her. Aaron returned to the driver's seat and pulled away from the curb as he made his path back to the corporate campus of Quillchem Industries.

"Sorry, Aaron, I don't mean to be rude," Cache said as she pushed one button on the center console to raise a privacy screen that separated her from Aaron. She picked up the phone in the car and called Nancy.

"Hey, Nancy, it's Cache. Is he still in?"

"Yes, he has been expecting your call. I'll put you through."

"Cache, what did we find out, do you have the journals?"

"We have them—at least most of them."

"What do you mean by that?"

"There were seventeen journals in the safe marked one through eighteen. Journal fifteen is missing."

"Could it be in his condo somewhere?"

"It's possible, but I don't think the police are going to let me tear through there until they are done with their investigation. At least we have most of them."

"Well, that is something to be thankful for, and for all we know the missing journal could be at his home. I should reach out to Mrs. Fischer to express my condolences and ask if you could come out and look through Lucas's study at some point. Do they have any idea who killed him?"

"If they do, the detective is not sharing with me, and I think I pissed him off, so I'm not sure if he will be helpful. But I got a contact in the Justice Department that could be useful."

"The journals are our top priority, not to sound callous. Lucas was a friend and I want his killer found, but we need to figure out the formula to EBSM."

"What do you want me to do with the journals in the meantime?"

"How legible are his notes?"

"Not at all; they're all in some special code the other scientists on the team spoke about."

There was a pause in the conversation. "So without Lucas it might be hopeless," he said.

"Unless we can crack the code."

"The army has specialists that might be able to help us with that. Bring the journals back to Quillchem and hand them over to Chase. I will ask her to wait around until you get here. I want them locked up on our premises until we can figure out what they say. Good work, Cache, have a good night."

Cache hung up the phone, picked up one of the journals and flipped through it. She put it down beside her and brought the privacy screen down.

"Sorry about that, Aaron, just some things I can't say in public."

"It's okay, Cache, I understand, it goes with the job."

"How long until we get back to the office?"

"About twenty-five minutes. Traffic is rather light at the moment, except for our tail behind us."

Cache looked out the tinted back window and noticed a black sedan behind them. "How long have they been back there?"

"Can't say. I noticed them about ten minutes ago; when I speed up, they speed up. I've slowed down to see if they would pass us, but they haven't." Cache repositioned herself so she could see better out the back window. She couldn't make out the driver, and a shadow suggested that someone was in the passenger seat. She turned the flash off on the camera on her smartphone, took a few pictures and sat back down. The letters and numbers of the license plate couldn't be determined even when she zoomed in on the image. All she noticed was a blue background with a red arching design on top. As Aaron pulled into Quillchem Industries, the dark sedan continued on past the facilities, speeding up as it passed. Cache watched the sedan but could see no indication of who these mysterious strangers were.

# 6

I t was seven a.m. on Saturday morning when Cache awoke from her slumber to the rocking beat of her favorite band. Unlike the previous day, she hadn't trusted her internal clock to wake her at the appropriate hour and set an alarm instead. She glanced around her suite as sunlight was trying to make its way in from behind the drawn shades. A large stack of photocopy paper still sat at the end of the bed, where she had left it the night before. After returning to Quillchem Industries, she'd turned the journals in her possession over to the company's lawyers, who photocopied them for over an hour to produce a copy for Cache and the army's team of code breakers. The originals were to be secured in the vault, maintained as confidential documents in the legal offices at Quillchem. As Cache played with different ideas, marking thoughts in the margins, she wasn't convinced that she would have any hope of determining the meaning of Dr. Fischer's proprietary code and hoped that the code breakers would have better luck. She pulled herself from the warmth of her bed and walked straight into the shower before calling the kitchen to order breakfast. She had planned a hot date that weekend with Chase to go and check out some of the local attractions in Boston. Cache wanted to visit the Museum of Fine Art, a by-product of her art history degree from Dartmouth; Fenway Park; the Old North Church; and the USS *Constitution*.

As she dried her hair and threw on the television set to see what weather was predicted for this weekend, the phone rang. She expected the call to be from either Chase, asking if they could reschedule the day's events, or the kitchen, saying there was a problem with her order.

"Hello, Cache, it's, ah... Detective Boone. Did I catch you at a good time?"

"Just getting ready for my day. Is there any news?"

"Yeah, that's one reason I'm calling. The coroner expedited their work on Dr. Fischer and is turning the body over to the family later today."

"What were their findings?"

"As suspected, Dr. Fischer was strangled to death; there were no other signs of injury to his body."

"No defensive wounds?"

"Nothing identified in the report. Toxicology put his blood alcohol at 0.09 percent. He would have had some level of impairment, which would have hindered his ability to fight off his attacker."

"And the murder weapon, was it the tie?"

"We believe so. Bruising on the neck is consistent with the width of the tie, and fibers found in the skin match the fabric of the tie found at the scene. On closer examination, the tie had small monogrammed stitching on the inside with the initials JA. I just wanted to know if you would know anyone with those initials."

Cache pulled the phone away from her ear and stared at it. Does this guy think I'm a complete twat?

"Yeah, I can think of someone with those initials, and I

would be a little surprised if you haven't already come to the same conclusion."

"I just wanted to see where your loyalties lie."

"My loyalties lie with my boss. He considered Dr. Fischer a friend and wants to see the killer found. Have you spoken to Dr. Allen on the matter?"

"He's agreed to meet with us tomorrow with his lawyer present, so we'll see what light he can shed on this."

"You know it could be a coincidence; it could be someone else's initials, or someone could easily have stitched it on the tie to shine the light on Dr. Allen."

"We have considered that. I can let you know what we find out after we've spoken tomorrow."

"That would be great. What was the other thing that you wanted to talk to me about?"

"I... I just wanted to apologize if I came across as a bit of a..."

"Dipshit?"

"Not my words, but kind of. Anyway, I thought if you weren't doing anything today, maybe I could take you out and show you the sights."

"As it so happens, I have a colleague who is doing the same thing, but you are more than welcome to join us."

"Um... you know, maybe another time."

"Okay. Any idea what the Fischer's are planning on doing with the remains?"

"It sounds like they're planning for a quick funeral; they're doing something for Monday."

"Seems a bit soon. Doesn't that sound a little suspicious?"

"Not really. Their only son has flown in from the United Kingdom and has to return to school there shortly, so they want to have a quick service so he can attend and then I guess he has to get back."

"Well, Detective Boone, thank you for calling. If you change your mind and want to join us, the offer is open, and if you learn anything from Dr. Allen and can share with me, I would appreciate it."

"You got it."

"Hey, Detective?"

"Yes?"

"One other question I wanted to ask about."

"Which is...?"

"I noticed the alarm panel by the front door. Was the alarm on when the cleaners came to clean the apartment?"

"They told us it wasn't on when they entered the apartment, so they called out, expecting one of the Fischer's to be there. When they heard nothing, they went inside and discovered the body."

"Was there any sign of forced entry into the home?"

"That makes two questions."

"Was there?"

"According to their system, someone in the residence buzzed up someone in the evening on Wednesday night. We are assuming it was Dr. Fischer that buzzed someone up."

"Did the security cameras catch anything?"

"Not much; whoever it was tried to avoid the cameras."

"You said 'tried.'"

"We have a figure in the building around the time that Dr. Fischer buzzed someone in. From what we could observe they appeared to be wearing a blue bomber jacket and may have been bald or wearing a white cap of some sort."

Cache reflected on this for a moment and thanked Detective Boone for the information. She hung up the phone, pushed the antenna into her chin and rotated it around. Maybe it would have been better to go out with him instead of Chase, as he may have been more open to sharing, but she had made plans, and whether it would have improved their dynamic would be anyone's guess. As she thought about the detective, a knock came from the door and Cache went to open it, allowing the kitchen staff to bring in her morning breakfast.

Cache spent the balance of the weekend going out on the town with Chase. That day they hit the attractions that Cache wanted to see and then went shopping at the stores that Chase frequented the most. They dined on seafood in the heart of Boston and returned to the campus, only to venture out again on Sunday. Cache had called Nancy and left a message for her to see if Graydon was going to be attending the services on Monday and whether she could accompany him to give her the opportunity to speak with the family without being overly intrusive in their time of grief.

———

The services for Dr. Fischer started at ten o'clock a.m. in a community outside of Boston called Liberty Crossroads. Cache had spoken with Graydon Quill on Sunday afternoon, and he'd invited Cache to come out to his residence just outside of Boston, stay the night and go with him and his wife, Jacqueline, in the morning. Cache cut her excursion with Chase short to return to the campus and have Aaron drive her out to the Quill estate. Their house sat on well over one hundred acres, with a large black driveway that stretched beyond the front gates for more than a mile. The estate housed over a dozen bedrooms and bathrooms, and the Quills and their staff made Cache feel right at home, though she felt she was intruding on their privacy.

The next morning they woke up, shared breakfast together and took the Quillchem limousine out to a church in Liberty Crossroads, where the minister spoke of the departed, shared appropriate passages for the circumstance from the Bible and had the Fischers' only child, Jonas, stand up and share family memories of time with his dad and mom growing up. Cache looked around the service, which seemed to be well attended, with almost every pew in a moderately large church filled to capacity. She first noticed Dr. Allen and Dr. Zhou in one section of the church together and noted that he must have provided the police with a reason not to arrest him on the spot. The next person whom she noted was Dr. Tanaka, who was conversing with the man beside her, who was of Japanese descent and had black hair and a pointy black beard, was thin, and wore a black suit and black tie. She watched as the man held her hand up in his and kiss it and remembering the wedding ring on her finger assumed this was her husband. Behind the Tanaka's, Cache spotted Dr. Wright, who seemed to be more fixated on the woman at the front of the church dressed all in black.

Cache focused her attention on Mrs. Fischer, who sat in the front row with her son and just looked at the coffin, never breaking her gaze to focus her attention elsewhere. At the end of the service, Cache joined the Quills and the rest of the guests from the company in the cemetery behind the church as they lowered Dr. Fischer's coffin into its last resting spot. Friends surrounded Mrs. Fischer, and approaching her at the service for anything other than expressing condolences would have been inappropriate. And yet Cache knew she would need some time alone with her if she was going to catch the doctor's killer. As the people in attendance approached her to share their wishes with her, Cache asked Graydon if they were going to proceed as well and he advised they would do it later as they and the members of his team had been invited back to the Fischer residence, about fifteen minutes away. This would provide a more intimate setting to talk with the widow, if for no other reason than to try to set up a time to speak with her later in the week.

———

The Fischer residence was breathtaking to Cache. The house consisted of multiple barn-style gables, with a three-car garage with wooden doors that looked like they belonged to an antique carriage house. There were stained glass windows throughout the front of the home, and a lush green lawn and manicured hedges led up to a stained cedar door. The house had a long driveway that could accommodate nine parked cars and a small set of gates on white wooden posts with coach lamps that were more decorative than functional. Flowers and plants in a variety of colors flowed over the front of the property in several garden beds full of red cedar mulch, and there was not a weed in sight. Cars lined the streets as people proceeded up the walkway and let themselves into the home. Graydon had his driver drop the three of them at the front of the house, and Cache and Jacqueline went inside as Graydon stopped to talk to various people who had worked with Dr. Fischer at Quillchem Industries. The inside of the house was even more impressive than the exterior. The residence looked like it could have graced many magazines dedicated to interior decorating. Everything in the home had its place. There was an abundance of warmth that exuded from the different rooms, which were uncluttered. Cache walked behind Jacqueline as they approached Mrs. Fischer. She wore a black dress to her knees, black stockings, and black leather heels. She stood tall and Cache figured that she might be an inch or two taller than her without the shoes on. She had an athletic looking figure and looked like someone who exercised regularly. She had short blond hair with streaks of gray running through it. She wore diamond stud earrings and a pair of thin silver-framed glasses that rested near the tip of her nose. Jacqueline grabbed Mrs. Fischer's hands in hers.

"Petra, I am so sorry about Lucas. Graydon and I are heartbroken over what has happened."

"Thank you, Jacqueline, I'm glad that you and Graydon could be here. Lucas would be happy that you're here."

"If you or Jonas need anything, you just call me or Graydon and we'll be happy to help."

"Thank you, I think I'll be okay. Jonas will go back to his life in the UK and I will be here, by myself."

"No, you call me. We will get you out of here, we'll find someplace for you to channel those energies. Petra, I would like to introduce you to someone. She never met Lucas, but Graydon brought her in to try to help out. Petra, this is Cache Iron. Cache, this is Petra Fischer."

Cache reached out for her hand and squeezed it in hers. "I am so sorry about your loss. I never knew your husband but I have heard nothing but great things about him, and I promise you, we are going to find out who did this to him."

"I'm sorry, Cache, did you say—are you not a scientist?"

"No, Petra," Jacqueline said, "Cache here is an investigator. She is now the head of investigations for Quillchem. Graydon hired her himself."

"Won't the police object to your involvement, Cache?"

"They can try, but I have a connection on the force who will prove helpful, as well as people in the Justice Department and military. We will turn over every stone and stop anyone that gets in our way."

Petra pulled her hand from Cache's and fiddled with her collar with her right hand. "Oh my, well, if there is anything I can do..."

"If you have some time later this week, I would love to come out and sit with you for a while. Maybe something you remember might point me in the right direction."

"I have already told the police everything I know. I'm not sure there's anything more to say," she said as she continued to fiddle with the top of her black dress.

"You have to remember the police are overworked and under-resourced, whereas I'm only focusing on this case."

"Okay, if Graydon thinks it will help, I look forward to our conversation."

Cache and Jacqueline walked away from Petra as she talked to other guests approaching her to offer their condolences. They made their way to the kitchen, where servers provided a selection of foods and glasses of wine, and they each made their choice and headed out to the backyard, where they found Graydon talking with a couple of gentlemen. Cache excused herself from Jacqueline and made her way over to Dr. Allen, who was nibbling on some cheese and crackers and looking on at the crowd.

"How did your interview go?"

"What interview is that, Ms. Iron?"

"Weren't you meeting with the Boston police yesterday?"

Dr. Allen looked around to see if anyone had overheard her. "Who told you that?"

"I have my sources. Is it true?"

"Does Graydon know?"

"Not yet. I gather information in chunks and then present it to him. I don't run to him with every little thing I hear. So how did your meeting go?"

He scratched his head and flipped the hair away from his forehead. "I don't know. Can you find out for me?"

"Find out what?"

"Find out if they're looking at me as a suspect?"

"Why don't you tell me what happened and I'll see what I can do."

"They think Lucas was killed with a necktie I own."

"Was it your necktie?"

"Yes... but I haven't seen it for weeks." He scratched the back of his neck and continued to look around as they spoke. "As you saw the other day, we are a casual bunch, but whenever the military showed up for a briefing, Lucas wanted us to look prim and proper, so I keep a few ties at the office in my cupboard. Just in case they show up out of the blue."

"Is this cupboard locked up?"

"It has a lock on it, but I don't use it. I hang my coat in there when I come in in the morning. Maybe I put my briefcase in there, but you've seen our security. It makes sense for the women to lock up their purses, but I keep my wallet on me."

"So anyone could have grabbed your tie, is what you're telling me?"

"Exactly. I mean, Lucas and I had our differences, but I didn't want the guy killed."

Cache reflected on this for a moment, the ease of access to the murder weapon. Any one of several people with admittance to the labs could have gotten it. She scanned the backyard of the Fischer residence. There were several garden beds with red cedar mulch scattered throughout the back of the house; different beds contained flowers of different species but all of the same color. There was a patch of white flowers in one garden bed, a patch of red flowers in the next, and several sitting nooks scattered throughout the property. A cobblestone path led from the back deck down to a large rectangular pool about fifty feet away. As Cache surveyed all the different people who had come to pay their respects, she couldn't help but notice Dr. Zhou off to the side under a shade tree speaking with Jonas Fischer. Jonas was a tall man in his twenties with auburn wavy hair combed back, a neatly trimmed beard and dark-framed glasses. Her hand rested on his arm, and she laughed as they talked. She had worn a skintight black dress to the event; some would say it was in poor taste, others may have felt it stylish. She looked like a schoolgirl smitten with a new boy in her class.

"Dr. Zhou looks like she's having a good time."

"I don't know what it is about those Fischer men that has

her so enthralled. I think she's making a fool of herself. I should go and put a stop to this."

"I'll go with you."

Cache and Dr. Allen walked over toward the shade, squeezing through small groups of people sharing stories or catching up. Dr. Zhou's demeanor turned from warm and enthusiastic to cold and aloof as she saw the two of them approach.

"Dr. Zhou, it's nice to see you again. We were just talking about you. And I understand you're Jonas; my condolences on your father's death," Cache said as she extended her hand and shook his.

"Dr. Zhou, may I have a word with you in private?" Dr. Allen said as he motioned for her to follow him, and they parted ways and headed back inside the house.

"Did you work with my father?"

"No, unfortunately I never met him, but they hired me to help find his killer."

"So you work for the police?"

"I work for Graydon Quill and Quillchem Industries. I hear you live in the UK?"

"Yes, I'm at Cambridge studying economics."

He had this air of being an academic, like a future professor of economics or philosophy. His cologne smelled of burned cedar and was very distinctive. As Cache eyed him up and down, she noticed a men's dress watch with a black leather band, a white face and roman numerals with a gold outer circle. With everyone wearing smartwatches these days, it was nice to find a young man who still liked the classics.

"I love your watch."

He pulled his shirt cuff back to show Cache. It was an Abreo.

"A present from my parents for getting accepted at Cambridge."

"It's beautiful and looks expensive."

"I would give it away if I could have one more conversation with my dad."

"I wish I could tell you something that would comfort you. All I can tell you is I will do my best to find out who killed him."

"Do you have any leads you can share with me? I promise I won't tell."

"Not at the moment. I'm still trying to decipher your father's journals. They're in this crazy language—I mean, I don't know what to call it."

"Atlantian."

"Excuse me?"

"Atlantian, as in the lost city of Atlantis." He had a big grin on his face and he quietly reflected on his thoughts for a moment. He laughed and rubbed his chin. "Thank you, thank you very much. I needed that on a day like today."

"I'm sorry, I don't follow you."

"When I was young, my father would tell me stories about the lost city of Atlantis. It was kind of our thing. Even over the years, when scientists would publish new ideas suggesting where the lost city might actually be on the Earth, we would share them with one another and discuss them at length. Just thinking about it brings back such wonderful memories of my dad. When I was about five, we created our own language, which we called Atlantian. He would write these cryptic messages to me and I would have to decode them, and then I would write back to him in Atlantian. It was just a crazy thing that we did."

"Do you remember this code that you call Atlantian?"

"Oh, after a decade of doing it, I could probably read it in my sleep. The language is based partially on Egyptian hiero-glyphs, with Athenian thrown in. It was rather a complex idea of my father's and it took me some time to learn it, but once I did it was the only way we would write to one another, even to this day. When I went off to school, we would talk via the internet, so there was no need to write, but even in a birthday card this year he wrote a brief message for me to figure out."

"If I brought you some documents, do you think you could help me decipher them?"

"I probably could. I could at least give you a frame of reference to work from, but it would have to be in the next few days. I'm heading back to school once I know my mom is settled and will be okay."

"I can call you tomorrow. Maybe we can set up a time to sit down over coffee. It would really help in the work that I'm doing and it might shed some light on any concerns that your father might have had."

"I'll give you my cell phone number."

Cache reached into her clutch and handed her phone to him. He was entering his number when an older couple approached them and apologized for the intrusion. They obviously knew each other, and Cache felt that she had taken up a lot of his time, so she told him she would call him and parted ways with him. She walked toward the house. She could no longer see the Quills out in the backyard, and Dr. Allen and Dr. Zhou were nowhere to be seen. As Cache entered the living room, she could hear someone yell, "*Pozhaluysta, ne trogay eto*," and as she and the others looked in the voice's direction, she could see the words originated from Mrs. Fischer, who directed them at a guest who had pulled a ceramic vase down from the fireplace mantel to more closely examine it. She regained her composure, cleared her throat and said, "Please don't touch that." Cache could see that she was a little embarrassed as she exited the room, heading toward the back of the house. Cache wandered through the crowds until she found Graydon and Jacqueline talking to a few other people.

"Are you interested in heading out?" Graydon asked.

"Sure, but don't rush on my account, I'll just wait for you out front."

Cache exited the house as others were still coming in the front door. She stood on the front steps and was searching for the Quills' limousine when she spied a black sedan that looked similar to the one that had followed her back to Quillchem Industries the other night. This might be an opportunity to introduce myself, she thought as she started to make her way in the sedan's direction.

"Ms. Iron, yoo-hoo."

Cache turned to see Dr. Zhou walking toward her, with Dr. Wright beside her.

"Are you leaving as well?"

"Yes, I came with the Quills and I think they're heading out soon."

"Poor Petra, she looked so devastated today," Dr. Wright said.

"Well, be a sweetheart and wait a good week before you hit on her," Dr. Zhou said.

"You know, you can be a real bitch sometimes. Ms. Iron, good day." He left, heading down the sidewalk.

Cache made small talk with Dr. Zhou and maneuvered her so that she could take a better look at the dark sedan, while not making it obvious that she was studying it, to try to determine the occupants.

"Where is Dr. Allen?"

"Off sulking somewhere, I suspect."

"Why?"

"We went out once or twice; it was nothing. He got it into his head that there was more there. Since then he acts like he's my boyfriend at times; it can be really embarrassing."

Cache continued to study the sedan, barely listening to Dr. Zhou going on about her relationships.

"Oh, my neck is so sore."

Cache turned to look at her as she rubbed her neck.

"I need a good massage, to get the kinks out."

As Cache turned to look over her shoulder, she could see the dark sedan driving down the street, getting farther and farther away.

"Maybe we should go for a massage together?"

Cache shifted her focus back to Dr. Zhou. "Pardon?"

"Maybe we should get a massage together, a little girl bonding time?"

"That sounds interesting. I would definitely like to pick your brain on a few things, if you don't mind."

As they continued to chat, Graydon Quill and his wife approached Cache, as they were now ready to depart. Cache was eager to get back to her suite and draw out some of the more common characters from Dr. Fischer's notes, so she could have Jonas teach her Atlantian when they got together. The limousine took them back to the Quill residence and then continued back to Quillchem Industries to drop Cache off. She had her night already planned in her head.

## 7

Cache had worked until the early hours of Wednesday morning compiling a list of similar-looking characters and symbols found in the various journals that Dr. Fischer had created. Each of Dr. Fischer's journals averaged about an inch in thickness. Cache knew she had limited time with Jonas before he would go back to school and a mountain of paperwork to get through. She envisioned creating an Atlantian dictionary with his help that would aid her and others as they made their way through the journals. She had spent most of Tuesday locked in her suite, poring over the journals, subsisting on coffee and sugary treats sent up from the kitchen. As she compiled the images on a notepad, she wondered whether each symbol represented an individual letter, word or phrase, or some combination of them all. When she woke at seven o'clock on Wednesday, she was operating on full adrenaline. The night had been restless for her as she kept thinking about the code and her being the one to decipher the journals ahead of the code breakers. Even with all the journals decoded, it still wouldn't explain where journal fifteen was, and she knew she would need to look at both the Fischers' main residence and their place at the Dawes.

She had a quick breakfast before picking up the phone and calling Jonas. His phone went straight to voice mail and Cache left a message asking him to call her as soon as possible. Over the next hour she paced in her room, continuously waiting for the phone to ring, but nothing came. At ten o'clock the wait was killing her; she tried him again, and again her call went straight to voice mail. She left another message for him to call her as she tried not to appear desperate, like they had just hooked up the night before and now she wanted to know if he liked her. Cache kept weighing out in her mind what to do next. She needed to hunt for journal fifteen. She needed to figure out whether the mysterious sedan had anything to do with all this, and she needed to find Dr. Fischer's killer, but the code, the code, weighed heaviest on her mind. Cache kept pacing back and forth in her suite, and then expanded her distance by going down the hall and back. She stopped once at Chase's suite and knocked, but there was no answer and Cache presumed she was probably busy doing her job somewhere in the building, which was what she should have been doing.

At 11:55 a.m., her phone began to buzz and she pulled it from her back pocket as she made her way back into her suite.

"Hello, Jonas, is that you?"

"No, do you know where Jonas is?" a female voice asked her.

"No, who is this?"

"It's Petra Fischer. I called Graydon, and he told me to call you."

"Why, what's happened?"

"He hasn't been home in two days."

"Who, Jonas?"

"Yes, we got into a huge fight after everyone left. He stormed out. I assumed he would just cool down and then come home, but he never did. Now I'm worried sick. First Lucas, now Jonas."

"Does he have many friends?"

"A few. Most are away at school but a few came home on short noticed for the service. I called them, they haven't seen him." Cache could hear a tremor in her voice, as if she had been crying for hours. "I don't know what to do."

"Did you call the police?"

"Yes, I called last night. They thought he was probably off somewhere, cooling off. They said I could file a missing persons report."

"Did you file a missing persons report?"

"Maybe I'm making too big a deal out of it."

"You should file a report. I'll tell you what I can do. Give me a list of his friends that he may have gone to and I'll look into it for you." She jotted down the names of some of his friends who were at home. His mother may not have been able to get anything out of them, but Cache thought she might be able to bring the wrath of the heavens on them if they were hiding something. She gave her Detective Boone's number and asked her to call him right after she hung up and let him know the situation. In the meantime she had a couple of ideas on places to check.

She started dialing his friends one by one, and one by one, they told her when last they had spoken with Jonas and that they hadn't seen him since the service. Cache believed them, and she thought about what he and his mother might have been fighting about, but it wasn't necessarily her place to ask, at least not now. She also needed to find Jonas, as he may have been the only link out there to this mysterious language known as Atlantian.

Cache reflected on the events of the service and the time she'd observed Dr. Zhou flirting with Jonas in the backyard. Perhaps he had shared something with her, something that would provide a clue to his whereabouts. Cache grabbed the list of extensions by the phone and looked for Dr. Wright's number. He had expressed some interest in Petra and might be the most willing to help Cache find her son. The phone rang once, twice, three times, and on the fourth a voice answered.

"Dr. Wright here, who is this?"

"It's Cache Iron. Do you have a minute to talk?"

"We're kind of swamped today, trying to figure out where we go next, and we're one man down."

"What do you mean by that?"

"Dr. Zhou called in sick again, so now it's three of us to unravel the mystery instead of four. Her best skill is getting coffee, but you know, you need coffee."

"Does she call in sick a lot?"

A moment of silence from the other end. "Funny that you mention it. Not really, she's very health conscious; I guess the service just impacted her more than the rest of us. So what did you want to talk to me about?"

"By any chance have you heard from Jonas Fischer at all?"

"No, why?"

"He seems to have gone missing. I am helping Mrs. Fischer track him down."

"Haven't heard from him, we're not really chums. Is there anything else?

"I had hoped to speak with Dr. Zhou."

"Can't help you there, you might want to try her at home, do you want to speak with anyone who actually showed up for work today?"

"You know, you're swamped and I don't want to hold you up. I'll touch base later, good luck with your work."

"Thanks, we'll need it."

Cache questioned the series of events. She needed Jonas to figure out the code, and he had said he would be available. Dr. Zhou had seemed overly friendly, and maybe she was just trying to be comforting in his hour of need, but she was not at work today. Could Jonas be with her? Cache grabbed for one of her pads of paper and began flipping through the pages until she came to a note written by Dr. Zhou with her phone number and address on it.

———

Cache called Aaron for the car and instructed him to take her to the address Dr. Zhou had given her. As they pulled up to Dr. Zhou's residence, Cache glanced around at the neighborhood. The doctor lived in an affluent part of Boston. A series of brownstones lined both sides of the street. There were full green hickory trees with little black metal fences around them every ten feet along the cobblestone sidewalks. The lampposts looked like they had once been gas fitted, now changed to electricity. The cream-colored brick building that Dr. Zhou called home was five, possibly six levels. A set of black French doors and a coach lamp sat ten feet down a path from the sidewalk. Small green hedges about two feet tall flanked the path. The second floor had two arched windows, the third and fourth bay windows. Cache told Aaron to park somewhere out of sight, figuring Dr. Zhou might be more inclined to let her come in if she felt she had no ride home.

Cache walked up the walkway and looked around. A few people were on the street that afternoon, but there was not much activity. Cache rang the doorbell and waited for a few minutes. She could hear someone wrestling with something on the other side of the door before it opened a few inches.

"Emily, it's Cache. Remember, we were talking about a spa day the other day?"

There was hesitation for a few moments. "Oh, how did you find me?"

"You gave me your address. I took a taxi here. Is this a bad time?"

A few seconds passed, and the door opened wider. "I don't recall that. Well, I'm not really feeling up to visitors right now. I might be coming down with something." She was dressed in an oversized gray wool sweater and tight black leggings with gray wool socks. If she was sick and wanted to be comfortable, this was certainly the way someone would dress for that.

"I've come all this way. I understand if you're not up to a spa day, but would it be possible to use your washroom and then I can call a cab to come pick me up?"

"You know, you're here. I can at least offer you a tea or coffee. Would you come in?"

Cache walked through the main entrance of the house. On the left-hand side was a staircase leading to the second floor. Two doors were on the right.

"The washroom is behind the second door to the right. When you're done, I'll be up in the kitchen; it's two flights up. Do you prefer coffee or tea?"

"Coffee please."

She tried to put a smile on her face, but it was clear to Cache that a snooping visitor was the last thing she wanted.

Cache popped into the washroom and waited an appropriate amount of time before flushing the toilet, turning on the sink, washing her hands and exiting the facilities. As she made her way to the stairs, she opened the other door to see a small closet filled with jackets and an assortment of shoes.

The second floor contained doors to two rooms and a staircase to the third floor. One room looked like it was being used as a guest bedroom, but there was no sign that it had been used recently. The other door led into Dr. Zhou's home office. There was a glass-topped desk, computer, bookcases, and a small table and chair by the door. The walls held several degrees from prestigious universities, including a bachelor of science from one, a master's from another, and a doctorate from a third. As Cache was leaving the room, a blue blazer hung over one chair caught her eye. Three gold buttons were on the cuff, and three out of four gold buttons were on the front of the jacket. Cache grabbed her smartphone, took a picture of the buttons and zoomed in on the photo. The buttons had an etching of a dragon on them, similar to the one she'd found in Dr. Fischer's office. The last buttonhole was missing a corresponding button. She stepped out of the room, closed the door behind her and made her way to the kitchen on the third floor. Dr. Zhou was brewing a cup of tea for herself as Cache's mug of coffee waited for her in the small sitting room opposite the kitchen.

Cache sat down, poured cream and sugar into her coffee and stirred it as Emily sat down in the seat beside her.

"Cold coming on?"

"No, without Lucas being there, I just wasn't motivated to go into the lab and took yesterday off. Seemed like a good idea to take today off as well. I'm sorry to ruin your plans for a spa day; it would have been fun."

"It's okay. I know what it's like to lose someone you're close to. It's like someone kicked the wind out of you. You have a beautiful home. Is it just you living here?"

"Just me. I have an office below us and a room above that I use for yoga and working out. The master bedroom is above that, and there's a small terrace where you can walk out and see the city."

Cache got up and roamed around the room. She noticed several framed fashion magazine covers on the wall, with a young Asian girl on the cover.

"Are these you?" Cache asked as she pointed to the photographs.

"Yes, I was a fashion model in my earlier days; helped pay my way through university."

"You're gorgeous in these. Don't get me wrong," she said as

she turned to face her, "you're beautiful now, but the pictures are breathtaking."

"Thanks, it's a blessing and a curse."

Cache returned to her seat and folded one leg under the other. "I don't follow."

Emily turned her palms inward and brought her hands down from her head to her stomach. "When you look like this and you have a brain in your head, men don't want to hear your opinion. They just want to screw you and be done. My looks paid for university and my master's and PhD, and then my looks ensured very few people would take me seriously. Lucas looked past the superficial and saw me for my mind. Now I get to go back and work with a bunch of people who think I'm a bubblehead who must have screwed her professors to get ahead." She sat back and sipped her tea quietly.

"I can relate somewhat. I didn't look like that in my early twenties, but I always found I had to do better than the next guy to stand out from the crowd—be more daring, be more driven."

She looked at Cache. "I know, it can be exhausting, right?"

"Do you think you'll stay at Quillchem?"

"Are you asking me, or are you asking for Graydon?"

"Just my curiosity."

"I might just pack it up. I may go home, see my folks; I haven't seen them in years."

"Where do they live?"

"They're in a small village outside of Bingyang."

Cache asked in a surprised tone, "You're from Criza?"

"My parents left when I was young. I grew up in Europe and the States, and then for some strange reason they went back."

"Was it hard for them? How were they treated?"

"I think it was rough at first. They're both academics, but slowly they were able to harmonize with living back in Criza."

"You know, I would love to see the rest of your place, if you don't mind showing it to me."

"Sure."

Emily got off the love seat, and Cache followed her to the floor above. There was little furniture in the room. On top of the hardwood floors, a black sponge mat ran throughout the entire room. One wall was covered in mirrors, making the room look double the size it was. A yoga mat and yoga ball sat in the corner. An exercise bike sat closest to the window, a stand-up punching bag was in the middle of the room with boxing gloves lying underneath, and a weight bench with a series of weights lined the wall. In the far corner, she had a small refreshment center with a tiny fridge that looked like it held bottled water, and a small wooden radio with large dials sat on a counter. Cache followed Emily up to the top floor of the house, which contained her master bedroom. The hallway had a set of double French doors painted in white with crown molding running along the ceiling to the right; a set of black wrought iron circular stairs was at the back of the hall, heading to the floor above. Emily opened up one door and the two women proceeded inside. There was a large king-size bed with a white embroidered headboard in the middle of the room. The bedsheets were messed up and a large duvet was scrunched together in the middle of the bed. Two white-painted wooden tables sat on either side of the bed with Crizan-style lanterns on each one. There was a large walk-in closet that Emily quickly went to shut as Cache walked into the room and a series of chests along a wall. As she opened up the bathroom to show her the large en suite, she ran to pick up a small black negligee that rested on the floor near the shower.

"Sorry, I didn't know you were coming over. I would have tidied up more." She took the nightgown, walked over to one drawer in the chest next to the far wall and threw it inside.

Cache glanced down at one nightstand and picked up a watch with a black leather band, white face and roman numerals.

"What a beautiful watch," she said.

"Oh... that's where I left it." Emily walked over, took the watch from Cache and put it on her tiny left wrist. The hole she chose caused the watch to swivel around to the inside of her wrist. "My head is not on straight today, can't find anything."

She motioned for Cache to follow her and she led her to a small black metal winding staircase that went to a rooftop terrace. Sure enough, you could see the surrounding neighborhoods from up there. There was a small bistro set made of black-painted steel. Emily sat down in one chair and put her tea on the table. "This is my happy place."

There was a half wall that surrounded the terrace. Flower planters sat on top of the walls in all directions. A few empty bottles of wine stood silently in one corner as testament to the fact that they had once been on duty not too long ago.

Cache looked at her. "What a wonderful view, just a great place to come up and relax—but you know, I left my coffee downstairs, I'm going to just grab it and be back up."

"No, you're a guest, I'll get it."

"Please let me. I feel being here has put you out and you're not feeling well. I'll just go grab it and be back up."

Cache ran down the stairs and back into Emily's bedroom. She opened the walk-in closet door and noticed that everything in there was neatly arranged. Shoes and boots had a place, dresses, skirts, blouses, and behind the closet door a selection of black leather corsets and whips. Cache opened the drawers next to the bed and rummaged through them to see if there was anything that might be a clue. As she opened the drawer on the right-hand side of the bed, where she had found the watch, the faint scent of burned cedar hovered over part of the bed. Cache leaned over the area and breathed in deeply to make sure she smelled what she thought she smelled and then came to focus on the top part of the bed. She grabbed the pillow and brought it up close to her nose. Yep, smells like burned cedar. She looked at the chest of drawers across the room, ran over there, opened the top drawer and pulled out the black nightgown. It was small and would barely cover up much of Emily. It was black lace and was mostly see-through, but it also had the faint smell of burned cedar. Cache threw it back in the drawer and opened up the remaining drawers, then took a quick look under the bed. She knew she had to be fast. Much more time would seem abnormal and would invite Emily's attention. She exited the room, shutting the doors behind her, and ran down the stairs, jumping two at a time to make up for the time she had taken to snoop through Emily's bedroom. She grabbed her coffee and then made her way up to the terrace without spilling any.

When she got to the top floor, Cache paused for a second to catch her breath and then walked up the stairs slowly, sat down beside Emily, took a sip of her coffee and looked around at the scenery.

"Can I ask you something?" Cache said.

"Yes, go ahead."

"I noticed you were talking to Jonas yesterday."

"He's a sweet boy, misses his dad, like all of us do."

"His mom called me this morning as I was heading out to come see you."

"Why... what did she want?"

Cache thought a moment of deceit might work in her favor. "It's a little embarrassing."

"Why? It's only us, you can tell me."

"She thought he and I had hooked up the other night. Maybe I had taken pity on him and brought him back to my bed the night of the service. Wanted to know if he was still at my place."

"She said that to you? What a bitch," Emily said.

"Not going to ask if it was true?" Cache asked.

"Not really any of my business. He's an attractive young man, but he is an adult. He can be with whoever he wants. Not his mother's place to say anything, at least in my opinion," Emily said.

"Between you and me, if he had come back to my place, I wouldn't be here right now. We would still be making the trees shake, if you know what I mean. I told her I hadn't seen him; we were going to get a coffee before he goes back to school, but that was it. Maybe something else will happen but for now coffee is the only thing on the table, unless he wants to put me there. You wouldn't have any idea where he's gotten off to?"

"Me? No, why would I have any idea?"

"You guys were talking for a bit after the service; thought he might have said something."

"Nope, not to me, but if you want to talk with someone I would talk to Dr. Wright."

Cache was puzzled that she would throw Dr. Wright's name out like that. "Why Dr. Wright?"

"Before you and Graydon got there, Jeffrey and I observed him and Dr. Wright having what looked like a heated conversation off to the side. I asked him about it later when we talked in the backyard and he said Dr. Wright thought he should quit school and come home and look after his mother like his father was supposed to."

The thought puzzled Cache, and she reflected on it for a few moments. "What do you think he meant by that?"

Emily had a surprised look on her face, as if everyone in the room knew the joke but one person. "You don't know? I thought you were the investigator. He has the hots for Petra, has for years going back to her time in East Germany."

"What about East Germany?"

"You need to talk to Mr. Quill about the details. All I know is that apparently before she was Mrs. Fischer she was Petra

Sokolov and met Ian at some conference. She was a rising star in the scientific community and then gave it all up to marry Lucas."

Cache leaned in on her chair to close the gap between her and Emily. "Is there any more?"

Emily leaned in so they were only a few feet apart. "Lucas told me once that he believes Ian had an affair with Petra shortly after they were married and always had suspicions that it hadn't ended."

Cache sat back. "He does seem rather defensive when it comes to Petra."

Emily leaned back and sipped on her tea. "Makes you wonder if he has a reason to feel that way, doesn't it?"

"Wow, your little group has a lot of drama for only five people."

"It's our own little soap opera, and don't get me started on Dr. Tanaka."

"She seemed fine to me, what's her story?"

"Akiko is our own little gossip queen. I heard the story about Ian and Petra from her, and heaven only knows what she says behind my back. About a third of the things she says are true and the other two-thirds are ideas she has concocted in her own mind to see if she can get a rise out of people. She told everyone that would listen that Lucas and I were sleeping together, that that's why our offices were so close together, because we couldn't keep our hands off one another."

"Should I ask?"

"Please. I like them a little younger, with more gas in the tank. Lucas was a mentor to me, that was it. Like I said before, he saw me for my mind and nothing else, but Akiko couldn't accept the fact that he saw more in me than he did in her. So she started a vicious lie about me. People already weren't taking me seriously, and for my colleagues to believe they hired me for my looks to be Lucas's plaything was more than I could handle some days. There were days I would just come up here and cry for an hour or more. You think high school bullies are rough, try intellectual ones who have been saving it up for years."

Cache sat there in silence, uncertain how to respond. She knew she would need to talk with Dr. Wright and Dr. Tanaka as they might be able to shed more light on what might have happened to Dr. Fischer, but Cache was certain she knew where Jonas had gone after the service; the question for her was, where was he now?

Cache finished up her afternoon with Emily Zhou and left her place, telling her she would probably have better luck getting a cab by flagging one down than ordering one. She thanked her for her hospitality and hoped that she felt better. She was convinced Emily knew more about what was going on with Jonas than she was prepared to say, and her comments about Dr. Wright had weighed on her mind; he was someone who needed further investigating. What she knew for certain was that the more eyes out looking for Jonas, the better. She walked a few blocks north of Dr. Zhou's residence and then called Aaron to come pick her up. As Aaron made a path to take Cache back to the offices of Quillchem, she pulled out Detective Boone's card and called him. The phone rang four or five times before it was picked up.

"Detective Boone, Boston Police Department, how can I help you?"

"Hi, Cache Iron calling, did I catch you at a good time?"

"Just doing some paperwork. So did you have an enjoyable weekend? Did you catch all the places you wanted to visit?"

"I did, and you should have come, it would have been fun."

"Thought about calling you afterward, but then I figured it was too late. So what can I do for you today, Iron?"

"I just wanted to follow up on the missing persons report on Jonas Fischer."

"No formal report has been made. Mrs. Fischer called, and I told her she would need to come in to file a formal report, but she hasn't come in yet. Why, has anything happened?"

"I just have an odd feeling that we should be worried. I'll follow up with Mrs. Fischer and get back to you."

"Hey, Iron, are you interested in maybe getting a drink later?"

"I don't know, Boone, let me first figure out what's happening with Mrs. Fischer and then we can talk."

Cache hung up the phone and leaned over to the front seat to advise Aaron that there was a change in plans. She now wanted him to head toward the Fischer residence in Liberty Crossroads as fast as he could without getting them pulled over for speeding. Cache looked through her phone directory for the number to the Fischer residence. She worried that something might have happened to Petra. The phone rang and rang, and with each ring, a knot in Cache's stomach grew tighter and tighter.

"Hello, who is this?"

"Petra, this is Cache Iron, are you okay?"

"I'm fine, just sitting in this house all alone."

"Have you not heard from Jonas?"

"Not a peep, he must really hate me to stay away without contacting me."

"I just talked to Detective Boone, he said you haven't come in to file a formal missing persons report?"

"I was going to, and then I thought maybe I was making too big a deal about it, maybe I should just give it some more time."

"That is not a good idea. I don't have proof but I think you need to file the report as soon as possible. I'm on my way to your place." She tapped Aaron on the shoulder and asked him, "How long before we get there?"

"About twenty-five minutes, barring accidents or construction."

"Petra, I'm about a half an hour from your place. Can you be ready to go in thirty minutes? I'll pick you up and take you down to the precinct that Detective Boone works out of and you can file the report."

"What if he comes home and thinks I made too big a deal about this?"

"Then he'll be angry for a little bit. On the other hand, he could be in trouble and will appreciate that you didn't sit idly by."

"Okay, I will be ready."

Cache made it to the Fischer residence in just under thirty minutes. In that short period of time, Petra had changed her mind again, and Cache had to coerce her to come with her to the precinct. She appeared frail to Cache, maybe a little too thin. She was wearing a polo shirt, a jacket, jeans and tennis shoes when Cache picked her up. Attempts at small talk on the ride to the police station did little to ignite a conversation between the two of them. Cache watched her as she gazed out the car window, continuously playing with the top button of her polo shirt. Cache brought up Ian Wright's name, but it did little to raise any interest from Petra. As they made their way to the downtown core of Boston, Petra caught sight of the Dawes hovering over the skyline. "Do you think they would let me stay at our place downtown tonight?"

"I don't know. They may still have it closed off as a crime scene, but we can ask. If not, I'll have Aaron give you a ride back to your place."

"How will you get home?"

"I can take a cab or I can call a friend who also lives at Quillchem to see if she could come down and pick me up. I might even take in some sights when I'm down there, and Aaron can come and fetch me later." Aaron pulled up alongside of the precinct and Cache walked inside with Petra. The desk sergeant directed them up three flights of stairs until they found their way to the detective squad. As Cache entered the room, she sparked attention from a few male officers and noticed Boone standing up at his desk and motioning for them to come to him.

"Good to see you again, Iron, Mrs. Fischer. Thank you for coming down."

Petra took the seat closest to Detective Boone's desk as Cache hovered behind her. Most of the desks in the squad room were messy, covered with stacks of papers, file folders and two or three used coffee cups. In comparison, Boone's desk was the opposite. He had three stacks of files. Folders in one pile, notes paper-clipped together in another and books neatly stacked on top of one another. He had a mug with the police department logo on it and no sign of any paper cups in the trash. The calendar blotter on his desk had small notes around the white edges, but the calendar itself looked clean, with precise notations on certain days. When he opened up a desk drawer to retrieve something, everything was tidy, as if it all had its own special place. Petra provided details of when she had seen Jonas last. She described the fight as a difference of opinion on what he should do with the rest of his school year. She had wanted him to leave school and come home and be close to her. He, on the other hand, was determined to return and continue on with the life that he had forged for himself there. They proposed different arguments to one another as to what Dr. Fischer would have wanted, and with a growing sense of frustration, he had stormed out of the house. Petra had chosen not to follow, figuring that he would walk around the block a few times like he had when he was younger and then cooler heads would prevail and they could talk about it more reasonably. But not this time; he hadn't come back. He didn't have a car. She did not know where he could have gone. She'd turned on the computer in Lucas's study, where they had all their contact information for friends and relatives, and she had called all of his friends, but none had seen him, or at least none were willing to share with her if they had. Detective Boone asked Petra for that list of friends and she told him she would send it to him. Cache piped up and told him she also had the list, and had already called them and come to the same conclusion, but she would send it to him. And that way Petra wouldn't have to do anything further on the matter.

The report was printed off and Petra signed it to make it official. Cache told Boone she would be back and took Petra downstairs and put her into the car with Aaron, asking him to take her back to her place. Cache looked up at the precinct and suggested that she might get a ride home with someone else.

Cache returned to the detectives' room and parked herself in the seat that Petra had vacated.

"If I were you, one of the people I would talk to first is Dr. Emily Zhou."

"Iron, why do you think we should talk to her?"

"What is with you and last names? I have a first name, it's Cache; you can use that."

"Why, Iron, does it bother you?" he asked with a silly smirk on his face.

"Yeah, and I think you're doing it on purpose, to piss me off. Now, getting back to Dr. Zhou, I was at her place this afternoon. I noticed a man's watch on the nightstand beside the bed that looked exactly like the one Jonas was wearing at the service, but when I spotted it, she made it out that it was hers."

"Could have been. Some women like a heavier man's watch rather than the more dainty variety created for women."

"Fair enough, but I smelled his cologne, a burned cedar smell, on her pillow and on her nightgown."

"You smelled her nightgown? Was she wearing it at the time? What were the two of you doing, if it's okay for me to ask?"

"Not what you're thinking. She was in another room, fully dressed. She hid the nightgown when I spotted it on her bathroom floor. When I smelled Jonas's scent on her pillow, I checked to see if it was on her nightgown. I could pick up the faint lingering smell of his cologne."

"Even if they did hook up, it doesn't mean she had anything to do with his disappearance."

"True, but it wouldn't hurt to talk with her. But can you leave my name out of it? I'm still trying to work on Dr. Fischer's death and deciphering his journals, and I don't need walls to go up blocking me from my work. Also, I would talk to Dr. Wright as well."

"Why him, Iron?"

His using her last name and his tone was getting under her skin. She gritted her teeth, opened and closed her right fist and remembered to center herself and breathe.

"Dr. Zhou said that her and Dr. Allen witnessed Dr. Wright getting into some sort of argument at the Fischers' residence after the memorial service with Jonas prior to my arrival with the Quills."

"So you didn't see this argument firsthand?"

"No, just heard about it. I haven't talked to Dr. Allen about it yet, but you could always ask him to confirm."

"Thanks, Iron, I think I know how to do my job."

"I'm not saying that you don't. I'm just sharing with you what I know. I have to figure out the mystery around Dr. Fischer's journals."

"I have to ask, what is so important about those journals? Is Quillchem trying to bring out a new television or music player? We have plenty of them already, we don't need any more. Tell your boss that. We will figure out who killed Dr. Fischer. He wants his own people to look into it, it's his money, but I would tell him to not be so worried about his journals. That thing with the Justice Department was a little over-the-top."

"Were you ever in the military?"

"No, I wasn't, and I know you were. What does that have to do with any of this?"

"I can't tell you the details, but those journals could save the next soldier's life who comes under fire while doing their job. It could save the next SWAT team member who has to bust through a door into an unknown situation because someone is shooting up a high school. Or it could save the next detective entering a room, unaware that a perpetrator is sitting in a closet with a twelve-gauge shotgun. That's what those journals are about. I know people that lost their lives performing their duty, I have friends that lost love ones—that is why it's so important that those journals be found and deciphered."

"What do you mean 'found'? I was there when you found them."

"One is missing, and we don't know where it is or why it wasn't with the group of them, and because of some made-up language called Atlantian, we may never know what they say. As far as I know, there are only two people that speak Atlantian: Dr. Fischer, who has been buried, and his son, Jonas."

"Which is why you're eager to find him?"

"I am eager to find him because my gut tells me he is in trouble and needs our help, which is why I need your help. I wouldn't be killing myself if this was over a new model of television about to come onto the market; this is important."

Cache sat back in her chair. She hadn't meant to get all preachy and stand on a soapbox, but she understood the importance of figuring out what the formula was to EBSM.

"Can I buy you dinner, Cache?"

She looked up at him, trying not to smile and trying to force a frown onto her face. His piercing blue eyes seemed to see right through her.

"Are you thinking burgers and beers?" she asked.

"I think I have to do better than that to win you over."

"Is that what you're trying to do, win me over? And how will you know when you've won?"

"Hopefully it will be obvious to the two of us."

"So you're hoping for sex?"

"I'm hoping to have a nice dinner with a beautiful woman. Are you hungry?"

Cache looked at him. His smile was inviting, she was hungry in more ways than one and her only other option was to go back to Quillchem and sit alone and eat something in her room, so this seemed like the best option for the night. She reflected on her last relationship for a moment; she had been struggling with where she now fit in. The fact that she was attracted to this man, with his irritating last-name calling, made her feel that she was back in more familiar territory. She knew that her investigation would also be helped by all the resources she had at her disposal, and having someone in the Boston Police Department who thought highly of her could only provide an advantage to her. Besides which, how could she say no to those blue eyes? They were like the Sirens calling out to sailors in a storm to come to them. She thought about what she was wearing. Was she dressed for wherever he wanted to go? The thought of their doing something after she brought Petra here hadn't occurred to her, and had it, she might have worn something more appropriate for the situation than jeans, a T-shirt and a fleece, but unlike a lot of men she had met, he spent little time staring at her chest; in fact, his eyes barely ever went below her chin.

"If I say okay, I can't stay out too late. Tomorrow is a workday."

"Same here. Besides, the place I'm thinking about is four or five blocks down the street."

"Is it a cop bar?"

"No, I can't say we won't run into other officers there but it's not a cop bar."

"Okay, you convinced me, let's go."

He grabbed the sports jacket from the back of his chair and motioned for her to follow him out. She could see his comrades giving him a virtual high five as they left the room. She didn't mind, because whatever level sparked their approval, she must have met the bar.

## 9

C ache walked with Detective Boone out of the precinct. Old-fashioned white glass globes from a century past were lit on two large columns with the precinct number in solid black numerals. Cache had told him that she could call for her car service or they could take a cab, but the detective insisted that they would be safe walking down five blocks to the restaurant he had in mind. After all, he was a cop, and he was packing; he flipped open his jacket to reveal his pistol. Cache was quick to point out that he was safe with her and lifted up the back of her fleece to reveal the top of her Quillchem-issued semi-automatic handgun.

"Do you have a permit for that, Iron?" he asked.

"Yep, do you want to see it?"

"If you wouldn't mind."

Cache fished around in her fleece pocket for the billfold that Quillchem had given her. She kept the permit in a small pocket underneath the badge and handed it to Detective Boone. He examined it and handed it back to her.

"How did you get that?"

"Luckily the Pentagon has friends in the State government, they were able to fast track it for me." She tucked the permit back into the billfold sleeve and put her badge back in her fleece pocket.

The streets were alive with activity. Street artists stood on the corner, serenading the passersby with their renditions of the classics. People were walking their dogs or out window shopping. A block away from the police precinct, the neighborhood became more trendy, with little bistros scattered throughout the area. Customers probably felt safe in this part of town, with a police station close by and cruisers going up and down the street.

"Here, you look cold," Detective Boone said as he took his jacket off and tried to put it around Cache's shoulders, but she waved him off.

"I'm from Montana; this isn't cold. You come out my way and I will teach you a thing about cold weather."

"Is that an invitation to come home and meet your folks?"

"Slow down, buddy, you haven't even made it through the appetizer."

Every twelve feet the city had planted a tree with little white lights that were aglow this evening. Lampposts displayed banners reminding people that this was the home of independence. They approached a red brick building with tan wooden doors with frosted glass panel inserts and lit gaslights adorning the outside of the building. On one window was the word *Monterey's*.

The restaurant had about three dozen small round tables scattered throughout. A large tree stood in the middle with little lights similar to those in the trees outside. The tables were all lit by candlelight, with only a hint of light coming from the ceiling to guide the servers to the appropriate tables. White linen, fine china and a hint of soft jazz playing in the background sent the message that he was going to go down swinging tonight trying to get a hit.

"Carlos, my friend, how are you this evening?" he said to the maître d'.

"Mr. Michael, I'm quite well, and you? Table for two for tonight?"

Cache glanced around the room. The restaurant was busy and most tables already had occupants.

"You know, we can always sit at the bar."

"No, we always keep a few tables free in case friends drop in."

He showed them to their table, next to the far wall and away from the door. The setting provided an extra level of intimacy. Cache asked him if he handled their parking tickets and that was why he got preferential treatment, and he explained that the owner was a childhood friend of his. So he could pretty much always secure a table, even on the busiest of nights. Cache felt significantly underdressed for the location and that maybe she would have been more appropriately dressed for a cop bar, but he assured her that she was fine and should just enjoy the evening.

"He called you Michael, not Boone or Detective."

"Yeah, it's my name."

"Haven't heard you use it much, Michael, or do you prefer Mike? I bet you're a closet Mikey."

"No, Michael is all right with me. What about Cache? I've never met anyone named Cache before."

The server interrupted the conversation to share the evening specials with them and provide them with the menus. They ordered a bottle of white wine for the table from a region in Italy as the server put down small bite-size pieces of freshly baked bread, drizzled in butter, and two plates for dipping in one of several bottles of olive oil sitting on the table.

"My great-great-grandfather moved to the United States in the late 1800s and headed out west. The family name was Iron-cache, but to him it sounded too French or Belgian and he dropped the last part, so the family name became Iron. I was the first girl born into the family in four generations, so my parents used the *cache* part of our surname that was dropped as my name."

"So what is your middle name, or do you have one?"

"Cache is my middle name. My first name is Julie, which is my mother's first name, but everyone for as long as I can remember always called me Cache, so that's what I go with. What about you? Did you come to Boston or did you grow up here?"

"I grew up here. My parents retired and sold the family home a few years ago and moved to Florida; I have an older brother who is married and living in North Carolina with two boys of his own. Still have a few close friends from growing up, like George, who owns this place."

The server interrupted the conversation to let them know that their meals would be out shortly and gathered the remains of the bread from the small table to give them room to eat their main course. Cache sipped on her wine as she stared into Boone's piercing blue eyes and noticed that his gaze never left her face.

"At the risk of screwing this evening up..." He leaned in, put his hand around her neck and planted his lips firmly on hers. Their mouths got lost in each other for a moment, until Cache realized that they were in a public place and not in the backseat of a car.

"Well, you didn't bolt or slap my face, so that's a good sign."

"Why, do you get slapped a lot?"

"Not a lot, but I have been wanting to do that for some time."

"Well, you don't have to worry, I'm not bolting and I don't slap; I punch. I have two older brothers and one younger; you learn to scrap in our family at a young age no matter what gender you are."

"So you have two older brothers I should be worried about?"

"Nah, just one. Cooper will let you know he is not pleased with you. Tommy will shoot you and bury you somewhere in the woods."

The server returned from the kitchen and put down roasted chicken for Michael and a strip loin steak, medium well, for Cache. The server filled their glasses with wine and then they continued to share stories about growing up in their respective communities. It was nice to have a night off, though in the back of her mind lay concern for Jonas's safety. She hoped he was all right, but short of scouring every home and building in Boston and the surrounding neighborhoods, there was little that she was going to accomplish until some semblance of a clue came knocking. They had been talking and eating for almost an hour when the server came to clear the plates and offer them dessert. The two of them ordered the crème brûlée and finished off their wine, then moved to coffee. Straight black for him; two creams, two sugars for her.

"What happens when you're done, when we find Dr. Fischer's killer and hopefully you've solved the mystery around the journals? Will you be staying in Boston?"

"You know, we never talked about it. Graydon was interested in getting me in on this case. I was surprised to learn that they listed me as the lead investigator for the company. I'm not sure if in his mind this job is more permanent than I think."

"So you plan on leaving when you're done?"

"Home is Hart, Montana, and the Iron & Sons ranch."

"Not Iron & Sons & Daughter?"

"Don't get me started on that. Like I said earlier, first girl in four generations. The ranch had been around a long time before I came along. It's something that has never sat right with my mom, but I've never felt I didn't belong."

"So what is Hart like?"

"A Boston suburb is bigger than Hart. We have around twenty-three hundred people, mainly ranchers and farmers, in the area. Four major streets, a couple of side streets that intersect. We have a bank, two gas stations, shops, a few restaurants —nothing like this, but it's home. I lived in Italy and Tokyo when I was in the army; I went to school in New Hampshire."

"What for?"

"Art history. But Hart was always home."

"You know you can have two homes, Cache, it's not one or the other."

They finished their dessert, got a refill on their coffee and settled the bill. While Cache insisted she pay half for dinner, Michael was determined to look after it and compromised on the premise that she would pick up their next meal, hopefully securing him a second date. They exited the restaurant around eleven o'clock; most of the other patrons had departed for the evening, and as she looked at him in the cold night air, the steam coming from their breath as they exhaled, she grabbed him by the shirt collar and pulled him into her, ensuring he knew exactly what her tongue tasted like. As they broke apart, she looked at him to tell him she didn't want the evening to end.

"I would invite you back to my place but we have armed guards, dogs and security cameras everywhere. Sneaking you in would be a challenge."

"Do you live at a bank?"

"Banks don't have this level of security."

"Come home with me."

"Is that a question or an invitation?"

He leaned in and kissed her again, holding her hands with his as he stared into her eyes and kissed her lips. "Definitely an invitation."

"Should we get a cab?"

As taxis raced up and down the street, all occupied, he said, "We'll wait forever. We can grab the subway, I'm just up four stops."

"Okay then, you lead the way."

They walked to the subway, jumped on the train and exited on Young Avenue. From the subway stop Michael's place was five blocks to the west on the north side of the street. As they headed to his place, they stopped every now and again for Michael to say hello to people in his neighborhood. He was well liked from what Cache observed.

Michael's place was like a lot of homes in that area of town, built in the early nineteen hundreds and longer than it was wide. The aging bricks that appeared on several homes had been covered up with cream-colored vinyl siding. The place was three stories tall and had a basement with a bricked-up window. There was a small concrete staircase of three steps up to the front door, which was painted in black with a shiny bronze kick plate and door knocker. There were two windows above the front door, one on top of the other for each of the upper two floors, and bay windows rose from street level.

The house was very tidy for a single guy living alone. If Cache didn't know his mother was in Florida, she would have assumed that she came over regularly to clean. The front hall was tiny, with a small bench and a series of coat hooks, one of which he hung his jacket on. The front of the house had a bay window with two chairs and a small table. Books stacked on the table showed an interest in the classics, including Dickens and Hemingway. He walked over to a bookcase on the far wall, pulled down a record and put it on the record player. There were at least two hundred record albums in his bookcase, with little flags identifying the genres. The sounds of Billie Holiday came through the room, and he walked up to Cache, took her in his arms and began to dance with her around the room. She leaned into him and kissed his lips. "Does this place have a bedroom?"

They walked up two flights of stairs, and he turned on the lights in a small bedroom. A cat lay curled in a ball at the foot of the bed.

"Who is that little guy?"

Michael walked over, picked up his cat in his arms and brought him over to Cache. "This is Sam; Sam, this is Cache."

Cache rubbed his ears as Michael suggested that he might want to find someplace else to sleep that night.

He returned to Cache, pulled her fleece and T-shirt off and put them on a chair. It was the first time he became aware that she had a hatred of bras and offered enough for men to gawk at. She put her hand on his chin and raised it so their eyes met. "Up here; you can play with those later."

He took her in his arms, and their mouths exchanged drops of sweet saliva. His hand fell on the grip of her gun. "We might want to take our guns off."

"Yeah, we don't want anyone to get shot."

He took off his shoulder holster and hung it around the top of the chair. Cache walked over to the bureau, pulled out her handgun, placed it on top and walked back toward him. He maneuvered behind her. She felt his muscular arms come around her. He reached down to the top of her jeans and popped open the top button. Her breathing became deeper as she could feel his hot breath against her left earlobe. The sounds of outside had disappeared. All she could hear was his breathing and the smell of his cologne, fresh, vibrant. He ran one of his fingers across her skin, just below the top of her panties. His finger passed back and forth along the edge, moving lower with each pass. As his hand grew closer to her honeypot, her breathing became more rapid, filled with anticipation. Her nipples came to full attention. She bit her lip, waiting for his hand to reach the end zone, but he pulled it away from the goal line and placed his hands on her waist. He whispered in her ear, "Don't move."

He unbuttoned his shirt and tossed it to the side, feeling her back press against his chest. She reached her hands up over his head and ran them through his hair. She lowered her left hand, reached around to grab his and brought it down into her panties so he could feel the heat coming from the honeypot. He could feel the energy building inside her. She tried to swallow. Her mouth was dry, and she became more aware of what his hands were doing with each passing stroke until her honeypot started to crack and the contents spilled out.

He pulled his hands up to her waist and spun her around so he could stare into her eyes. She slipped her hands underneath her jeans and let them fall to the ground. He gripped the back of her head with his right hand, running it through her long brunette hair. He grabbed her breasts with his left hand as she pulled his pants down and took hold of his manhood with a firm grip. He pushed her back toward the bed, and she spun him around and pushed him down on the bedsheets. She mounted him like he was a bronco looking to be challenged at the county fair and dug her heels into his sides. With each thrust, she ground against him, until they expended all of their energies and she fell down on top of him. He pulled the covers over them as she kissed the side of his face. They spent the next several hours gliding over one another, the sweat from their bodies clinging to one another's skin, and getting to know each other in the deepest way possible.

———

The morning came way too soon for the two of them. They had spent most of the night tuckering each other out and only managed about an hour of rest before the alarm went off. They lay together, Cache's naked body draped over his, with the bedsheets pulled up to the top of their chests. Michael turned to face her and kissed the tattoo on her right shoulder, a pair of crossed flintlocks and a skull in the middle. He reached down for her left wrist and brought it up to his mouth, forcing Cache to climb on top of him.

On the inside of her arm, a phrase in Latin was tattooed.

"What does this mean?"

"It says, 'If I cannot move heaven, then I will raise hell.'"

He laughed and told her that it suited no other person that he'd met more than her. Michael had several tattoos in black down his left arm, including portraits of three Hollywood legends from the fifties, their images intertwined, and a Celtic cross on his right shoulder. As the alarm clock rang again, they both knew that the evening was behind them. For Michael it meant getting back to work solving several crimes that had come across his desk in the past week. For Cache, it meant getting back on Jonas's trail to see if she could find him and help solve the mystery of what was in the journals. In order to conserve water and better protect the planet, Michael suggested they shower together. Cache thought it was a lame excuse for his wanting to see her naked one more time, but she didn't care. In the time they were together, he'd caused the honeypot to break on more than one occasion. For a few weeks Cache had felt that she was adrift, not sure what lane she was supposed to drive in when it came to her sexuality; he'd helped clarify that she liked his lane, and if she crossed over into the other lane occasionally, that was okay too. What should have been a quick soaping of two individuals turned into Cache's being pinned against one of the shower walls, her right leg gripping his waist; hot water splashed on them as he entered her and they moved in harmonious motion with one another. After about twenty minutes, he reached over and turned the taps off. Cache reached back and turned the taps back on, and then did something that made him care less whether he was late for work.

They managed to break from their embrace and find their clothes and respective firearms. Cache grabbed her smartphone and called Aaron to come pick them up. She would drop Michael at the precinct and then head back to Quillchem, hoping to catch Chase before she became unavailable for the day. The two of them had a quick breakfast, and Aaron pulled up in the black Baumann to whisk them off to the day ahead. Michael asked to be dropped off a few blocks from the police station to avoid a day of ribbing from his fellow officers if they spied him being dropped off in a chauffeur-driven Baumann. They agreed that whatever this was, whether it would lead to something more, they would take it as it came. Cache still did not know how long she would be in Boston and felt that trying to nail something down would just ruin the fun that they had with each other.

They both agreed that they would call each other at some point during the week and see if a time was convenient for the two of them to see each other again. Cache didn't want a fancy dinner or a night out on the town and would have been happy to crawl into his bed and make their own fun. After dropping Michael off, Aaron made a straight path to get Cache back to Quillchem Industries. The drive ahead, with morning traffic, was going to take about an hour, and she decided to call Chase instead of hoping to catch her in between meetings.

"Hey, Chase, it's Cache."

"Where were you last night?"

"Why?"

"I came by around ten thirty, thought you might want to hang out, and there was no answer."

"Stayed at a friend's place."

"Does this friend have a name?"

"He does, but not why I called. Can you get me the personnel files for Dr. Fischer from Human Resources?"

"I can, anything in particular that you're interested in?"

"A story I heard about the Fischers' being in East Germany at one point."

"You don't need Human Resources; I can fill you in on what we know. The Fischer's used to work for a government-run facility in East Germany before the Berlin Wall came down. When it did, they took the first opportunity available to them to flee. Dr. Fischer ended up working for a small company in Paris that was acquired by Quillchem Industries and he became part of the Quillchem global family."

"How much do we know about Petra?"

"Let me check." Cache could hear Chase typing. "I'm just looking at Dr. Fischer's security clearance. We have information on her place of birth, education, work history, parents, siblings. There is a note to the file, that reads part of information taken at face value as resources to support in East Germany were limited. As I read through the rest of the notes, there was nothing flagged as a concern to hold up Dr. Fischer's clearance.

Where are you going with this, Cache?"

"It was suggested to me that Petra and Dr. Wright may have been involved in an affair at one point that could still be going on. He seems awfully defensive when it comes to her, and I'm wondering whether he has more to do with all of this than he's letting on."

"Do you think he could be involved in Dr. Fischer's death?"

"If he had a relationship with his wife and wanted it to go farther, Dr. Fischer could have been an impediment to this happening. Maybe he did something, and maybe Jonas found out."

"Why, what does Jonas have to do with any of this?"

"Jonas may be our only hope of deciphering Dr. Fischer's notes on EBSM, and now he's gone missing. Dr. Zhou said that she observed Jonas and Dr. Wright having an argument after the service. When Dr. Zhou asked him about it, Jonas said that Dr. Wright felt he should quit school to come home and look after his mother."

"What the hell business is that of his? He's not his father."

"I know, but he's acting like it. He's overreaching, which makes me suspicious. And what if Jonas happened on something that could implicate Dr. Wright in his father's death? Dr. Wright could have seen Jonas as another impediment to his happiness and maybe gotten rid of the son like he got rid of the father. I mean, this is all speculation; if I had any actual proof I would take it to the police. Chase, are you there? You're too quiet."

"Mmm... Yeah, I'm still here. I'm just accessing some internal grievances filed by Dr. Wright over the years. Just give me a sec."

Chase scanned the documents that were kept in internal memos on the Quillchem Industries computers.

"Well, it doesn't appear that there was love between the two of them. There are several instances where Dr. Wright filed complaints about Dr. Fischer and said that he should be the one running the EBSM project, not Dr. Fischer, but it just looks like professional jealousy. There was one note from Human Resources after following up with Dr. Fischer, who praised Dr. Wright's work but made a vague comment that he has always wanted what Dr. Fischer has. Human Resources made some observation that they thought it pertained to his position at Quillchem heading up EBSM."

"But what if it's not related to EBSM but related to his wife instead? Maybe something triggered Dr. Wright into doing something—maybe Dr. Fischer's breakthrough in discovering the formula for EBSM sent him over the top. The accolades that Dr. Fischer would receive, maybe that was just too much."

"Do you want me to request the files on Dr. Fischer from Human Resources?"

"No... I don't think they're going to tell me what I want to know, and I don't think I can approach Petra on it. I picked her up last night and took her to the police station to file a formal missing persons report on Jonas. She seems frail and distant; the experience of losing her husband has been devastating to her. I don't think I could go over there this morning and start asking her whether she was having an affair with Dr. Wright and whether Dr. Fischer or Jonas knew about it. Could send the poor woman over the edge."

"So what are you going to do?"

"Can you put me through to the Franklin Facility, I want to see if I can set up a meeting with Dr. Wright, maybe I can get to the bottom of this by going to him directly."

Chase put Cache on hold and a few moments later she could hear the phone ringing. On the fourth ring a female voice answered.

"Hello, Dr. Tanaka speaking, how can I help you?"

"Dr. Tanaka its Cache Iron, is Dr. Wright in the lab, I want to talk with him."

"No, he called in, said he wouldn't be in today."

"Did he give a reason why?"

"No. You can try him at home."

Cache thanked her for the information and hung up and called Chase back.

"Hey it's me."

"Did you get your meeting set up?"

"No, he is not in the lab. Could you dig me up his home address?"

"I'll check with someone in HR and email you the address."

Cache hung up the phone and told Aaron to drive around

until they knew where they were heading. About fifteen minutes later, Cache received an email with Dr. Wright's home address, and she gave it to Aaron and asked him to drive like he was piloting a rocket. If Cache's fears were correct, she might find Jonas tied to a chair in the doctor's basement or, worse, buried in the back garden.

## 10

Aaron drove like a man on a mission, weaving the Baumann in and out of traffic while trying not to raise the attention of the authorities. As Aaron drove down Alcott Drive in the Boston suburb of Madison, he caught sight of a police car parked up ahead and pulled to the side to let Cache get out. Cache walked toward the house. It was two stories and primarily consisted of yellow brick, with a bay window on the second floor. Ian Wright stood at his mailbox holding a towel to his forehead, speaking to a uniformed police officer. Cache waited off to the side on the sidewalk until they were done and the police officer departed. Dr. Wright looked over to see Cache standing there.

"Ms. Iron, it's not a good time for whatever you are doing here."

She walked toward him. "What happened to you?"

"If you must know, I came home from running some errands before heading into the lab and found two guys rummaging through my house. I grabbed the only thing handy, a bamboo umbrella that I have in my front hall, to defend myself and my home. One took a swing at me and ended up clocking me in the forehead. I fell backward as they exited out the rear of the house."

Cache pulled the cloth that he was holding against his head away and looked at the wound. "I don't think you need stitches but we should get some ice on that."

"Are you a doctor and a private investigator?"

"I was in the army for six years. I've had some training in looking after wounds. Let's go inside and try to deal with this."

Dr. Wright walked into his house, and Cache followed him. As she passed into the house, she observed the front door. There was no damage to the side of it. They had not forced the door open, so whoever had gained entry had either a key or the skills to pick the lock. Cache closed the door behind her. Jackets were on the floor. The contents of the hall closet lay as a mess, blocking a clear path toward the back of the house. The small living room in the front had cushions removed from furniture, magazines thrown on the floor and books pulled from two bookshelves about eight feet high. They walked to the back of the residence, which consisted of a kitchen and a small family room with a flat-panel television. The kitchen was small but had a gas range and a large double-door fridge in a chrome finish. Expensive appliances, including a coffeemaker, sat on the counter. Recipe books had been thrown across the room, drawers pulled out and the contents scattered over the kitchen floor.

Ian sat in a chair next to a small brown table. A broken vase lay on the ground, and puddles of water had settled underneath the chairs. Cache went to the freezer, got out an ice tray and inquired where he kept his clean towels. She then fashioned an ice pack and handed it to him as she sat down beside him.

"Did they steal much?"

"The police and I went through the house. They didn't steal anything. Look, the flat-panel television is still here; that costs two thousand alone. Computer equipment is still here; some books that I own that are first editions that could easily fetch twenty thousand from the right buyer are all still here. It was almost as if they broke in just for kicks."

"I realize this is not the best time to talk with you, but I wanted to follow up with you on a couple of things. But I think it can wait. I wouldn't mind if you took me through the house afterward just to see if we can identify if anything is missing. You said you went out to do some errands. When was that?"

"I don't know, maybe around seven o'clock this morning. I wanted to pick up some fresh fish, a few vegetables, a nice bottle of wine. I was hoping a friend might stop in this evening for dinner. I guess that won't be happening."

"Did you lock the door?"

"Of course I locked the door, what a silly question to ask."

"The police may or may not have pointed this out to you, but there is no sign of forced entry, which means they either had a key, picked the lock or the door wasn't locked in the first place."

"I am positive that I locked the door."

"Did you notice anything odd in the neighborhood this morning?"

"Nothing unusual, saw my neighbors, said hello, some were out walking their dogs—everything was ordinary."

"So no unusual faces, or cars, or anything like that?"

Ian paused for a few moments without saying a word.

"Ian, did that ring a bell?"

He held his finger to his lips for a moment and sat in silence. "There was something odd—well, not odd, but out of place."

"Which was...?"

"As I walked to the market, I noticed a black sedan parked on the street."

"What's unusual about that?"

"This one had diplomatic plates. I'm sure it's normal in Washington but not around this neighborhood."

"How do you know they were diplomat plates?"

"They had the blue face on the plate with a red arch over the top with the word *Diplomat* in white on the red portion."

"Interesting."

"What, no aha moment for you?"

"There could be several reasons for a diplomat vehicle to be in the area. Unless we canvass the neighborhood and hope everyone tells us the truth, we have no way of knowing what they were doing in the area. How does your head feel?"

"Sore, but a bit better. What did you come to talk to me about?"

"Jonas Fischer is still missing, I wanted to talk to you about a few things."

"Yeah, Petra called me the other night and filled me in on the details, you really didn't tell me much when you called earlier."

"I take it you two are close?"

"We've known each other a long time. She was too good for Lucas and he never appreciated what he had. He would easily have thrown it all away for a pretty face."

"Any pretty face in particular?"

"Not my place to say, and Petra doesn't know. I don't see how it helps her now for me to share my suspicions with her."

"And you never shared your thoughts with her in the past?"

"Never. What type of guy do you think I am?"

"What happened with you and Jonas at the service?"

"Nothing. I paid my respects, and that was it."

"You didn't get into a fight with him? I heard from a few sources that there was some sort of tussle."

"There was no fistfight, if that's what you're getting at. Look, the kid is just like his father, doesn't think about anyone but himself. His poor mother is sitting home all by herself, her world shaken, and he's planning on going back to school and leaving her here. It's not like we don't have great universities here. He could easily transfer and be close to home, but no, he wants to get back to school, back to Cynthia, the little tramp."

"Who is Cynthia?"

"According to Petra, his latest girlfriend. He's known her for a few months; he's known his mother his entire life. I just wanted to smack some sense into him, but no, I did not lay a hand on him."

"Did the police search the entire house?"

"Top to bottom. They poked around the basement for a bit; not much down there. Just storage. In fact, I think if something's missing down there, it could be years before I'll realize it."

Cache asked if he had a dustpan and picked up the broken glass from the vase and wiped the water up with a paper towel. She closed the drawers in the kitchen and put everything back into some semblance of order, allowing her to snoop while appearing helpful. Dr. Wright told her that she didn't have to bother, but she insisted and said that it was best he keep that ice pack in place. She moved into the family room and straightened up the cushions while making small talk with him and inspecting everything she came across as she pulled the room together.

They moved into the living room, and Cache started to put the books on the floor back on the shelves. Dr. Wright told her there was a logic in how he had the books positioned, and she suggested that she get the room in order and then later he could arrange the books to satisfy his needs. When they were finished, Cache had him take her up to the second floor, where his bedroom and washroom resided, as well as a second bedroom that he had turned into an office. As Cache opened the door to the office, she saw papers were everywhere and the top drawer of his desk was ajar.

"I think one of them was just starting in on my office when I came home. One threw something at me, hitting me in the head, while the other came down the stairs and ran out the back door."

"Did you see their faces at all?"

"No, they were dressed in black with ski masks on, couldn't see any details. I told the police already that unless they catch them with something that belongs to me, I would have a problem making a positive identification."

Cache walked into the room, picked up the papers on the floor and banged them on the desk, so the piles took a more uniform shape. Dr. Wright will need to organize this later, she thought. She created separate piles on the desk and then gathered books that were on the floor. As she sat at his desk, she saw something shiny behind one of the painted slats in the closet door. She motioned for him to stay where he was as she drew her gun from the back of her waistband and walked softly toward the closet door.

She grabbed the handle with her left hand, her right hand tight around the grip of her gun, and with a heave she threw the door open to see another bookcase, with glass front doors with brass fixtures and a shiny metal crisscross pattern on the glass.

"I told you the police checked everything."

"Why do you have a bookcase in your closet?"

"This is where I keep my prized books. I don't keep them downstairs, I keep them up here." Cache opened up the door to the cabinet. The books were all hardcover, some leather bound with gold leaf imprinted on the spines sharing with the world their existence. There was *Moby-Dick*, *The Great Gatsby*, *A Tale of Two Cities*. Cache scanned the books until something caught her eye—something that seemed out of place—but she decided not to let on with Dr. Wright what she'd seen, and she closed the cabinet door and returned to the desk.

"How bad is your bedroom, did they destroy it?" she asked.

"They didn't touch it, probably never got to it."

Cache got up and walked across the hall to the master bedroom. It was a pleasant room, not overly masculine and filled with average-priced furniture. In fact, compared to the residences maintained by the Fischer's and Dr. Zhou, Dr. Wright's home was small and average. Where his wealth went besides first editions and a nice kitchen, Cache had no idea. On a dark walnut chest of drawers against one wall, she noted an expensive men's watch, cuff links and a pair of pearl earrings sitting on a base of gold that looked like five golden petals, which didn't look like something Dr. Wright would wear. She walked around the room eagerly, wanting to go through the drawers, but restrained herself as this was his private residence and she was not a police officer with a warrant. Cache went over to one side of the bed and got down on the ground to look underneath.

"Do you see anything interesting down there?" Dr. Wright asked.

Cache stretched her hand underneath the bed, pulled free a soft pink bra and threw it on top of the bed. "Just that. I don't think pink is your color."

"Someone I know must have left it. Thanks for finding it and embarrassing me in my home."

Cache got up and proceeded to the top of the stairs. "You're right, none of my business, and this is your home with your personal possessions, but I have one question."

"What's that?"

Cache walked back to his study and opened up the closet door. She opened up the glass door on the bookcase and ran her fingers along the hardcover spines until she got to a book comprised of a manila paper cover with the word *Quillchem* on it and removed it from the bookshelf. As she pulled it loose, she could see the number 15, written in blue ink with a circle around it, in the top right-hand corner.

"Why is it, Ian, that I've been turning over every rock in Boston looking for Dr. Fischer's journal number fifteen and you've had it all the time?"

Dr. Wright's eyebrows pointed upward, his mouth dropped open. "I have never seen that before. I have no idea how that got there."

"According to you, this is your private collection of your most personal things, and yet here is the missing journal sitting among them. How do you explain that?"

He pondered for a few minutes and attempted to snap the fingers of his left hand at Cache while he held the ice pack with his right hand.

"Those guys, those intruders, that is what they were here for. Not to take something but to put something here. Something that would make me look guilty!"

"You mean they tore your house apart to hide the fact that they were leaving something? It wouldn't have taken them long to put the journal there. Why spend all the time trashing your place?"

"Don't you see? It's to throw you off. Like the sleight of hand that a magician does. He wants you to look at one hand, while the other hand is actually doing the trick."

"I'm sorry, Ian, I don't buy it. Given that this is the property of Quillchem Industries and written by Dr. Fischer," she said as she scanned the contents, noting the same strange symbols as she'd found in the other journals, "you won't mind me taking this, will you?"

Cache walked back behind the desk and sat down, putting the journal flat on the desk.

Dr. Wright was quiet for a few moments. "Since it's Quillchem property, it's probably safer in your hands."

"Good call." Cache flipped through the journal, noting the

Atlantian language, as Jonas had described it, marked on all the pages, until she found herself toward the end of the book and noticed several pages had been torn from the journal. She counted the snippets of paper still clinging to the spine of the journal and identified that four pages had been removed.

"Okay, what did you do with the missing pages?"

"What missing pages?"

"There are pages torn from the back of the journal. Ian, I am not playing games with you."

"Ms. Iron, given that I have never seen that journal despite where you found it, I have no idea where any pages are that are missing from that journal."

"Why do you keep saying that you've never seen that journal, since you all were keenly aware of the journals Dr. Fischer kept?"

"Lucas would write in his journals occasionally out in the lab; that's where we would come across them. But most of the time, he wrote in them in his office with the door closed. When we would comment on the funny notations that we saw, he would simply say that the code was too sophisticated for us and that we should focus on our own work. So yes, I have seen the journals being written in, but I have never had the opportunity to sit down and go through them cover to cover."

Cache was uncertain about whether or not she believed him. Given the police had searched the house from top to bottom, if Jonas was being held prisoner by Dr. Wright, it was not being done here. Unfortunately, as she flipped the pages in the journal, she knew only Jonas offered any real opportunity for her to get an understanding of what was contained in the writings of Dr. Fischer.

"Ian, do you know where Jonas is right now?" Cache asked, knowing that sometimes the most direct question will lead you to the answer that you seek.

"I think I would like you to leave my home. Take that

journal and get the hell out of here."

Cache grabbed the journal and walked out the front of the house as Dr. Wright slammed the door behind her. He never said no, she thought. Cache called Aaron to come pick her up, and once inside the back of the car she called Graydon to inform him that she had recovered the missing journal but pages had been torn out. He asked her where she found the journal and she pretended as if she hadn't heard his question. She avoided telling him where she had found the journal, fearing that he would muddy the waters, like a little kid splashing in puddles on the way home from school. They still didn't know who killed Dr. Fischer or where Jonas was, and she didn't want to agitate things until they found Jonas. Graydon's only request was for her to bring the journal back to Quillchem and turn it over to Chase for safekeeping. Like the other journals, copies would be made for Cache to work from, and a copy would be sent to the code breakers to work on. Cache put the journal beside her and looked out the window. Her mind went to the soft pink lace bra and pearl earrings. Neither one seemed to fit the picture of Petra Fischer from what she had gathered through her interactions with her. Petra seemed more like the type of woman who would wear a plain white bra like a female gym coach would wear during gym class. On all the occasions they had been in contact with one another, she'd favored diamond earrings.

"Jonas, where are you?" she muttered. She grabbed her phone and accessed her pictures, looking for the one that she'd snapped the other day as she and Aaron were being followed. Light blue license plate with red on top and a white smudge where the word *diplomat* might appear. Why would someone with diplomatic plates be involved? It would make more sense for someone to try to steal the journals. Foreign governments would be eager to get their hands on this technology, but why would you break into someone's house and leave a journal there? The police investigating it could look at it directly and not make the connection that it was something of importance to Quillchem. On the other hand, if you were looking for a safe place to hide it so you would not be caught with it, Dr. Wright's closet may have been an ideal location.

Aaron pulled through the gates at Quillchem and drove up to the main building. Cache jumped out and made her way past security to the elevators that would take her upstairs to the legal department. As the elevator doors opened, Cache could see Chase sitting in one of two dark blue leather chairs reading a magazine and gazing at her watch.

Chase looked up from her magazine and put it down beside her.

"I was on my way home after a long day and I got a call from Graydon asking me to stay put because you were bringing me something that needed to be addressed today."

"Sorry about that," Cache said as she handed the journal to her.

"This is the elusive number fifteen." Chase took the journal from Cache and Cache followed her into the copy room, watching her hips swing left and right in a tight red flannel skirt. Cache sat in the legal receptionist's seat and swiveled back and forth while Chase made copies of the journal and locked the original one up with its brothers and sisters. As she emerged from an office, locking the door behind her, she said, "I think someone owes me a drink."

"Do you want to go out or stay here on site?"

"Too tired to go out to the club, thinking a more relaxing girls' night in, if that's okay with you?"

"That works for me. So do you want to go to your place or mine?" Cache asked.

"I've been to your place, so why don't you come across the hall to mine. I have a larger liquor selection. Anything you have, you ordered from the kitchen staff; anything I have, I brought from my place in town." The two of them took the elevator down and walked back to their suites. Cache popped into her place to see if she had any messages, but nothing was flashing. She pulled off her fleece, threw it on the couch and went across the hall to Chase's residence. Cache had hoped for a little sleep that night, as the night before had proven to be anything but restful. Unlike Cache's suite, Chase's felt more like a home. Personal photos of friends and family were dispersed around the suite. A diffuser in the corner of the room was piping a cinnamon scent into the air. Magazines sat on the table in front of the television, including legal journals and gossip magazines. Clothes hung over chairs, and books were stacked on tables, mostly of a romantic genre, with guys with big bulging muscles on the front cover and women wearing something they eagerly wanted to get out of. She walked over to the music player she had hooked up to speakers, each about a foot tall, and scrolled through the menu, looking for her playlist of soft rock tunes. Chase grabbed a pair of crystal rocks glasses from the bar and a bottle of eighteen-year-old scotch from one of the cupboards and placed them down on the table between the two of them as they sat back on the couch only a few feet apart. Cache kicked off her boots, leaned forward to grab the bottle and poured them each a glass of about two fingers of scotch. They grabbed their glasses and toasted to a night free from the worries of the day. Cache sipped on the scotch, which was not her preference, and watched Chase toss back the scotch and set the glass back down on the table next to the bottle.

"Want another one?" Cache asked as she opened the bottle and poured scotch into the empty glass.

Chase leaned back on the couch, rubbed her neck and flipped her long, wavy black hair behind her. Cache reached for her glass and raised it in the air, saying, "Here's to whatever comes next."

# 11

M onday morning came a little too quickly for Cache as she opened her eyes to see the sun trying to peek in through the window shades in her room. She wiped the sleep from her eyes and sat up in bed. Her head was pounding and all she could remember of last night was singing eighties pop songs with Chase after they got home, using the toilet tube rolls from their bathrooms as makeshift microphones. On Friday Cache called back some of Jonas's friends who she had previously spoken with to put together a list of his old haunts where he liked to go. She spent most of Friday and part of Saturday checking out those locations hoping she might find a lead, but nothing panned out. Drinks with Chase after a day of searching on Saturday had led to the two of them sharing their thoughts and feelings with one another into the early hours of the morning. Luckily for Cache, living across the hall on a floor with only two suites and an elevator made getting home a lot easier. Cache had spent Sunday researching the members of the scientific team on the internet, reading papers they'd published, which all looked foreign to Cache. When she had enough for the day and wanted female contact, she got dressed and walked across the hall and knocked on Chase's door. They both felt they needed to get away from Quillchem for the rest of the day and ventured into Boston's downtown for seafood and a little karaoke. As far as she could recall, the taxi had dropped them off at the Quillchem security gates at around one o'clock in the morning, and had either of them shown any sign of common sense they would have gone straight to bed, but instead they went back to Chase's suite, cranked the music and drank the good stuff.

She pulled herself from the bed and immediately hit the ground. Gravity can be a nasty demon when it wants to be. Cache walked over to her duffel bag and rummaged around in one of the side pockets for a plastic baggy that she kept with stuff for headaches and muscle aches, bandages, cotton swabs and alcohol pads. She grabbed two of the headache pills, walked into the bathroom to fill up a glass of water and tossed them back. Hopefully that would take care of the jackhammer thumping between her ears. She wandered into the living room and sat down on the couch. Cache questioned whether she could hold breakfast down, but coffee sounded like a miracle drug right about then. She called to the kitchen and ordered pancakes with a side of bacon, toast and a pot of coffee.

After enjoying a quiet breakfast in her room, she turned to her yellow notepad to reflect on the notes that she'd jotted down as she investigated the research team online. Michael hadn't called professionally or personally, and so she operated on the premise that Jonas was still missing. She knew she couldn't compel Petra to answer any lingering questions that she had, but there were still four people who worked for Quillchem who should be more cooperative. Cache called Nancy, and they exchanged tales of what they'd done that weekend. Nancy and her husband had cleaned their gutters, so their weekend was more productive, but Cache's was more fun. She asked that Nancy set up a meeting in the Explorer Room in the Franklin Facility just after lunch and let the four members of the team know that she wanted to meet with them separately, beginning with Dr. Allen. Attempts to hold a civilized meeting with all four of them at one time had proven to be counterproductive, and she thought each of them might be willing to share their thoughts if the others weren't present. She had already learned about some of the suspicions that existed among the group. She speculated on whether meeting with them, taking their answers to her questions and rephrasing them to other members of the team might extract important information. She had set the expected meeting duration to be about thirty minutes per person and would begin with Dr. Allen, followed by Dr. Zhou and Dr. Tanaka and concluding with Dr. Wright.

———

Just after lunch, Cache took a golf cart over to the Franklin Facility, made her way past security and parked herself in the Explorer Room. The conference room had a medium-sized mahogany table with six leather chairs on wheels surrounding it. Single chairs on opposite ends faced one another, and then two pairs of side-by-side chairs sat opposite one another. The wall the conference room door was on was all glass, and Cache drew the shade so no one could get a sense of what the conversations that would take place between her and the other participants were like. A large oil painting hung on the far wall, and two small windows on the other side of the room showcased the manicured lawns that surrounded the facility. At one thirty p.m., Dr. Jeffrey Allen was right on time.

"Dr. Allen, thank you for coming in. I just wanted to go over a few things with each of you one-on-one. Whatever we talk about here is private and will remain between the two of us," Cache said.

"I understand. I heard Ian's home got burglarized last week, and you were there?"

"Are you suggesting that I had something to do with the robbery?"

"No, just stating a fact."

"I had gone to see Dr. Wright on something that had come up as part of the investigation and given what had transpired, I felt it was better to give him some time to deal with the aftermath of the break-in and continue the conversation here at Quillchem."

"Okay, that's fine, but why drag the rest of us in here?"

"Because he is not the only one I had questions for. Last week I was able to recover the missing journal of Dr. Fischer's, the elusive journal fifteen."

"Really... where was it? If I can ask."

"All I can share at this point in time was that it wasn't any place that Dr. Fischer would have had access to. So, Dr. Allen, I wanted to ask you point-blank, were you ever in possession of the journals that Dr. Fischer kept, especially journal fifteen?"

"That is preposterous. Lucas kept better security over those than his wife's chastity belt."

"What do you mean by that?"

"I mean, Lucas kept those journals under lock and key. He wouldn't let us look at them. Let alone ever take them with us anywhere."

"That wasn't what I was referring to. You made a comment about Petra's chastity belt. What aren't you telling me?"

Jeffrey appeared flustered, thinking back about his earlier response. "I probably misspoke."

"I don't think you did. It's just the two of us. What are you not telling me?"

"Let me put it this way: a male member of our team favors the company of married women, and it's not me, to be clear."

"Dr. Zhou told me you witnessed Dr. Wright and Jonas arguing at the service, is that correct?"

"Yeah, the two of them were going at it for a while. Ian grabbed Jonas by the arm at one point and he yanked it away, knocking a tray from a server who was passing by. Caused a lot of noise. I think everyone saw that. Ian realized everyone was staring, and so he backed off. Ian doesn't know when to let his foot off the gas. He is so headstrong, he can't see what he is doing sometimes."

"Could he be responsible for Lucas's death?"

A few seconds of silence and Cache asked again, "Jeffrey, is it possible for Ian to have killed Dr. Fischer?"

He shrugged and moved his head from side to side. "I don't believe so, but who knows."

"Let me talk to you about a rumor I heard about a relationship between Emily and Lucas."

Dr. Allen sat up straight. His neck appeared to tighten. "Anything Emily did, she needed to do for her career. Lucas couldn't take the hint that she wasn't interested in him that way, only professionally."

"You mean she slept with him to help her career?"

"No, no, no, you are way off base. She flirted here and there, she laughed at his jokes, she played to his ego—no, she would never go that far, her and I—"

"Her and you?"

"We had a thing a few years ago and got off track. Now we're trying to find our way back to each other. She knows something like that would be the end of us. No, I know her, she wouldn't cross that line."

"If you say so, but I will have to ask her; I have her scheduled to come in next."

"She isn't here."

"What do you mean, she isn't here? I specifically requested a meeting with the four of you."

"She texted Akiko this morning and told her she was taking another personal day, wasn't feeling well."

"I know I talked to her a few days ago and she said she might be coming down with something. I didn't know Akiko and her were that close."

"They're not. Akiko hates Emily and Emily doesn't think that much of her."

"Why would she text Akiko and not you?"

"You would have to ask her. I saw the text myself but company protocol says you're supposed to call your supervisor to advise them. I guess with Lucas not here anymore she didn't know who to call."

Cache jotted down some notes on her pad, away from Jeffrey's eyes.

"All right, well, can you ask Akiko to come in then?"

"No more questions for me?"

"None at the moment."

Jeffrey shoved the chair back from the table, got up and exited the room. Cache thought it was odd that Emily would text Akiko. Given their conversation the other day and knowing that Cache wanted to meet with her, it would have been more appropriate for Emily to call Cache.

———

After about ten minutes, the door opened, and Dr. Akiko Tanaka came in and sat down in the chair previously occupied by Dr. Allen. She wore a cream-colored knit skirt with reds and oranges running in a crisscross pattern, a light pink blouse and a jacket that matched her skirt. She had on white stockings and black flat shoes. As she sat down, she brushed her hair behind her ears and smiled.

"Thank you, Dr. Tanaka, for meeting with me. I had a couple of questions I wanted to ask you and thought in a more private setting, you might feel more comfortable sharing your thoughts with me."

"So you're saying this meeting is optional?"

"Only if you don't want to work at Quillchem any longer."

Cache looked at her. The scowl upon her face told Cache a lot about her.

"I love your earrings. Pearls, right? Looks like they're sitting on a golden flower; beautiful."

"Thank you, they were a gift from my husband. So what are your questions?"

"I understand Emily is off sick?"

"Yeah, probably on her back somewhere, that's where she does her best work."

"I take it you don't like Dr. Zhou much?"

"Try spending your entire career in a male-dominated world and then seeing someone with a fraction of your experience blow by you because they are attractive."

"Must be rough, but you can't blame her for how she looks."

"It's not her looks that I blame her for, it's her actions."

"I heard she could be flirtatious with Dr. Fischer."

"Flirtatious is one thing; I caught them on more than one occasion kissing in the lab, when they thought no one else was around, and from what I saw, she was the aggressor."

"How do you know that?"

"I came back into the lab one night to retrieve some notes that I had left on experiments run that day. I could see her putting her hands on his chest, and he made several attempts to back away from her. Then, when he couldn't retreat any farther, she put her arms around him and kissed him. He had a deer-in-the-headlights look. Next thing you know, his hands were everywhere. It was disgusting."

Cache made some quick notes out of sight of Dr. Tanaka on her notepad, then flipped back to her notes from her discussion with Dr. Allen.

"So I thought Emily had a thing for Dr. Allen."

"Oh please, maybe in his mind. No, she knew what she wanted. She is a class A manipulator. She has Jeffrey wrapped around her finger, he would do anything she commanded, but she shows no sign of interest in him from what I've observed."

"What about a past relationship?"

She shook her head. "No, can't see it. She goes after big game; that is not him. He will always be a small fish."

"Okay, well, moving on, I just wanted to tell you that we found the missing journal of Dr. Fischer's."

She showed no response on her face at the news.

"I want to ask you directly, have the journals, including journal fifteen, ever been in your possession?"

She tapped her fingers on the desk for a few moments. "No. Next question."

"Did you kill Dr. Fischer?"

"Are you out of your mind? Why would I kill Dr. Fischer?"

"It's just a question. Sometimes a direct question is best."

"No, not me. I hope you asked Jeffrey that question. That's who I put my money on."

"Why?"

"Because of Emily. What are you, blind? Emily has a thing for Lucas. Jeffrey sees Lucas as an obstacle to get Emily, hence you get rid of the obstacle and it's smooth sailing. That is who I would put money on. Mark my words," she said, pointing her finger at Cache.

Cache continued to jot down notes out of her sight.

"I just had one other question. I hear you see all around here. What can you tell me about Dr. Wright? I heard he had a thing for Petra Fischer."

"Please. Ian has no interest in someone like that. He likes a more refined woman, someone with taste who can give him what he needs."

"I don't know, I can kind of see the two of them together. I mean, if she was single. I heard they had a thing in the past."

"That was in the past. Ian told me there is nothing…"

"Nothing what? Nothing anymore? Why, because you're his current lover?"

The question resulted in her squirming in her seat, and her pale skin flushed. "I don't have to take that from you!"

"You know Ian's place was robbed last week. I was there to ask him a few questions and saw earrings that looked just like yours on a chest that he has in his bedroom."

"They're pretty common, I see them everywhere."

"No, they're not. My guess is the set you're wearing is a replacement set, because you couldn't remember where you left them and didn't want your husband to find out."

She sat there in silence and stared at her lap. Cache tapped her pen on her pad of paper and just looked at her, waiting for her to say something. After a few minutes she looked up at Cache, a tear rolling down her right cheek.

"You can't say anything, please. This needs to stay between us."

"How long has it been going on?"

"About a year. We were working late and one thing led to another. No one else knows. We were always very discreet. My marriage would be over if my husband found out, and I don't know what he would do to Ian."

"I won't say anything, but you have to be honest with me."

"About what?"

"Were Lucas and Emily having an affair? I'm looking for truth here, not gossip."

She wiped the tear from her cheek. Cache got up and walked over to a box of tissues on a far table, brought them closer to her and sat back down.

"Truth."

"I told you the truth. From what I saw, there was something going on between them."

"And Dr. Allen?"

"No, Emily never showed any interest in him."

"Petra?"

She took a minute before she answered, "He told me there was something there once, but it was over."

"Did you believe him?"

She took a few more seconds to think about it. "No."

Cache pushed back in her chair. "Akiko, I'm not here to pass judgment on anyone. What you and Dr. Wright do on your personal time is your business. My job is to figure out who killed Dr. Fischer and find his son. Do you know where Jonas is?"

"No, last I saw of him was at the service. I asked Ian about the altercation between the two of them but he told me to leave it alone."

"Could Dr. Wright have done something to Jonas?"

"I don't know. Ian can get in a rage sometimes. Lucas just brought it out of him. He believed he should have been heading up the EBSM project, not Lucas. I can't believe he would do something to Jonas, but I can't be sure." She took a deep breath. "So you're not going to say anything about... about me and Ian?"

"Nope, you're free to go. Can you ask Ian to come in next but tell him to wait about fifteen minutes? I want to gather my notes." Dr. Tanaka stood up from her chair and pushed the chair back toward the table. She gathered a few more tissues in her hand and walked out of the room. Cache walked to the other end of the conference room and opened up the cabinet against the wall. She fished around in the coffee pods, looking for one that read "Irish Cream," and brewed herself a cup of coffee. She retrieved two creams from the small fridge at the bottom and poured in a generous amount of sugar. Cache closed the cabinet doors, walked back to her chair and sifted through her notes. She had already gotten many of her answers from Dr. Wright on Thursday but didn't want to give the appearance that he wasn't being questioned that day, so it only made sense to bring him in even if it was merely to talk about the weather. After fifteen minutes had passed, a knock came at the conference room door.

"It's open."

Dr. Wright walked in, saw the open chair close to Cache and decided that the chair opposite her at the end of the desk was the more appropriate place for him. "Is this going to take long, Ms. Iron? I have a lab to run."

"Funny thing, Ian, Graydon hasn't told me you're in charge. Do you want me to call him?"

Ian scratched his ear; he had a small bandage on top of his head from his injury sustained on Thursday. "No need to bother him. What would you like to know? And for the record I have no idea how that journal got into my book cabinet."

"I believe you."

His eyebrows narrowed and Cache could see a few lines on his forehead form. "Why don't I think you're being sincere?"

"Because up until a few moments ago, I thought the only way that journal could have gotten there was if you put it there, but what if Akiko put it there?"

"Where are you going with this? I thought we agreed that the intruders put it there."

"No, that is what you would like me to believe. If they were going to break into your home to leave the journal, the last thing they would do is ransack the place. I can believe they broke in looking for the journal, which has me wondering why they would think that you had it in the first place, but if you're off boinking Dr. Tanaka in your spare time, maybe she put it there."

"There is nothing going on between me and Dr. Tanaka. I don't know where you get off making an accusation like that!"

"Ian, calm down, she admitted to it. I noticed earrings just like hers on top of your dresser, and even though I've only been here a short while, I've noticed she likes to wear pink, so I'm guessing that undergarment is hers."

He tapped his fingers on the desk for a few minutes and then cracked his knuckles. "How is this any of your business?"

"I don't care what the two of you do to one another. Her husband might, but right now I am trying to figure out who killed Dr. Fischer, where Jonas is and what the journals say. I need Jonas to help me figure out what is in those journals. You and Dr. Fischer have a long history of rivalry. Is it enough to kill someone over? Probably not, unless you're sleeping with his wife."

Ian stood up and pushed the chair back. He slammed his hands down on the desk. "Listen, you little bitch, why don't you pack your bags and go home and fuck a cow? I don't have to take your bullshit."

Cache pushed her chair back, pulled her firearm out from behind her belt and put it on the desk in front of him. "You want to dance, old man, I'll break you in more pieces than that glass vase you had in your kitchen. Now sit the fuck down." Cache sat back in her chair and waited for Dr. Wright to seat himself. "Were you having an affair with Petra Fischer?"

"None of your fucking business. Next question."

"Do you know where Jonas is?"

"Haven't seen him. Next question."

"Could Dr. Tanaka have put Dr. Fischer's journal in your bookcase?"

"I don't know, it's possible."

"Did you ever see Dr. Fischer and Dr. Zhou in any situation that could be construed as romantic?"

"No."

"No?"

"I only heard what Akiko said she saw. I believe her."

Cache jotted down some details on her notepad.

"Ian, I haven't told Graydon where I found journal fifteen, but at some point I may have to. You may end up being questioned by the police and possibly the army. I would work on your temper. That's not going to play well with them."

"Are we done?"

"For now. Thank you for your time."

Dr. Wright got to his feet, walked over to the conference room door and threw it open, almost taking it from its hinges. Cache watched as the door swung open wide and then slammed back into place. She was left with plenty of suspects but was no farther in figuring out where Jonas was. She tapped her pen on the notepad. Two of them had told her that they had never been in possession of the journals, and one was taking the position that one of the journals was planted in his home to throw suspicion on him. This meant if they were being truthful, none of them would be in possession of the missing pages. The only person whom she hadn't had a frank discussion with was Emily Zhou; she wrote Emily's name on her pad of paper and circled it several times. This series of meetings had taken its toll on Cache, and the headache that she had managed to beat this morning was coming back with a vengeance. Tomorrow she would try to get a one-on-one meeting with Emily if she made it into work. If not, she might have to drive back over to her residence to see if she would have an honest discussion about herself and her relationships with Lucas and Jeffrey, and whether she knew that Ian and Akiko were involved. Tonight, she just wanted to be alone with her thoughts. No drinks with Chase, no poring over the internet looking for a clue. She wrote Michael's name next to Emily's and circled it a few times. Maybe he'd had had some luck at figuring out where Jonas was, she thought. She was a bit annoyed that he hadn't even called her to see how she was. Why do we have to play these games about who is going to call who first? she wondered. She thought about it for a few minutes. What the hell am I doing? I need to focus on Jonas. She would call him tonight for an update and nothing else. If he wanted to read something into it, let him. She hadn't mooned over a guy since she was in high school and wasn't planning on starting to now. What she needed to do was get some answers. She went back to Emily's name and drew stars around it. "I'm not sure why, but I can't help feeling that you're the key to this whole thing."

---

## 12

The yellow pad of paper with multiple pages folded over the top was where she had left it the night before. Tempers had flared with one interviewee, and Cache took that as a sign that she was on the right trail. As she read through her notes from her meetings with Dr. Allen, Dr. Tanaka and Dr. Wright, she kept coming back to one annoying question that only Emily Zhou could answer for her. After she prepared herself for the day ahead, she called Dr. Zhou's office over at the lab facilities. It rang repeatedly until the voice message kicked in. Cache opted not to leave a message, as she was eager to get an answer to her question and didn't like the idea of waiting for Emily to get back to her. She next called Dr. Tanaka.

"Hello, Akiko here, who is this?"

"Akiko, this is Cache Iron."

Her tone of voice was cool and unfriendly. "Hello. I thought you weren't going to say anything."

"To who, Ian or your husband? Ian already knows you're sleeping with him, and as far as your husband goes, if it isn't tied to this case, I have no reason to interfere in your personal life."

"Fine. What can I do for you?"

"Is Emily there? I was trying to reach her and it went to voicemail."

"No, she didn't bother showing up, didn't call, didn't send a text. I sent her a text asking where the hell she was but haven't received a reply."

"What time was that at?"

"Would have been nine o'clock a.m. We all start at eight o'clock, so being an hour late when we are swamped with trying to figure out the formula for EBSM doesn't help anyone, but when you're a little princess, you think you can do what the hell you please."

"Thanks for the info. If I reach her, I'll ask her to contact you."

"Great. Not like she contributes anything but at least she can get the actual scientists coffee."

Cache hung up the phone and rested her chin on top of it. Yesterday a text and today nothing. Her stomach started to twist, and she felt eager to talk with Emily. She called Aaron next and asked him to bring the car around for her. She wanted to drive back to Dr. Zhou's residence, and this time he could wait outside. No pretenses about why she was there. She had one question, and she needed an answer for it.

The drive out to Dr. Zhou's neighborhood was calming that morning. A light rain was coming down. Few people were out and about as cars whizzed by, splashing the sidewalks with the water that accumulated on the street. As they came down Emily's street, Aaron caught sight of a black sedan with diplomatic plates coming toward them.

"Cache, the car coming toward us looks like the one that tailed us the other day. Do you want me to turn around and follow him?"

Cache leaned forward, hovering over Aaron's shoulder. "Let's see if we can catch the license plate number. I'm a little concerned about why they're in this neighborhood."

As the car passed, she saw the windows were heavily tinted, preventing anyone from seeing the occupants in any great detail. Cache thought she had spotted a T and an S on the license plate, and Aaron was sure he saw a 5 as well. Cache scribbled the details down on her notepad and would call Michael later to see if he could run a search on the plates. As they pulled up to Dr. Zhou's residence, everything looked normal. She exited the vehicle and told Aaron to wait there. She walked up the path to the house and noticed a rolled-up newspaper beside the front door. Cache bent down, picked up the paper, turned it over to see the masthead and noticed that it was the Sunday edition of the *Boston Globe*. It had been sitting out there for two days, waiting to be collected. She pressed the doorbell, waited a few seconds and pressed again, and there was no answer. She stepped back to look up at the windows above to see if she could spot any movement, but all the drapes on the front of the house had been pulled closed. Cache rang the doorbell again and then knocked several times and pressed her ear to the door, but she heard nothing. She grabbed her cell phone and searched her contact list for Emily Zhou's residential number and initiated the call. She could hear the phone ringing inside the house, and after several rings it went to voice mail.

Cache reached down for the doorknob, grasped it in her palm and turned it to the right. She expected it to be locked, but the knob turned all the way and the door swung open.

She called out, "Emily, it's Cache Iron, are you okay?" but silence was the only answer that she heard. Cache motioned for Aaron to stay put, and she reached for her handgun and gripped it in her right hand as she entered the house. She opened the doors on the bottom level but saw nothing unusual.

She leaned against the staircase and looked up at the floors above. There was darkness on the second floor, with light moving on the third. Cache crept up the stairs as quietly as she could. She reached the second floor, opened the door to the office and flipped on a light. No sign of Emily, but she could hear rustling from the floor above her. Cache closed the door behind her and made her way to the third floor. The shades at the front of the house were closed. The drapes at the back of the house fluttered in a breeze coming from an open window. Cache made her way into the kitchen, stopping and listening every few steps. As she came into the living room, the shadow of a figure was ahead of her in the dark. Cache raised her firearm. "Emily, is that you?" The figure didn't move. Cache walked over to the end table closest to her and reached underneath the shade of a table lamp to fumble with the switch.

*Click.* The light went on and Cache could see Emily sitting on the love seat with her head pulled back and a silk tie around her neck. Cache walked over to her and put her fingers against her neck, but there was no pulse. Dr. Emily Zhou was dead. Cache sat down across from the body and reached for her cell phone to call Michael and report what she'd found. She was about to press the connect button when she stopped. The moment the police arrived, this was going to be a crime scene and any information that she had that could help Cache find Jonas was going to be hidden from her behind a sea of yellow crime scene tape. Cache went downstairs to the hall closet where Emily had kept her coats and looked for a pair of gloves. She found a pair of leather gloves that were a little tight on Cache's hands but would help ensure she didn't leave any fingerprints. Cache then proceeded upstairs, taking the stairs one at a time on the off chance that whoever killed Emily might still be in the house. She made a sweep of the bedroom and top terrace to ensure that she was alone. Cache went downstairs to her office and poked around, looking for a safe or a hiding place of some sort, but nothing could be found. She sat down in the chair behind the desk and turned on the light. There were scientific papers on the desk, magazines, books on chemistry and engineering, nothing out of the ordinary for a scientist. Cache opened the scientific textbooks and flipped through them. But nothing seemed unusual. She began flipping through the magazines, and a few photographs fell out onto the desk. The photos were deeply personal, showing Emily and Jeffrey Allen out on the town, dining and holding each other like two people in love would. Why they were hidden away in the magazines and not in a picture frame was unclear. Cache grabbed the photos, shoved them back into the magazines and stacked everything on the desk.

She opened the drawers and fumbled through the papers but found nothing incriminating or helpful. She looked around the room and noticed that Emily's master's degree hung to one side, leaning to the left, while her other degrees were straight. Cache stood up and went over to straighten it, but the moment she raised the corner, it fell back again. She pulled the degree down from the wall and looked behind it to see that an eight-and-a-half-by-eleven-inch manila envelope about a half inch thick was taped to the back of the degree. Cache placed the degree down on the desk and pulled the papers from inside the envelope. It was a collection of notes on all members of the scientific team—personal habits, education, where they grew up, friends, family. Separate pages existed for Dr. Fischer, Dr. Tanaka, Dr. Allen and Dr. Wright. There were handwritten notes in the margin that appeared to be in a woman's handwriting. Cache laid each paper flat on the desk and took a picture with the camera on her smartphone, then reassembled everything and returned it to the wall for the police to discover upon their search of the home. Cache returned to the floor where Emily's body rested and noticed a small notepad with the Quillchem Industries logo on it sat next to the phone. The top page had the remains of a third of a piece of paper torn from the pad. Cache grabbed the notepad and returned to the office, looking for a pencil. When she found one in the second drawer of the desk, she shaded the piece of paper directly under the torn page to reveal a name, *Welterhouse.*

Cache pulled the paper from the pad as carefully as possible and tucked the page into her back pocket. She returned upstairs and put the pad of paper back where she had found it. Cache then went upstairs to the master bedroom and searched through the drawers and the closet, under the mattress and under the bed. There she found an orange silk tie with the letters JA stitched on the inside. Another Jeffrey Allen tie, she muttered, and took a photo of it and returned it to the location where she'd discovered it. She sat down on the floor, crossed her legs and looked around the room, trying to determine whether there was anywhere she hadn't looked. Cache stared at the dresser where she had found the black see-through nightgown covered in Jonas's scent. There was nothing further to be found in the drawers, so she removed each of the drawers and placed them on the bed. Upon removing the last drawer at the bottom, she found a small envelope taped to the back of the dresser. Cache peeled it off and opened up the envelope. A single passport issued by the Republic of Criza only a few years earlier was contained inside. Cache flipped it open to the photo, which matched Emily Zhou, the details a carbon copy of what Cache knew of her. But the name listed was Beatrice Yu. She grabbed her smartphone, photographed the details of the passport, returned it to where she had found it and placed all the drawers back in their correct spots. She pondered whether anything could be found behind the drawers in the bathroom and pulled the drawers out. Cache found nothing taped behind the drawers, but one drawer, containing various makeup items, seemed shallower than it should have been.

Cache poked around on the inside of the drawer, tapped the bottom of it and heard something that suggested a hollow cavity. With the help of a nail file, she was able to pull up the white bottom of the drawer to reveal a small automatic pistol with a star and a diamond engraved into the grip. Touching it was not something she would consider doing on the off chance it could be tied back to a murder or other crime. Dr. Zhou or Beatrice Yu, or whoever she was, certainly led an interesting life outside of the office. Cache straightened everything back up, tucked her firearm down into her waistband and went outside to fill Aaron in on the fact that there was a dead body inside. Cache pulled the gloves off, tossed them inside the car and suggested that Aaron find a place to park and wait for her call. Once the police arrived, they would detain him and ask him questions that Cache didn't want him answering just yet.

Cache returned to the front of the house, sat down on the step and pulled out her smartphone. She looked for Michael's contact info and called him.

"Iron, good to hear from you. I was just thinking about you, meant to give you a call, but it's been busy—"

"Save it, this is not a 'let's get together' call, I'm calling to report a murder."

"Who was murdered?"

"Dr. Emily Zhou, she's one of our scientists at Quillchem. I came by to see her as she hasn't been in the office yesterday or today and found the front door unlocked."

"And you went inside?"

"I wanted to make sure she was okay."

"Obviously not."

"No. She's upstairs in her living room. Looks like strangulation. She has a silk tie around her neck, might be like the one you found with Dr. Fischer."

"Did you touch the body?"

"Just to feel for a pulse. There was none, so I came down here to call you."

"Have you looked around the rest of the house? Someone could still be there."

"Nope, just found her and came down to call you."

"Why don't I believe you?"

"I don't know, must be some internal issues you have around trust; you need to work on that. I was going to call 911 but you're already involved in Dr. Fischer's murder, and it just seems like this is connected somehow."

Cache gave him the details. And she sat down on the front stoop and stretched out her legs. After about fifteen minutes she could hear the sounds of sirens growing louder and louder until two police cruisers with lights flashing pulled up in front of the residence, followed by an unmarked police car. Michael walked up to her and told the uniformed police officers to go upstairs and make sure the house was clear while he spoke to Ms. Iron. After a few minutes of searching, the officers returned to tell him the house was clear and that indeed a dead body was upstairs. He looked at Cache as if she knew more than she was telling and told her to wait outside while he went into the house. Cache spent the next half hour sitting around waiting for Michael to be done. The forensics team arrived to document the scene and remove the body. Michael took an official statement from Cache before trying to play the sympathetic boyfriend and offering to take her out for coffee in case she was too scared to go back to one of the securest compounds in Boston. They walked a couple of blocks away from Dr. Zhou's residence. As she suspected, as they walked away, the yellow tape was being put up as uniformed officers stood guard and various law enforcement professionals went in and out of the house. After a few minutes of quiet walking, they found Andy's Bistro and went inside to get two cups of coffee, black for him and two creams, two sugars for her, and found a small table tucked away in the corner. The bistro had a glass display in front of the server, with an assortment of cakes, cookies and small sandwiches that could be heated in the microwave. A large antique brass coffee machine sat on the far counter opposite the display, and the only person who appeared to be working, at least according to his name tag, wasn't Andy. The bistro was longer than it was wide, with a glass window in the front, and a wooden front door with a frosted glass panel insert. The floors looked vintage and likely originated from a previous owner, before Andy came along and occupied the space. There were two rows of small tables opposite the display counter. The ones against the wall ran from the front of the bistro all the way to the back, where the washroom facilities were located. Michael chose a table as far away as possible from the front door for the two of them to sit down at.

"Okay, cards on the table. What is it you're not telling me?"

Cache thought for a few seconds. "Okay, here it is: I enjoy being on top. Deal with it. You want to cuddle far too much, and the scruff might look great in the office, but it can be hard on the skin."

"What? No, that is not what I am talking about, and what do you mean I want to cuddle too much? You want to know what you do that I don't like?"

"Not really."

He let out a big sigh. "I'm talking about the case. Look, we want the same things. Unfortunately, I have a dozen other cases I'm working on and can't give my undivided attention to this one."

"Understood. That's why Graydon brought me in."

"But that doesn't mean we should hold back on info the other one can use. Look, I want to find the killer of Dr. Fischer and so do you. I want to find Jonas and get him home to his mom, and so do you. The fact that you need Jonas for those journals of yours, that is a Quillchem matter and doesn't involve us, but you still need Jonas to help you, so what aren't you telling me?"

"I was tailed the other day."

"What do you mean you were tailed?"

"My driver, Aaron, saw a car following us. I snapped a picture of the front of the car trying to get a detailed photo of the license plate." Cache pulled out her smartphone, scrolled to the picture and showed it to Michael.

"That's pretty blurry."

"But do you see the colors of the plates? Not the traditional Massachusetts white; those are diplomatic plates."

Michael enlarged the photo by zooming in with his fingers. "Okay, it's possible but it's pretty blurry."

"We think we saw the same car heading away from Emily's place as we were driving there."

"Did you get a look at the driver?"

"No, the windows were tinted out. We have an idea on the license plate: we think there was a T, S and five in the plate number."

Michael pulled out a small notebook from his inside jacket breast pocket and wrote down the details. "I'll look into it. We may not be able to figure out who was driving it but we might be able to figure out to which embassy the car belongs."

Michael could feel his front pocket shaking, and he reached down and grabbed his phone.

"Detective Boone here... You did. Well, isn't that convenient... Was it like the other one? Okay, I'll reach out to the doctor and ask if he and his lawyer can come down to the station and sit with us again." Michael hung up the phone and put it down on the table.

"Problem?"

"Maybe we found the killer. What can you tell me about Dr. Allen?"

"Dr. Allen is an employee of Quillchem. I can't discuss that with you."

"Cache, I need something."

"So what I am going to tell you is off the record. I will deny ever saying anything about it."

"Fine, what do you have?"

"The team was rather dysfunctional, so it's surprising that they could figure out a solution to the project they were working on. Emily—Dr. Zhou—indicated to me that she had a working relationship with Dr. Fischer. Dr. Tanaka has suggested to me that she caught them, on more than one occasion, involved in a romantic embrace. Dr. Allen has suggested that Dr. Fischer's advances toward Emily were not reciprocated by her and that she had feelings for him, an idea that Dr. Tanaka believes to be false."

"And how does Dr. Tanaka fit into this?"

"From what I've learned, she's the office gossip queen."

"Okay, well, the team went through Dr. Zhou's residence. They found a tie underneath the bed in the master bedroom with the same JA monogram that was found near Dr. Fischer's body. We also found photographs of Dr. Allen and Dr. Zhou together, which suggests to me that your Ms. Tanaka was mistaken."

"Was that all you found?"

"Why, what did you find that we haven't found yet!"

"Nothing, I'm just curious, maybe you found something that could help me out." The reality was that if Dr. Zhou was involved with the Crizan government, any efforts Michael put forward would bear no fruit. Cache had someone else in mind who might be able to help, with ties that ran deeper into the US government. Cache sipped on her coffee and Michael tried to note everything she said.

"So you think this is one of those classic love triangles?"

"Well, it's a triangle, but I'm not sure I would define it as classic. Beyond those three, I found evidence that Dr. Tanaka is having an affair with Dr. Wright, and it is possible that Dr. Wright was also engaged with Petra Fischer, so you could have a weird triangle there."

Michael sat back and rubbed his chin. He looked around the bistro. There was only one other couple in the place at the time, and they were seated far away from them, so they could not pick up on what they were discussing.

"So who do you think killed Dr. Fischer and Dr. Zhou?" he said in a whisper, leaning in toward Cache.

"When it was just Dr. Fischer, my money was on Dr. Wright. They have a history of butting heads, Dr. Wright felt slighted when Dr. Fischer was chosen to head up the project and if the rumors about Petra Fischer are true, that could be another reason."

"Do you think it's possible that he got rid of Jonas? Maybe the son was another obstacle?"

"That is what I'm thinking, but when you add in Dr. Zhou's murder, then I'm no longer fully set on Dr. Wright. From what he's said, he didn't think much of Emily but I couldn't see him killing her. With Dr. Fischer gone, if he had feelings for Petra, then he has removed a barrier. If Jonas proved another obstacle, maybe he removed a second barrier, but what did Dr. Zhou have to do with it?"

"Maybe she found out. If she was romantically involved with Dr. Fischer, she may have found proof and confronted him."

"It's possible. I'm not sure if I mentioned it, but of the journals that we recovered from Dr. Fischer's safe, one was missing. Then it wasn't."

"I don't follow."

"I found the missing journal not in Dr. Fischer's possession, but in Dr. Wright's home. The only other person that may have had access to put the journal there is Dr. Tanaka, but everyone swears that Dr. Fischer never let anyone look at his journals, so how did they get their hands on the missing one?"

Michael took a sip of his coffee as his phone buzzed. He picked it up.

"Detective Boone here... You found what?... Could it be fake?... Hold on." He covered the phone mouthpiece with his hand. "Have you heard of Beatrice Yu?"

Trying not to look smug, Cache asked, "Who is that?"

"Where else should we be looking? We are on the same side."

"I would tell them to check the master bathroom and have a good look at her degrees in her office."

Michael relayed the information to the team, hung up the phone and put it down on the table again.

"Are we going to find your fingerprints on any of these items?"

"I wore gloves."

"So we have a scientist who may not be who she said she was, but she's dead and can't answer our questions."

"She told me her parents are back in Criza."

"Of course they are, provided that wasn't a lie. What are my people going to find in the bathroom and home office?"

Cache leaned into him, motioning with her finger for him to come closer. When he was a few inches away from her, she grabbed his cheeks and kissed him on the lips. "Why ruin the surprise?"

Michael sat back in his chair. "Well, you're anything but boring."

"Does the name Welterhouse mean anything to you?"

"You mean like Jacob Welterhouse?"

"I have no idea, just the name Welterhouse."

"Well, Jacob Welterhouse was a shipping magnate that made a fortune in the eighteen hundreds, had a house in downtown Boston at one point that was purchased and demolished, and they erected a group of high-rises on the land. Why?"

"Let's just say I found something at Emily's that said Welterhouse on it and leave it at that."

"So you removed evidence?"

"It might be nothing. I shaded a piece of paper on the pad by the phone. The top sheet was torn away from the pad. I'm telling you now, all that was on the pad was one word. Depending on how hard she wrote, you could probably shade the next piece of paper and come up with the same evidence."

"Maybe she was interested in something to do with the land or the street."

"What street?"

"Welterhouse Avenue. It runs for about eighteen or nineteen blocks down near the harbor."

"Are there a lot of buildings on the street?"

"Maybe a hundred or so."

"So Jonas could be in one of those buildings."

"That's a pretty big leap. Some of the buildings are abandoned, some have offices and homes; you would need a warrant to go through them all, and that would require a lot of evidence, not just one name."

Cache sat back in her seat and reflected on this. How could she check every nook and cranny of over a hundred buildings? She changed her focus to a different subject. "Are you meeting with Dr. Allen any time soon?"

"I don't know yet. We'll ask him to come back down to the station, though it probably won't do much good."

"When you have your meeting with him, can you let me know?"

"Why?"

"He's an employee of Quillchem, I should let Graydon know." Cache picked up her coffee and sipped on it and thought, It also means he won't be at home.

## 13

C ache opted not to go over to Michael's place after his attempt at a police interrogation at the bistro. She knew she would need to return to Quillchem and bring Graydon up to speed on the developments. He could then decide how best to inform the team, though from what Cache had experienced with the group of four, it didn't seem like any love would be lost. They might have to fake caring that a colleague was murdered only a short time after Dr. Fischer had been killed. They would also need to face that the pool of suspects had gotten narrower, with light being focused on the remaining three. Cache wrestled with the fact that while Emily had not gotten on swimmingly with her colleagues, there was nothing to be gained by her death unless it was as Michael suspected: She had learned who killed Lucas Fischer and attempted to blackmail them or threatened to take what she knew to the police.

Cache spent part of the evening on a closed conference call between her, Graydon Quill, General Douglas and an assortment of Pentagon personnel, and representatives from the FBI, CIA and Homeland Security. All wanted to know who Emily

Zhou really was and why she was carrying a Crizan passport under a different name. The various agencies got off the call around midnight, with the CIA tasked with learning what it could about Beatrice Yu through their channels overseas. Graydon was concerned about how much information may have passed from Dr. Fischer to Dr. Zhou and then where she had passed that on to. The military was concerned about a foreign government's having access to EBSM to outfit their own troops, especially when domestically the project was stalled until someone could break the code.

Cache woke around seven o'clock that morning and went for a run around the campus to clear her mind. Of the three remaining members of the team, she had questions about Dr. Allen's relationship with Dr. Zhou. She was uncertain about their relationship, maybe it was genuine love, maybe Dr. Zhou was using it for alternative purposes, but these were answers best gotten from Emily, who could no longer offer input. Jeffrey would tell Cache what she wanted to hear, which didn't suit the investigation. No, what Cache needed was an unbiased view of their relationship. She had uncovered photos of the two of them hidden at Emily's place, which got Cache wondering what she might find at his place. Michael had told her he would text her details when Dr. Allen and his lawyer agreed to meet with the police to answer further questions about evidence discovered at Dr. Zhou's home. Cache estimated that given this was the second interview in several days, the meeting would be brief unless the police were prepared to charge him with one or two of the murders. Cache hoped to gain access to his home, have a look around and be gone by the time he arrived home. An old friend who'd had a run-in with the law had taught her a useful skill that had proven handy on more than one occasion. Cache, in pulling her bag together to come out to Boston, had packed a small black nylon pouch filled with all the tools necessary to pick a lock. What she hoped was that a security system in the form of an alarm or hungry dog wasn't waiting for her on the other side of the door, but she saw no other way to get the answers to her questions. When she got back from her run, she showered, had breakfast and called home to talk with her parents and update them on what was going on with her and the case to the extent she was allowed to disclose.

During the talk with her mom, Cache received a text from Michael advising her that the meeting with Dr. Allen was scheduled for one thirty in the afternoon at his precinct in downtown Boston. Chase had pulled the residential address for Dr. Allen from personnel records and made it very clear to Cache that she had no interest in knowing why she wanted that information, given her easy access to Dr. Allen at the company's lab facilities.

At noon, Cache had Aaron drive her out to the community of Beacon Hill, which Dr. Allen called home. His residence was part of a series of three-story town homes with a possible attic from the appearance of a small dormer window built into the roof. The town homes had a light-colored red brick exterior with black window frames and shutters, and two sets of windows on each floor facing the street above the main entrance to the residence. There was a small window beside the front door. Dr. Allen's particular home was on a small side street with two town homes on either side of the street. There were people walking by on the sidewalk, but none paid too much attention to what was occurring on the smaller side streets. Cache pulled on a pair of gloves that she'd brought with her, so she didn't have to improvise. She began by ringing the doorbell on the off chance that someone was still at home. After a few minutes of pressing the button and no one coming to answer, she proceeded to pick the lock to the front door. Cache inserted her tension wrench into the door lock and then inserted the pick and jimmied the tumblers until she heard a click and put the picks away in her pocket. As she opened the door, she listened for the sound of an alarm beeping or something scurrying around inside the residence but found the home quiet.

She darted inside and locked the door behind her. In front of her on the right-hand side was a lightly stained wooden staircase with a white-painted banister. There were three doors in the hallway. The first opened to a small powder room with a window facing onto the street; the second door was a walk-in closet. Cache flipped on the light and examined the coats. Almost all the coats were male oriented, except for a blue bomber-style jacket with *Quillchem Industries* stitched on the right and the name *Emily* embroidered on the left chest. Cache walked to the end of the hall and opened the door to a small storage room filled with bikes, canned food, a small wine rack and an assortment of boxes. She closed the door behind her and made her way to the second floor.

The stairs led to the main living area of the house. At the top of the stairs was the kitchen, with a dark brown wall of cupboards in an L-shape flanking two walls. The farmhouse-style sink sat below a window that looked out to a small yard with a single building behind the house to hold a car. There was a door at the back of the kitchen that led to a small deck and a staircase descending to a path that took you to the garage. There were chrome appliances throughout the kitchen and a small kitchen table near the back door, where it looked like Dr. Allen kept his mail. Cache flipped through the opened mail on the table but saw nothing that sparked her curiosity. She walked down the hallway. There was a large opening to her right that went into a small dining room with a dark stained wooden table, six chairs surrounding it, and a chandelier with white electric candles hanging down. A curio cabinet sat against the back wall and Cache rummaged through it, only to find a selection of dishes and sterling silver cutlery.

The front room of the residence was the main living area, with two couches in the corner, a television off to the side and a large coffee table. As Cache poked through the magazines and books in the room, she found nothing of interest. Cache then made her way up the stairs to the third floor. There were three doors in the hallway, and unlike Emily's place, no staircase to take you to an upper level. Cache went to the end of the hall and opened up the first door. Jeffrey's master bedroom consisted of a large four-poster bed with a cream-colored canopy, a dresser and chest in cherrywood with bright brass fixtures, and an entertainment unit to complement the other pieces in the room. She rummaged through his drawers, but there was nothing alarming hidden within their compartments. The small walk-in closet had several suits hanging against the wall and several dress shoes along the bottom of the floor. She walked over to the bed and sat down on the right-hand side, and noticed a large picture frame on the nightstand. She picked it up to take a closer look at it; from the age on the faces she guessed it had been taken a few years ago. Mountains and a pristine blue lake appeared in the background, and what looked like a tent, but the primary subject matter was what got her attention most. It was a selfie taken of Jeffrey and Emily together, her arms around him and one of his arms around her as he held the camera with the other. There was no sign of anyone else accompanying them on this trip, and it played heavier in Cache's mind that a relationship between the two of them was a real possibility. She stood up and walked to the door on the other end of the room opposite the front of the house. It was a small bathroom with walk-in shower, toilet and double sink. Another door led to the third-floor hallway. Cache rummaged through the bathroom drawers to find the usual items: toothpaste, tooth floss, over-the-counter medicine. She opened up the medicine cabinet built into the wall. There were a few pill containers prescribed over the years to Dr. Allen and a bottle of pills for anxiety prescribed to Emily Zhou. She put the bottles back and exited into the hallway. Cache glanced down at her watch. It was now 2:10 in the afternoon, and she knew she needed to speed things up and get out of there. She approached the last room on the floor by the top of the stairs and opened the door to a small guest bedroom that had been converted into an office. Like most of the offices of his colleagues, there were bookcases along the back wall, flanking a small window with blinds that looked onto the tiny backyard. A chair and large desk with papers everywhere sat in front of the bookcase with two chairs on the other side of the desk. The walls contained degrees from various universities and the desk held two more photos, one solely of Emily and another of the two of them taken at some formal event, given the tuxedo Jeffrey was wearing in the photograph. Cache sat down at the desk, lifted the papers and tried to see what was contained in the mess without disturbing it too much. To the left of the desk was a large black steel mesh garbage bin with lots of crumpled-up paper in it. Cache reached down for a few of them and put them in front of her on the desk. She uncrumpled the first and smoothed it out. It had some of the same symbols in the Atlantian language that Dr. Fischer had created, and different letter-number combinations below. She grabbed the next crumpled piece of paper and the one after that, and all appeared to be attempting to crack the code, but what was he using as a source? All the journals were now accounted for and locked up in the legal department's safe. Cache poked further through the mess of papers on the desk, and down toward the bottom she found a series of eight-by-ten photographs that someone had taken of the journals. She was uncertain which journals they were and lined all the images up on the desk and took a picture with her smartphone so she could compare them with the photocopies she had back at Quillchem. Cache returned the pictures to their original location, folded one of the crumpled pieces of paper into a square and tucked it into her jeans pocket. She scrunched the remaining pieces of paper back up and returned them to the wastepaper basket.

Cache then poked through the desk to see what goodies were buried there. In the second drawer, she found a series of letters written by Emily to Jeffrey. She flipped through them; they were very personal, as she poured her heart out to him in them. One that caught her interest read,

*My Dearest Jeffrey,*

*I know what you saw must confuse you. I never meant for you to find out. There are things that I must do, things that I am compelled to do to protect the people I love, including you. The predicament that I find myself in requires me to use everything at my disposal to get closer to Lucas. I see the way he looks at me. I know what's on his mind when he asks me to work late and the rest of you have gone home. For the time being I have to pretend interested in his attentions, to accept his affections without hesitation, wherever that decision will take me. Know that for now, I must follow this course of action. We will have our time together in the future, when it is just you and me.*

*Love*

*Emily xxox*

Cache sat back in the chair and thought to herself that Dr. Tanaka was way off on that one. She was so focused on the content of the letters that she didn't hear the garage door open and close in the back of the house. She heard a voice from outside. Dr. Allen had arrived home and stopped to take a phone call. Cache folded the letters back up, returned them to the desk and exited into the hall, closing the door behind her. She could hear him fidgeting at the back door to his home as she moved down the stairs as quickly as possible. As she approached the back door, it swung open, and she retreated up the stairs. She could hear him on the floor below. She looked around for a place to hide and spotted a closet. Maybe she should hide in there. What if he went to access the closet, and she was in there? No, that wouldn't work. The shower; maybe she should hide in the shower. She could hear him coming up the stairs. She felt her heart beating faster. Cache moved quickly to the end of the hall; opened up the master bedroom door, closing it behind her; and squeezed under the frame of the bed. As he made his way to the upstairs, Cache could hear his footsteps grow louder and louder until she saw the bedroom door swing open and his black socks moving into the room, closer to where she was hidden. Cache looked around underneath the bed. She could feel her nose wanting to sneeze. Dust everywhere, and she was allergic to dust. One sneeze and the jig was up. She pinched her nose and breathed with her mouth. Cache felt him sit down on the bed as he talked to someone on the phone.

"This is getting really aggravating. This is the second time they have called me down to the police station. No, they don't have anything, they're just fishing. Okay, so a tie of mine was used to strangle her. It doesn't mean I did it. It was her idea that I monogram my initials on the backs of my ties. At the time I thought it had to do with everyone borrowing them. Lucas, Ian, they couldn't keep their own ties at the office. They knew when the army showed up we had to put them on. She probably wanted me to monogram them so she could keep them straight with everyone else she was sleeping with. Damn right I sound bitter! Do you like having that Quillchem bitch hauling us into meetings all the time to grill us? We just have to play it cool. I am working on it. If we can crack the code, we will be rich. Then we can say goodbye to this place and find someplace that doesn't have an extradition treaty with the US. Okay I got to go, I'll see you at the lab tomorrow."

Cache watched as he got up off the bed and walked toward the bathroom. She could see him drop his trousers and throw his shirt on the ground. A few minutes passed and the sound of water running came from the bathroom. Cache squeezed out of her hiding place and tiptoed past the washroom and down the stairs to the ground floor.

Part of her wanted to confront him, to find out where he had gotten the photos from, but it appeared that he had yet to crack the code and time was still on her side, though she feared time might run out for Jonas. She made her way to the front door and eased her way out. Now she needed to lock it from the outside to ensure that Jeffrey would remain completely in the dark about her intrusion into his home. Once the door was secured, Cache headed for the sidewalk, took her gloves off and put them into her pockets, and grabbed her smartphone to call Aaron to come pick her up.

————

Cache arrived back at Quillchem at just after four o'clock p.m. and called Michael from the car. He wouldn't provide her any details about his discussion with Dr. Allen and his attorney but suggested that she come over to his place for a late-night dinner so he could catch her up. She knew this was just a ploy to have sex—anything he'd learned from his meeting with Dr. Allen he would keep to himself until they had enough evidence to move forward with the case—but given the choice of sleeping with him or sleeping alone tonight, the prospect of his warm bed appealed to her. In her suite, Cache laid out the copies of the journals on the living room floor and scanned each one, comparing it to the pictures on her phone of the items found in Dr. Allen's home office. After spending almost an hour comparing the photos of Dr. Fischer's gibberish, she determined that Dr. Allen's pictures originated from journals one, five and the elusive number fifteen. She questioned whether she should return to Dr. Allen's and look through the mess of papers to see if somewhere she could locate the pages that had been torn out of journal fifteen or whether the police could get a warrant to search his home, hopefully discovering the documents in the search.

She then shifted her focus to the letter that she had read from Emily to Jeffrey and then the phone conversation she'd overhead when Jeffrey had returned home. Of the two remaining people in the lab, the one that Cache pegged as the probable person on the other end was Akiko Tanaka. Was it possible that she was not only engaged in an extramarital affair with Dr. Wright but with Dr. Allen as well? Alternatively, he could have been talking to someone else at Quillchem; however, the only three people feeling burdened by her line of questioning were Dr. Wright, Dr. Tanaka and Dr. Allen, though of course it was always possible that Ian and Jeffrey were also involved in a relationship. Cache sat on the couch with her pad of paper and tried to reason out the flow of activity between the individuals involved. Somehow Jeffrey had come into possession of photographs of the journals. How, Cache could not definitively answer, but if Emily and Lucas were involved in some sort of relationship, it was possible that she may have been able to get the copies. If Dr. Allen had at one time had in his possession journal fifteen, it was conceivable that he'd used his relationship with Dr. Tanaka to plant the journal in the possession of Dr. Wright, thereby forcing suspicion off of them and onto him.

As she worked out the dynamics of the three remaining members of the team, the what-if scenarios grew for her until she felt it was time to go deal with a mindless distraction and called Aaron to bring the car around and take her out to Michael Boone's residence. After a long, quiet car ride while Cache sat alone with her thoughts, he dropped her at the front of Michael's and she told him to go home and that she would see him tomorrow. She walked up the steps to the front door and rang the bell. Michael opened the door, wearing jeans and a blue T-shirt with the Boston police logo on the upper left-hand chest. Flour was dusted across the material and a tea towel hung over his shoulder.

She looked at him. "I'm such a dunce, I should have brought wine. Maybe I can go pick something—"

He stopped her in midsentence, grabbing her by her ass and pulling her in tight to kiss her. "You talk too much sometimes."

She smiled and kissed him back and went inside, closing the door behind her.

"What is that smell? I could eat that aroma."

"Give it forty minutes, you can. I'm making for you my mother's lasagna. There is a glass of wine waiting for you. How was your day? Why did you want to know when we were meeting with Dr. Allen?"

"I wanted to snoop inside his house."

"You broke into his house? You know, we consider that illegal in this part of the country. In fact, it's illegal in all parts of the country."

"Are you going to arrest me? You know, I can think of something more fun to do with your handcuffs, if you don't want to take me downtown and book me."

"I'm going to pretend that I didn't hear any of that." He went back to the oven, flipped on the oven light and crouched down. "You can see the cheese bubbling." He turned to her. "So what did you find?"

"Find where?"

"At Dr. Allen's."

"I thought you didn't hear that."

He stood up, walked over to his glass of wine and took a sip. "Don't be funny. I think he killed Dr. Zhou and Dr. Fischer, but the evidence is circumstantial at best. If you found something that we could find using a warrant, well, I'm happier to see murderers go to prison than go free."

"Funny thing is, the stuff I found points to the fact that he and Emily Zhou were in a serious relationship, or at least that's what he wants people to think. I found some copies of journals that he should not be in possession of but nothing that's going to point you to who killed Lucas or Emily, and I'm no closer to finding Jonas."

"Well, for what it's worth, I asked a couple of uniformed officers that work the area that Welterhouse Avenue is in to keep an eye out for anything suspicious. It's a long shot but they're down there anyway; who knows what they might come up with."

Cache walked over to him, put her arms around his neck and pulled him in tight against her. "Thank you for doing that for me," she said, and placed her lips against his.

"Don't get your hopes up, it's a sizable area to cover and we're looking for something to say, 'Come look this way.'"

They continued talking about the letters from Emily to Jeffrey, and Michael shared that they hadn't learned anything new from their meeting that day between Jeffrey, his lawyer and themselves. He acknowledged the tie found around her neck was one of his and that they were involved in a relationship. He was always leaving belongings at her place, as she was with him. Cache shared that she had found a jacket of Emily's in the front closet tucked among other jackets, so it wasn't as if it was on display to be found. Other ties, shirts and articles of clothing that belonged to Jeffrey had been found in the drawers, closet and laundry hamper of Emily's place. Nothing out of the ordinary for two people in a relationship. Dr. Allen's lawyer had pointed out to the police that the weapon was a weapon of convenience, no different from a perpetrator grabbing a knife from a knife block found in most kitchens. Other than his ties' being used to kill both victims, there was nothing else to link him to the murders, and his ties were easily accessible to someone visiting Emily's home or the lab.

Dr. Allen's lawyer further established that the ties were an everyday variety and anyone could have purchased a tie and had a similar monogram sewn on the inside in the hopes that it would throw attention for the killings onto Dr. Allen. His lawyer made it clear that there was no reason for him to want to kill either victim. Cache paused on that thought and shared her belief that there was a cause. Dr. Fischer was taking the person whom he loved away from him. That is enough reason for anyone to want to take action against someone like Dr. Fischer. If by some chance Dr. Allen had learned that Emily was involved in a relationship with Dr. Fischer voluntarily and not as she had made it out to be, that may have given him reason to want her dead, too.

The two of them went back and forth over the next few hours, enjoying Mrs. Boone's lasagna recipe and a second bottle of white wine. They proposed different theories as to who the culprit could be and their motives until it grew late and their attraction for one another took over. Michael threw Cache over his shoulder, turned the lights off in the kitchen and carried her upstairs, thinking about her earlier comments about what he could do with his handcuffs.

## 14

Cache stared up at the ceiling. She was lying there in Michael's bed straight as a board with his arm reaching over her chest and his right leg draped across her like he was a bear trying to hug a tree. Most men want to get some distance after they have sex; Michael hugged her, afraid that she would escape out a window in the middle of the night if he didn't hold on for dear life. She could hear his snoring in her ear, and gentle attempts to shove him off her and over to the other side of the bed proved challenging, resulting in defeat, so she lay there, feeling the heat of their twisted bodies under the covers. She pondered why this bothered her. Was it the fact that she was from Montana, a place she expected to return to after she wrapped this case up, and here on the East Coast was someone she had been searching for? Would he be interested in giving up all that he had worked for to become a sheriff or sheriff's deputy in Hart, Montana? Could she take this city boy and turn him into a rancher? As she looked down at him, she knew there was as much chance of that occurring as his turning her into a domestic homemaker who would stand eagerly at the door awaiting his return each day, with a beer in one hand, food on the stove and a pregnant belly waiting to add to a growing litter of kids. Yet over the years she'd had just one steady boyfriend, from high school, whom she'd lost because of distance when they went away to school. Then there had been a few on-and-off relationships in college and the service and one brief encounter with someone she tried not to think about.

She pushed at his shoulder. "Hey, Mikey, hey, Mikey."

"What, is there a problem?" he said in a groggy voice.

"I can't breathe. Can you move over?"

He turned over onto his side, pulling a good stretch of the covers with him. "Are you happy?"

"Thank you, now go back to sleep."

"Anything for the woman I love," he said as he drifted back to sleep and began to snore again.

Cache shot up in bed, sitting at almost a ninety-degree angle. "What?" She looked at him as he continued to snore away. "You're kidding, right?" But there was no answer. She fell back against her pillow. Nah, he was dreaming; he couldn't feel that way after just a short time. She liked him, and the sex was what she needed to satisfy a void she had been struggling with, but this was just fun, something to do while she was in town. There was no room for that word to be used. She wanted to wake him up and make him take it back or deny he'd even said it, but she just looked at the back of his head and turned to stare at the ceiling. She needed to get some sleep, but the case continued to haunt the back of her thoughts, and now Michael had just added a level of complexity that she wasn't prepared to handle.

The case involved seven people. On one side there were the Fischer's, husband, wife and son. On the other side there was Dr. Fischer's team, four individuals who either admired or despised him, depending on who you asked. There were straight lines all over the place, but two lines still remained dotted and she needed clarity on them. Was Dr. Allen in a relationship with Dr. Tanaka, and was Dr. Wright in a relationship with Petra Fischer? And what about Jonas? Where are you? she continued to ask herself repeatedly, until mental exhaustion gave way to slumber and she fell back asleep.

At six o'clock a.m., she felt hot breath against her face as moisture fell across her lips, and she woke to find someone who had slept well and wanted to play before going to work. She opted for a couple's shower as she had two questions that she needed to get to work on today. They dressed and made their way downstairs, and Michael made scrambled eggs for the two of them with brown toast while Cache pulled together the coffee. She grabbed her smartphone and texted Aaron to see if he could come pick her up. She offered to drop him at work, but he felt it could ruin his reputation as a down-to-earth guy if his colleagues spotted him getting out of her German luxury sedan and decided that he would take the train that morning.

They sat and ate breakfast at a small table in the kitchen. Cache desperately wanted to ask him about what he'd said in the middle of the night, but she wanted to have enough time to talk about it in detail, as opposed to giving him an opportunity to say he had to go. His phone vibrated and rang with a familiar eighties pop tune that Cache was surprised he would have as his ringtone.

"Got to get that," he said as he stood up from the kitchen table.

"Just let it go to voice mail."

"No, it's the station calling. Something must be up." He grabbed the phone from the inside of his jacket hanging in the hall and returned to the kitchen. "Hello, Detective Boone here... Hey, Murphy. Did they leave a name?" He waved in Cache's direction as she scrolled through her emails. "No name, just a sighting. Okay, where did they say the sighting happened, Welterhouse?"

The name Welterhouse caused Cache to stop and put all her focus on Michael and his phone conversation.

"Do we have a number?... Okay, I asked a couple of uniforms to keep an eye out in the area. You said there were two stained glass windows in front, one with broken glass and pink and blue graffiti on the wall. Thanks, I'll look into it."

He hung up the phone and put it down on the table.

"What about Welterhouse?" Cache asked.

"The precinct got a tip a few hours ago that made its way up to the detective squad. That was my partner Dennis Murphy. The caller said that they think they saw someone matching Jonas's description going into a building on Welterhouse."

"Do we have a number?"

"No, just a vague description of the front of the building, and the caller didn't leave their details so we can't call them back to get further info."

"What was the building description? I'll have Aaron drive me up and down the street until I find it."

"And then what?"

"Then I'm going in there to look for Jonas."

"And then be arrested? This has to be done legally. When Aaron gets here, we—you and me—will go with Aaron and try to identify the building. Once we have an identification, I will call Murphy back and he will go to a judge and try to get a search warrant."

"You think that's going to stop me from going in?"

"I will handcuff you to the door of the car if I have to. We wait for the warrant and backup. We don't know if Jonas is there on his own or if he was taken by someone or a group of people, and we are not going in without backup."

"Okay, fine. We'll do it your way. Give me the building details."

"No."

"What do you mean, no?"

"I have a feeling that if I give them to you, you'll ditch me somehow and go do this on your own. I will give you the details once we are in the car."

"You know, trust is important in a relationship."

"Is that what we have?"

"Based on what you muttered in your sleep, you seem to think so."

"Why, what do you think you heard?"

"I'll give you the details when we're in the car."

———

They waited for another twenty minutes in silence, staring at one another, trying to see which one of them would blink first. Would Michael share the details of the building with her or would she tell him what he had uttered to her in the middle of the night? They each resisted saying anything to the other and turned to frivolous conversation about the weather.

When Aaron arrived, Michael leaned over the seat and whispered into Aaron's ear that he should take them to the intersection of Elderwood Street and Welterhouse Avenue. Elderwood Street ran north and south, and that intersection was at the southernmost point in the city. Cache demanded that Aaron tell her what Michael had shared with him, but he advised her that Michael was a police officer and she wasn't, which didn't sit well with her.

"This feels like when my brothers used to gang up on me."

"What happened to them?" Aaron asked.

"They got the worst of it and learned not to do it again."

As they reached the intersection of Elderwood Street and Welterhouse Avenue, Michael shared with Aaron and Cache that they were looking for an abandoned building with a series of windows above the front entrance, of which two of them appeared to be stained glass, one with a significantly broken corner. The building was red brick with graffiti sprayed on it with different tags in primarily pink and blue spray paint. Aaron began driving slowly along Welterhouse Avenue, staying to the right-hand side as much as possible. But parked cars often forced him into the left-hand side, which annoyed some drivers behind him. The street was two lanes running in opposite directions, with street parking on both sides. The initial area the search had begun in was more trendy, with restaurants and shops and a few formerly abandoned buildings receiving restorations to turn them into the next hot spots. As Aaron continued to drive down the street, the upscale area turned more middle-class, with shops that had been there for forty years or more, and then turned into a more industrial area as they drove away from the city. A number of the factory-style buildings had broken windows, and a few were boarded up, with graffiti sprayed on the plywood where windows and doors used to be. The scent of the harbor drifted into the area as Cache spotted rats running for cover under wooden pallets, chased by stray cats looking for their next meal. Building by building, they searched. The cars behind Aaron disappeared as they moved into this stretch of Welterhouse Avenue, with very little traffic going in either direction. As they approached the fourteenth block, Michael saw something and asked Aaron to pull over to the curb. There was a building matching the description on his right. He went with his first instinct without thinking and reached down behind his jacket and pulled out his handcuffs. Cache didn't see it coming. He grabbed her by the right wrist and place one cuff on, then cuffed the other to Aaron's headrest in front of her.

"What the fuck, Michael? Take it off right now."

"No."

She looked over to his side and saw the building he'd spotted. "That's the place, get these off of me." Her face tightened up, her eyebrows raised and she gritted her teeth. "Take them off or it's the last time you will—"

"Will you shut up for one minute and look? Aaron, reverse and stop when you get to the alley back there."

Aaron put the car in reverse and backed up, stopping at the alleyway between the building they were seeking and the one next door to it. A black sedan with tinted windows was parked in the alleyway. The familiar diplomatic plates were on the back of the car.

"That has to be the car that was tailing us."

"Yeah, and that could make this more complicated."

"Why?"

"Because if this property is owned by an embassy we may have a problem going in."

"You will have a problem, not me."

"If there is a complication like that, then we will both go in."

"Won't you get in trouble?"

"Probably."

She leaned forward as close as she could to him, being handcuffed to Aaron's seat, and kissed him.

"Thanks. I'm not sure the kiss is worth my pension, but I don't like the idea of Jonas being in there."

He grabbed his phone, called Detective Murphy and gave him the address details. Murphy would take the information to a judge to see if they could get a warrant as they sat and waited. After about forty minutes of sitting in the car and staring at the building, they caught sight of some activity in the alleyway. Two men dressed in black exited out a side door and got into the vehicle. One man had a briefcase with him, and the car drove down the alleyway.

"Now is our chance to go in."

"No, we're still waiting on the warrant, but, Aaron, can you follow that car? Don't get too close but let's see where it goes."

Michael looked at Cache and could see she was dying to go

into the building. Getting her away from the building as they waited on a warrant seemed like a good idea, and it might provide them with some information about which country the sedan belonged to.

Aaron almost lost the car coming out of the alleyway as the sedan turned right along Warner Springs Road and sped up. With few cars traveling the roads in this part of town, Michael instructed Aaron to stay way back for fear that someone might spot them; he didn't want them doubling back to the warehouse to deal with any potential loose ends. The car in front continued to pull away from them and Michael urged Aaron to speed up but not get spotted.

After they had passed several blocks, Michael took the cuffs off Cache, operating on the assumption that even if she were to jump from the vehicle, they were far enough away that Michael could beat her back there if she was on foot.

Cache was conflicted on how to feel about Michael at this point and hoped that the decision to tail the car in front of them would not be one that came back to haunt her. The car in front, after several blocks, turned left, moving away from the harbor toward central Boston. As traffic picked up, Aaron could move up on the black sedan so that he was only a car's length away from them. The tinting on the back window prevented any of them from gaining insight into the car's occupants. They continued down several city blocks, heading toward downtown Boston, until Aaron spotted them signaling to turn into a white concrete building on the left-hand side. The building was three stories, with light red tinted glass on all the windows facing onto the street. There were white slab planter boxes with a variety of shrubs separating the sidewalk from the building, and a number of professionally dressed people were coming in and out of the front entrance. Aaron signaled to pull off to the right and parked the car while the three of them saw the sedan pull up to a black gate with a guard post at the side of the building. A uniformed security officer approached the window and appeared to talk with the driver for a few minutes before returning to the guard post. A few seconds later, the gate lifted, and the sedan drove down to what must have been an underground parking garage.

"If I ask you to wait here while I go talk to the guard, will you still be here when I get back?" he said, looking at Cache. He thought about it for a second and turned to face Aaron. "Aaron, if you leave I will have you charged with something and ensure you spend at least six months in county jail, so don't listen to her."

Michael ran across the street, stopping cars in both directions to safely cross, holding up his badge when a few of them honked at him. Cache watched him speak to the security officer for a few minutes, shake his hand and return to the car.

"What did he say?"

"So the building holds various professional services, including several law firms and consulting firms. I asked about the car with diplomatic plates that just entered and he indicated they were here to meet with one of the law firms but couldn't give out more information without a warrant."

"So there is no embassy in the building?"

"Afraid not, and we do not know who they're meeting with."

Cache raised her cell phone, took a picture of the building and marked the GPS coordinates. "I'll pass it on to our contacts with the army. They may have a better idea of who is in that building."

Michael's phone played the pop eighties tune again, and he reached inside his jacket to grab it.

"Hello, Detective Boone here... Did you have any trouble? ... Okay, we'll meet you back at the warehouse. Bring some backup, I don't know what we're dealing with. We just followed two guys who came out of the warehouse to an office downtown. The car had diplomatic plates... Okay, if we get back there before you, we'll sit tight." He hung up the phone and returned it to his inside pocket. "Aaron, can you take us back to the warehouse?"

"Good news?"

"Yeah, the judge signed off on the search warrant. Murphy is going to meet us there with a couple of patrolmen, so we won't be going in alone."

Cache looked at Michael and muttered, "I hope Jonas is there and he is still alive."

# 15

Aaron drove directly to the warehouse, where the three of them sat out front for about thirty minutes waiting for Detective Murphy to arrive with two squad cars. As Cache grew more restless in the back of the vehicle, a dark blue sedan pulled up alongside followed by two police cruisers. A man in his late forties, heavier with dark hair and a beard emerged from the blue sedan. Michael exited the back and walked over to talk with him as Cache climbed out of the vehicle onto the sidewalk. Michael motioned for her to come over where he formally introduced her to his partner Detective Murphy. With the front of the building boarded up, they walked down the alleyway to the side of the building, where the two men in the diplomatic sedan had emerged from. There was a glass-paned door with steel mesh; the windows were painted on the inside, preventing anyone from seeing in. Michael pulled a lock pick set from his jacket and worked on the lock. After several attempts where he expressed that he almost had it, Cache pushed him aside and took over, opening the lock in just a few minutes. The officers and Cache drew their weapons, and they entered the building. Detective Murphy looked back at Cache.

"Do you have a permit for that thing?"

Before she could answer, Michael said, "it's okay, I've already asked and verified it."

There was a damp musky smell in the air as they walked up a set of stairs, with dirty white linoleum peeling away from the surface into a shell of a building. The first floor had all the walls gutted, and you could see from one end of the building to the other. Creatures could be seen scurrying about, and broken walls and other debris were scattered throughout. As the group walked along the inside perimeter of the building, they came across a staircase leading to the floors above. The two uniformed officers stayed on the ground floor, ensuring anyone caught entering the building would be detained. Cache, Michael and Detective Murphy proceeded to the second floor. There was a series of offices running down the hallway. The three of them walked down the corridor, guns firmly in their grasp and holding flashlights with their other hands. As was to be expected, electricity to the building had been turned off. As the three of them approached each room, they stopped to listen for the sound of anyone or anything in the office. They then tried the doorknob, and if the room wasn't locked, they would open the door and scan the room with their flashlights. For any rooms that were locked, they identified they would need to come back to those rooms later and pick the locks one by one or try to force the door open.

Room by room they went along the corridor until they got to the end of the hallway. A hallway ran perpendicular to the main corridor, with rooms on both sides of the walls. Michael and Cache went to the left and Detective Murphy to the right. Each room they came across was deserted. In some rooms there was evidence that homeless or druggies had taken up residence there, with empty food containers, torn blankets and dirty needles littering them. They returned to the stairwell and continued up to the third floor and then the fourth, searching room by room, concerned that at one point a door would open and something horrific would be waiting for them on the other side. As they approached the last floor, Cache's optimism that they would find Jonas had fallen away. Now it just seemed like a pointless exercise. She started thinking about packing it in. Without Jonas it could be years before the code was broken. She was no farther in figuring out who'd killed Dr. Fischer and subsequently Emily Zhou, and all she had really learned was that his team of scientists was rather dysfunctional. As the three of them made their way down one of the last hallways on the top floor, Cache spotted something in the distance: a set of double doors with a chain and lock around the knobs. She rushed to the doors and put her ear against one. She could hear something behind the doors, something moving. As she glanced down at the bottom of the door, she could see light flickering off the floor. Michael attempted to pull her away from the door but she brushed him off. "Jonas, is that you?"

The light underneath the door flickered. "Help get me out of here!" came from the other side. Cache ran and pushed her shoulder against it, but the doors were solid and would not budge. Michael joined in, and then Detective Murphy, and they kept running and hitting the door with their shoulders until Cache noticed dust coming from the ceiling with the last strike. Detective Murphy radioed for one of the uniformed officers to grab a pair of bolt cutters from their cruiser and bring it up to the fifth floor.

"The chain looks too thick for bolt cutters," Cache said.

Detective Murphy grabbed the bolt cutters, but the blades could not get around the chain.

"Mind if I try something?" she asked as she pulled her handgun from her waistband.

Cache yelled out to Jonas to stand away from the door, and

she aimed at the lock and pulled the trigger, breaking the lock open.

"That was going to be my next option," Michael said as Detective Murphy concurred with him.

Cache pulled the lock, took the chains off the door and opened it. The room was dingy and reeked of feces and stale urine wafting over to them from a series of metal buckets in the corner. Cache ran to Jonas and hugged him. He smelled of sweat and filth. The wonderful burned cedar aroma that he'd first had on when she met him was gone. He was wearing a plaid shirt and khakis with dirt all over him. An old mattress lay on the floor, with some musty blankets lying on top of it. A battery-operated lantern was his only source of light other than a few cracks of sunshine that were coming from an old window that could be seen through a hole in the ceiling. In the middle of the room, there was an old wooden table and a metal chair. Notepads were stacked on top of one another, with photographs in another pile and a bunch of pens in a box. Food containers were piled in a corner near the metal buckets, which had maggots crawling over them, and empty water bottles were found around the base of the desk, with a few unopened ones in the corner.

Michael brought a flashlight close to Jonas's face. A cut around his lip had scabbed over and a purplish bruise was forming underneath his right eye.

"What happened?" Cache asked. "We've been hunting everywhere for you, your mother is worried sick."

"Emily, is she okay?" Jonas asked.

Cache looked at Michael and didn't know what to say.

Michael stepped in. "She's fine, she's been worried sick about you."

"I was hoping somehow she would get away. They dragged her out of here by her hair, kicking and screaming, and told me what they were going to do to her if I didn't cooperate. I kept asking to see her but they would never produce her, which meant either she was dead and I would be next if I didn't help them or maybe, just maybe, she had escaped and it would only be a matter of time before you guys came to get me out of here."

"What did they have you doing?" Michael asked.

Jonas walked over to the table, grabbed a series of photographs and brought them over to Michael and Cache. "They had these. They said they were pictures of my father's journals; they wanted me to translate them. The more I helped them, the safer Emily and I would be."

Cache took the photographs while Michael and Detective Murphy held up their flashlights and flipped through them. "How would they have gotten these?" she asked.

"I don't know, and it was hard to follow what my dad wrote. The pictures they had had no flow to them. It was like they gave me one page from one journal and then three pages from another. I did my best to translate them. You have to understand my dad and I always just used the language to send messages to one another, not stacks of books."

"There were two men here earlier. Are those the ones who grabbed you?" Michael asked.

"I don't know if they were the ones who grabbed us but they were definitely the ones in charge. Every day since they kidnapped me, they've brought food, water and a new stack of photos for me to work on deciphering. I would fill up the pads of paper with what I think my dad wrote. They took them and put them into a briefcase and then locked me in. What day is it?"

"Thursday," Detective Murphy said.

"My mom must be worried sick. I feel so horrible, we got into a big fight, if I... if we hadn't, none of this would have happened."

"You said they grabbed you?"

"Yeah, after my mom and I had a fight, Emily—she was so sweet at the service and told me if there was anything she could do to call her. I didn't know where to turn, so I called her. She came and picked me up. One thing led to another, and we got a lot closer. The next day she suggested we take a walk. The fresh air would do me good to clear my head. I remember it was cool. She had forgotten to grab a sweater and went back inside to get one. We were about twenty minutes from the house, walking down this path that she likes to go down, and I just remember being grabbed from behind, a bag thrown over my head, my wrists taped behind me. I could hear her plead for our lives. They must have knocked us out with something; we came to here in this room. We didn't know what was going to happen to us next. They came in, making their demands. The tall one punched me in the face and dragged her out of here and told me she was very attractive and they were going to take turns with her before they killed her unless I did what they said. Emily, she must have gone to you. That's how you found me, right?"

"Someone called in a tip, kid. I don't know if it was Emily," Detective Murphy said.

Cache rubbed his shoulder and looked around the room. "I think we need to get you out of here." She walked over to the table, gathered the photographs and pads of paper and walked with Jonas down to the car, where Aaron was waiting. Michael made it clear to him that he would need to make a statement about the events but it was fine if he wanted to go home first with Cache to see his mother. As he got into the backseat of the car, Michael mouthed the words, "Tell him," to her as he climbed into Detective Murphy's car and drove away, heading back to the precinct. Cache took one last look at the building that had served as a prison for Jonas for more than a week. She hopped in the backseat and told Aaron to drive to the Fischer residence.

"Do you need anything from me at the moment? We can stop and get you anything you like."

He looked out the window. "I just need to get home, see my mom and take a hot shower. Once I've done that I'll give Emily a call and thank her and make sure she's all right."

"You have a special connection with her?"

He turned to face Cache. "I know what you're going to say—the age difference, can it really work. She just gets me. It's like we're two of the same person."

"I thought there was someone special back at school. Did I misunderstand?"

"No, you probably mean Cynthia. I should call her as well. We've been going together for the past year. She's great, but she doesn't get me like Emily does."

"Jonas, you connected with Emily for what, a few days, and I'm guessing you hooked up, but don't throw away your relationship with Cynthia over this."

"You don't get it. It's okay. I'm just thankful that you came and found me."

Cache patted his leg. "You could still do me a favor."

"I suppose it has to do with Atlantian?"

"I'm not going to ask you to translate the journals for us. I can't say the military won't ask you, and you need to figure out what you're going to say there, but teach me and then I can work at decoding the journals and any other correspondence from your father that we come across."

"I suppose it's not a big favor to ask."

"I put together a list of symbols that I found throughout his journals. Help me create a sort of dictionary and then we'll have that as the master blueprint. The military may even be able to program a computer to do the deciphering for us."

As they drove into his neighborhood, Jonas began pointing out the homes of different people that he knew and sharing stories about the individuals with Cache. She knew the car ride would be over soon as they pulled into the Fischers' driveway, but she had an unfinished piece of business that she had to deal with.

"Aaron, can you pull over to the side and park?" Aaron did as she asked, and Jonas seemed a little bewildered by her actions given how close to his home they were. She leaned down and pressed the button to raise the privacy screen between her and the front seat. "Sorry, Aaron. Jonas, I have to talk to you about something and I need you to listen to me carefully."

"Okay."

"Emily is dead."

"What? That can't be, that is impossible. She came to you to come rescue me!"

"As Detective Murphy told you, the police got a tip. I went with your mother to the police station to file a missing persons report on you. They circulated information to the public and someone called in and said they saw you going into the warehouse and told the police what the building looked like. We drove down Welterhouse Avenue looking for a similar building; that's how we found you. The day after we believe you went missing, I met with Emily at her place and spent part of the afternoon with her. I told her we were looking for you and she said nothing."

"No, they probably told her if she said anything they would kill me."

"It's possible. All I can tell you is she was killed in her own home. I know because I'm the one that found her. Maybe she was trying to protect you, but before you go and throw away your relationship with Cynthia, stop and think. Emily is not there waiting for you and she has left us with several questions.

The answers, if they come in time, might be unsettling for you."

"Like what?"

"It's just speculation at this point, and it would be premature to say without further evidence."

"Tell me, I have a right to know."

"It's possible that she was working with your abductors, that she set the whole thing up to help decipher your father's journals."

"That can't be, there is no way that was the case."

"Maybe not, but your father kept those journals off site in that special language that the two of you had in a safe with a biometric lock in your parents' residence at the Dawes. I am sure you're aware the Dawes has pretty tight security, and yet I have found photographs of those journals now in two places. Did your abductors say anything to you?"

"They asked about the missing pages. On some of the photographs you have, you can see pages had been torn out from one journal. They wanted me to tell them where my father put them but I had no idea. That's how I got this cut underneath my lip; they weren't happy with my answer."

"Yeah, well, a lot of people want to know where those missing pages are. I am one of them, but I am not going to hit you over it. Look, you need to figure some of this out on your own. If you want to talk, you have my number, call me. I will go with you when you need to make your police statement."

"Going to hold my hand?"

"Detective Boone won't bite; I'm more the biter."

"What?"

"Sorry, inside joke. Promise me you won't break up with your girlfriend until you've had a chance to process everything."

"Okay, no breakups, at least not now."

Cache bent over and pressed the button to bring down the

privacy screen and asked Aaron to continue driving toward the Fischer residence. As they pulled into the driveway, they could see Petra tending to her flowers in the front garden, standing up, holding a pair of pruning scissors in her hand. She dropped them and ran to Jonas as she saw him get out of the car. She grabbed him so tight that he had a hard time breathing, and eventually she loosened her grip. They talked for a few minutes until her English changed to what Cache suspected was Russian and then back to English as she kept hugging him and rubbing his head, promising there would be no more fights about anything. Jonas went into the house as Petra approached Cache.

"Thank you for bringing him home to me. First to lose Lucas and then Jonas—a wife and mother shouldn't suffer such grief." She gripped Cache's hand and held it tight, more strongly than her small frame would suggest she was capable of. "I'm so glad you talked me into filing the police report. If they hadn't gotten that tip, who knows if we would have ever found him." She turned to look at the front door to the house.

"How did you know they got a tip?" Cache asked.

"The detective, the tall one with wavy hair, he told me. I was on pins and needles waiting to hear if you found him."

"You always work in the garden when you're feeling anxious?"

"Oh, dear, you should try it," she said as her grip around Cache's hand grew tighter. "It's very relaxing." She loosened her grip and rubbed her hands down on her apron. "Would you come in for some tea or coffee?"

"Sure, that sounds great." Cache went to the car and told Aaron that she would be a few minutes, as she hadn't really had a chance to sit down with Petra and get details that might be helpful to the case.

Cache followed her inside and closed the door behind her. She had been in the house briefly for the service after Dr.

Fischer's burial, but it had been filled with people. Now it was just three of them. Cache walked into the kitchen; a large set of double doors that she remembered using the last time she was here led out onto the deck. The kitchen was enormous, with a gas-powered burner and copper range hood. Petra went to a cupboard and pulled down a mug, then plopped a tea bag in it as she turned on a burner to heat a kettle on the stove.

"Do you prefer tea or coffee?"

"Coffee, if it's not too much of a bother."

"You brought my only son home to me, it's worth a little bother." She walked to a cabinet above their microwave and pulled down a bag of coffee beans.

Cache could hear the sound of the water running somewhere in the house and thought it must be Jonas taking the long, hot shower he'd been thinking about.

Petra scooped out the beans, and then the sound of the grinder drowned out the sound of running water elsewhere in the house. She then dropped the grounds into a filter, and the coffee machine dripped into a glass pot stationed below it. The kettle on the stove whistled, and as she grabbed for it she was distracted by the coffeemaker and burned her finger, exclaiming, "*Der'mo*," and then went to the sink to run her finger under some water.

"Are you okay, can I help you?"

"It's a little burn, my dear, I got worse for years working in the labs. Sit, relax, everything is okay."

She returned to the stove, turned the burner off, poured boiling water into her cup and set the kettle back down. She returned to the coffee machine, turned it off, poured the coffee into a cup similar to hers, brought it over to the table and sat it down in front of Cache. Petra grabbed the cream from the fridge as Cache spotted a small silver bowl with sugar in it.

"That word you said?"

Petra thought about it for a second. "*Der'mo*, it means...

'crap' in English. Sometimes when my brain is stuck for a phrase it goes back to my first language."

"Russian is your first language?"

"Yes. I grew up there, went to university there, and then I got transferred to a lab facility in East Germany. This is long before the wall came down. I met Lucas and"—she waved her hands in the air—"is history, as you say."

"What did you do in the lab?"

"I was a chemist, a very good chemist. When the wall came down, we had a chance to escape to the West, and we took it. Lucas ended up taking a job in France at a lab that was later purchased by Quillchem. I did contract work in the region at various labs until Jonas came along and decided to stay home to look after him."

"Dr. Wright told me the two of you have known each other a long time."

"That pig, don't listen to that fool. He was always jealous of what Lucas and I had, a long, loving, faithful relationship. We were devoted to each other. Ian worked every angle to try and find a weakness."

"A weakness?"

"Oh, he made it very clear to me what he wanted, but when I said no, it infuriated him. He saw something where there was nothing to be seen. I had my happy life and he couldn't accept that."

Jonas walked into the kitchen in a fresh set of clothes, with wet hair and that smell of burned cedar once again. He had a towel around his neck and poked his head into the fridge to retrieve a beer, then left the kitchen.

"He will need to make a statement to the police, you know."

"Why... why should he? He is home safe."

"The people that took him are still out there. They grabbed him once, they could grab him again. I can talk to Graydon about maybe putting one or two of our security personnel out here, if that would make you feel better, at least until we catch them."

Petra rested her hand on top of Cache's. "No, we will be okay," she said, and smiled at her.

"Well, he still needs to make a statement with the police. I can come pick him up and take him there if he likes, and I want him to teach me that language that he and his father made up."

"Oh, that gibberish of Lucas's again. Why couldn't he keep regular notes like everyone else, always thought he was smarter than everyone else."

"Did he ever teach you Atlantian?"

"No, that was their thing, and honestly I couldn't care less. It was fun for a grown-up man to do that with his young son, but then to bring it into his work environment... I don't know what got into Lucas's head sometimes, always making impulsive decisions that would come back to haunt him later."

They continued their conversation for almost an hour, with Cache asking what it was like to live in East Germany behind the wall. The more she asked about Petra directly, the more Petra shared about her life before Lucas. She avoided talking further about Ian Wright. Cache glanced down at her watch and felt it was time to depart. She thanked Petra for her hospitality and checked in with Jonas one more time before leaving. Petra walked her to the front door of the house.

"Are you sure I can't get some security people out here? I think I would feel better."

"No, we will be fine. You worry too much, dear, that lovely brown hair of yours will turn gray early if you don't give up the worry."

"Maybe you should get yourself a gun, just for safety's sake."

"We have several in the house already. I learned to shoot from my grandfather when I was a little girl back in Russia. No, if someone tries to break in here and take my Jonas again, they will be the ones calling the police."

Cache hugged Petra and left the house. She observed Petra watching her depart behind a curtain in one of the front rooms of the house. Cache got back into the car and asked Aaron to head back to Quillchem. She would need to brief Graydon on the latest developments and wanted to talk to Michael about what he had told Petra about the tip they had received.

ache had someone to call who might be able to offer her some needed insight, but the thought of phoning them left her stomach feeling queasy. She started by calling Graydon to advise him that they had found Jonas alive and that he had agreed to teach her the special language he had concocted with his father. Cache also informed him that Jonas's captors had obtained copies of the journals and had been making him translate them, so she was uncertain how much of the information has been passed on to whatever party was behind the kidnapping. Graydon expressed anger at the betrayal and soon realized he was voicing his concerns to the wrong person. He advised her that he would need to inform the military and they might have further questions for her and Jonas. She hung up the phone in the car.

"I could hear him yelling from here," Aaron said as he drove along the highway, heading back to the Quillchem campus.

"Yeah, he is not happy. I can't blame him; years of work and we have no idea what the secret formula is, and that formula might be making the rounds through a foreign government or being put up for sale on the black market as we speak. I need to call Detective Boone about something personal," she said as she reached for the button on the center console and raised the privacy screen between her and Aaron. She called Michael's cell phone.

"Hello, Detective Boone here."

"Hey, it's me."

"Did you get him home safe?"

"Yeah, he headed for the shower after his mother tried to hug all the air out of him."

"We did good work today, Iron, it's something to be proud of."

"Hey, I have a question for you."

"Sure, shoot."

"Did you tell Mrs. Fischer about receiving the anonymous tip?"

"No, typically we don't do that. A lot of times they don't pan out and we don't want to create false hope. Why?"

"She said you told her."

"Wasn't me. Wait a minute." Cache could hear him shout to someone. "I asked Murphy, he didn't say anything either. Why does it matter?"

"It's probably nothing. It just struck me as odd. Can you do me another favor?"

"You keep asking for favors and your tab is going to get pretty steep."

"It's okay, I'm sure I can cover it."

"What's the favor?"

"Can you listen to the tip that came in and tell me if it was a woman or a man's voice that left it?"

As Cache looked out the side window of the car, she could see that they had arrived at Quillchem, as they were passing through the front gates of the facility. Aaron drove to the front doors and Cache jumped out, expecting not to need his services for the rest of the night. She made it up to her suite and was tempted to knock on Chase's door to see what was going on in her life, but she knew it wasn't because she was interested, rather because she was trying to avoid making a phone call to the one person who might be able to get her some answers. Cache pulled open her laptop and typed the words "Mayhem Gallery" into the search engine. The website came up in the search results, along with addresses for art galleries in California, Brazil and France. She noted the California gallery and looked at her watch; if she was lucky someone would be there to at least pass her message along. If the person she wanted to talk to didn't want to call her back, then she would know she had traveled down the path as far as it would let her go. The phone rang twice before being picked up. "Hello, Mayhem Gallery, Janine speaking. How can I help you?"

"Hi, this is Cache Iron. Is Nina there by any chance?"

"Madame Mayhem is in a meeting. Was she expecting your call?"

"No, I was hoping to catch her, but if she's unavailable—"

"Can you hold on for one second?"

Cache could hear the sound of a light classical concerto as she waited on hold.

"Hello, did you say your name is Cache Iron?"

Janine proceeded to give Cache a phone number to call and a five-digit code and asked that she not try to reach Ms. Mayhem again. Her business was no longer welcome there. Cache got off the phone and looked at the number she had been given. What on earth is this? Cache thought. She could have just said no and hung up. Now Cache had to start calling mystery phone numbers. Cache dialed the 1-800 number that Janine had provided her.

"Hello, you have reached the offices of Lunar Tradicity, please enter your consultant's number at the sound of the beep." Cache had briefly learned about Lunar Tradicity when she was in California and had a sinking suspicion about the people behind the company. Cache entered the code 21975, and the operator told her the call was being connected.

"Hello, Cache, it's good to hear your voice."

"Nina, is that you?"

"Yes. I was wondering if I would ever hear from you again."

"Wasn't sure you would want to talk to me."

"What happened in California, that wasn't of your making. I imagine it was a tough decision."

"Harder than you know. Do you hear from them at all?"

"Once or twice. Do you want to know if they ask about you?"

"Yes and no."

"Well, when it's a firm yes, I will tell you. So what can I do for you?"

"What's Lunar Tradicity?"

"I suspect you already have your suspicions."

"Are you a spy?"

"Past life. Now I just sell expensive art to people who want to get rid of money."

"I heard you were someone who could always come up with a solution if you have a problem."

"I have a lot of friends. We help each other out. What do you need help with?"

"I'm working a case out in Boston, the Lucas Fischer murder, and need some help with it."

"Fischer, Fischer... I think I read something about that. Did he work for Quillchem Industries? Yeah, yeah, Lucas Fischer, he's working on Electrified Ballistic Stopping Material, right?"

"That's top secret. How do you know about that?"

"I told you I have friends everywhere."

"Can you check with your friends to see if they know anything about a Dr. Emily Zhou? She was also murdered. I found a Crizan passport and military service weapon hidden at her place."

"Interesting..."

"There's more. We tailed a couple of guys to a building who had diplomatic plates. I can send you the address if that would help."

"Cache, why aren't you going to your military contacts with this? This was a joint military operation with Quillchem. I would think they would be all over it."

"I did and they are, but it's a one-way door. I learn something, I share it with them, and then they never tell me anything they find out, so I knew I needed to go to my own contacts if I was going to figure this mess out." There was a pause on the line for a few seconds.

"Hmm, hmm... thinking, thinking. You said you are in Boston?"

"Yeah."

"You need Dong Zhang. He is a friend. He owns a small bookshop selling vintage and rare books. Wait one second while I look something up." Cache waited for a few minutes. "Here it is. Thank heaven for database management tools. In the old days, this type of stuff was on tiny microfiche. If you want to find out this information, go to Benny's Books on Crocket Court. When you get there, look for a man in his midseventies. Last time I saw Dong, he had long black hair. He was portly back then and I suspect he still is; he has a terrible sweet tooth. When you see him, tell him you are looking for a first edition, *The Great Gatsby*. Wherever he directs you to, say to him, 'You know, Fitzgerald preferred cocoa.' If it's him, he will reply, 'He preferred gin in his ale.' Tell him what you need and hopefully he will be able to get the information for you."

"Thanks, Nina, for doing this for me."

"I lost a few good friends over the years to their bodies' consuming excessive amounts of lead. Hazard of the job. I will tell you about it sometime. If something like EBSM had existed back then, they might still be here today. I get the significance of what you are doing. This breakthrough that I heard about through back channels could be a lifesaver for our people in the military, so anything I can do to help, I will. Dong is a good starting point, and he owes me a favor or two. I helped get him into the country. Cache, if you need me in the future, call Lunar Tradicity; don't call the gallery unless you want me to get you a Picasso or a Monet. The line with Lunar is secure; no one can eavesdrop on our call."

"Okay, I will."

"Oh, and, Cache, if you are available in a few months, I'm looking at opening up my fourth gallery, in Brussels. I would love for you to come to the opening."

"I would love to."

"Good, I will have Janine add you to the guest list."

The call ended and Cache searched the web to find out where Crocket Court was. It was not too far from a collection of restaurants and shops. She didn't want to call Aaron back but wanted to talk to Dong as soon as possible. A knock came at the door and Cache walked over, knowing there was only one person this could be.

"Hey, neighbor, haven't seen you much. What are you up to?"

"How would you like to go to a bookstore?"

"I wouldn't really, but we could go to a club."

"There's a book my dad wants, and I found a dealer in town who might have a copy. I just sent Aaron home. How about you drive us down there and then I'll buy us dinner?"

Chase seemed agreeable to that and went next door to change into some casual wear, and the two of them headed off in search of *Gatsby*.

———

Crocket Court proved to be about forty minutes from Quillchem in a small community outside of Boston. There were many shops and restaurants with façades that dated back to the mid-1800s. The cobblestone sidewalks were lined with arched black iron posts with flower baskets hanging from them. Small bistros were scattered throughout the area, with couples sitting on small makeshift patios as the smell of fresh baked bread and sound of clanging glasses filled the space around them. The one thing Crocket Court did not offer was a place for cars to park, and Chase needed to find a space a few blocks away. There were buskers on street corners and musicians playing live in some of the restaurants. The people around them all looked like they were having a good time. Chase and Cache had stopped to take a look at a clothing shop when Cache noticed, a few doors down, a building painted in teal, with carts of used books out front and a book hanging from a sign that read "Benny" in big gold letters. Cache mentioned to Chase the store that she had come down to see was just a few doors down and encouraged her to continue looking at the clothing store while she went to see if they had the book she wanted.

The bells above the door clanged together as Cache walked into the small shop. There were shelves of books running as high as the ceiling, with ladders on rollers attached to many of the shelves, allowing access to the books higher up. Leather-backed chairs were in small pockets of the shop, with readers poring over their latest finds as Cache spotted people sitting on the floor leaning against the book stacks, absorbed in their latest discovery. The carpet was dated and must have been red at one point, as continuous traffic along certain paths had rubbed the color out of the carpet. At the front there was an antique brass cash register, though it appeared to be more for decoration. An older gentleman with gray short hair, and thin —was working a small digital tablet as a customer stood there with a stack of books on the counter. An orange cat rested near the cash register, keeping an eye on its domain. Cache walked to the back of the store and found a kid, about sixteen years old with messy black hair and pimples on his face, helping a customer. He had on white high-tops, jeans and a blue vest with the words *Benny's Books* stitched across the front. Cache waited until he was done with a customer and asked if Benny still worked there. To her surprise, the kid told her that the man at the front of the store was Benny, but he was far from the way Nina had described him.

Cache walked to the front of the store, looked at the man and thought, What the hell.

"Can I help you find something, miss?"

"I'm looking for a first edition *The Great Gatsby.*"

"Oh, a woman of impeccable taste. You might find that in aisle seven, way at the top. We try to keep the more expensive items there, away from people who are happy with a current edition."

Cache looked at him like someone thinking about diving off a cliff and having thoughts that this might not be a good idea. As she started to walk away she turned to him and said, "You know, Fitzgerald preferred cocoa."

He looked at her, astonished by what she had just uttered, and without thinking said, "He preferred gin in his ale." Cache looked at him, shocked that this was the friend that Nina had sent her to see. "Hey, Justin, are you free?"

The young kid walked to the front of the store.

"Can you look after the cash register? This young lady is looking for an exquisite book and I must help her find it."

Justin took over at the front of the store as Benny asked her to follow him. They walked to the back of the shop, ducked behind a black closed curtain and then entered a door on his left and made their way down underneath the store. There were books stacked to the ceiling on three shelves, but he approached a solid wooden wall with two brass lamp fixtures and turned one fixture ninety degrees, causing a panel in the wall to open up. He motioned for Cache to go through the opening, and he followed, pushing the panel shut behind him. The two stood in the dark for a few seconds, and Cache reached around to the back of her jeans and gripped the handle of her gun as Benny flicked on the lights. There was a small office in the room, with a laptop in a docking station on a desk, connected to a large computer screen. He went behind the desk and motioned for Cache to sit down in one of the two chairs in front of the desk.

"Who sent you? MI6? CIA? German intelligence?"

"Nina Mayhem."

The sound of those two words brought a smile to his face. "How is Nina?"

"Doing well last time I saw her. She says she's opening a new gallery in a few months."

He reached down into his desk and pulled up a bottle with two glasses. "Brandy?"

"Sure."

He poured them each a drink as he shared a couple of stories from his past that pertained to Nina Mayhem.

"So do you prefer Dong or Benny?"

"Please, no Dong. Dong Zhang, as far as the Crizan Intelligence Service is concerned, died in a car crash; dental records proved it. I can thank Nina for that. Now it's just Benny Smith, all-American boy."

"Well, Benny, Nina thought you could help me with a problem. I am trying to find out some information about a Dr. Emily Zhou. She also holds a Crizan passport under the name Beatrice Yu." Cache shared with him the photos of the passport that she had taken as well as the hidden service weapon and detailed the story of the people with diplomatic plates who were following her and the building in downtown Boston that they had disappeared into.

"I'll look into it for you. May take a few days. I have a couple of contacts that I can reach out to and see what they have heard. My guess off the top of my head is it's Crizan intelligence, given the passport, military service weapon and your description of who was following you, but let's see what I can come up with. Sometimes with foreign operatives, one government wants to give the impression that it's another government doing the activity so they take the heat; classic misdirection. Leave me your phone number or email so I have a way to contact you." Cache provided him with her contact information. He got up from his chair and motioned for Cache to follow him. As he came to the wall, he reached down to press a black button that looked like a doorbell, and the wall panel popped open again. They went through the passageway back to the stacks of books in the basement. As Cache went up the stairs, he told her to wait and then went to scan the books on the shelves until he found a copy of *The Great Gatsby*, not a first edition but later. Cache opened up the cover and saw that it had a small sticker that read "$100."

"A hundred dollars?"

"Don't worry, I'll give you the friends and family discount, ten percent off."

"You must not like your family."

Cache proceeded up the stairs, her new book under her arm, and darted back into the main shop from behind the curtain. She noticed Chase roaming through the store.

"I thought I lost you, couldn't find you anywhere."

Cache held up the book under her arm. "They keep the good stuff under lock and key," she said, and made her way to the front counter, where Justin rang up the purchase and then stuffed the book into a recycled plastic Benny's Books bag. Benny stood beside Justin as he was ringing up the order to ensure she got her discount.

"I will let you know if I find out anything further about those additional books you inquired about."

Cache picked up her purchase and walked out of the store with Chase. They sauntered down the street, looking at the various menus posted out in front of the restaurants, and settled for a place called the Velvet Turtle. Seated outside on the patio, Chase perused the book that Cache had just purchased and pointed out to her that it wasn't a first edition. Cache said that it didn't matter, her father would love it anyway, and that today was a day to celebrate. They had brought Jonas home safe to his mother. With his help, Cache would hopefully be able to decode the journals, and Quillchem stood a chance of figuring out the formula for EBSM. They looked over the menu and Cache, true to her word, told Chase that dinner was on her. Once the wine was served and then the meal, the two of them relaxed for the balance of the evening. They listened as a street musician stopped near their table to serenade them. For the first time in days, Cache did not think about the murders. Benny would hopefully provide some insight into who Dr. Zhou really was, and unless evidence presented itself in the coming days, the murder of Dr. Fischer could very well become a cold case waiting for something to happen in the future. Cache still suspected that Dr. Allen knew more than he was saying. As she sipped her coffee after a scrumptious meal, she tapped her fingers on the table.

"What's wrong, where are you?" Chase said.

"I'm here. Why, can't you see me? Maybe I should drive us home."

"The finger tapping. We were having a friendly discussion and then you disappeared and the finger tapping began."

"The missing pages to Dr. Fischer's journal. I'm just wondering what ever happened to them. And Dr. Tanaka, how well do you know her?"

"Not at all. If you asked me to point her out in a crowd, I would be lost, but she might say the same about me."

"I just think there's more to the relationship between Dr. Tanaka and Dr. Allen than we're seeing, and given that Dr. Allen and Dr. Zhou were close... Wait, wait one minute."

"I'm waiting," Chase said, looking puzzled.

"The photographs."

"What photographs?"

"When we rescued Jonas, he had large photographs of all of Dr. Fischer's journals, and I found similar photographs at Dr. Allen's place as he was attempting to break the code."

"Okay, and... ?"

"And let me run with this idea for a moment. I found evidence in Dr. Allen's home that showed that he was in a relationship with Emily Zhou at one point. There are pictures of the two of them, some of her clothes are at his place."

"When were you at Dr. Allen's place?"

Cache looked up as she tried to piece this together in her mind and dismissed the question with a wave of her hand. "Dr. Zhou and Dr. Fischer were in some sort of relationship. Who pursued who is up for debate, but what if Dr. Zhou went to visit Dr. Fischer at his place downtown? Something happens. She kills him and photographs his journals. She then gives the photographs to Jeffrey Allen to decipher, and when he fails to be successful at it, she hires a couple of guys to abduct Jonas to translate the journals. That makes sense, doesn't it?"

"She was a tiny thing. Would she be able to strangle Dr. Fischer?"

"When I went to her place, she had a fully stocked gym with punching bag and weights, and if you saw her figure, you knew she was in great shape."

"Then who would kill her?"

"I don't know, that's where I keep getting lost. It's also possible that she took journal number fifteen and gave it to Dr.

Allen to convince Dr. Tanaka to hide it at Dr. Wright's place to incriminate him."

"I'm getting lost. There are too many doctors in your scenario. Why kill Dr. Fischer in the first place?"

"Maybe it was like her letters to Jeffrey Allen said, she was trapped in a relationship with her boss and couldn't get out. Or maybe Dr. Fischer caught her photographing his journals and she reacted."

"But to immediately react, are you going to strangle someone? I could see her picking something up and hitting him with something, but strangling?" Chase said as she twisted a small gold cross hanging around her neck, rotating it between her thumb and index finger.

"Oh... I'm sorry, Chase, this puzzle is driving me nuts. I didn't think about it throughout dinner and the musician played a song that reminded me of music that was playing in the elevator when I went up to Dr. Fischer's condo. Aagghhhh, I hate this thing. I keep feeling that there's something that I'm seeing and at the same time is completely invisible to me, right there in front of me, taunting me."

"So meet with Jonas, decode the journals. Who knows, maybe Dr. Fischer might have documented something in his journals that will point you in the right direction."

"Like someone calling out from the grave?"

"Exactly. You just need to figure out what Dr. Fischer is trying to tell you and then you might have a clearer picture of what is going on." Cache knew Chase was right; this approach of going over the facts in her head day in and day out wasn't resolving anything for her. Maybe the journals might tell her more of what was going on in the lab than just their work on EBSM.

## 17

I t was ten thirty on Friday morning when Cache met up with Jonas at Jay Jones Java, named for two heroes from the Revolutionary War. The small coffee shop was located in Liberty Crossroads, about twenty minutes away from the Fischer residence, in the heart of the village. Like most small villages, it had one primary drag where most of the shops were. Here in Liberty Crossroads, it was Lincoln Lane. Two other streets ran north and south, perpendicular to Lincoln Lane: Adams Avenue to the east and Paine Parkway to the west. Given the ordeal that Jonas had suffered over the past week, Cache wanted to make this as easy on him as possible and had Aaron drive her out in the morning. She offered to pick him up, but he said he wanted to ride his bike to clear his head. Cache was thankful for any help he could provide in decoding the journals. Jay Jones Java was semi-busy that morning. The crowd stopping in on their way to work had long since gone and now there were people popping in as they went to the discount store across the street or the dry cleaner next door. Most of the buildings in the village dated back to its founding in the late 1700s and had been updated with modern conveniences while maintaining that historical charm. Cache walked into the shop. There was a mother with a small child in a stroller in front of her. A few couples were at little round tables opposite the counter, where a lone barista was tending to the visitors' needs. After a few minutes of watching the mother in front of her decide whether she felt like a chocolate powdered scone or tea biscuits that day, Cache made her way to the till.

"What can I get you today?" the tall, slender barista with brown curly hair asked.

Cache looked at the name tag clinging to his white apron. "Well, Todd, I think I am going to have a large Colombian roast, two creams, two sugars."

"Are you staying or going?" he said with a goofy grin on his face.

"I'll have it here." Cache spotted a table in the back of the café that would suit her purposes well and pointed to where she would be sitting. She paid for her drink, and he told her he would bring it over to her when it was ready. Cache walked to the rear of the café. A long bench ran across the side wall with a leather padded backing, and a series of small tables with chairs sat opposite the bench. She parked herself down so that she could see the front door and keep an eye out for Jonas as patrons came in and out. After a few minutes Todd brought her coffee over to her as the bells above the front door chimed and Cache could see Jonas coming into the café. She waved for him to come to the back, where she was sitting. As he approached, he looked at Todd and went to shake his hand. There was an exchange of words for a few moments, and a smile and a laugh between the two of them as Jonas sat down at the table.

"I take it you know each other?"

"One of my best friend's younger brothers. Haven't seen him in a few years. My buddy is out west at college. Sorry to make you come all this way."

"No, look, your dad's journals have been weighing heavy on

my mind. Any help you can give, I'm here. I'm just appreciative that after everything you went through, you're still willing to meet with me."

"How could I say no to the woman that saved my life?"

"I'm sure the police would disagree with you on that." She reached over and gripped his hand. She could smell the burned cedar cologne he was wearing. "We're just glad we got you home in one piece," she said as she stared at him. She could see the appeal he would have for someone like Emily, who was a few years older than her; Jonas was several years younger. If it weren't for her knowledge of Cynthia waiting for him back at college, the thought of the two of them getting it on in the back alley would have been stirring in her. Young men are more eager to please, like they have something to prove, she thought. She reached down into a bag that she'd brought with her and pulled out photocopies of one of the journals and a makeshift document she had created from the various images found among Dr. Fischer's notes.

He glanced down at the documents. "I wonder if my father had any idea this language he created would cause so much trouble."

"Secrets are meant to be kept secret. I suspect that is why he used it. The project he was working on could save a tremendous number of lives. People putting themselves in harm's way to protect us all." She flashed a smile at him and tucked her hair behind her right ear as he stopped to look into her eyes. How easy it would be to put her hand around his head and bring him in closer.

"Tall cappuccino and biscotti with chocolate syrup," Todd said as he put the plate and drink down in front of Jonas. He looked at the photocopies of the papers. "Something your kids drew?" he asked as he looked at Cache.

"No kids, thanks."

Jonas smiled at her, pulled a pen from his backpack and

started to explain to Cache how the language was created. When he was little he was fascinated with mummies and the pyramids, and so his father had taken the time to explain the hieroglyphs that they found on the pyramid walls. He based the foundation of Atlantian on those images. To make it more complicated, he blended in the ancient language of Athenian as the middle point between the English language and the hieroglyphs. While it seemed confusing to most people, it was no different from any other language, and once you learned it and used it, it flowed easily when reading and writing in the language.

Some of the symbols represented entire words, some represented phrases and others specific letters. Cache sipped on her coffee and watched as he explained the different images to her. She could tell, despite the trouble Atlantian had caused in his life, as he described it to her, someone eager to learn it, that he took a great deal of pride in it, and his enthusiasm for the made-up language could be seen across his face. They spent the next hour refueling on coffee and cappuccinos as they worked to document a makeshift dictionary for Cache and then start to apply it to the copies that she'd brought of journal one.

The first journal was a combination of Dr. Fischer's early results in working on the chemical compound for EBSM. It also documented his thoughts on the members of the team that Graydon had assembled for him. The notes identified that no love existed between him and Ian Wright, that Akiko Tanaka was a quiet but competent scientist, that Jeffrey Allen was pretentious and somewhat full of himself and Emily Zhou was strikingly beautiful for a scientist and might prove a distraction from their overall work for both himself and his team members. Buried in his notes were his pride in his son's accomplishments and the challenges of keeping a long marriage fresh.

As Cache sat back and read some of the personal notes that

were transcribed from journal one, she deliberated for a moment. "I never thought... I mean, I just assumed your dad's notes would reflect his work, not everything in his personal life."

"You will see a lot of it as you go through his journals."

"Was it hard for you to read it as you worked to decode the journals in that hellhole they threw you into?"

"It kept my mind off of everything. I could feel my dad's love for me and my mom come out in the writing. I also saw things about their marriage that were more behind the scenes than I was aware of."

"Like what, if I can ask?"

"Just troubles I guess they have had over the past few years. I guess I never thought how my going off to school abroad would affect them. When I got accepted to Cambridge, they were both so proud, maybe they hadn't stopped to think about what it would be like for the two of them with me not at home."

"Your captors, did they give you any clue as to who they were?"

"I can tell you they were Asian, Japanese, Crizan or Chinese, if I had to guess."

"How do you know that? Was it how they spoke?"

"Partially. It was more how they looked."

"What, you saw their faces?"

"Yeah, they did not try to conceal their identities from me. Why?"

"My guess is that they figured you weren't going to leave there alive, so they didn't care if you saw what they looked like. Have you talked to Detective Boone at all?"

"This morning I spoke to him for more than an hour before I headed out to meet you. I was planning on meeting him tomorrow to sign the statement. He wants me to sit down with a sketch artist so they can keep an eye out for them."

"Did you hear any foreign words that you remember that might give us a clue as to where they were from?

"Nothing I can remember. When they spoke to me, one of them spoke in English, but I would hear them on the phone. They weren't using English then. I don't know what they said though I do know they were very upset when it came to the torn-out pages, like I would know what was on them."

"Did you translate all the journals for them?"

"I don't think so. They had maybe about three dozen photographs in total; some they took with them and the rest I think you grabbed the other day. If they had pictures of all the journals they had yet to show me everything."

Cache sat back and felt a little bit easier. They had gotten their hands on the journals, but it was possible that they did not have a complete set and might only have limited knowledge of Dr. Fischer's work on EBSM.

The café had emptied out. Two guys sat in the far corner with a laptop open, discussing something. A man in a suit was ordering at the counter, while two men in construction clothing waited behind him.

Cache started to talk to Jonas about Cambridge and could see he was lost in thought. "What's wrong?" she asked.

"That man who just came in." He motioned with his head toward the front of the shop. He was a midsize gentleman dressed in black jeans, a black leather jacket and black leather gloves. He had a round face and appeared to be of Crizan descent, with black hair cut close to the scalp and a neck tattoo from what Cache could see from where she sat.

"What about him?"

"I think that was one of the guys that was at the building."

Cache reached for the back of her jeans and grabbed her gun, but surveyed the room and thought there was too much of a chance for collateral damage. She gathered up the papers on the desk, put them into the bag that she had brought and instructed Jonas to follow her. As they proceeded to the back of the café, the man in black pushed through the line shoving one of the construction workers to the side. The man pushed back and Cache turned to see the man in black do a roundhouse kick to one of the construction workers, sending him flying against the glass display counter and smashing the glass. Cache ran to the rear of the café and pushed against the back door. But it would not budge. She looked over her shoulder and could only see the other construction worker fly across a table and hit the leather padded piece that was fixed to the wall. She grabbed Jonas by the hand and pulled him into the women's washroom. A broom leaning against the corner of the door would provide her with some time; she wedged it through the door handle, hoping it would prevent the stranger from opening the door. She looked around the room to see what was available to her. Two bathroom stalls, two sinks, a dispenser of feminine products attached to the wall and an old metal trash can. She opened the first bathroom stall and saw nothing but toilet paper. Then they heard the shot. One shot and then a second, and she could hear someone walking down the hall. Cache opened the second bathroom stall, and a small glass window was in the upper corner. She braced herself against the back of the toilet with one foot and then rested her other foot on the toilet roll dispenser attached to the wall. She could hear someone yelling in the hall but didn't know what they were saying. The door pushed in, as someone was doing something on the other side to get into the room. Cache pulled her gun from the back of her jeans, grabbed it by the barrel and smashed the glass with the handle.

Again, a large bang came from the bathroom door. Flecks of wood were flying into the air with each hit. Jonas looked white as fear started to run through his veins. Cache hopped down and cupped her hands together. "Here, we should be able to fit through the window. You go first."

"No, you should go."

"Why?"

"Because—"

"Do not say because I am a woman. I've got the gun. Do you have much experience with firearms?"

"Never held one."

"Okay then, I have. I can't take the risk of you getting hit. When you get out the window, I want you to find a place to hide. If I don't make it out, find somewhere safe and call the police."

He put his foot in Cache's hands as a louder bang came from the bathroom door, and Cache hoisted Jonas out the bathroom window. She moved out of the bathroom stall and could see a large crack forming in the wooden broom. It wouldn't hold much longer. The door thumped again as parts of the handle broke apart and the door started to budge. Cache stepped up on the toilet roll holder and threw her bag and gun out the window. As she looked over the bathroom stall, she heard the wooden broom stick snap and saw the top of the door, open to the small bathroom. She squeezed her way through the opening and felt as if something grabbed at her foot as she came flying out the other end. She clutched her bag, tucked her gun down into her jeans, crouched down and made her way up an alley at the back of the café, where she found Jonas hiding behind a large metal dumpster.

"You made it."

"Was cutting it close but we are not out of the woods yet."

Cache grabbed her phone and called up one of her map applications to see where she was. The closest street to her position was Adams Avenue, and she looked for Aaron's contact information and called him.

It rang once, as Jonas looked around and she thought she

could hear voices in the distance; rang twice—the voices sounded angry; rang a third time, and Aaron picked up.

"Hey, are you ready to go?"

"We're being chased."

"By who?"

"My guess is the guys that grabbed Jonas. I expect they are not done with him. I need you to go to Adams Avenue and drive up and pull to the side and keep the car running. We will try to get to you and then I need you to get us the hell out of here as fast as you can."

"Should I call the police?"

"They won't get here in time. We will when we're out of here."

Cache hung up the phone and told Jonas to stay where he was. She crawled along the alleyway, staying low to the ground, until she came to an alleyway running north and south. She popped her head out and spotted two men of Asian descent heading down from the north side, a handgun in one man's hands, a machine gun in the other's. Cache glanced in the other direction to see the man from the café heading toward her position from the opposite direction with another man beside him as they checked various areas where someone could be hiding. Cache could see what looked like Adams Avenue two blocks in the distance, but it would require them to cross the path that the four men were heading down. While she may have been able to pick off two of the men, the odds were stacked against them with four.

"So are we fucked?" Jonas asked.

"Give me a minute." Cache looked around and noticed the large metal dumpster that they were hiding behind was on wheels. She got up and opened the lid. The dumpster reeked from bags of garbage that sat inside waiting to be removed.

"Here, help me move this over toward the corner there."

They pushed the dumpster over toward the intersection

with the path their assailants were walking down to locate them.

"Okay, I want you to get in the dumpster."

"Why?"

"Because I'm hoping it will provide you with some protection."

"What are you going to do?"

"I'm going to take a run at it and hopefully jump in with you, and it will take us to the other side. Once we get across that path, I want you to get out and don't look back and run to Adams Avenue. Look for a black Baumann; that will be Aaron. If I don't make it, you get the hell out of here."

"I can't leave you here."

"Yes, you can."

Jonas climbed into the dumpster with Cache's bag as she walked about ten feet back from it. She didn't know how far away the men hunting them were and she took a run at the dumpster, pushing it out into the open, and jumped in. Cache could hear the sound of gunfire as bullets struck the metal container as it sped across the alleyway to the other side. She grabbed Jonas by the back of his shirt and pushed him forward.

"Come on, let's get out of here."

They ran to the opening that led onto Adams Avenue. Cache spotted Aaron parked a few blocks down, waved at him and pointed Jonas to the destination he needed to make it to. She could hear shots above her head as bullets struck the bricks of the old building, shattering clay and mortar to the ground. Cache took cover behind the wall and returned fire, squeezing the trigger. She looked over her shoulder as Jonas made his way to the back of the car. She held her position as Aaron sped to her until she had emptied her clip, then ran to the car, dove into the back with Jonas and pulled the door shut.

"Where to?" Aaron asked.

"Anywhere but here," Cache said. "Are you okay?" she asked
Jonas.

"Yeah, just shaken up. How the hell did they find me?"

"My guess is someone followed you from your house. We
had our own security people watching the warehouse but I
haven't heard from them." Cache dialed the number for one of
their security officers, but it rang repeatedly until it went to
voice mail. The same for his partner. Cache then called Detective Boone, figuring there would be less of an explanation to
offer him than any local law enforcement in the area. She was
wrong. She spent the next twenty minutes detailing the events
of the morning to him. Cache wasn't so sure whether his
expressed concerns were that of a dutiful lawman or a potential
boyfriend. After he scolded her as if she could have predicted a
visit to a coffee shop would end in gunfire, Michael got off the
phone with her and proceeded to her location with his partner
Detective Murphy. From the car he planned on calling for local
backup and told her to circle the area until she heard from him
and then have Aaron make his way back to the coffee shop. The
sight of an expansive police presence in the area would likely
result in the assailants' fleeing to ensure they weren't picked up
for questioning.

After about forty minutes of driving around, Cache got the
call from Michael. It was not a call that she wanted to receive.
The two construction workers in the café had died of trauma
from the beating that they'd received. One of the gunshots
she'd heard had been to the chest of the man at the counter
when the man in black entered the café, and the second had
been a head shot to the barista named Todd. Todd had been
killed instantly, and they had taken the man with the gunshot
wound to the chest to the local hospital with life-threatening
injuries. Detective Boone instructed her to go directly to the
local police station giving her the address, where officers would
have questions for them as to what transpired.

For the next two hours Cache and Jonas were interviewed by officers about the events that took place in the café. A small camera that the café had installed in the back corner of the room had recorded all the events of that morning and the video had been saved by a cloud server; the company that owned the café had provided the footage to the police to help catch the killers. Cache had called Graydon to advise him about what had happened. Upon further investigation by the Boston Police Department, they found the two Quillchem security personnel who had been staking out the warehouse shot to death in their car. As news of the events spread throughout the community of agencies involved in the project, the small police station in Liberty Crossroads became a hub for every government law enforcement agency that had an acronym for its name. The CIA, the FBI, Army Intelligence, the Justice Department—all of them had representatives descend on the local police station. The military and the Justice Department argued that Jonas and his knowledge could be a national security issue and suggested putting him in the hands of the US Marshals. While local law enforcement felt that they might need him to testify if the culprits ever came before a judge, Cache argued that if they were members of an embassy with diplomatic immunity, expulsion from the country was the best they could hope for. They would have her and camera footage if they ever required it in a court of law.

It wasn't long before the next level of authority showed up at the station: Petra Fischer and Cache's boss, Graydon Quill, armed with home phone numbers for a half dozen or more US senators and congressional representatives. As the parties argued in a small conference room, Cache sat outside and rubbed Jonas's back. The thought of his having to tell one of his best friends that he may have gotten his little brother killed weighed heavily on him. Cache tried to reassure him that the events that had been set in motion when his father was strangled to death were nothing that he had caused, nor had he contributed to them. She knew that there was nothing she could say to him to ease his conscience, and only time and distance from this storm would help him feel right again. For now, all they could do was sit in the small waiting room drinking terrible coffee in Styrofoam cups while the suits in the other room argued about his future.

## 18

C ache returned to her suite late in the evening. She knew she would not have a voice or even be allowed to offer an opinion on the boy's future. Cache decided the best thing she could do was to use the notes she had made during her time with Jonas to work on the journals of Dr. Fischer. She gathered the photocopied documents that the legal department had made for her and laid them out all over her room. There were eighteen journals in total; the stack of photocopies, which depicted two journal pages each, was over a foot thick. Journals one through five lay across her bed. Journals six through ten were in piles across the floor by the window, and journals eleven through eighteen were in assorted stacks around the main table in the living room. Common sense would have told her to wait until morning before trying to tackle such an enormous task, but she felt like a kid the night before Christmas knowing that stacks of presents with her name on them sat beneath the tree down in the family's living room.

She ordered up snacks and two pots of coffee and tried to determine where the best place to begin was. There was potentially a month or more of work ahead of her as she scanned all the piles. In the morning she would take her notes to legal and have them copied, with a set going over to the military to see if they could program a computer with character recognition software that might speed up the process. As she weighed whether to start with the first journal and begin to work her way through or the last journal, there was a knock at the door. Cache jumped up off the couch, expecting it to be her coffee, and instead was greeted by Chase in a pair of tight satin shorts and a T-shirt with the faded image of a boy band that had seen some success a decade or more ago.

"Hey, not a good time. As you can see, I have a lot of work ahead of me."

"What are you doing?"

"Jonas gave me a lesson on the language that he and his father used to communicate with, and now I'm going to see if I can make heads or tails of these journals."

"Want some help?"

"Do you really want to spend your night trying to figure this out?"

"I can think of something else I would rather be doing, but who knows what's in these journals? Let me grab my reading glasses."

As she went next door to grab her glasses, the kitchen staff brought up the coffee and snacks and laid them out in her room. Chase returned wearing black-rimmed glasses and had put her hair up. She had the look of the librarian that all teenage boys would like to have seen in their school.

"Where should we begin?" she asked.

"We can start at the beginning to see how this unfolded, or start at the end to try to get some sense of Dr. Fischer's last days."

"Where do you want to start?"

"All the journals are intact except for journal fifteen. I think we should start there and try to determine what was going on."

Cache went over her notes from her time with Jonas with Chase. From the dictionary she had compiled, she and Jonas had determined that Dr. Fischer used initials to refer to different people. On the list that she shared with Chase, there were two symbols representing E and Z, for Dr. Emily Zhou. There were similar patterns of two-letter combinations that repeated themselves through all the documents: IW for Ian Wright, AT for Akiko Tanaka, JA for Jeffrey Allen, GQ for Graydon Quill, JF for Jonas Fischer, PF for Petra Fischer and MT for someone she had not identified. There were also special symbols representing the lab, his home, their condo at the Dawes and an assortment of other locations that Cache hoped to deduce in time.

Chase sat across one chair, her long legs hanging off the arm of the chair, with a pen in her mouth, referring to the notes that Cache had created. She looked like someone engaged in a crossword puzzle on Sunday morning. Cache sat on the floor taking Chase's notes and circling repeated word patterns that she might have to ask Jonas about in the future if she was ever allowed to speak with him again. Cache tackled small groups of words to try to gain a sense of what the major themes of the journal were, knowing that everything would need to be translated in the future. The hours ticked by as the coffee dwindled. The kitchen staff brought up a second round at three thirty in the morning as Cache fought to stay awake and Chase had drifted off to dreamland. At nine o'clock a.m., Cache woke to the sound of the doorbell to the suite ringing. She looked around. Chase was still asleep in the chair. Piles of notes on yellow paper were all around Cache, as they had started to gather an understanding of what was in journals fifteen and sixteen. Cache stood up; her back ached as she stumbled to the door, like she had spent the previous night on a bender going from bar to bar. She opened the door to see Graydon Quill standing there with coffee and donuts.

"Hey, boss, what brings you here?"

He walked into the room and spotted Chase asleep in the chair and papers all over the floor. "I had a feeling you would jump right into it. I know you better than you know yourself." He walked over to Chase, grabbed her foot and wagged it back and forth. "Don't tell Human Resources."

"Or legal," Cache added.

"One more minute, Mom, I promise I'll get up and take out the garbage," Chase said.

Graydon went over and put his hand down on her shoulder to give it a little jiggle. "Hey, sleepyhead, wake up."

Her eyes opened slightly until she realized it was her boss standing over her, and then they widened as she sat upright. "Did I doze off? I am so sorry."

"It's okay, don't worry about it," Cache said.

Graydon took one cup of coffee and sat down on the chair opposite Chase. "Have we learned anything?"

"What happened to Jonas?"

He let out a deep sigh. "It took a lot of wrangling—they wanted to put him in a safe house—but they agreed that his returning to school in the United Kingdom might be best."

"Whoever grabbed him could go looking for him there," Cache said.

"We agreed the CIA would reach out to their contacts at MI5 to monitor him. The FBI has a field office in London. If he sees anything strange, he is to contact them right away and make his way to the US embassy, and they will take it from there. I only secured his freedom because I convinced the army that you now knew the language and you would work with their code breakers so we all understand it. This makes Jonas less valuable to the government."

"There's also the fact that the kidnappers may not have had

a complete picture of all the journals, so even if they grab him, they may have nothing for him to decipher."

"I hope you're right; too many years of research have gone into this project. So what do you have for me?"

Cache spun around to face him, pulling some of her notes away from the base of Chase's chair. "The journals are not so much scientific journals, as we started out believing, but more a diary of Dr. Fischer's thoughts. There is stuff about the research, trials and errors, and there are some points about different people in the lab and his observations on them. There is talk about his son and Dr. Fischer's hopes for the future about his relationship with his wife."

"You got that from what you could decode so far?"

"Yeah, there are certain patterns that start to emerge when you stare at it long enough. I suspect all the journals, when they're decoded, will share Dr. Fischer's deepest thoughts about everything around him, not just EBSM."

"But it's EBSM I'm interested in; that's the kettle of fish."

"From what I could tell, as you read toward the end of journal fifteen, you can see that Dr. Fischer thought he was onto something. Previous tests that failed because of differences in ballistic ranges and bullet compositions seem to have been resolved, and then we get to the pages torn out and it goes quiet. When we begin to read the start of journal sixteen, it talks about the incredible break-through that he made, that he had solved the problem. Testing had proven favorable with the most recent develop-ment, but so far there is no mention of the formula. If the formula was written down, it was written down in those torn-out pages."

"And we don't know where they are?"

"Nope. Jonas said his captors were angry that pages were missing and took it out on him that he didn't know what his father had written on those pages. Maybe Dr. Fischer removed those pages himself to hide them away somewhere. They could be at his house or his place at the Dawes."

Graydon rubbed his face. "Or they could be at their place in Martha's Vineyard."

"What place in Martha's Vineyard?"

"They have a small place down on the water."

"So a third place we need to get access to, to try and locate those pages. Do you think Mrs. Fischer will let me go and check it out or do you think we would need the military to try and get a warrant?"

"They may have a problem getting a judge to sign off on a search warrant if all we have is a hunch and I am not even sure we have that. I think they would need something more substantial, what do you think Chase?" Graydon asked.

Chase thought about it for a few minutes, "I can reach out to them and talk to them. I can see several issues coming into play that might prevent a search warrant from being issued given there is no evidence suggesting that the pages are in any of the Fischer's homes. It would be much easier on everyone if she would just grant you access to the properties."

"She might not have before, but given you have saved her son's life twice now, she might be more agreeable," Graydon said.

"You should know before you talk with her that there was something funny going on with your team in the lab."

"Funny how?"

"There was a passage toward the beginning of journal fifteen that said one day, Ian Wright came into the lab with hints of orchid perfume on him."

"That can't be, we have a zero-fragrance policy in the lab."

"And yet he did, and Dr. Fischer noted it, because it is the same perfume that his wife, Petra Fischer, wears."

"So do you think the two of them were or are..."

"It's possible. There have been allegations made by other

members of your scientific team that might suggest it, but Petra seemed to be insulted by the accusation when I very delicately brought it up with her, and Dr. Fischer, from his own notes, suspected that Dr. Wright went out and purchased that perfume just to get under his skin."

Graydon shook his head and rolled his neck from side to side. "Lucas came to me frequently wanting to fire Ian; I always had to talk him down. Dr. Wright is a gifted scientist, though he could make an ass of himself when he wanted. I didn't realize it was that bad. Lucas never said a word about it. Cache, there were rumors that I turned a blind eye to about him and Dr. Zhou, just water-cooler-type gossip."

Chase jumped in. "That is strange, because I came across entries that Dr. Fischer made suggesting that, as they made more progress on the project, Emily started becoming more flirtatious with him. Even to the point of being sexually aggressive."

"No, not Emily, she was always very prim, proper, professional."

"No, Chase is right. There are a couple of passages where Dr. Fischer noticed a top button being undone and her leaning over his desk. I got the impression that the attention made him uncomfortable, and yet he talks about the first time she kissed him being exhilarating and making him feel alive."

"She kissed him?"

"At least from his point of view. Dr. Tanaka had mentioned that she had seen it with her own eyes on more than one occasion. Dr. Allen suggested and I might add, I came across a letter from Emily to Jeffrey that would have led him to believe that it was Dr. Fischer forcing himself on her, but as we read his personal notes, it seems like it was the other way around."

"Do you have the letter? Can I see it?"

"I don't have it with me."

"Can you get it for me? I would like to read it for myself, not that I'm doubting you."

"I came across it when I broke into Dr. Allen's home to snoop around."

He looked at her and looked at one of his attorneys sitting across from him. "I probably didn't hear that. So where are we now?"

"There are groups of symbols that I need to send to Jonas to see if he can help us out. We can continue on with journals sixteen to eighteen to see if they provide any clues as to where the missing pages might be if Dr. Fischer was the one who tore them from the journal. If you can talk to Mrs. Fischer to see if I could have a look through their residences for the missing pages, that would probably be our next step. If I had to place a bet on the outcome, that is where I suspect the formula for EBSM lies."

"Well, ladies, I am going to leave you to it. Cache, please keep the army up-to-date on what you learn. The more we share with them, the easier they will be on Jonas." He pulled himself up and out of the chair, stepped over the piles and made his way to the door. "People died yesterday over this. We need to figure this out to ensure we don't lose any more." He grabbed the door handle and departed the suite. Cache pulled herself off the floor and plunked herself down on the couch, looking at all the papers scattered across the floor. Chase turned around, crawled over to the couch and pulled herself up onto the cushion beside Cache.

"We did good work here," she said as she put her arm around Cache.

Cache leaned forward, putting her elbows on her knees and resting her head on her hands. She glanced back at Chase. "Minor victories don't mean we will win the war."

# 19

---

On Sunday morning Cache awoke. She gazed out into the living room and reflected on the progress that had been made. She thought about Michael, the smell of his cologne on her skin, the feeling of his embrace. Since California she'd felt like she was in a fog, after a first-time romance with another woman sent her world spinning in a direction she hadn't seen coming. It had caused her to question things in her life that she had taken as a forgone conclusion, but now, thinking of Michael, it felt like the fog had lifted. He just felt right.

Her deciphering partner had wandered back to her place around five o'clock in the morning, and Cache had shoved the papers off of the bed and crawled under the covers. After about five hours of rest, she was up again, sitting on the couch, hair wet from the shower and poring over the journals with her master document of words and symbols. She heard her phone buzz from across the room and went to pick it up. Much to her surprise, she'd received an email from Professor Elise Marchand. Professor Marchand had been one of her favorite teachers at Dartmouth, teaching renaissance art. A year after she'd graduated from university, while she was stationed in Italy with the army, she'd received an email from Professor Marchand, who had left Dartmouth and accepted a position at the Sorbonne in Paris. The two of them got together in Paris and toured the galleries. Every year or so, Cache would hear from her about some exciting project she was working on or some new artist that she had discovered. That morning the email simply read, "Read an article about you regarding the Pinup Killer, so proud of you, call me whenever you get a chance."

Cache continued to scan through the journals, highlighting common phrases throughout Dr. Fischer's notes to help separate his comments on the people around him from the notation regarding his research. Based on her tally, Cache identified that there were at least ninety-two separate passages related to IW. Emily came in second with seventy-one passages related to EZ, Petra came in a close third at sixty-eight, forty-one were about someone or something identified as MT and there were smaller sets for Dr. Tanaka, Dr. Allen, Graydon and Jonas. Cache wondered if Jonas was back in England yet and jumped on her email. She had identified other symbolic phrases that they had not discussed, so she composed an email attaching several photos of her notes and sent it to the address he'd provided. Hopefully, once he got settled back into his life, he would see her note and respond to him. Cache called down to the kitchen and ordered up a hamburger and Coke. Not her traditional breakfast, but she was famished. She began to poke her way through journal eighteen, hoping the last entries would highlight anything going on with Dr. Fischer at the time of his death.

She sat there and scribbled her notes, looking at what she had written over and over again. In the days leading up to his death, there were more entries related to MT than in previous journals. Since Dr. Fischer had chosen not to date any of his entries, it was impossible to tell when they were written, but there were comments suggesting that MT was "getting more frequently agitated by the situation." He was worried that he "may have made a mistake." There was no indication of what the mistake was. Her meal arrived, and she took a break from her work and shoveled it in.

Her phone buzzed again, and she grabbed it to look at a message from Benny. "Found some info for you. Can we meet today?" She looked around the room. The only thing she had to do today was to continue working out what the journals said. She looked at her watch. It was Aaron's day off. She struggled with whether to bother him and have him come back to the office to pick her up. Another option was to have Chase take her, but she had already asked a lot from her the night before. The best option seemed to be to take a cab. Cache researched it online, called a cab from her suite and headed out, closing the door quietly so Chase wouldn't know she was leaving. Cache walked down to the main guardhouse and talked to the guards on duty while she waited for a white and blue taxi to arrive.

There was very little traffic on the road that day as she made her way back to Benny's Books. The store itself had one or two customers in it, and when Benny saw Cache, he motioned for her to wait a minute while he finished up with a customer. A young woman named Audrey was working in the store that day and tended to the cash register as Cache followed Benny downstairs to the hidden room behind the panel.

"Thanks for coming in. This wasn't something I wanted to talk about over the phone."

"No problem, I appreciate anything you could find out."

"It wasn't easy. I had to go through an old contact at Interpol to find this out. Not sure how helpful this will be but it's important you know what you are up against."

Cache sat down in the chair opposite Benny and leaned forward, eager to hear what he had to say.

"As you could guess, Emily Zhou and Beatrice Yu are the same person."

"Explains the passport."

"Beatrice Yu was the daughter of two academics that fled Criza when she was just a teenager. She did well in school, very strong in science and mathematics, and was easy on the eyes. However, her biggest contributions weren't in advancing science but in reporting the findings of others back to the Crizan government."

"She was a spy?"

"Yes, though not a willing participant."

"I don't follow."

"When she was eighteen, the Crizan Intelligence Service captured her parents and brought them back to Criza. They faced years in labor camps, likely never to see each other again. However, it was Beatrice the intelligence service was really interested in."

"How?"

"In exchange for leniency, Beatrice went to work for the intelligence service. She underwent plastic surgery to enhance her looks and was educated by some of the top minds to ensure that she would excel at a foreign university, and excel she had to, because her parents' fate lay in her hands. In negotiating this deal, her parents would remain under the watchful eye of the Communist Party and would teach together at a university in Criza, never to leave the country again. Beatrice had her name changed to Emily Zhou; modeled; went to university; was placed in company after company, rising in the ranks—all the while, spying and stealing trade secrets."

Cache sat back and rubbed her chin. "I don't know if I should be mad at her or feel sympathy for her."

"My contacts tell me that the building in downtown Boston that you followed the car to houses several law firms, one of which is a front for the Crizan Intelligence Service. The US government keeps a watchful eye on them, so it's not like they're fooling anyone, it's just the game spymasters play."

"Benny, thanks, that helps a lot." She got up from her chair and followed him out of the room.

"Can I interest you in a third edition of *Tom Sawyer* by Mark Twain? Great price."

Cache touched his elbow and politely declined the offer. She went upstairs and exited the store. There was a light sprinkle of rain in the air and she hadn't thought to bring an umbrella. She walked to a local café, ordered herself a coffee and sat in a booth by the window so she could watch the people darting in and out of the shops. She thought about what Benny had told her. It made sense somewhat, but then opened up other questions. Emily must have gotten access to Dr. Fischer's journals at different points in time and taken pictures of what she could get. Realizing they were in some special code that he refused to teach her, her handlers grabbed Jonas, figuring he could decode the journals. Maybe she was in a relationship with Dr. Allen that she couldn't focus on because of the impact it might have had on her parents. Maybe she forced a relationship with Dr. Fischer in order to get access to the journals that he kept away from work in his private residence downtown. She tapped her fingers on the table. Why would she kill Dr. Fischer? By all accounts she only had a partial collection of photographs. It would have made more sense to continue on in the relationship that she was trying to forge with him to gain greater access, or if she was going to go for broke, order him at gunpoint to turn over the journals. But strangling him made no sense. You can't stand across a room and threaten to strangle someone and have them take you seriously, especially if your body size is smaller than your victim's. No, as Cache played out the different scenarios in her head, she decided the death of Dr. Fischer served no purpose for Emily. However, Dr. Allen was a different story. Could this simply be the result of jealousy from a former lover oblivious to the foreign influences over Emily's life? After all, it was one of Jeffrey Allen's ties, or one made to look like one of his ties, that was the murder weapon.

Then who killed Emily? Was it the intelligence service, unhappy with the work that she was doing for them, or were they cleaning up loose ends? That didn't make sense. She was an asset that could have had years of value to them. Why kill her now? Could Dr. Allen have killed her? Maybe he found something out from Dr. Fischer that suggested she wasn't as innocent as she made herself out to be? Then there was a completely different angle that she had considered at one point that could still be plausible: Ian Wright.

The rain had picked up its intensity and puddles started to form on the sidewalk. People splashed about as they hurried to get out of the rain. She looked around the café. More people had come in to get out of the elements of the day. Large chalkboards hung on a far red brick wall, announcing the specials for the day. Cache read through the soups and sandwiches and flagged a server down to order a bowl of their signature chicken noodle soup. Nothing would taste better on a day like today, she thought. She wasn't in a hurry to return to her suite and the journals. She had been so keen to dig right into them and now the desire had faded as she was looking at months of work to try to figure them out. Maybe she could take them home with her; maybe spending some time back on the ranch away from everything in Boston would allow her to focus and take breaks where necessary so it didn't feel like she was pushing paper all day long.

The server plunked down a large white ceramic bowl with a red-painted rim and a large spoon inside a yellowish broth, with chunks of chicken bobbing up and down in the liquid. The smell was heavenly as she leaned over it to breathe it in. The server dropped off a few packs of crackers as Cache scooped up a spoonful, blew on it and let the broth glide over her taste buds. "Oh, that is so good," she mumbled to herself.

She felt a vibration from her phone and pulled it from her jeans to look at a text. It read, "Lunar Tradicity would like to talk."

Cache went to her contact list on her phone to find the phone number and consultant identification that Nina had provided her. She called the number back as she looked at her soup and punched in the code.

"Cache, did I catch you at a good time?" Nina asked.

"Just having some chicken noodle soup."

"You're in Boston, you should have the chowder."

"Chowder, I didn't even think to check."

"Did you get ahold of Benny?"

"I did. In fact, I just came from his place, it's a few doors down. He was able to dig up some info for me. Thanks for putting me in touch with him."

"That's good. Listen, after I got off the phone with you, I did a little digging. Something about the name Lucas Fischer rang some bells for me and I made some inquiries."

"What did you find out?"

"Dr. Fischer used to work in East Germany before the wall came down."

"Yep, both him and his wife, and then they got out and Dr. Fischer went to work for a company that Quillchem later purchased."

"How much do you know about Mrs. Fischer?"

"Quillchem had some info on her when they did the security clearance for Dr. Fischer and then the rest is stuff she shared with me."

"Well, I will share this with you. A friend of mine who spent a lifetime at MI6 said that Mrs. Fischer used to go by her maiden name in East Germany. There they knew her as Petra Sokolov. Petra Sokolov at one point was employed by the KGB."

"What?"

"You heard me right. Whether or not she still is, my friend couldn't tell me, but MI6 had a file on her at one point. Grew up in Russia, excelled at academics and worked for the Russian government in several scientific positions. Which makes me wonder if their efforts to flee to the West were their choice or whether she was being pushed to do it."

"Sounds like Dr. Zhou. Benny believes she was coerced into working for the Crizan Intelligence Service, gathering scientific intel and funneling it back to her handlers."

"It's not really new; every government does it. They put their people in positions where they can monitor things and report back when they learn something."

"But it's not like Petra worked in a lab. She stayed home and took care of her son, while Dr. Fischer went to work."

"Yes, but when Dr. Fischer came home, did he share his day with his wife? Remember, she was a formidable scientist herself. She would fully comprehend what he was doing. In fact, she may have even offered an opinion or influenced him in some way."

"That's interesting."

"Anyway, I just thought you should know. And you're coming to my gallery opening, right?"

"Wouldn't miss it for the world. Thanks, Nina."

"Always, darling, hugs and kisses." And then the line went dead. Cache put her phone back into her pocket and ate a spoonful of her soup. It had grown cold as she talked with Nina. The incredible aroma had diffused into the air, and she ate spoonful after spoonful until it was done and she stared down at the bottom of the bowl.

Cache scratched her head. She was uncertain what to do with this new piece of information. If the military knew about it, they hadn't bothered to share it with her, and what was she going to do, ask Petra if it was true? Who would truthfully answer that question? Even if she was with the modern version of the KGB, why would she want her husband dead? Could the rumors about a relationship with Ian Wright be true? Was Ian her spy at work while she watched her husband at home? Was it not Petra who encouraged her husband to hire Ian in the first place? Could Ian also be a spy?

The questions circled around in Cache's mind. She looked outside. The weather had grown worse, as buckets of rain were coming down. Reluctant to go out onto the street and wait for a cab, she eyed the chocolate cheesecake the café had on its signage and ordered a big slice and another cup of coffee. Cache grabbed her phone and called Nancy, hoping to leave a message that she could look into tomorrow when she got into work, and was surprised when she answered.

"Hello, Graydon Quill's office, Nancy Grant, how can I help you?"

"Hey, Nancy, it's Cache. What are you doing in on your day off?"

"Oh, catching up on some work. What are you doing?"

"I'm in a café eating a big slice of chocolate cheesecake, waiting for the rain to stop so I can hail a cab."

"Do you want me to call Aaron to come get you?"

"No, it's his day off. I have paperwork waiting for me back in my room, so I don't mind just hanging out here for a while."

"So what can I do for you?"

"I had a question. I'm working through Dr. Fischer's journals and we identified different patterns of symbols for different people. I have everyone figured out except for one person. The initials are MT. Do you know anyone with those initials?"

"Could be dozens of people with those initials. I know there is Mike Trait, who works in accounting, and Maria Tabares, who is down in marketing, and Matthew Talbot—he's a nice old man, looks after the flowers and grounds crew that makes the campus look so nice."

"It's someone Dr. Fischer would have come in contact with. You don't know if there was anyone in the lab with those initials, do you? I mean, this can wait, I don't want to hold you up."

"Nonsense. If you can bear with me, I will have a look at the people that have worked at the Franklin Facility."

Cache could hear typing and humming in the background. After a few minutes, Nancy jumped back onto the phone.

"I looked through the list. The most likely person would be Michelle Travis."

"Is she still working at the facility?"

"One moment while I access her records... nope, it says here that she left the company about six months ago. She was an assistant of Dr. Allen's."

"Do we know why she left the company?" Cache asked.

"It just said she called in one day and gave notice without explanation. From the comments on her file from Human Resources, the abruptness of her resignation raised a few eyebrows and there is an indication not to rehire at Quillchem."

"Do we have a phone number for her?"

Nancy proceeded to give Cache the last phone number they had for Michelle. As Cache jotted down the number on a café napkin, she noticed the rain had stopped. She thanked Nancy for her help and told her she should go home. Cache looked down at the number and punched the digits into her phone. The phone rang a few times before a female voice answered.

"Hello, who is this?"

"Is this Michelle Travis?"

"Uh-huh, who is this?"

"My name is Cache Iron, I am a private investigator." It was one of the first times Cache had used those words out loud— "private investigator." "I'm wondering if you would have a few minutes to talk to me."

"About what?"

"I'm investigating the murder of Dr. Fischer at Quillchem Industries, and I just wanted to talk to you and find out why you left."

"Who told you to call me? Did he mention my name?"

"He who?"

"Jeffrey, did Jeffrey give you my name? You tell that lying son of a bitch he is lucky I didn't press charges. What gives him the right..."

"The right to what? I'm not following."

"If you want to talk to me, you can talk to my lawyer first. I have nothing further to say to you, don't call me again."

As Cache tried to point out that she hadn't really said anything to her in the first place, all Cache heard was the dial tone. On a normal day, that would have struck her as odd. The way today was going for her, it elicited the equivalent of a shrug. She looked down at the crumbs on her plate. The rain had stopped, and the sun was attempting to make an appearance. If she was going to catch a cab, it would be after she tried the red velvet cheesecake. She ordered a slice of that from the server floating around with a carafe of coffee, filling up customers who were low. Cache flipped through her contacts until she found Chase's cell phone number and pressed the connect button. The phone rang once with a quick pickup.

"Hey."

"Hi."

"Are you home? I thought I heard you go out earlier but I could be wrong."

"No, I had a meeting I had to go to," Cache said.

"On Sunday?"

"They had some information on the investigation that couldn't wait until tomorrow. I have something that popped up that I wanted to ask you about."

"What was that?"

"Michelle Travis. Ring any bells?"

"A couple. Why?" Chase asked.

"She used to work in the lab, right?"

"Yeah, and she quit."

"Do we know why? I just tried to talk to her, and she hung up on me and said if I want to talk further to her, I have to contact her lawyer."

"Why do you want to talk to her?" Chase asked.

"I'm thinking she might be the MT in Dr. Fischer's journals. These are the only initials so far that are unaccounted for."

"Cache, it's kind of a thorny issue. She alleged that Dr. Allen made unwanted advances toward her. She left and sought the advice of counsel. We are trying to work things out with her, under the radar, in a way that works in everyone's interest."

"That still doesn't mean she isn't the person that Dr. Fischer was writing about. Some of the comments regarding MT were rather racy. Is it possible that she was involved with Dr. Fischer?"

"I couldn't tell you, it hasn't come up yet. We can ask; the other side might use it as a bargaining chip to get what they want," Chase said.

"What Graydon wants is answers. What do you think his answer will be if I have to tell him that Michelle could be the mystery person identified in the journals?"

"I will reach out to her lawyer tomorrow and see if she would be willing to talk to us on the matter. Where are you?"

"I'm in a little café near the bookshop I went to the other day, eating cheesecake and drinking coffee."

"I like cheesecake."

Cache gave her the directions to where she was and told her she would wait for her at the café. Maybe Michelle would have the missing piece of the puzzle that would bring it all together. All Cache could do at this point was cross her fingers and eat cake.

## 20

"I hate Mondays" is a sentiment experienced by most people forced to work in order to make a living. Despite the fact that Cache had worked for most of the weekend, she still felt deep inside that Mondays sucked. Today, she needed to focus on a couple of key items. Chase would reach out to Michelle Travis's attorney to see if it would be possible to have a sit-down discussion to determine if she was indeed the MT written about in Dr. Fischer's notes. Graydon was supposed to have reached out to Petra over the weekend to see if Cache could visit her and have a look through their residences, to see if she could find the pages torn from journal fifteen. She had never been to Martha's Vineyard and might never have a chance again. The rain clouds of yesterday had disappeared and the weather woman predicted the day would be warm with sunny skies. The drive out should be more relaxing for Aaron than shuttling her around the downtown Boston core.

Cache poked around the suite, dividing her time between decoding more passages in Dr. Fischer's journals and pacing the floor, waiting for the go-ahead from Graydon. At 11:22 in the morning, her phone rang, and she stubbed her toe racing to get it.

"Hello?"

"Hello, it's Graydon. Did I catch you at a good time?"

"Yeah, just waiting for the go-ahead from you, hoping to make Martha's Vineyard tonight."

"If you're hoping to get into the Fischer residence, it's a no go," Graydon said.

"What? Why?"

"I talked to Petra; she said no."

"Did you remind her that I saved her son's life not once but twice?"

"I did in a more subtle way; she said she thinks the world of you and any time you want to come out to Liberty Crossroads, she would love to have you for dinner, but as far as poking around her house, she said no," Graydon said.

"Wouldn't you say that is odd? After all, this may be the crowning point in her husband's career. Not to mention it could shed some light on who killed him. If it was me, I would turn over every stone until I got the answer I was looking for."

"Her rationale, for what it's worth, is it has been a trying time for her. She just wants to get past it and move on. She said she would keep an eye out for the notes and if she ever comes across them, she will call me and turn the pages over to us. We can't compel her to open her house up to us; we are not the police."

"Maybe we can't search her home, at least not directly, and Martha's Vineyard sounds like it is out, but if the police still consider the condo at the Dawes an active crime scene, I might be able to convince Detective Boone to let me poke around."

"How are you going to do that?" Graydon asked.

"I have some pull with him. I can only ask, and he can say no, but right now it's the only shot we got, and we can rule out at least one of three locations if nothing is found there."

"Go for it then, and let me know if you find anything out. I will deal with Petra in the event she learns that you were over at their place snooping around."

"If you could maybe get her out for lunch sometime, maybe I could swing by their place and let myself in."

"Sorry, Cache, I seem to have some static on the line, didn't catch that last part, but keep me up-to-date with what you find out at the condo," Graydon said.

Cache hung up the phone, bewildered at Petra's refusal to let her come over and have a look around. Everyone handled loss differently. Maybe this was the way she handled it. She hadn't talked to Michael in a few days and wasn't sure how receptive he would be to letting her go over to the condo by herself and have a look around.

———

At two o'clock that afternoon, Cache found herself in the back of the Baumann sedan, Aaron at the wheel, heading to downtown Boston to look around the Fischer residence at the Dawes. As they pulled in front of the tower, Cache could see Michael leaning against a newspaper box, chowing down on a hot dog and drinking a cup of coffee. While he was open to her having a look around the condo before the police released it back to Petra Fischer, he wasn't okay with her having free unsupervised access to the place. After they'd bantered back and forth for twenty minutes on the phone, Cache realized that she wasn't getting in unless he was coming along. She relented in her argument, which must have soothed his ego to some extent, let him feel he had gotten one over on her. She popped out of the car and asked Aaron to go and park somewhere, as she didn't know how long she would be up there. This might be her only chance to take a good look around the place for the missing pages, as Petra would decline any requests in the future when

the police no longer had a say in the matter. Cache walked up
to Michael. The relish was falling down the side of the bun, and
a little mustard had splattered on the lapel of his brown suede
jacket. He had a goofy grin on his face. She grabbed the other
end of the hot dog and took off half of it in one bite, with a coy
look, as if she knew what he was thinking in that brief moment.

"You know you can get your own," he said.

"Why get my own when I can have yours?"

"We are talking hot dogs, right?"

"Come on, Michael, let's get this over with," Cache said as
she tugged his jacket and led him into the lobby of the
building.

They rode the elevator to the twenty-ninth floor as he stared
at her and she just focused on the elevator doors, not acknowl-
edging what he was thinking at that moment, feeling his eyes
trying to penetrate her skull. They got up and walked down the
hall to the front door. Cache crossed her arms and tapped her
foot on the ground as she waited for him to get the key out and
let them in. After a few minutes of watching him fumble
around with the keys, she wasn't certain whether he was having
trouble or was doing it just to piss her off. She grabbed the key
ring from his hand, shoved him to the side, found the correct
key and unlocked the door. A beeping sound started as soon as
the door opened and Cache spotted the set alarm flashing for a
code to be entered. She looked at Michael. "Well, aren't you
going to do something?"

"I was waiting for you. Is there a problem?"

"What's the code, Michael?"

"Eleven nineteen, Jonas's birthday, or so Mrs. Fischer
told us."

Cache punched the four-digit code into the alarm panel,
and the beeping stopped.

"So what are we looking for?" Michael asked.

"Sheets of paper, a light yellow in color, with strange

symbols on them, and the edges are torn, but if you find any papers like that set them aside; we're just assuming that the journals were everything. And, Michael..."

"What?"

"Thanks for doing this for me. Petra won't let us search the other residences, so I have my fingers crossed that the papers are here."

"Where do you want to start?" Michael asked.

"If you can take the living room and kitchen, check underneath and behind drawers, the insides of books. I'll take his office."

Cache walked into the home office space and tried to identify manageable chunks to tackle. She began by going through all the books in the bookcases, holding the books with the spines to the ceiling and fanning the pages to see if anything would fall out. Book by book, she went through five bookcases stuffed with textbooks on a variety of scientific disciplines, but nothing showed itself. Michael would occasionally shout out his status, which seemed to always be, "Haven't found anything, how about you?" Cache then turned her attention to the file folders of paper on the desk and chairs. She lined all the piles up against the far wall, and as she flipped through the contents, she reallocated them to the opposite end of the room. There were family photos tucked in between pages of notes on different theories, but no pages with special notation. File folder by file folder, Cache went through everything that was in the room. By the time she had finished, Michael came in and sat in one of the chairs, which were now completely empty, having searched the other rooms with no luck. Cache started to open the drawers to Dr. Fischer's desk. On the right-hand side, the top two contained an assortment of pens and pencils, and two staplers, one red and the other black. Paper clips, staples, highlighters in a rainbow of colors, but nothing of significance. His bottom left-hand drawer held stacks of paper that Cache flipped through, but nothing was written on them. His lower right-hand drawer was locked. She pulled on the handle but it would not budge. As she examined the lock, she thought it looked like something designed to keep your kids out, not someone trained in picking a lock. She pulled a couple of paper clips from the desk, fashioned them into different shapes and inserted them into the lock as Michael stood up to watch. A few minutes later, Cache said, "There she is. Now, show me your secrets."

Cache flipped through the file folders in the bottom drawer. Several of them related to bills for their properties, taxes, utilities, insurance, and then one folder was marked "Office." Cache pulled the folder out, put it down on the desk and flipped through the papers. She came to a memo from Niles Gaven and began reading it aloud.


Dear Dr. Fischer,


No doubt you have learned that the company is facing a lawsuit by a former lab associate claiming sexual harassment by a member of your team, Dr. Jeffrey Allen. I have spoken with our counsel and I am asking discreetly for your input on whether you believe the accusations have merit or whether it is a fabrication by the imagination of Ms. M. Travis. Please set up a time with my assistant so we can discuss this matter in greater detail.


Yours sincerely,


N. Gaven

VP of Human Resources


"That is interesting."

"Why? Things like that happen in big companies every day."

"I realize that, but I was trying to get a meeting with Michelle to see if she is the MT referred to in Lucas's journals."

Cache flipped the page over to see a handwritten note from Dr. Fischer with a few attempts at writing an appropriate response. She read through his notes and sat back in the chair.

"In the notes attached to the memo, Dr. Fischer said he had very few dealings with Ms. Travis other than to ask her where Dr. Allen was, but given Dr. Allen's propensity to strut around like a peacock, while he has no evidence to support or deny the claim, he unfortunately feels that Ms. Travis is probably telling the truth."

"Does that help you at all?"

"Not really. If he had no dealings with her, why would he write about her in his journals?" Cache said.

"Maybe he was fantasizing about her, maybe he had a crush on her—there could be a host of reasons why he wrote about her," Michael said.

"The passages I read were not about fantasy, they were about a real relationship."

Cache put the file back and looked around the room. There had been nothing in the safe after they recovered the journals and nothing in the apartment that hinted of the missing pages. Cache got up, walked over to Michael and touched him on the shoulder, wandered out to the living room and plunked herself down on the couch to look out onto the harbor. Michael joined her and put his arm around her, not saying anything. She gazed at the cream-colored carpeting, an outline still visible where Dr. Fischer's body had lain when it was discovered by the housekeepers coming to do their weekly clean.

"You checked everywhere?" she asked, turning to face Michael.

"I know my job. I'm sorry it's not here. No chance Mrs. Fischer will let you look in the other two locations?"

"Not at the moment. Maybe if we keep asking, we can wear her down, but it's not looking too good. She said she'll keep an eye out but the papers could be anywhere and may not be found for years."

Cache stared at a light purple ottoman with maple-colored legs that stood near the window and about twelve feet away from the couch. She noticed the brass vent cover underneath.

"You checked the vents, right?"

"No. If there are papers in there we should hear a flapping sound when either the heat or air-conditioning kicks in. Listen, the air is circulating right now and there is no sound."

Cache continued to stare at the vent and decided to humor herself. She got off the couch, walked over to the ottoman and moved it out of the way so that she could see the vent. She kneeled down, wedged the vent cover off, took out her smartphone, flipped on the flashlight feature and put it down into the hole. She reached in with her right arm for a few seconds and pulled it out.

"Any papers there?"

"No, but I can feel something. Can you hand me a pen?"

Michael reached into his jacket for a pen and went over to Cache and handed it to her. She put her arm back down into the vent and caught hold of something. She pulled her arm out and looked down into the vent.

Cache sat up and turned to him. "You will want to see this."

"See what?" he asked as he crawled beside her and peered into the vent hole. Cache shone her flashlight down so the light reflected off the aluminum vent. There, sitting on the elbow joint of the vent, was a gold pendant with what looked like blood on it.

Michael grabbed an evidence bag from his jacket, turned it inside out and put it around his hand and reached into the vent to retrieve it. He pulled it out and sealed the bag as the two of them stared at the gold pendant.

"I don't think it's blood. It could be lipstick," Michael said.

"It looks like there could be a partial fingerprint on it," Cache said.

"I will have the lab look at it. Excellent find."

Michael rotated the bag. "It looks like there is some writing on the back."

"Could be an engraving. What does it say?" Cache asked.

Michael got up off the floor, walked into the kitchen, put the light on above the range hood and held the evidence bag up to it.

"It appears to be two words: 'Moya Tigritsa.'"

Cache grabbed the bag from him, held it up to the light and read the inscription again. "Moya Tigritsa." She said it again even louder. "Moya Tigritsa."

"Yeah, I said that already."

"No, don't you see? Moya Tigritsa, that is the MT that Dr. Fischer was talking about in his journals. It must be. Whoever this Moya is, Dr. Fischer has some association with them, and maybe they have the torn out pages or maybe, just maybe, they know something about his death."

"Bit of a stretch, slugger, but I want to get the lab to analyze the fingerprint. If it belongs to this Moya person, hopefully they're in the system and we can find them."

Michael tucked the evidence bag down into his jacket as Cache replaced the vent cover and put the ottoman back where she'd found it. Feeling the trip was not a complete waste of time, they locked up the condo and reset the alarm. Cache wondered if the Fischer's used the same alarm code for all of their properties. People tend not to want to remember too many passwords and are creatures of habit. They took the elevator down as Cache called Aaron to bring the car around. She drove Michael to the precinct, pushing him to find out whose fingerprint was on the pendant and to be expedient about it. Cache, on the other hand, wanted to get back to the campus and research Moya. She called Nancy from the car and asked her to search the company's personnel to see if Moya had ever worked for the company. Next on her list was touching base with Graydon to advise him that the papers were not at the condo and to pick his brain on whether he'd ever had contact with someone named Moya. Graydon reflected on the name, but he could offer no insight to Cache about who this person was. Cache looked at her watch and presumed the team would be together working in the labs; she called them one by one. None of them admitted to knowing who the person was. She couldn't ask Petra who this was for fear that it was someone that Lucas had been involved with, which wouldn't be a memory that Cache wanted to serve up to a grieving widow.

Was Moya behind the death of Dr. Zhou? Was Emily the only person who could have told Cache how to find Moya, and was this now a secret that she had taken to the grave? No, somewhere out there, Moya was within reach, watching from the shadows; Cache could feel it. She looked out the window as she could see Quillchem's campus in the distance and muttered, "I don't know where you are, Moya, but I am coming for you."

## 21

Cache had spent the better part of last night's slumber time staring at the ceiling above her bed, weighing an important decision. She kept being taken back to an incident six years earlier when Corporal Rudi Globb of Lincoln, Nebraska, took two shots at close range, to be sent home to his parents in a flag-draped coffin for doing his job as they investigated an incident off base. It wasn't the risk that they accepted when they enlisted that bothered her. It was knowing that out there was a formula that could create a material that could have helped Rudi, let him marry his high school sweetheart, and have the requisite number of kids to be considered average, and live out his years working the family farm. Yes, Petra Fischer had the right to grieve the loss of her husband in whatever manner she saw fit, and certainly had the right to decide what happened on property that she owned. Cache wrestled with whether one woman's rights outweighed the lives of all the people the fabric could protect.

At nine forty-five that morning, as Aaron picked her up at the front of the main building, a tall coffee in hand, she had decided. Petra's wishes in this instance didn't count. Based on her calculations, the trip out from the office to the Fischer residence on Martha's Vineyard would be two and a half hours, including catching the ferry to bring the car over to the island. Cache spent the time researching the name Moya Tigritsa from her smartphone. A call from Nancy told her that Moya had never worked at Quillchem, despite the fact that the company had over ten thousand employees working worldwide. No one with that name had ever been directly associated with the organization. As far as external vendors or other outside organizations that Lucas Fischer may have had an association with, she couldn't say, but for Cache this was just another brick wall. Moya, from everything she had encountered so far, was a ghost.

The weather was cool that morning but partially sunny. The weatherman was calling for storms to move into the area over the next several days. The ride over on the ferry proved very scenic to her. When they landed in Martha's Vineyard it took a while to disembark and another half hour to find the Fischer residence. As Aaron pulled into the driveway, Cache asked him to stop the car so she could get out and survey the area. The nearest homes to the property were off in the distance, as Cache could only see the tops of the roofs from where she stood. Cache jumped back into the car and Aaron drove down the driveway for about ten minutes, arriving at a home that personified local architecture. Barn-style arches in the front of the house flanked the front door in the middle, with a gravel driveway and a small patch of green grass close to the house. There were numerous windows whose frames were painted in white along the front; the front door and window shutters were all painted black. The exterior of the house matched the roof, with cedar shakes protecting the interior of the house from the elements. A white-painted cupola sat in the middle of the roof with windows on all sides and a black-painted weathervane on top of the dome, showing that the wind was coming off the water that afternoon. As they pulled into the driveway, they saw that a similar barn-type structure covered in cedar shakes sat to the right of the house with two black-painted garage doors with small windows. Cache hopped out of the car and instructed Aaron to back the car up alongside the garage in the event her plan didn't work out and they had to make a swift getaway before the police arrived. She cupped her hands around her eyes and peered in through the garage windows. One area of the garage was void of any vehicles; a secondary vehicle was parked opposite with a car cover pulled over the top. This was a good sign. It might suggest that no one was home. Cache walked around the house and peered inside to see if there was any sign of movement. The last thing she wanted to do was enter the house and find Petra or someone else there. She'd brought her lock pick set with her and was relying on the Fischer's to use the same alarm code as the one they used at the Dawes.

Most of the windows had the drapes pulled shut. As she walked to the back of the house, she saw a small swimming pool with a white concrete patio and short-cut green grass filling a good portion of the backyard. A wooden boardwalk seemed to go on into the distance; it was a few hundred feet from the house to the beach. From where she stood, Cache could hear the waves in the distance crashing along the shore.

All the blinds on the ground level of the house in the back were closed tight. On the far side of the house she found a small crack in the blinds and observed that most of the furniture in the room had white dust covers over them, except for one chair near a desk that was uncovered, and the related sheet lay on the floor beside the desk.

Cache walked to the front of the house and pulled a pair of tight-fitting black leather gloves from her pocket and put them on. She then did what any respectable person who was about to break into a home would do. She rang the doorbell. After a few more attempts and no one coming to investigate, she took that as her cue to use her lock pick. After a few tries of playing with the lock, she heard the click and grasped the door handle. What was that alarm code again? she thought. Oh yeah. She rotated the knob and pushed the door open. As was to be expected, an alarm panel to her left had a red light on it and began to beep. Cache entered the code 1119, but nothing happened. She looked at the panel, and it was counting down until it would sound the alarm. At forty-five seconds she assumed she had pushed the wrong button and entered the code again, but it continued to beep, now at thirty-five seconds. She looked behind her to ensure there were no obstacles if she had to make a run to the car and get the hell out of there. Cache thought to herself, Jonas was twenty-three, which meant he would have been born in '99. She looked at the count; it was now at twenty-five seconds. No, 98, she thought, and entered the month and year of his birth, 1198, but the alarm continued to count down, nine, eight, seven... Cache thought about abandoning the plan as she keyed in the day and year—five, four, three—and 1998, but the alarm stopped beeping and the red "armed" light turned green. With two seconds to spare, she put her lock pick in her back pocket, rested her hands on her knees, hunched over and breathed deeply.

She walked outside, looked at Aaron, gave him the thumbs-up, returned inside the house and closed the door behind her. It was eerie. Little light was coming in from outside. The house was dark and she could hear the winds coming off the ocean and hitting the back of the house. She turned the light on in the hall. There was a sunken living room off to her left where the rolltop desk that she'd spied from outside sat, with most of the other furniture in the room covered in white cloths. She went into the living room, flipped on the light on top of the desk and sat down. She went through the drawers and flipped through the papers. There was some personal correspondence with friends, inviting them to various social engagements on the island; postage stamps in one drawer; pens and paper in another. There was no reason why this shouldn't have been covered up, but it yielded no new information to her. Cache lifted the dust cloth on every piece of furniture. Where drawers existed, she opened them, felt underneath for anything that could be taped there and went through the contents. For furniture she lifted the cushions, and for ones with zippers along the back she felt for any foreign object that could have been hidden between the fabric and the foam. Where vents existed, she lifted the vent cover up and looked inside. From the living room, she went to the dining room, to the kitchen and then to a family room, taking the same methodical approach to each room. The last room on the floor was behind a closed door close to the front entrance. Cache grasped the handle and opened it and felt for a light switch on the wall. A large desk sat near the window in the front of the house. A couple of filing cabinets and bookcases gave Cache about an hour's worth of work, to find nothing. As she sat in the office chair, she leaned forward to examine the framed photographs on the desk. There was a photo of Dr. Fischer and his family; one of his son, probably around the age of nine; and a group photo of the Fischer's with friends at what must have been a Halloween celebration. The six people in the photograph were dressed in clown-style costumes sporting bald heads with colorful hair jutting out the sides. The desk was empty of almost anything, a contradiction to his desk at the Dawes.

There were still plenty of rooms to have a look at, bedrooms on the next level, an attic perhaps. She saw no sign anywhere of a basement but thought she should also have a quick look in the garage before she and Aaron departed. As she got up from the chair, her leg brushed up against something. She looked underneath the desk and flipped on the light on her smartphone, and spotted a black wire mesh trash basket underneath the desk with a single piece of crumpled-up white paper sitting in the bottom. Cache reached down, retrieved the paper, flipped on a light sitting on the desk, unfolded the paper and smoothed it out. It was a handwritten note dated a few days before the doctor had died.

*My dearest Emily,*

*I wish I had the courage to say this to your face. As I look into your eyes, I lose all sensibility and the words don't come out. You have always been a trusted friend and confidant, and in my moments of weakness, when troubles brewed at home, I turned to you in ways that I know crossed the line on more than one occasion. I take responsibility for it all. Your beauty and your mind are not two things that go hand in hand too often and had we met years earlier, things might be different.*

*While things at home have been taxing for some time, I cannot in good conscience throw all the years Petra and I have been together away. The day when we discovered EBSM worked is my greatest moment of accomplishment, and in it I suffered my greatest moment of weakness, as I gave in to temptation and took our relationship to the extreme. I don't think I will ever look at my office desk again without thinking about what occurred between us.*

*You deserve someone that can love you with all of their heart. It is for this reason that I must transfer you out of my department. This is not a punishment. I just can't look at you and not desire you. I will speak with Graydon and ensure they name you to head up any project that you want, and if you decide to leave, I will give you the*

*highest recommendation possible to ensure you experience no harm*
*from my decision.*

*Love always,*

*Lucas*

Cache studied the letter and then folded it up. Common sense
told her to put it back in the trash bin so no one knew that she
had been there, but this was important information. She put it
into her pocket and went upstairs to check the bedrooms.
There were five bedrooms upstairs and two washrooms. The
ceiling at the end of the hall had a rectangle cut into it and a
rope hanging down, which must have led to the attic. All the
bedrooms, except the master, had white dust cloths covering all
the furniture. The dust on the oak floor that ran throughout the
top of the house had only been disturbed going into the master
bedroom. Cache nonetheless tiptoed from room to room, investigating every nook and cranny looking for the missing notes.
Room by room, there was nothing to be found. She walked into
the master bedroom. The dust cloth had been pulled from the
bed and lay in a ball by the window. Cache walked to the
window and peered out. She could see the backyard and
watched as the ocean came in and out along the beach. There
was nobody on the beach walking along; for a Tuesday, it was
deserted.

She went through the drawers and gained a sense of the
Fischers' lives in private when no one was watching. She
stepped into the master bathroom; toothpaste was left next to
the sink, a shampoo bottle stood near the shower. She checked
the drawers and found nothing related to why she had come.

As she returned to the master bedroom, she thought she heard footsteps and stopped in her tracks. Cache listened and thought it was probably just the wind, but then she heard it again. She grabbed her phone and texted Aaron.

"You're not in the house, are you?"

He texted back, "No, I'm in the car. Why?"

"I think I hear footsteps," Cache texted.

"Do you want me to come in?"

"No, but keep the engine running. I need to figure out where they're coming from," Cache texted.

"Will do, boss."

Cache walked out into the hallway and stood still. A crash came from above her in the attic. Had someone seen her coming up the lane and taken refuge in the space at the top of the house? She faced a dilemma. She had no legal right to be there; in fact, she'd broken the law entering the house. Smart money said make an exit and hope it doesn't come back to bite you. But her instincts told her she needed to find out who was up there. She walked toward the end of the hall. Another thud came from above. She reached for her handgun and pulled on the rope with her left hand, opening the trapdoor in the ceiling. A set of wooden stairs unfolded, providing her with a means to venture up. Cache stepped up on the first step and turned on the flashlight on her smartphone. She continued up until she was halfway in the attic, and there was no sound. Light from the small windows cast shadows in parts of the attic. She panned the light across the room, catching sight of boxes stacked on top of one another, and as it went from one stack of boxes to the next, the light reflected off eyes hiding behind them. Cache pulled her gun up.

"Come out into the open so I can see you or I will shoot."

Nothing ventured forward. She picked up her light and moved it to the spot until she caught sight of those eyes staring back at her. There they were, watching her movements. Cache climbed up into the attic, holding the gun in her right hand, her light in the other, and she stepped forward to the boxes, warning that the person should come out immediately or face the consequences. When she was within ten feet, the eyes moved, and Cache held the light in the direction the subject was going in. She saw the bushy tail of a racoon as it squeezed itself through an opening in the corner of the roof.

"Oh, that scared the crap out of me," she said.

She holstered the gun in the back of her jeans and shone the light around the room. A thick layer of dust coated the floorboards, showing multiple racoon prints and one set of footprints going to a set of boxes in the corner. Cache walked over and examined the boxes. The two on the bottom still remained taped; the one on top had the edges folded over. She pried the flaps back; a series of old tin cans. She opened them up. They were vintage but all appeared empty. A large coffee can in the middle must have been near a hundred years old. As she moved the can, she felt something shift in it and opened it again, but it was empty. Cache flipped it over and examined the bottom of the can carefully, noting a seam around the inner edge. She grasped the bottom and turned it counterclockwise until it opened, showing a small hiding place underneath the tin. A couple of pieces of paper fell out onto the floor. Cache bent down, scooped them up and took them downstairs to the study so that she could examine them under a brighter light.

All three were letters addressed to Petra and signed by Ian. In each one he laid out his case for why the two of them were meant for each other, saying that fate had brought them together years earlier only for them to find each other again now. There were no dates on the letters and nothing to suggest when they were sent, but all seemed to be offers of enticement with nothing talking about anything that might have already occurred between them. Cache took a picture of each letter, folded them back up and returned them to the tin in the back of the attic. She made her way back down and pushed the trap-door back up into the ceiling. She hadn't found any torn notes there in the house, which meant if Lucas had been the one to remove the journal pages, and they were still in existence, her only remaining hope was that they were at the family home in Liberty Crossroads. Cache did one last sweep of the house to ensure that there wasn't a place that had been missed. She went down to the front door, reactivated the alarm and shut the door behind her, locking it again with her lock pick set.

Cache walked around the house toward the back, where Aaron waited with the car. Upon seeing her, he hopped out of the driver's seat.

"Did you find out what it was?" he asked.

"Yeah, a racoon had taken up lodging, but I scared it away temporarily. I suspect it will be back sometime soon. Anyway, nothing to note in the house. I'm just going to have a quick look in the garage and then we can be on our way." Cache walked over to the far side of the garage. A door resided on the side, and she made quick work of the lock. The inside of the garage was neat and tidy. She flipped a light on overhead and pulled up the cover that was hiding a vehicle. A late-model Jeep was under the sheet. Cache had a look in the glove box and under-neath the seats, but there was nothing of interest, and she tucked the vehicle back in for its rest. To the right of the Jeep an empty vehicle bay sat. Signs of oil stained the concrete slab. Along the back there were shelves full of nuts and bolts, nails and staples, and power tools hung from hooks embedded into the wall. There was a series of tables attached with brackets that could be folded up if necessary and offered a selection of power tools that most people would have envied. She scanned the room and thought this must have been Lucas's man cave when they were out here vacationing. The decorating inside the house had Petra all over it. Even his office screamed more about her than it did about him. But here in the garage, yes, this was his spot. Cache noticed a small wooden set of stairs on the far side of the wall, leading to a space above the vehicles. She walked over and climbed the steps, which creaked with every step she took. At the top of the stairs, she flipped a switch that lit up the space. There were framed movie posters on the wall. A huge baggy leather couch and love seat sat in front of a large flat-panel television. Multiple gaming devices sat on black-painted shelves that provided a resting place for the television. Scientific magazines, car magazines and the odd girly magazine were in stacks on one table opposite the love seat. Wooden-planked floors with a dated thin carpet covered most of the floor. A small wooden bar in the corner with a fridge and a collection of glasses and bottles of alcohol made this the perfect retreat for him or his son. Cache walked over to the fridge, opened it up and counted about twenty cold cans of beer. She grabbed one and popped the top. With Lucas gone, Jonas in England and Petra probably never coming into this space, who was going to miss it? Cache searched through the magazines, checked the cushions and poked into every drawer. And still, the pages that she was seeking were not there. She turned the light off and returned downstairs. In the corner of the tool area was a red tool chest about five feet high with multiple drawers and stickers all over it from oil and gas companies, some that were now extinct or had been swallowed up by their bigger competitors. She went through each drawer, all of which held a variety of hand tools. One drawer was dedicated to hammers, another to mallets. One drawer held twenty screwdrivers of different lengths and screwdriver heads. A drawer was full of wrench parts and another dedicated to pliers and cutting tools. In the top drawer were a series of batteries for the power tools and a shiny metal case. She grabbed the case and opened it up. There were seven cigarettes on one side of the case and four on the other. She closed the cigarette case, walked over to a magnifying lamp that was attached to the corner of one table, flipped it on and examined the cigarette case under the light. The case looked to be made of silver. Fine etchings on the back of the case, on the front a hammer and sickle. Cache held the case close to the light. In the bottom were two letters etched into the silver: MT.

"Moya, we meet again," Cache said. She put the case down, took pictures of the exterior and interior, and put it back where she had found it. She glanced around the room, ensuring nothing had been missed; shut off the lights; turned the lock on the door; and pulled the door tight behind her, checking to make sure it was locked.

Cache walked back to the car and jumped in the backseat.

"Any luck?" Aaron asked.

"Not what I was hoping for but something puzzling nonetheless."

"What do you want to do now?"

Cache thought about going down to the water. But the last thing she needed was someone coming along and asking her what she was doing there.

"Let's get out of here."

Aaron threw the car into drive and had started to make his way up the driveway when they saw the headlights of a white BMW coming in the opposite direction.

"Heads up, we got company."

Cache looked over his shoulder. "Just pull up. If it's Petra, I'll tell her we were in the neighborhood and wanted to see if she was at home."

Aaron pulled up alongside the BMW as Cache rolled down her window to see a woman in her late fifties, with blond hair, tanned, wearing a pink sweater tied around her neck.

"Hello, who are you?" the woman asked.

"I might say the same to you."

"I'm Buffy Webb-Davies, my husband and I live just over there."

Cache had met these society types before, with their hyphenated names and came up with a name on the spot.

"Jackie Jordan-Jones, it's a pleasure to meet you," Cache said.

"Are you a friend of the Fischers'?" Buffy asked.

"I have known Lucas and Petra for years. I was at Lucas's service. I don't recall bumping into you there, Mrs. Davies."

"We wanted to be there, but we were on the coast and weren't able to get back in time."

"It's a pity. Jonas told me his mom was out here vacationing and I was in the area, but alas, I must have missed her," Cache said.

"Really? I didn't know she was out here. I saw your car and said to myself, 'Buffy, you should check that out.'"

"Well, Mrs. Davies, I must be going. It was really nice to meet you," Cache said as she brought the window up and told Aaron to get them the hell out of there.

"Anything you say, Ms. Jordan-Jones."

## 22

_____

Wednesday morning started out uneventful. Cache's trip to Martha's Vineyard had involved a brief standoff with a cagey racoon, a delightful conversation with someone named Buffy and no missing pages —the point of her trip. She'd learned more about the relationships between Emily and Lucas, and Ian and Petra, and that Moya had something to do with the USSR, though Cache had no idea what. What she did know was that if Lucas was the person who tore the pages out of the journals that she desperately needed to put her hands on, there were three possible known locations and thousands of unknown ones where he could have put them. Maybe he'd burned the pages, preventing them from ever seeing the light of day. Maybe they were in a safe deposit box in some foreign bank, or maybe they had been entrusted to a close friend for safekeeping. It was this line of thinking that Cache had in the back of her mind. Maybe he'd entrusted the pages to Moya. Where Moya could be found was what she had hoped her search of the internet and trusted contacts would provide, but all efforts had come up empty. What she had was one possible location that she knew of left to hunt for the papers. The question was how she was going to go about it. If she turned up for a visit, a friendly stop to say hello, Petra would provide her little opportunity to search their entire house, a rather large house on a large piece of property. No, the best opportunity would be to search when she was not there, which meant Cache could spend the next several weeks staking out her place, waiting for her to go out so she could seize on the opportunity. Or she could create the situation, and for that she would need help. Cache spent part of the morning continuing to work on decoding the journals by hand. She had received some positive news from the army. The code breakers had run sample tests on patterns that she had decoded by hand against those decoded by a computer after scanning the documents into a mainframe. Fingers crossed, what may have taken months to decipher might be done in the next few weeks, and then the army could determine what any additional papers that might surface in the future said on their own without involving her or Jonas. Cache sat down and wrote out a to-do list for the day. The local weather report advised that the day ahead was to be cloudy with the possibility of light showers. A storm was making its way up the Eastern Seaboard from the Caribbean and was expected to bring heavy rains over the next few days.

First on her to-do list was to enlist Graydon's help to get Petra out of the house. Take her for dinner and keep her occupied for a few hours. The presence of oncoming storms might be a deterrent for her to go out, but the sooner Cache could get into their property in Liberty Crossroads, the sooner she could cross it off her list. Besides, Graydon had more incentive than anyone to want to find those pages. Cache would need to bring him up to speed on what she had done yesterday and assure him that no one was the wiser. Following that, Cache had scheduled a call with Jonas at three o'clock her time. Given that Cambridge was five hours ahead, it was the ideal time for them to talk so as not to interfere with his studies. Beside his name, she wrote "MT" and circled it. He was the only one that she hadn't asked, besides Petra, and given that Lucas seemed to know MT, Jonas might be the better starting point; she would go to Petra as a last stop.

She could hear raindrops smacking against the windows. She was glad she wasn't making the trip out to the Vineyard today. The foul weather reminded her of being back home, and she ordered up hot chocolate and a pot of hot coffee from the kitchen downstairs. As she saw it, without a break in the case she might very well be home by the weekend. Then she would periodically follow up with Michael and Chase to see if anything new popped up that needed to be investigated, but sitting in a suite, no matter how nicely furnished it was, was not how she wanted to spend her life. She reached for the phone in the room and gave her boss a call to pitch him on the idea.

"Hello, Graydon Quill here," he said.

"Graydon, it's Cache. Did I catch you at a good time?"

"Do you have news?"

"Yeah, unfortunately it's bad," she said.

"Why don't you bring me up to speed."

"I went out to the Fischers' place on Martha's Vineyard yesterday to have a look for the papers."

"So Petra gave in. I knew she would."

"No, she wasn't there, I let myself in," Cache said.

"You mean you broke in?"

"I didn't get caught."

"Still."

"I thought this was important," Cache said.

There was a pause in the conversation. "No, you're right. I wish it didn't have to come to this but we need to explore every option we can to find that formula. Though I am not condoning it, I suppose it is necessary when one party to the situation is being unreasonable."

"I'm glad you feel that way, because I need your help. I

found some interesting things at their property out on the Vineyard but not what we're looking for."

"Anything that you want to share with me?"

"Not at this point."

"So what do you need from me?"

"We scoured the condo in downtown Boston and came up empty. I rummaged through their place in Martha's Vineyard and found nothing. The only place left to look is their place in Liberty Crossroads, and for that to happen, I need her not to be there."

"And that's where I come in?"

"If you and your wife could get her out of the house for a few hours, take her for dinner, it would give me a chance to take a look through the house. If the papers are not there, they could be anywhere, and, Graydon, I don't know if we will ever find them."

"When do you need this to happen?"

"Watching the weather, it's supposed to get nasty on Friday. If you could get her out tomorrow, that would help. Otherwise we may be waiting a week, and then we have to talk about what we do going forward, because I have to tell you, as it stands now, I am at a loss as far as what happened to those pages."

"You know I need you to be more optimistic than that. I am confident you're going to find them. Maybe we won't find them today but I know a day will come when you will call me to tell me that you have them."

"How do you know that?"

"One thing the army told me about you from your record is you're tenacious. That is why I know that day is coming. I'll talk with Jacqueline and ask her to reach out to Petra. Tell her that we want to make sure she's okay with the storm approaching, see if she needs anything. It's a good reason to call. I'll let you know more when I hear something. And, Cache..."

"What?"

"Don't get caught."

Graydon hung up the phone, and Cache reached for her pad of paper and scratched one thing off of her to-do list for the day. She looked at her watch. She had a few hours before her phone call with Jonas.

She hadn't called home for a few days, and given that the case might have been hitting a brick wall, she thought she should call to see what was going on. The phone rang and rang and Cache's mother picked up just as Cache was about to hang up.

"Hello."

"Hey, Mom, it's me."

"Hi, I was wondering when I was going to hear from you. Is everything going okay? I know you can't talk about the details, but how are you?"

"I'm okay. I've kind of hit a brick wall. I have a couple more leads to follow up on but if they don't pan out, I'll probably be heading for home."

"That doesn't sound good."

"No, it's not. I've been racking my brain trying to determine if there's anything I'm missing, but I keep coming up dry. I have paperwork I can do for Quillchem for the next several weeks, but I can just as easily do it at home as here."

"Sometimes a break can do you good, give you a clear perspective on things. You might just find you wake up one night in the middle of your sleep with a new perspective on the case."

"Thanks. I needed some encouraging words. Anything else happening?"

"Gayle Shellington called the other day; her daughter Hayley went into labor on Sunday. Had a baby girl. Still no official word on the name but it sounded like Marvin might have passed out watching the delivery."

"Marvin couldn't handle dissecting a frog in school, I'm not sure why he thought he could handle seeing a delivery. Anything else happening?"

"Your dad is looking at upcoming cattle auctions. Your brother Cooper was in here a little while ago, not sure where he got off to. Do you know what day you'll be coming home?"

"Not yet, but I'll call. Not sure if they'll let me take their jet home, given that I haven't accomplished what they hired me for. I'll need someone to come pick me up at the airport."

"I'll let your father know. I'm sure one of us will be available."

Cache thanked her mom and hung up. It sounded good to hear her voice. Being cooped up in her suite made her long for the wide open area that home offered. As the day wore on, she kept an eye on the time as she didn't want to miss the opportunity to talk with Jonas. There were a few things that she had forwarded to him, phrases that she hadn't come across when they met at the coffeehouse, and getting an idea of what they meant would help her in working through the passages. At three o'clock she called the number to the phone in Jonas's dorm room, hoping he was back from classes and everything else he had going on that day.

"Jonas?"

"Hey, Cache, is that you? Good to hear your voice."

"Are you settling back into school? You haven't had any people following you, have you?"

"No, no one following me, except for someone from the FBI. They contacted me shortly after I got back to my dorm and told me they would keep an eye out, that sort of stuff."

"You're sure it's them?"

"Yeah, after I spotted someone, I called them and they confirmed it was one of their people. Kind of got the feeling they were testing me. Haven't seen anyone since."

"Well, keep an eye out, but I have a feeling you won't be seeing anyone else. How's Cynthia? It was Cynthia, correct?"

"Yeah, she picked me up at the airport. She's been great, but I've been struggling about whether I should tell her about Emily."

"I wouldn't if I were you."

"So if it was you, you wouldn't want to know?"

"I might want to know and then after you told me I might wish you hadn't. You can't take it back."

"I just feel guilty."

"Guilt is like carrying around a heavy box. After a while you decide that you're going to pass that box off to Cynthia, and you are no longer carrying the heavy box, but it hasn't disappeared. Now she has to deal with the weight of the box; that's not fair to her."

"So what do I do?"

"Love her with your whole heart. If somewhere down the road you break up for other reasons, she never has to be impacted by a bad decision, and if it works out, then time will hopefully lighten your load, plus I might be able to help you with that now."

"Sorry, I'm not following you."

"Jonas, I think Emily was working for a foreign government to infiltrate Quillchem and steal secrets for them. I think she was the source of the photos you were asked to decipher. Your dad likely never left her alone with the journals long enough to photograph them all. That's why it was only random pictures you were given."

"That can't be. No, she wouldn't do that to me."

"I've found a fair bit of evidence that I can't go into with you that suggests she was in on it. I thought you should know. She may have liked you. I can't speak to that, but she was under pressure to get answers on your dad's project and after he was gone, you were the only one she knew of that could translate the photographs that she had."

There was silence from the other end. She had struggled

with whether or not to tell him but didn't want him to destroy his relationship based on a game that was rigged from the beginning.

"Yeah, I'm just processing it."

"Look, I can't absolve you of your guilt. The mouse still goes after the cheese, even if it's a trap. But I suspect Emily would have used every opportunity you afforded her to get close to you and get what she was after. It was like you were playing a card game that you thought was on the up-and-up, only to find out later the dealer was working from a stacked deck. That's why, if I were you, I wouldn't tell Cynthia anything. If you love her, just work extra hard loving her and learn from this lapse in judgment."

"Thanks. I got the pictures you sent."

Cache spent the next half hour going over the different images that she couldn't figure out with him. She advised him that the army had developed a program to read Atlantian and that with this new batch of images and further testing, the military would have less need to rely on him or her. Cache asked about school and his plans for the future. He asked if she was going to stay on with Quillchem or go home after this was done. They talked for a while. After all, Quillchem was paying for the phone call.

"Jonas, thanks for your help with this. I know it can't be easy trying to get on with your life not knowing what happened to your dad, but eventually the truth will come out."

"He would have wanted me to continue on."

"Any plans for tonight? Are you going out with Cynthia or staying in and catching up on your schoolwork?"

"I told the guys I had an important call with a Yank, but I'll probably head down to one of our local pubs for a pint. I'll grab a smoke outside first."

"I didn't know you smoked."

"Yeah, my parents weren't too happy about it. I never did in high school, it's a habit I picked up in university, just like my dad."

"Lucas smoked?"

"Yeah, both my parents did. Funny enough, that is how they met."

"How was that?"

"If you listen to the way my dad tells the story, they both worked for some company in East Germany before the wall came down. He remembered everyone in the building who smoked would go out on their breaks at ten o'clock in the morning and two o'clock in the afternoon to the loading docks to have a smoke. It could be raining like hell or freezing cold and the diehards were out there having a smoke. I guess my mom left her lighter or matches somewhere and my dad lit her cigarette, which gave him the chance to try some cheesy opening line. My mom makes the story sound a little more believable."

"Does your mom still smoke? The few times I've seen her, I haven't seen her smoke, and I would have thought the stress of dealing with your dad's demise would be enough for her to want a cigarette or two. In fact, I can't recall even smelling it on her."

"She smoked for a while until she was expecting me and then gave it up. The two of them gave it up, but my dad would still sneak off to have one now and again. She knew; she was always wise to his games, he just didn't know it."

"Maybe that was the reason your dad created your secret language, so he could hide things from your mother's eyes."

"Well, don't tell her I told you this, but Mom also could read Atlantian."

"How?"

"She asked me one day how it worked. My mom's mind is sharp. She picked it up in no time flat. So when my dad would leave me these little notes, I would test her to see if she could figure it out. She always did. In fact, I hadn't even thought about it until now. If you have problems with any of dad's journals, you might want to ask her. She's there, I'm here; you'll probably get your answers a lot quicker."

Cache took in this new piece of information. She started running different scenarios in her head. This wasn't an insignificant detail; this was big.

"Jonas, can I ask you another question?"

"Sure, you're the one paying for the call."

"Did your dad ever mention a Moya Tigritsa to you? I've been trying to reach him or her but I can't find them anywhere."

Jonas chuckled at the name Moya Tigritsa. "You already have spoken with them and didn't even know it."

"Spoken to who?"

"I haven't heard that name in almost a decade. It's funny how one thing can bring up so many memories from your childhood."

"Were they a friend of your dad's? Were they at the service?"

"They were at the service all right. I wouldn't use the name Moya Tigritsa; I prefer the term 'mom.'"

"Wait, Moya Tigritsa, that's your mom?"

"If you go to a search engine and translate those two words from Russian to English, it translates as 'my tigress.' It was a pet name my father gave my mother, so you can understand why I would never address my mom that way. Who wants to think of their mom as a tigress? But evidently my dad did."

Cache had been feeling like she was alone in a dark basement the last several days, not sure what direction to go in to escape the darkness, and in one conversation Jonas had flipped the light on for her. She thanked him for his help and told him to stay in touch and to call her if he needed anything. As soon as she got off the phone with Jonas, she called Graydon to fill him in on some new revelations and told him it was imperative that he get Petra out of the house so that she could have a look around. Based on what she had pieced together so far, she suspected that the pages, if they were still intact, would be in the Fischer residence, and if she was right, those pages would explain who had silenced Dr. Fischer and Dr. Zhou, and why.

## 23

The minutes seemed to take longer to pass for Cache on Thursday than any other day that she could recall. She paced around her suite, waiting for a call from Graydon to tell her everything was a go. She had put the national weather station on and watched as the weather people predicted when the effects of Hurricane Louise would be felt in Massachusetts. Weather prediction models were determining that the storm would reach land sometime in the early hours of Friday morning. As she watched the news, she felt as if she was losing her chance to investigate her suspicions. Any further delays would provide an opportunity to get rid of evidence if it hadn't already been disposed of. Shortly after the start of the lunch hour, her phone rang. She was wearing a groove in the carpet.

"Cache, it's Graydon. It wasn't easy, but we convinced her to come out to dinner tonight."

"How did you do that?"

"Jacqueline called and told her that we wanted to check in on her and wanted to take her out to dinner. When she politely declined, Jacqueline asked if we could stop in to make sure the house and she were all right. Jacqueline didn't let up until we had an agreed time this evening."

"Where are you going?"

"We were trying to get her as far away from home as possible, even suggesting she come stay with us for the evening, but she wouldn't hear of it. So we agreed to have an earlier dinner together at five thirty at a restaurant called Little Italy in Liberty Crossroads. Kid, you may not have an enormous window of time, so do your best with what we could get you, and watch yourself, this storm could be a nasty one."

"Thanks. Fingers crossed I'll find what I'm looking for."

Cache hung up the phone and scheduled for Aaron to pick her up around four o'clock in the afternoon. That should provide enough time to make it out to Liberty Crossroads and sit in wait for Petra to depart from her home. Then Cache would need to move like lightning to search an enormous house for a few sheets of paper in what might only be a few hours of time.

The afternoon dragged on worse than the morning. Cache made sure she had her gloves, a small metal flashlight, smartphone, her lock pick set and hopefully the right code for the alarm. She decided to leave her firearm locked away in the desk at her suite. Cache didn't perceive Petra as a threat. But if she was caught in her home without her permission, the fact that she had a gun might not play well with the police.

She and Aaron drove out to Liberty Crossroads late that afternoon. The rains had intensified, and the wipers were working like mad to provide a clear line of sight for Aaron as he whisked down the highway. Water had collected in some places, causing major splashing as the tires hit the puddles. He pulled up around the block a couple of doors down and turned off the car. They sat and waited, fearing that a change in weather could dampen the situation and force her to call the whole thing off. At about 4:40 p.m., Cache spotted a woman in a black trench coat with a clear umbrella darting from the front door of the Fischer residence to a black BMW parked in the driveway. After it started up, the reverse lights came on and the car pulled from the driveway and headed past their parked car. Cache grabbed her smartphone and sent Graydon a text.

PETRA ON WAY WE ARE GO.

"Should I wish you luck?" Aaron asked.

"Keep the car running like you did in Martha's Vineyard. If the alarm code I'm thinking they're using isn't the right one, I'm hightailing it out of there and we need to be gone. It won't take long for the police to get out this way."

"You got it."

Cache pulled on her leather gloves and opened the back door of the car. The winds pushed against her, trying to warn her not to move forward. She shoved as hard as she could as water poured into the car's interior, soaking her jeans and fleece pullover. She shut the door and raced across the street and up the walkway to the house. Cache held her back to the storm to shield her hands from the elements as she went to work on the front door lock. The first try didn't work, and the pick slipped from her hand. Her leather gloves were wet and cold, and she pulled them off to try to get a better grip. Cache bent down and grabbed the pick and made a second attempt, then a third, until the lock signaled it was time to come in. She pulled her gloves back on. The moment the door swung open, the beeping began. Cache thought about the other codes she'd used. The code was going to be either 1198, 111998 or something completely different, which meant that the effort would need to be abandoned and she would have to hope that she wasn't caught fleeing from a house with the alarm going off. She punched in the 1, then 1 again. She held her breath as she punched in the remaining two digits, and the "unarmed" light turned green. Cache locked the door behind her. She squished as she walked. Cache decided to take off her boots so as not to risk being detected later on by the wet footprints Petra would find all over her house. She thought about pulling everything off, but to be caught breaking into someone's home wearing only your panties was not the impression she wanted to leave with the police. Cache wandered down the hall. Petra had left lights on in the front living room, the kitchen and the study, which faced the front of the house. Cache walked into Lucas's home study. There were seven bookcases lining one wall, all in cherrywood, with an assortment of hardcover and softcover books. A large cherry desk sat in front of the window. A computer and a brass lamp that was turned on sat off to the side. Filing cabinets underneath the desk and a large cupboard with multiple drawers sat against the far wall. Degrees for both Lucas and Petra hung on the wall, as well as numerous photographs of the two of them in their early years. Cache sat down at the desk. None of the filing cabinets were locked, and she pulled out file folders one by one and flipped through the contents. Her gloves were damp. She knew the water would dry, and would have preferred to take them off but she didn't want to leave her fingerprints all over everything she touched. She sat back in the chair and looked at her smartphone. At five twenty she had received a text from Graydon:

PETRA HERE GO FAST.

It was now five thirty. Cache knew she might not be able to search all the contents of this house in the two to maybe three hours she would have, and if there was a safe on the premises, forget it. She didn't have the training or expertise to break into a safe. A front door was one thing; a safe was something completely different. Folder by folder, drawer by drawer, book by book, Cache went through the study and didn't find any of the missing pieces of paper. She walked toward the back of the house and entered what was designed to look like an old-fashioned movie theater, complete with three levels of seating, a concession stand and an old-fashioned popcorn machine. How nice it must be to be rich, she thought. She poked around in the drawers and under the cushions but found nothing. The next room was an exercise room, complete with dumbbells, strength training machines and a speed bag. Two yoga mats lay across the floor near a set of French doors to the backyard that were being soaked with water. Cache went from room to room throughout the large house and found nothing. As she crept through the upstairs bedrooms, she began with Jonas's room, then the guest rooms, bathrooms and master bedroom. The boom of thunder ripped through the house and the house shook. She went to the window and spotted part of a tree in the backyard split in two, with glowing embers being doused by the rain. Another flash lit up the windows like the high beams of a car, and the lights in the house flickered and then went out. Cache went over to a table lamp beside the bed and turned the switch, but nothing happened. She turned on her flashlight, made it to one of the bedrooms facing the front of the house and looked outside the windows. The sky was pitch-black and not a light could be spotted except for the car that Aaron sat in. The streetlights were out, and no lights were coming from any of the neighbors' homes, except for the odd bouncing light in a window caused by people walking around their homes using a flashlight.

Cache held her flashlight in her teeth as she poked around the drawers to see what unmentionables Lucas and Petra had hidden away, but she didn't find what she had come for. She sat down on the bed, leaving a wet impression behind her, and looked around the room. Her suspicions had not taken her where she wanted to go. She stood up and looked at the bed. "Oh man, hopefully that will dry before she spots it."

Cache walked downstairs, her bare feet sticking to the hardwood on the staircase. She needed her flashlight to see where she was going, as the house was covered in darkness. She walked back into the living room in the front where she'd left her boots and brushed too close to the mantel of the fireplace and felt something move against her shoulder. She dropped her flashlight as she reached forward, catching the vase that had been knocked over before it came crashing to the ground. How would she have been able to explain that? she thought. She sat the vase down and grabbed her flashlight to examine it. Everything appeared to be intact. This was the same vase that Petra had gotten irate over when someone had picked it up to look at it. It was oriental in design, potentially an antique, and may have been worth something more than a vase that you could pick up at a flea market. Cache went to put it up on the shelf and felt something stir inside of it. She sat it back down on the floor and examined the top with her flashlight. A black sponge was wedged into the top of it, and she pulled it out. Sticking her hand down into the vase, she was uncertain what she would find, when her fingertips felt the folded edges of paper and pulled them out of the vase. Cache unfolded the sheets of paper. There were four pages, Dr. Fischer's scribblings on all of them. Cache moved over toward the window to get a better look, sat down on the love seat against the window and scanned the pages, holding her flashlight in her teeth. Having spent days decoding the pages, she had developed a rhythm to it and started to read some of the details of the notes. What she read caused her eyes to open wider. There in blue ink was the formula for EBSM and, more important, the reason why Dr. Fischer had been killed.

Cache knew these pages were worth gold and certainly worth killing over. She wasn't going to take any chances. She laid each piece of paper down on the table in front of her and photographed it. When she was done, she compressed the photos into a standalone file, encrypted it with a fourteen-character letters-and-numbers password and sent the file to Graydon's email address at Quillchem. She looked down at her phone. Her cell phone signal was weakening because of the storm. Her phone only had two bars on it, and she gritted her teeth as the phone struggled to send the message out. She checked her outbox, and it was gone.

A bit of relief came as she did that. At least the formula had found its way home. The thunder continued to crackle overhead; the roof sounded like it was a snare drum in a drum kit used by a rock band. Cache next typed out an email to Chase, included the password and told her that she knew why Lucas and Emily had been killed and to give the details of the email to Graydon. She felt it was safer to send the password to Chase than Graydon on the off chance the government that Emily worked for may have hacked his email account. She looked at her phone; it was now down to one bar of signal. She hoped this message got out. The phone went to No Service, then back to one bar, and it held there as the message took a minute to send.

As she was focused on whether she had enough of a signal to get her email out to Chase, her ears picked up an unfamiliar sound hidden in the noise that Mother Nature was creating. A lone beeping sound and then silence. The house stood still as the rain smacked against the windows. Cache looked down at her smartphone and noticed that she had received a text from Graydon. With her smartphone tucked away in her wet jeans, it had hindered her feeling the vibration when it went off. She opened up the text.

PETRA HAS GONE, GOT PHONE CALL AND LEFT, COULDN'T STOP HER.

Cache looked at the time the text had been sent. It was almost a half hour ago. She was about to send a text back when she saw the words "No Service" across the top of her phone. Cache tucked the phone back into her jeans, pushed herself off the couch and lowered herself to the floor, wedged between the couch and table. She sat there and listened, trying to distinguish interior noises from external. She turned off her flashlight, reached up for the pages and folded them back up. Her jeans were still damp. She pushed them down between her skin and her panties, which were still dry. For the first time in a long time, she wished she had a bra on so she could tuck them down into her bosom for safekeeping. She could hear the floorboards above her creak. Cache felt like something was moving in the upstairs bedrooms. She gazed over to the corner where she'd left her boots. The front door to the house was twenty feet or more away from where she had crouched down, and getting to it would require her to run through the front hall, leaving herself exposed.

She could feel her heart beating faster, as if it had decided it was going to get the hell out of there and jump from her chest. Cache focused on her breathing, trying to center herself in the moment. She rose up on all fours and backed herself up behind the side of the couch as she heard a large crashing noise outside. Lightning lit up the room and Cache, from her position, could see a set of eyes in the hallway staring at her. Petra yelled at her, "I have a mouse in my house!" Another flash of light came from outside and Cache could detect something metallic in her hand. She bolted, her bare feet sticking to the hardwood, and made a dash through the back living room doors toward the dining room in the rear of the house. Cache found refuge underneath the dining room table. She grabbed her smartphone and checked to see if she had service, but there was nothing.

"Shit," she said. Cache fumbled through her apps and looked for an app that she used to record her voice for memos. She pressed record and put it into the pocket of her fleece.

"Cache, sweetheart, you can come out. I know it's you. I promise to make it painless," Petra said.

Cache looked around the room. There was a closed set of doors to the right and a set close to her on the left. She crawled over to the left, raised her hand above her, opened the door and peered inside. It was a closet. If she were to hide in there and was discovered, there would be no direction for a retreat. She closed the door and crawled toward the other set of doors.

"If you make me hunt you down, I will make you suffer," Petra yelled.

Cache crawled to the other side of the room, opened the doors and crawled inside the butler's pantry. She reached for the back of her jeans to grab her gun and remembered that it was locked away, back at Quillchem. Cache stood up and looked around the pantry in the dark. She feared turning on her flashlight might give her position away. She felt a couple of items on the counter. One felt like a coffeemaker and another like a toaster. There was a block with handles protruding from it. She gripped a handle and pulled it out of the block and lightly touched the edge with her finger. "Yep, that's a knife."

She tiptoed out the other side of the pantry. The lightning continued to fill the rooms with moments of brightness giving way to stillness. The kitchen she remembered was large, with an island in the middle and seating at the far end. She took small steps. The surface had turned smooth and slippery to her bare feet. She extended her left hand in the darkness as her right gripped the handle of the knife. One foot in front of another. Her knee bumped up against something, and Cache put her hand down to feel the granite of the kitchen island. She moved with the edge until she was at the corner farthest from the entryway to the kitchen from the main hall.

"You know, if I shoot an intruder, they might give me a medal. After all, I am a poor defenseless widow and you're someone that has broken into my house."

Cache listened to her voice to try to gauge where in the house she might be. Staying on the main level made the most sense. Going downstairs or upstairs would provide no exit from the house unless she were to jump from a window or squeeze her way through one of the small basement windows.

"Buffy phoned me while I was at dinner," Petra called out in the dark. "I had phoned her to check on our place in the Vineyard. Much to my surprise, an old friend by the name of Jordan-Jones came out to visit me the other day."

Cache could estimate that her voice was coming from the midpoint of the front of the house. Between the study and living room near the front door. Cache knew that to get outside through the front, she would have to go right by her.

"Here is the funny thing. I don't know anyone named Jordan-Jones, but when she said she was a pretty brunette in her midthirties in a black Baumann, well, I know someone just like that, don't I, Cache?"

Cache braced herself against the side of the island and stared out toward the kitchen entrance. Even by what little light existed, she could see movement in the hall in front of the kitchen's entrance. Another loud crash came from overhead and a flash of light drew Cache's attention to the set of double doors out at the back of the kitchen that she had gone through on the day of the memorial service. The problem was that they were about twenty feet in front of the entrance to the kitchen from the hall. Cache crawled over to the doors, stopping and holding her breath every time she heard footsteps in the front hall.

"If you had just left it alone, a few months from now, even a few years from now, I would have slipped some info on EBSM to Ian. He could have said I found it in some old papers. Of course it wouldn't be the actual pages, but Graydon wouldn't care as long as he got his precious formula. Even in the end, Lucas tried to protect Emily. He loved me like that once. I thought of her with him as I pulled on the ends of the tie I slipped around his neck. I could picture them laughing at me in my mind and I pulled tighter. My jaw clenched as I pulled on the ends with all my might, snuffing his last breath from his body. What was I to do? He brought shame on us, if it got out, it always gets out, people would look at me with pity. I don't need anyone's pity. The only way for me to face our friends after what he had done was if he was dead. That formula took my marriage. That slut Graydon hired almost took my son. So why not make Graydon wait. Ian has lusted after me for years. He would have been a good boy and done what he was told, but no, you needed to do things on your timeline. Where has that gotten you?" she screamed above the roar of the thunder.

Cache crawled a few steps forward from the island and didn't realize she was near the table and chairs before she bumped into a chair, causing it to scrape along the floor. She froze and didn't move. Did she hear that? she wondered. There were no footsteps, no movement whatsoever. Had she gone upstairs, or was she standing in the doorway to the kitchen? Cache put the knife down and extended her hand forward to feel for the remaining chairs and legs to the table.

Another crash from above, like a drummer pounding on their cymbals, and a flash of light outside the back door, hidden by the door's shades, cast light on Cache's position, throwing her shadow across the room and into the hallway. The sound of breaking china came from behind her.

"You little bitch. I see you have something that belongs to me. I will make you a deal. You give it back and I will let you leave. That sounds fair, doesn't it? That whore that Lucas had as an assistant, she had something of mine; it's amazing how talkative she became before I squeezed the life out of her. Then all I had to do was a little investigation, drop an anonymous tip, and you and your friends got mine back."

The sound of the voice was coming from behind her in the direction of the living room. In the dark room, she must have come in contact with the vase that Cache had left on the floor.

Cache crawled to the door. She had little blocking her from the kitchen entrance that she could use as cover. If she grabbed a chair, the scraping sound along the floor would give her position away. Cache reached for the handle of the door, feeling for a dead bolt, but there was none. Instead, a double-sided lock. In order to get out of the house she would need to pick the lock, and for that she would need to turn on her flashlight, which might tell Petra where she was hiding.

Cache listened for her, hoping to start work on the door when it sounded as if she was far away in the house. A sound came from a few feet from the kitchen entrance door, and Cache scrambled to the far wall, pushed her back up against it and stayed low, gripping the handle of the knife with both hands.

"Cache, are you still here? I don't hear you, sweetheart. Let me know you're okay."

Cache could feel her pulse racing. She thought about smashing the glass to see if she could push her way out the door, but Petra could strike as she tried to force her way through the shards of glass, only to bleed out on the back patio. Cache heard the steps get fainter and fainter as it sounded like she was heading toward the far end of the house, where the Fischer's kept the movie theater and workout room. She could make a run for the front door, unless Petra knew Cache was hiding in the kitchen and was really only a few feet outside the entranceway, standing in the dark waiting for Cache to make a desperate run for freedom. Staying in the house was like being cornered by an animal with few options. If she could get outside she would be on more even ground. The weather might play in her favor; she was used to the elements, and she might have the ability to surprise her hunter. She listened but heard nothing. She crawled back toward the door, turned the flashlight on and held it in her teeth.

She put the knife down, pulled out her lock pick set, inserted the picks into the lock and fidgeted with it. The sound of footsteps resumed. She felt a tumbler give, and then a second. The steps grew louder. A third tumbler and a fourth gave way. The steps were outside the kitchen entrance. The sound of breathing. Hers, or was it Petra's?

A fifth tumbler gave way. Hopefully, only one more.

A flash of light.

Thunder roared.

A sound behind her.

"There you are, my poor little mouse."

A sixth tumbler released.

Cache turned to see a gun barrel.

She gripped the handle.

Cache pulled it down.

A loud noise from inside the kitchen.

An explosion in the dark.

Shattered glass everywhere.

## 24

C ache dove forward into the storm, her hands hitting the wet flagstone of the back patio, and tumbled forward. The shot from behind ricocheted off the door. There were two more shots in the air as Cache clung to the ground and pushed herself forward. Her jeans were soaked and clung to her legs. She crawled around a stone garden planter and looked toward the opening in the kitchen. The knife. Where is the knife? she thought. She'd left it on the kitchen floor. Cache wasn't going back in for that. She wasn't sure whether Petra would follow her out into the storm, but the winds caused the door to continue to open and close, smashing against the wall and the door frame. Cache looked around the yard. The rain and the darkness reduced her visibility. She reflected on the day of the service, when she'd walked back here and talked to people, trying to make chitchat. She recalled a large metal fence surrounding the property with triangle ends at the top. Trying to get over the fence could be more of a challenge than she wanted to take on. The metal would be extra slick in the storm, and if she lost her grip while on top, she could impale herself on one of the ends and bleed out before anyone would find her body. She looked over her shoulder. A pathway ran down to the pool. A black object appeared about twenty feet to her left but wasn't moving. She crouched down, the cold wet grass underneath her feet. Cache debated whether she might move more freely if she took her jeans off, but they were protecting the papers that she carried underneath. The storm raged as if it were as angry as Petra was that someone had come into her house. Cache made it to within five feet of the dark object and shone her flashlight on it. An old shed stood there in the yard, a six-pane glass insert in the middle of its door. She moved toward it and peered inside. The door was locked. She grabbed her flashlight by the lens and smashed the metal tube through the glass in the bottom of the door's window. She reached inside, fumbled for the lock and slid it to the opposite position. Cache pushed the door open and walked inside, stepping on the broken glass. "Ouch!" she screeched as she hobbled over to a small table to pull glass shards from her left foot. Blood was streaming down. Cache pulled the phone from her fleece and set it down beside her. It was still recording. She pulled her fleece top off and looked around for something to cut it with. There was a gas-powered weed whacker, an electric leaf blower, several bags of fertilizer, a small table, hand tools, brown clay pots for planting and a red plastic container. She found a large pair of garden shears, cut one of her sleeves off her fleece top and tied it around her foot. She then pulled the fleece top back on minus one sleeve. Her phone still showed no service. She reflected on her options. If she gave herself up, Petra would shoot her. Petra could always claim she was an intruder and that she didn't recognize Cache in the dark. For now, she was out of the elements. She picked up her phone and stopped the recording. She saved the file and began recording a new message. Cache left a detailed account of what she had heard Petra say in the event she didn't make it out of the situation alive. She didn't have time to review what had previously been recorded and whether anyone listening to it would hear what she'd heard. Cache sent an email that went to her outbox. She hoped if the service were to return, the message would go out. She had sent it to Graydon and Michael, advising them that Petra was the killer and now she was hunting her. In the event she didn't survive, a recording of the events could be found in the shed in the backyard of the Fischers' property. Cache shone her flashlight around the small room, looking for somewhere she could hide her phone. As she pulled back bags of fertilizer on the ground and removed stacks of clay pots, she discovered a red rusty toolbox hidden in the back. She pulled it up and sat it down on the small table. There was an assortment of screws, nuts and bolts scattered throughout the box. An open pack of cigarettes, a fresh pack of cigarettes and a rusty old flip lighter with the hammer and sickle on the outside. She pocketed the lighter and lifted the tray. She was hoping for a gun or knife hidden in the bottom, but all that was there was an old rubber mallet with a wooden handle, stained with years of use. Cache put her smartphone in the bottom of the box for safekeeping; tucked the folded pieces of paper, which were wet on the outside, beside the phone; and put the tray back on top. She shoved the toolbox back to where it came from piling the pots and fertilizer bags in front of it. Cache poked around inside and thought about how long she might be able to stay here. A movement in the yard startled her; a figure moved around the property. She picked up the glass pieces and threw them to the side of the door. Reaching over, she grabbed the red container and could feel something sloshing around inside. She pulled the lid off and could smell fumes from gasoline. Cache patted her jeans and felt the lighter she'd put into her pocket. Grabbing the rubber mallet and gas can, she made her way back out into the storm, shut the door behind her and crawled along a small stone retaining wall, hiding behind several clay pots.

Thunder roared again, but this time it didn't come from above, but from the direction of a figure in black, shattering two pots to her left. Cache grabbed the mallet and gas can and crawled along the ground, seeking refuge behind a tree—not the ideal spot in a lightning storm. The figure continued to move in front of the entrance to the kitchen, like a goalie trying to protect the net. Cache felt around the ground beneath her and could feel the top edges of rocks buried in the dirt. Digging around the rocks, she was able to loosen them and provide her with a means to see what she was up against.

Cache threw a rock about twenty feet away toward the house. She could hear a boom go off and see a flash of fire coming from the figure. She threw another rock in the same direction, and again thunder roared from just outside the entrance to the kitchen. As she suspected, Petra had retrieved a shotgun from somewhere in the house.

She looked around the yard and then back in the pool's direction. She kept low and made her way down to the pool. Chairs left out had been toppled over. A patio set rested against a small building with windows and a front door. It must be a pool house, she thought. She moved along to the door, found that it was not locked and made her way inside, setting down the gas can and mallet by the front door. The pool was rectangular, about forty feet long and twenty feet wide. She could see the raindrops hitting the surface of the pool and splashing up the pool water from inside the pool house about ten feet away from the entrance to the shallow end. Cache turned on her flashlight. She noticed a phone on top of a desk, grabbed it, pressed the talk button and put the phone to her ear. There was no dial tone, only silence. She glanced down at a red light fading in and out as what battery power it relied on began to die next to the words 'intercom.' As she listened, she could hear the sound of someone's breath.

"Hello?"

"My dear, why do you make this hard on yourself? Just give me what I want and I will make it painless. I'll even send your parents some nice flowers from my garden."

"You know you're nuts, right?"

"I think you're the one that is crazy. There is no phone service, no one is coming to your rescue, there is no way to signal for help. When the storm lets up, I can come down there and deal with you myself, but, Cache, if you're going to make me walk all that way, that is going to be very painful for you. Come up to the house, we will have a nice cup of tea together, you can kneel on the ground, you won't even see it coming."

Cache hung up the phone and tossed it against the wall. Aaron was still sitting out in the car, with no sign that there was a problem. Somehow, she needed to signal him. Otherwise she might as well go and have tea. She looked around the pool house for something she could use. A gas furnace to heat the pool was in a room with the pool pump. There were chairs and couches for relaxing on, and wooden shelves that contained books and an assortment of knickknacks. Cache stepped out into the storm, clung to the side of the pool house and moved around back. A separate shed was attached to the back. As she opened it, she spotted what she had hoped to find. A tank for fuel to help provide heat to the pool. She returned inside the pool house, grabbed the red gasoline canister from the front door and opened it. Cache poured the contents over the chairs and couches and ran a stream of gasoline to the room where the furnace and pump resided. Maybe she couldn't get the attention that she needed by phone, but a big fireball on a property in a well-to-do area might do the trick. She looked around for the best place to situate herself. The pool might provide adequate cover for her. Her jeans and top were soaked. Trying to maneuver in them could prove difficult, and she was hoping to entice Petra to leave the comfort of her home, to come down here and deal with her now. Cache slid out of her jeans and rolled them up. She pulled off her fleece top. Cache left the pool house, walked to the far end of the pool, grabbed the lighter from her pocket and put her jeans and top on the ground with two lawn chairs over them to ensure they would still be there when she needed them again. It had been a while that she had been in the backyard. The rain was coming down so hard that she had stopped noticing it was there. She was already soaked to the bone and couldn't get any wetter. Cache grabbed her rubber mallet and brought it down toward the deep end, where the pool had a metal ladder. She went back into the pool house and flipped open the lighter. Cache rotated the flint once and had a small spark but no flame. She tried it again and again, but it wouldn't give her what she was looking for. Cache banged it as hard as she could onto the desk and tried one more time. The spark ignited. A beautiful flame. Cache walked over to the couch and tossed it on. She exited and made her way to the deep end of the pool, where she lowered herself into the water and placed the rubber mallet on the top step of the ladder.

She could see the flames flickering in the window. Smoke poured out of the front door as sparks floated up into the air. I wonder if she can see this from wherever she's perched, Cache thought. The flames grew in intensity, the remaining furniture ignited, the drapes evaporated as flames crawled up the walls and she could see the flames traveling to the right of the structure. She pushed herself down into the water so her nose was just above the waterline. As the pump room started to become consumed by the fire, she dove under the water. Even submerged, she could hear the roar of the gas tank catching fire. From under the water, she saw a fireball rise into the sky. As she came up to the surface of the water and looked around, she saw the pool house had been reduced to its substructure.

In the distance, a woman's screams became louder and

louder. Cache grabbed hold of the mallet and clung to the side of the pool.

"What the fuck? Where are you, you little bitch? I'm going to skin you like a rabbit and boil you in oil when I get my hands on you."

Petra circled around the pool house, looking everywhere for Cache, her shotgun in her hands. She pointed it at the shadows the flames cast around the edge of the pool and fired. She continued to scream into the darkness at someone who wasn't there. Cache watched her move around the pool. She came toward the ladder. Cache submerged herself underwater and watched Petra move closer to the ladder. Cache pulled herself up. With the mallet in her right hand, she swung it with all her might, smashing down on Petra's right leg, causing her to tumble to the ground. The shotgun broke from her grip and bounced over the pavement, landing in the pool, and sank to the bottom. Cache made a run for the house. Her bare feet clung to the steps as she pounced toward the back entrance. Cache ran into the kitchen and then down the hallway and out the front door. She made her way to the car, where Aaron was sitting, as he lowered his window to see a half-dressed woman running toward him.

"Are you okay?" he asked.

"No, do you have cell service?"

Aaron reached for his phone. "No, it's still out."

"Look, I don't have time to go into details. Petra is the one who killed Lucas and Emily. I found what I was looking for. You need to go and find a police officer and bring them back here. If they need further convincing, tell them to call Detective Boone."

"Get in, I'll take you to the police station."

Cache looked back at the house. "She'll be gone by the time we get back. I hid the evidence but there is no guarantee she won't find it. Go and get somebody." Cache ran back toward the house as Aaron pulled out to go find backup.

She crept back into the house and crouched down to listen. She could hear moaning coming from the kitchen, as Petra was cursing in a foreign dialect. Cache closed the front door behind her. The door hinges squealed.

"Is that you? How dare you come into my home and assault me the way that you did," Petra yelled from the kitchen.

Cache crept toward the kitchen doorway. She could see the silhouette of someone sitting at the table. She also spotted the handgun Petra had been using earlier, hoping that Cache would be brash enough to walk in and give her a clean shot. Cache decided that was not how this was going to play out. She continued to move east into the house, toward the movie room. They had constructed the room not to let light in and interfere with a movie, and without electricity it might be the best place to get a jump on her.

As she moved away from the entrance to the kitchen, she called out, "Did you fall down, you old bat?" Cache could hear the kitchen chair scrape along the floor. That seemed to have put some spark in the tigress. Cache continued to walk at a quicker pace toward the movie room. She opened the doors and left them open. She wanted Petra to know where she could find her. The room was pitch-black. Her flashlight was back in her jeans near the pool. She crawled along the carpet until she came to the far wall and then moved down a step to wait.

Hidden behind one chair on the top riser, Cache listened for the sound of movement. The house went quiet. Petra wasn't making any more threats. As she approached the darkened room, she didn't want to indicate where she was. Yet Cache could hear her breathing. The weather, being struck in the leg, running around in a storm—the old girl had tired. Her breathing was telling Cache exactly where she was. Cache sensed she was around the opening to the room and rose up into the pose a sprinter makes at the start of a race. She counted down in her head, three, two, one, and pushed off on her right foot, running toward the door as fast as she could. As she shortened the distance between her and Petra, the electricity in the house flipped on, lights lit the dark rooms of the house and Petra could see Cache coming toward her.

She raised the gun and squeezed the trigger as Cache's shoulder contacted her ribs, sending Petra flying backward and the gun falling to the ground. Cache fell forward, landing on her knees, and looked in front of her as Petra scrambled to her feet. She glanced from side to side in the hallway but didn't see the gun anywhere. Petra searched the area, looking in all directions. Cache got to her feet and moved toward Petra, bringing her fists in front of her face. "You tried to kill me. This ends now, you old bitch."

Petra sized up the situation and ran in the opposite direction toward the living room. Cache chased after her until she saw Petra reemerge from the living room, with her hands around the grip of a silver metal fire poker. She raced toward Cache. "Why won't you fucking die?"

She swung and made contact with Cache's shoulder, sending her into the wall. "That's for blowing up my pool house." She swung again, trying to make contact with Cache's head. Cache ducked, and the swing caught nothing but air. Cache grabbed one of her arms and slammed the palm of her fist up into her rib cage. "That's for almost blowing my head off with a shotgun." Petra leaned forward, her right hand clutching her ribs, the poker held firmly in her left hand. Cache brought her arms close to her chest to protect her rib cage. Petra spotted exposure. She swung again. The metal shaft made contact with the side of Cache's left knee, bringing her to the ground. She screamed in pain as her kneecap felt like someone had poured gasoline on it and lit it on fire. "That's for breaking my vase." Petra towered over Cache, bringing the metal iron to the ground as Cache lay on her back and jostled from side to side, hoping to avoid a blow to her ribs. Cache fought back the pain, tears coming to her eyes. Petra moved in closer, confident she could end this. Cache bent her right leg and kicked Petra, sending her backward. Cache hobbled to her feet. Petra came again. Cache tried to center herself, but putting pressure on her left knee just sent searing pain up her leg. She watched Petra as she closed in. Closer, closer. Cache drove her palm up into the middle of Petra's face; she could hear the crack as her palm contacted Petra's nose, sending her off of her feet and down to the ground. Cache looked around. There on the floor behind one of the double doors that led to the kitchen, the gun lay. Cache limped over to the door, picked up the gun and drew the slide back, sending a round into the barrel.

She limped into the kitchen and put the gun down on the counter. Cache grabbed a tea towel and some ice from the freezer and made an ice pack. She pushed the gun down into the back of her briefs. How she missed having her jeans on. Hopefully, they'd survived the blast. Cache walked out into the hall, put the ice pack on Petra's face and told her to hold it there while she helped her to her feet and dragged her by her arm into the kitchen and parked her at the table.

She reached for a phone on a small desk. There was a dial tone. She called 911, reported what had occurred and requested that they contact Detective Boone. Cache turned on the lights in the kitchen and sat down at the table at the opposite end. She rubbed her knee. The pain was throbbing, but she didn't want to take her eyes off Petra. Who knew what other guns were in the house. She extended her leg, pulled the gun from her briefs and put it on the table.

"I'll take that cup of tea now, if the offer is still open."

# EPILOGUE

The next several hours went by in a blur. The police arrived, and at first Petra made it sound as if Cache were the criminal and she the innocent party. That changed when Detective Boone and his partner arrived on the scene. Cache had grabbed a blanket to wrap herself in and walked down to the garden shed to turn over the evidence she had collected. She held her breath, fearing that what she had recorded would be muffled, but when she turned the volume all the way up, you could hear what Petra had been yelling at her.

Cache held on to the yellow pieces of paper. Michael knew taking them from her would only lead to a fight and he would only have them in his hands for a short while before suits from Washington arrived to take possession of them. She gathered her belongings and Aaron drove her out to the Quills' residence to stay for the next couple of days. Graydon wanted a briefing in the morning as to what had transpired after Petra left the restaurant, and given that the worst of the storm was on its way, he was more inclined to have a houseguest than have to face the storm and drive into the office.

Cache slept later than normal for her. Her eyes opened, and she looked at the ceiling. A small chandelier hung in the middle of the room. She looked around at the large queen-sized bed with overstuffed pillows she had slept in and realized the job she had been tasked to do was pretty much done. The rain continued to spatter on the window. The drapes were pulled tight, preventing her from seeing what the storm had brought that day. Cache pulled herself from the warm cocoon she had created with the covers and walked to what she thought was a closet, only to discover it was a large guest washroom, with tub, shower and two sinks. Her clothes from the night before had been washed, folded and left on the vanity for her. She held up her fleece to her nose. She could smell springtime. She looked to the side of the pile and saw a blue sweatshirt with the word *Quillchem* printed on the front. She looked at her one arm fleece and thought the sweatshirt was a good substitute. A long, hot shower was what that day called for. Cache dressed and went to the window to pull back the drapes. She had thought last night was bad; today looked even worse, but she wasn't out in it and had no intention of going back out into it until the faucets turned off and it was just a drizzle.

Cache made her way down a large, sweeping staircase made of white marble. A red runner took her to the bottom, where one of the Quill staff directed her toward the back of the house, where Graydon and Jacqueline were taking morning coffee and watching a weather channel on television. Graydon sat closest to a set of doors that led outside. Water poured down the outside of the glass like someone was standing on the other side washing the windows with a fire hose. Cache could hear winds howling beyond the doors. Mother Nature clearly wanted everyone on the property to know that she was in charge.

Cache walked in as Graydon turned his attention away from the television and Jacqueline put down her newspaper.

Graydon motioned for her to take the seat next to him, opposite his wife. As Cache sat down, one of the staff asked her what she wanted to eat and poured her a cup of coffee from the pot in her hands.

"Louisa, do we have any of the strawberry scones left?" Graydon asked.

"I can check for you."

"You have to try the strawberry scones," he said as he reached over and grabbed Cache's arm.

"Did you sleep well?" Jacqueline asked.

"As soon as I pulled the covers over my head, I was out cold."

"Well, dear, you stay as long as you like. I still can't believe that Petra was responsible for Lucas's death, and that poor Dr. Zhou. Do you have any idea why?" Jacqueline asked.

Cache reached down into her pocket and pulled out the yellow pieces of folded-up paper, faded in places from where the water droplets had dried, and handed them over to Graydon.

"I feel an enormous weight has been lifted from me. Detective Boone wanted to take these from me, but he didn't want another incident with the Justice Department."

"Smart man." He took them and unfolded them in front of him. A series of graphic images that meant nothing to him. "Did Picasso draw these?" he asked as he unfolded the pages and flipped them over, examining all the strange notations that Dr. Fischer had written on the page. "You can read this?" he asked.

"I've gotten better at it."

"So what does it say?"

"The first part talks about one of the last changes he made to the formula. All the other journals, from what we've gathered so far, talk about the formula, the testing, the results and subsequent changes to the formula. Previous versions of the formula would stop ballistics at certain ranges but not at others. Others would stop certain alloys, but not all. Then he had success with the latest formula, which is written about on the second page." She pointed to a set of four images on the page. "These symbols mean 'Electrified Ballistic Stopping Material.' Wherever you see those symbols in any of Dr. Fischer's journals, his notations are about the science behind the research. The last test they did"—Cache pointed to the bottom of the second page—"met all the test requirements."

Jacqueline stood up, walked behind Graydon and looked down at the page. "I don't know how you read that."

Cache sat back in her chair and sipped her coffee. "As I told you before, these are more a diary than just scientific journals. In those pages, it talks about the night Dr. Zhou and Lucas consummated their working relationship by making love on his desk at the office."

Jacqueline ran her finger along the images. "Cache, where does it say that?"

"Jackie, this is not a soap opera," Graydon said.

"The journals identify each person with two symbols, one for each of their initials." Cache pointed at one set of symbols. "This is EZ, for Emily Zhou. When you read through the passage, it talks about them getting it on at the office. Apparently, buttons were flying everywhere as they worked to get each other undressed. I found one of those buttons underneath Lucas's desk and matched it to a blazer that Emily had in her home. In the passages that followed afterward he talked about his lust for Emily and how he feared his marriage to Petra might be over."

"He said that in these pages?" Graydon asked.

"In these pages briefly, from what I could decode. In journals sixteen through eighteen, he documented his growing feelings for Emily. At some point he must have left journal fifteen with the successful formula in it lying around. As far as he was aware, only he and Jonas knew this language. He didn't know that Jonas had taught Petra how to read these journals. I suspect, being a scientist herself, she wanted to see what the final formula looked like and read more than she wanted."

"And that was the reason she killed him?" Jacqueline asked, looking up at Cache.

"The last passage in journal eighteen must have been written only a few weeks ago. Somewhere in that time frame, Petra learned the truth about what had happened between Emily and him. There was some sign at their home in the Vineyard of his recently visiting and a letter that he wrote to Emily telling her that he wanted to stay with Petra. I don't know if he ever sent that letter or was conflicted, but he went from staying out in the Vineyard to their place at the Dawes."

"Which is where he was found dead," Graydon said.

"From his blood alcohol content, he had a few drinks that night. She must have known he was going there; maybe he called her. Something happened between the two of them that led her to strangle him with a tie that he must have borrowed at some point from Jeffrey Allen. During the altercation—"

"You mean murder, my dear."

"During the murder, he must have struggled with her, grabbing at a pendant that he had given her and tearing it from her neck. Detective Boone and I found it lodged in a vent underneath a chair. The police found a partial print on it belonging to Dr. Fischer. That is why she has been fidgeting with her collar; she must be used to fidgeting with the pendant, and in its absence her brain has her playing with her collar."

"Do you think she went there determined to kill him?" Graydon asked.

"I think so. The night the medical examiner believes Dr. Fischer was killed, the police found security video footage of an unidentified man in the building. I think it was Petra dressed in a Quillchem bomber jacket, perhaps Lucas's, with a bald cap on. She knew where the cameras were and also knew that anyone that might spot her from behind might believe it was Dr. Wright that had gone there to see Lucas. Her efforts to avoid being detected suggest to me that she meant to do harm to her husband."

"So do you think she took out Lucas and then Emily was next because she was the one he was having an affair with?" Jacqueline asked.

"No, I think she was fine with leaving her alone, at least for the time being. From what I found out about Dr. Zhou, I'm speculating that at some point in her life she was forced to work for the Crizan Intelligence Service. Lots of governments are going to want this formula and she was working to get it for them. My guess is when Jonas disappeared, Petra believed Emily was involved but likely didn't know her relationship with the Crizan government or didn't care."

"But didn't you find Jonas through an anonymous tip?"

"That was Petra. She forced Emily to tell her where Jonas was and to write down the street name on a piece of paper before she killed her. Petra did her own research over the next few days and realized there was too much muscle guarding him for her to get him out by herself. She couldn't really tell the police how she got the info, so she dropped an anonymous tip and I went with the police to find Jonas."

Jacqueline sat back down opposite Cache and reflected on what Cache had shared with her, sipping her tea and looking down at the papers in front of her.

"How do you know she killed Lucas and Emily? Lucas was already dead, so he couldn't write about it. Is there anything in these pages that we are going to have to turn over to the police for them to prosecute Petra?" Graydon asked.

Cache took a sip of her coffee and put it back down. "Nope, not that I can imagine. Last night, she was confident she was going to kill me. My cell phone had no service, so I couldn't call anyone, but I had a fully charged battery, so I put it on record and put it into my fleece pocket for safekeeping. As Petra got angrier that she couldn't find me, she admitted killing Lucas and Emily."

"And you have that on tape?" Graydon asked as Jacqueline looked up from the papers.

"I was worried that it might just come out as muffled noises, but if you turn up the volume loud enough, you can hear what she said. Whether her attorney can come up with a reason it can't be used in court is another question."

"But, Cache, you heard her, right?" Jacqueline asked.

"Yep, so I will be a witness at trial, but the recording backs up my account of what she said, so hopefully it won't get thrown out of court."

Graydon opened his palms toward the yellow pages that were laid out in front of him. "I guess it makes sense now, why she was adamant that we not have access to her properties to look for the pages, if the contents of these pages were going to throw suspicion on her."

"She had the pages all along, but she knew they would incriminate her, and so she couldn't afford to let me find them, but she also recognized the importance of the work as a former scientist herself, so she couldn't bring herself to destroy the documents with the working formula on them."

"So what about Drs. Wright, Tanaka and Allen? Were they in on this at all?"

"You have a very dysfunctional group there, there is no denying that, but no, I don't believe they had a direct hand in the murders. Ian had romantic feelings for Petra. She used him to make Lucas jealous. Emily was working for a foreign government to secure the formula, but Lucas didn't trust anyone with his journals since they contained his innermost thoughts and feelings. I suspect when she had the opportunity to get close to them, she photographed what she could but could never get a complete set. She used her looks to entice him and pursued him in an effort to secure access to the journals. That's what Dr. Tanaka saw on more than one occasion, a secret that she shared with Dr. Allen, who she was also involved with. At one point Jeffrey and Emily appear to have had something together, or that was also part of her plan. We will never know. Jeffrey is convinced it was real, and that secret has gone with her to the grave. From what I gathered, when Petra confronted Lucas at the Dawes, she knew his account of his betrayal was documented in journal fifteen. She probably feared that one day Jonas might learn the truth, so she grabbed journal fifteen, leaving the rest in the safe. At some point, she removed the pages that documented his infidelity with Dr. Zhou. Unfortunately for us, the formula for EBSM was on the same page. My guess is that Dr. Zhou got possession of journal fifteen from the Fischer residence at some point; it may have even been the day of the memorial service. She wouldn't have known that the important pages had been torn out. She photographed the journal's contents and then the journal fell into Dr. Allen's hands. Graydon you should be aware that when I let myself into Dr. Allen's residence he came home, and I had to hide to avoid being discovered. While I was hiding, I overheard him on the phone with who I believe was Dr. Tanaka. He was trying to decipher the code with the intent on selling the formula to someone and then leave the country. I suspect he then had Dr. Tanaka, who had gotten friendly with Dr. Wright, plant the journal in his home, thinking the discovery of the journal would cast suspicion on him."

Graydon sat back in his chair and put his hand over his mouth and rubbed his chin.

"Well, I think Dr. Allen's and Dr. Tanaka's days at Quillchem are numbered. I will need to talk with the military about this information, I would imagine they will want to take charge of the situation."

Cache reached for her cup of coffee and sipped it as Graydon folded the pages back up and tucked them into his shirt pocket.

"It will be hard on Jonas, finding out that his mother killed his father and his assistant," Graydon said.

"Well, there is no way to sugarcoat it. He will either learn about it from her or the media. I suspect when word gets out it will be all over social media."

"Well, Cache, thank you." Graydon sipped his coffee and put it down. "With Lucas's work, we might be able to save a lot of lives in the future. They will owe a debt of gratitude to you, but unfortunately no one can ever know."

"It's okay, I remember the nondisclosure agreement I signed."

"It's funny, I suspect Petra will be able to use our need for secrecy against us. She might be able to get a reduced sentence in exchange for agreeing not to publicly disclose any of this."

Cache took another sip of her coffee and watched the rain pound against the patio stones.

"So what's next for Cache Iron?" Graydon asked.

"Well, my work for you is done here. Assuming you're not going to kick me out of my suite until the weather clears up, I'll grab a flight home. I appreciate you having faith in me. I'm thinking I might set up a private investigation company, take on a case here and there."

Graydon nodded in approval. "Or you can come work for me full-time."

"Doing what? You have a head of security—and you don't need a full-time investigator."

"No, but I can afford one."

"I don't want to sit around waiting for something to happen."

"How about this then: I keep you on retainer. If something

comes up, I will call you, and when there's nothing you can pursue your own work."

"It's a generous offer, I'll have to think about it."

"What's to think about? You get a paying job, use of a corporate jet, accommodations and infinite resources at your disposal —you only get that if you work for me."

Cache smirked, looking at Jacqueline, who was trying hard not to laugh.

"You like getting your way, don't you?" Cache said.

"I always do."

# THANK YOU

*Thank you for reading!*

Dear Reader,

I hope you enjoyed *Iron Proof*. I have to tell you that I really loved developing the character of Cache Iron. What's next for Cache? Well, be sure to stay tuned. Cache will be back next in the book *Charged Iron*.

I need to ask you a favor. If you are so inclined, I would love it if you would post a review of *Iron Proof*. Loved it, hated it - I would just love to hear your feedback. Reviews can be tough to come by these days, and you, the reader, have the power to make or break a book.

Thank you so much for reading Iron Proof and for spending time with me.

In gratitude,

Alex Blakely

# ABOUT THE AUTHOR

Alex Blakely is a Canadian author who grew up loving works of fiction in the classic "who dunnit style." A university graduate in the study of economics, he spent a number of years working in the area of finance before embarking on his writing career. He lives with his family in a community, west of Toronto, Ontario.

facebook.com/AlexBlakelyBooks

twitter.com/alexblakelybook

instagram.com/alexblakelybooks

bookbub.com/profile/alex-blakely

goodreads.com/alexblakely

tiktok.com/@alexblakelybooks

# ALSO BY ALEX BLAKELY

Cold Iron

Hot Iron

Iron Proof

Charged Iron (expected 2022)

# AUTHOR'S NOTES

## Join Author's Notes

If you want to stay up to date on the latest work from author Alex Blakely, join his monthly newsletter called Author's Notes. There he will share with you behind the scenes info on his current and future books as well as things going on in his personal life.

You will get to see book covers before they are released to the public and get to download exclusive content created solely for subscribers. To subscribe go to: https://alexblakelybooks.com/newsletter

# THE IRONHEADS

If you enjoyed this book consider joining our Facebook Group called The Ironheads to talk about all things about Cache Iron and future Books from Alex Blakely.

To join go to: https://www.facebook.com/groups/theironheads